# DARK SIDE
## OF
## SUNSET POINTE
## A Lance Underphal Mystery

by

# MICHAEL ALLAN SCOTT

**TELEMACHUS PRESS**

# WARNING

**THIS IS A MURDER MYSTERY INTENDED FOR ADULTS
IT CONTAINS EXPLICIT LANGUAGE, SEX & VIOLENCE.
IF YOU ARE OFFENDED BY THIS TYPE OF MATERIAL,**

# PLEASE DON'T READ IT.

This book is a work of fiction. Names, characters, places and incidents are either the product of the author's imagination or are used fictitiously. Any resemblance to actual persons, living or dead, or to actual events or locales is entirely coincidental.

**DARK SIDE OF SUNSET POINTE**

Cover design by David Prescott of DPMediaPro.com

Photograph by Cynthia A. Scott

Logo design by Michael Manoogian of Michael Manoogian Logo Design
http://www.michaelmanoogian.com

Published by Telemachus Press, LLC
http://www.telemachuspress.com

Visit the author website:
http://www.michaelallanscott.com

ISBN: 978-1-938701-94-8 (eBook)
ISBN: 978-1-938701-95-5 (Paperback)

Version 2013.11.11

Printed in the United States of America

10  9  8  7  6  5  4  3  2  1

This book is dedicated to my father:
Ernest E. Scott, Jr.
1923–2012

Until we meet again …

# PROLOGUE

There are few persons, even among the calmest thinkers, who have not occasionally been startled into a vague yet thrilling half-credence in the supernatural, by coincidences of so seemingly marvellous a character that, as mere coincidences, the intellect has been unable to receive them.

–Edgar Allan Poe

# THE CALL

**[6:47 PM – Tuesday, August 24, 2010]**

A BLAZING SUN still high above Phoenix's western horizon. One hundred nine degrees in the shade. Those with the wherewithal and accumulated vacation time have fled north to the cool pines or west to the balmy California coast weeks ago. Only the dregs of humanity, conscripted company workers and hardcore entrepreneurs are left to bake in the Valley of the Sun's August heat. Yet beneath the surface layer of superheated atmosphere and social veneers there is another, more subliminal furnace raging—its fumes stoking the fires of Hell.

Just off the intersection of Greenway and Tatum a white stucco box of an office building squats under a clay tile roof, heat rising off the reddish tiles in shimmering sheets. Mounted on the wrought-iron entry gate, the building directory announces the tenants: Suite 101—Whiting Realty & Development. The office is closed for the day yet the overburdened air conditioning units grind away, sheltering the last remaining occupant from the sweltering heat.

Bloodshot eyes stare at a spreadsheet, the monitor's image glares with the harsh reality. Too many negative numbers expose an ugly truth. Anxiously perched on the edge of his high-backed leather executive chair, Gary Whiting waits with the phone to his ear. Dreading the final ring, Whiting lets it go to voicemail, again. He needs to talk to his partner, Rodriguez. He loosens the knot in his power tie and hangs up. This time, without leaving a message.

The four Excedrin have knocked his headache down to a dull throbbing at the base of his skull, but his eyes still ache. He's been crunching numbers for their Sunset Pointe development project, staring at the monitor all damn day. He rubs at the knots in his stomach through his rumpled white dress shirt, thinking maybe he should eat or maybe he should just shoot himself. He taps the return key with a jittery thumb, hitting it too many times, trying to put the numbers out of his mind. His pulse pounds in his temples. *Shit! Got to get ahold of that asshole, Rodriguez.*

Whiting runs a trembling hand through thinning hair, his scalp hot and moist. They've got to do something about these numbers. Short stubble on raw cheeks twitches as he anxiously works his jaws. They could lose the whole damn project. *Thirty million!* He can't believe it, he's bet everything on this project. And with the hard-money loan, they've got a bigger nut than ever. *Shit!* Those hard-money bastards, they're Rodriguez's contacts. Of course they *had* to have the money to finish—all the construction cost overruns. *Fucking Rodriguez.* His fingers manically drum on the hardwood desktop, their nails ragged, bitten to the quick. They're in way too deep to quit now.

Chewing his bottom lip, Whiting redials Rodriguez's cell.

"Damn Gary, whaddaya want?" Rodriguez sounds out of breath, frustrated.

"Mike, we need to go over some numbers. Ya got a minute?"

Rodriguez gives a short chuckle then lowers his voice. "I'm kinda in the middle of somethin'."

"Yeah, but ..." Gary hears a thump, then a woman's muffled words. "Hey, are you at the office? Who's with you?"

"Yeah, like I said, we're kinda in the middle of somethin' here."

Whiting hears giggling in the background.

"Stop that," Rodriguez says to Diane. To Gary, he says, "Diane's never done it on the desk before."

Whiting can almost hear Rodriguez's leering grin.

In the background Diane laughs. "Do I get overtime for this?"

Now they're both laughing.

"Damn ... Mike, you guys ... in the office?"

"Hey, don't sweat it. It's almost seven, no one's around, yard gates are locked, lights are off. No one's gonna know."

Whiting hears Diane coo … more giggling.

Rodriguez speaks closer into the phone. "That is, as long as you keep your mouth shut."

"Hey, no problem. I don't care what you do with Diane. She's *your* bookkeeper."

Diane lets out a short yelp. "What was that?"

"Shit," whispers Rodriguez. "Shit."

"Mike, what's going on?"

"Hold on, I think someone's here."

Whiting hears grunting, rustling, probably scrambling for clothes, the metallic snap of window blinds.

"Who's that?" says Rodriguez under his breath. "Get your panties on."

Whiting hears Diane whine. "I'm trying."

He hears Rodriguez whispering to himself. "Who is that? Is that …? I'll get that bastard."

"Gary, hold on, I gotta take a picture with this thing, hold on."

"Okay." Whiting hears the blinds clacking.

He hears Rodriguez talking to himself. "Damn, it's dark … but I think I got 'em."

"Mike … Mike?"

"Yeah, I'm back, hold on. Gotta check this out."

Whiting clutches the phone in a sweaty hand, pressed hard against his ear. He hears a loud bang. A door slamming the wall? *Too weird.* He needs a Valium.

Diane screams.

"*You*, you asshole!" yells Rodriguez. "What the fuck do *you* want!?!"

Whiting hears POP, POP! Screeching, a low grunt, loud thumps … POP, POP, POP! "Uh, uh, uh …" Guttural gasps. A long wail. High-pitched keening, its otherworldly echo raising every hair on goose flesh. Whiting drops the receiver, horrified. The plastic handset bounces off the desktop as it sinks in. *They've been shot!*

His first reaction, call nine-one-one! And say what, his partner and his partner's bookkeeper were fucking? … in his partner's office? … and someone broke in and is trying to kill them? *Holy shit!* What if he's dead? What if his partner is really dead? *Mike Rodriguez dead* … He's a real asshole, but dead?

The gunshots ring in his ears, echoing in his head. Whiting can't get the sounds out of his mind. Horrible. And as he dwells on it, his heart rate ramps up past panic levels, the overworked organ hammering in his chest. *Was that Diane?* That high-pitched wail, unearthly, frightening. And those grunts, that gasping, as if bullets were ripping them apart, choking, drowning in their own blood. He's never heard anything like it—visceral, haunting. Too terrible to think about, but he can't get it out of his mind. *This is bad, very bad.*

Gary's mind flits, beefing up his anxiety. He dare not think about it: What about Sunset Pointe? What if Mike Rodriguez is really dead? What happens now? The cost overruns, the big loans, draining their development project, running it into the ground. And if Diane's dead too … *What happens if they're both dead?* The new numbers, the hard-money assholes will be looking for him. Terror stains his pits with acrid musk. He can't let anyone see these numbers, can't let anyone find out. Probably too late to do anything anyway. They're probably already dead. Gingerly, he picks the receiver off the desk and puts it back in the cradle. *Gotta get outta here!*

Shaking, he tries to tap a Valium out of the bottle, spilling pills all over. A few, rolling off the desktop, bouncing on the carpet and rolling under the desk. *Shit!* He nervously scrapes up the pills, trying to scoop them back into the bottle as they stick to his sweaty palm. *Gotta hurry.* Finally downing the Valium, he jerks back to his computer. He passwords the Sunset Pointe Projections spreadsheet, copying it to his thumb drive and deleting it from the server.

Whiting opens his browser and punches up his fave, fidgeting as the browser opens to the Tangiers Casino site, agonizingly slow. The showgirls graphic starts up—a herky-jerky streaming digital dance, their hip-swaying welcome a grotesque parody. Eventually, it lets him check his Tangiers Club account balance and comp a room. He worries the mouse, clicking the WesternAir icon, booking an eight-thirty flight to Vegas. *I'm outta here.*

The searing heat hits Whiting like a blast furnace. On his way to the car, Whiting wrestles with the moment. He'll have to call his shrewish wife,

Lydia, tell her he needs a break, been working too hard. A quick overnight to Vegas and he'll be back in the morning, just needs to get away for a few hours. She'll hate it, but what's new? She ought to be used to it by now. He doesn't care, hasn't cared in years. She certainly can't threaten to withhold sex anymore. Can't even remember the last time they had sex. It wasn't ever that good anyway. And at least she can't badger him when she's giving him the silent treatment. He'll call her when he hits Sky Harbor, hopefully get her voicemail while she's yakking at her battle-ax mother.

# WAKING UP

**[10:11 PM – Tuesday, August 24, 2010]**

THE TEMPERATURE JUST dropped below a hundred degrees for the first time since midmorning. A pit-bull's bark reverberates in the deep-fried night, accompanied by the traffic noise from nearby Indian School Road. The din from the heavily traveled arterial permeates the early sixties neighborhood, smothering it in a deafening blanket of tire hum and growling exhausts. Traffic fumes superheat the dead air into a toxic mix of $CO_2$ and petroleum-charged gases. A typical August night in central Phoenix.

Beneath the thick layer of late-summer pollution, an empty side street lays dormant. A decrepit ranch-style squats on the street's south side, windows dark and lifeless. Its overworked window A/C units rattle and buzz, competing with the noisy traffic. Hidden by night's deep shadows, cheap off-white house paint peels away from ancient cinderblock. Tilted chunks of broken concrete form a narrow driveway. A beat-up Sentra sits at a slight list in the single-car carport under sagging eaves. Sparse clumps of dead Bermuda cling to bare dirt. The barren yard, anchored by two mangy junipers. The worst kept home on the block, everyone in the neighborhood knows it's a rental. No self-respecting human being would live there if they could afford to live anywhere else. None of the neighbors know the crusty old fart that lives there, rarely seen and never heard from. And they're fine with that.

Inside, the sole occupant snores away, splayed belly-up in a worn out recliner. Three-day stubble and a stained pair of briefs are the only cover for the pasty-white flesh on the downhill side of middle age. Gnarled arms and legs, battered and flaccid, covered with bald patches and spotty smudges of thin black hair—a roll of whale blubber clinging to a bloated gut. Life rumbles on by as Lance Underphal lies oblivious—dreaming.

*Crusin' with the top down, Sonja by my side. We're free at last.*

My cell rings. Annoying. There it goes again. Need to change that obnoxious ringtone.

Go to roll over, but can't. Stuck. Must've fallen asleep in my chair ... again. *Damn. Why am I wet?*

Blinking. Stinging eyes open to blurred images on an old flatscreen. *What movie is this?* Trying to rock forward and sit up. *Did I piss myself? Oh ... spilled my beer.*

I collapse the foot rest, my ratty recliner's springs shove me upright, and I stumble off to find the phone. That damned chirping, like some three-hundred-pound robotic sparrow, obnoxious as hell. I've GOT to change that ringtone. Maybe get Jimi on there, or Led Zeppelin, or even Lyle Lovett, anything but that damned chirping. *Where's that fucking phone?* I hear it—on the table somewhere, maybe under these proofs.

"Yeah."

"Lance?"

"Whaddaya want, Lacey?"

"Got a job for ya."

"Yeah? At this time of night?"

"Lance, It's only a little after ten."

"Ten's way past my bedtime."

"Yeah, well, do you want it or do I call someone else?"

"Yeah, maybe. What's up?"

"Guy and his girlfriend shot. He's dead, she's in a coma. Just picked it up off the scanner."

"Where at?"

"Construction company in Deer Valley. MJR Development. I'm on my way. I'll text ya the address. Get your butt over there ASAP."

"Yup, see ya over there in a few."

I pick my way through the clutter, my hand in my beer-soaked underwear scratching my nuts, heading for the shower.

Lacey's a good kid most of the time. A little too ambitious for a left-wing Socialist, yet she means well. But this freelance shit is for the birds, the worst sort of photography, especially for a free-press rag that doesn't pay shit. Lacey's kidding herself thinking it will ever get her a Pulitzer. Still, a buck is a buck, and the settlement checks don't make it to the end of the month, no matter how I stretch them.

I stand under the streaming showerhead, eyes closed, water running out of my open mouth, propped up against the back wall, my back and knees aching. Fifty-seven is a bitch. Can hardly wait until I'm sixty. The cool water helps my thick head. Times like these, little moments, in the middle of some mindless chore, that I end up missing her most. I know it's too late. Won't ever find another woman I like, much less love, at my age. She was my best chance and I'll never give her up. Can't help it, I still miss her.

Sonja's lilting voice pops into my head with a bad Mick Jagger impression. "Can't always get what you want, but if you try sometime ..."

"You never could sing."

"And your point is ...?"

"Whaddaya want now?"

She laughs. "*You*, to stop whining."

I drop from cynical to sullen. "How is it you always catch me feeling sorry for myself?"

"Not hard, you spend a lotta time at it."

"Just wishing you were here."

"I am here."

"You know what I mean. So I can see you, touch you, feel you."

"Minor details. You still have the best of me. Eventually you'll come to understand."

"I don't know ..."

"You need to know something. I'm here for you, more than ever."

"What about a little help? What about the exhaustion, the sleeplessness, the headaches, the loneliness?"

As she chuckles I can almost see her head wag. "See what I mean? Feeling sorry for yourself. I can't do it for you, you know."

She's starting to piss me off. "Yeah, but ... sometimes, I wish you'd leave me alone. I mean, after all, you're dead."

She laughs. "Dead? Do I seem dead to you?" Her tone softens, turning faintly melodic. "It's far better here. More freedom than you know. Just wait, a bright new future lies ahead."

"Great, now you want me to kick it, I suppose."

I hear the warmth of her smile. "You've got a few chores to do first, but we'll get there."

"Sounds like a helluva honey-do list."

She blatantly ignores me. "This one—the one you're going to."

"The shooting?"

"Yeah, with Lacey. It's not pretty. You be careful. Keep your guard up. There's a lotta turbulent energy surrounding this shooting."

"Sonja, I know this. There's always turbulence around violent crime."

"Yeah, but this one—more than usual. I'll tell you more when you're ready, you're going to need it. Lance, just be careful and it'll be alright."

*Shit!* I hate when she does that. Wish I could tell if she's for real. Or am I just talking to myself? Mental masturbation. Shit, who knows? But I don't dare let anyone else know or they'll cart me off to the nearest funny farm. Two voices, one head, they'd probably be justified. Yet most times, I'd swear she's really here, really speaking to me. Problem is, she's always right. I *hate* this! Now I'll be looking over my shoulder the whole fucking time.

# THE SCENE

**[11:03 PM – Tuesday, August 24, 2010]**

MY CELL'S CHIRP makes me jump as I turn off the street and through the chain-link gate. What with rushing, too much coffee and Sonja's enigmatic warning, my head is beginning to throb—my nerves, on the ragged edge. I glance at the number. It's Lacey. *Dammit.*

"Lance, where the hell *are* you?"

"I'm just pulling up."

"Well, get your ass over here. I need pictures."

I've known for a few miles now that I'm on the right track. Could tell by the circling news choppers. As I pull in, the night sky pulses with red and blue flashes from all the emergency light bars. Floodlights everywhere, bright as day, really help my headache. Emergency vehicles and cop cars are haphazardly jammed into the parking lot. They're boxed in by news vans with dishes telescoped, transmitting every scrap of juicy gore they can scrape up. Nothing like a good murder to boost ratings. God, I hate the news media. And here I am working for them. Figures.

The four majors are here. Reporters, network-badged mikes in hand, stand in front of crime scene tape for maximum visual impact. Their camera operators shine the light of truth on the reporters' politically correct, ethnically diverse, well rehearsed facades as they dutifully articulate the "shocking details" of "tragic events"—lenses focused to crystal clarity. If the viewing public only knew, they would slip in their own vomit running to unplug their TVs. Controversy and sensationalism, the news media's single-minded pursuit. It's all about the ratings, any way they can spin it. My cynicism often gets the best of me. A "shocking detail" of a "tragic event" I laughingly call my life.

I squeeze my beat-up Sentra onto a wedge of crumbling asphalt between the backside of the Channel 9 news van and a chain-link perimeter fence topped with curls of razor wire.

As I put my Canon together and drag my butt out, I see Lacey bending Detective Salmon's ear. At this distance I can't tell if Frank Salmon is nodding in agreement or simply tolerating a typical Lacey Friends verbal barrage. Late twenties, early thirties, it's getting to where I can't tell anymore. Anyway she's kinda cute, decent figure, I can see how the detective might put up with it. My cynical side wonders if she's fucking him. Though I've got to give her credit, most reporters barely get the time of day—usually, only a sanitized department-issue press release. Yet she manages to worm her way into the damndest places, extracting inside info you just don't see anywhere else. Probably why that free-press rag keeps her around. Guess I'm lucky she likes my work. But then, I'm cheap and easy, a good bargain for the *Valley Free Press.*

Heading for the Lacey and Salmon show, I unsteadily weave my way through uniforms and EMTs. Glaring floodlight bounces off everything, nearly blinding. As a photographer, every shade of light and dark is my chosen profession. Yet sometimes, I pray for darkness.

Squinting, I glance to my right, noticing the squat, tilt-up concrete box. It's typical of light-industrial buildings in the last Phoenix real estate boom—now bust. Nothing fancy, probably a few offices and the rest, warehouse. Construction equipment yard in the rear. The storefront door is propped open. A large sign in bold font on the fascia above reads "MJR Development Group." Never heard of them, at least not until tonight. Now, through the miracle of instant global media, the whole world will know that name. My stomach gurgles then tightens into knots as a slight wave of dizziness passes.

Doctors have all sorts of technical diagnoses for my various symptoms and conditions, describing them with long-winded, serious-sounding medical terminology. But when I get them to bottom-line it, they tell me I'm getting old. Sonja insists it's all bullshit and I'm just a silly hypochondriac with a sensitive system and ESP I simply can't control. *Well shit, no wonder!*

Believe me, I've tried all the meds. Too expensive. And if they work at all, they cover up the symptoms for a while, but then make things worse. Sometimes, much worse. When it comes to modern pharmacology, I've decided you just can't win—God damn the pusher. Obviously, drugs are not the answer. There are better ways. Still though, I can vaguely recall the days when a fat joint of Acapulco Gold could cure one's ills. Though that certainly wasn't the intent when we fired it up.

*Ah, the good ol' days.* Distracting myself with nostalgia seems to help me cope with the inevitable hell I feel coming. And it's coming on like wildfire through dry weeds on a hot and windy desert night.

# THE PHOTO SHOOT

**[11:09 PM – Tuesday, August 24, 2010]**

LACEY SPOTS ME coming and turns back to Salmon. "Frank, you remember my photographer, Lance Underphal."

Salmon gives me a dismissive nod and turns back to Lacey.

"Hi," I mumble foolishly.

I uncomfortably shift from one foot to the other as Lacey continues to engage Detective Salmon.

Lacey smiles at Salmon. "Have any clues yet?"

Salmon gives a slight smirk. "Not sure, too early to tell, but we found the vic's cell. Looks like it received calls and has a couple new photos about the time of the shooting. Could be nothing. We'll know more after the techs process everything."

A uniform strides up.

Salmon turns to him. "Forensics are about done. It's okay to take them through, but be careful. Don't let them touch anything."

Lacey is positively beaming. "Thanks, Frank."

"Sure. You owe me." Salmon turns, headed for an unmarked Mercury Marauder bristling with antennae.

Who does he think he's fooling? Helluva car though. He's got some seniority to get a ride like that.

I duck beneath the crime scene tape, trudging along behind Lacey and the uniform, headed for the main entry door. The sign shines brightly in the glare from the floods, "MJR Development Group."

The uniform is all business as he orders us to put on protective footies.

"Watch your step."

As if we could do anything else. The place is crawling with forensic techs chatting amongst themselves—standard government workforce, the proverbial road crew with five guys leaning on shovels while one digs. Our tax dollars at work. I'm sure CSI and its knockoffs have done wonders for Forensic Department budgets throughout the free world—the CSI effect. Sometimes that cynic in me just won't shut up.

The stench hits me like a Mack truck, that chemical smell of forensics and gunpowder. And lurking underneath, that unmistakable mix of odors— sweat, blood, urine, bowel gases, feces and worst of all, decaying human flesh—the vile reek of death. My stomach lurches up my throat and I break out in a cold sweat as I try to keep down whatever's left of my dinner. Probably pale as a ghost.

The uniform spots my distress. "Hey, if you've gotta throw up, do it outside. Don't contaminate the scene."

"Yeah … no, I'll be okay," I reply sheepishly.

He watches me like a hawk.

Suddenly, ice picks stab deep into my temples. *Great, just what I need.* It hits hard as a sledgehammer. I hide behind my camera, clicking off shots, trying to look professional in spite of the thundering migraine.

Rings of blinding light invade my vision. I can't see, yet staring back at me through the painful glare are wavering images. I can't look away.

Trembling, I experience everything, all senses on full blast across all energy spectrums. Shimmering black pools of blood stain mottled grey carpet. Reddish-brown blood-smears dance on a vibrating wall peppered with bullet holes. A broken, light oak desk lists to one side, groaning. Reddish-brown blood spots spatter its caved-in desktop. Blood spray fans the far wall, the ceiling, everywhere. A reddish-black aura hangs in the atmosphere like a poisonous mist. I wonder how anyone could have lived through this. Crackling with intensity—there's so much blood, so many bullet holes.

Pictures flash through my mind. High-beams and running lights blasting through window blinds, cutting through the gloom like white-hot targeting lasers. More pictures, probably the dead guy and his lover, a black stain of terror boiling off them in a turbulent frenzy. I'm feeling bullets sting like hot hornets, seeing the silhouette of the shooter in the doorway as muzzle blasts flash and pop. Now they're flailing, jerking, screaming, writhing, their blood blossoming like a dark red kaleidoscope blotting out the light. Excruciating pain. My vision tunnels. *Shit!* I hit my knees, shaking. And everything goes dark. As I go down, I hope I got the pictures Lacey needs. *Dammit!* Why is it that Sonja's always right?

# THE NEWS

### [11:21 PM – Tuesday, August 24, 2010]

THE TV'S COLORED light dances off the polished mahogany bar, sparkles through the hanging glasses and reverses itself in the back wall's endless mirror. Hanging over the far end of the long bar, the TV keeps a silent vigil over clinking glasses, the murmur of scattered small talk and the drone of Muzik's Country Mix channel.

A Chuck Wagon Steaks & Ribs regular, Johnny Chavez sits on a barstool three-quarters of the way down, slamming shots of cheap tequila and boasting about his latest sexual conquest. Shaggy black hair with sun-bleached streaks of mud brown, loosely pulled back in a ponytail that bobs with his grating laugh. Braying like a mule at his own joke, his wide mouth splits a broad leathery face with rubbery lips, exposing big yellow teeth.

Two stools farther down, Jeremy Gott, the Chuck Wagon's manager, smiles and nods, his narrow shoulders hunched as he pretends to listen to the big construction contractor's redneck humor, absently contemplating the final take on what's turning out to be a slow night. Tuesdays in August usually are.

The TV's Breaking News flash catches Jeremy's eye. Too far away to read the closed captioning, he waves over his bleach-blond bartender with the big bolt-ons.

Sally puts down the glass she's drying and gives him a practiced smile. "Whaddaya need?"

"Wouldya turn up the TV?"

"Got it, boss."

Jeremy's eyes are glued to images of Breaking News. Chavez, curious why Jeremy's suddenly so interested, shifts dark eyes to the screen. An overhead shot from the news chopper reveals small clusters of people gathered in a parking lot bright with floods, pulsing with red and blue emergency lights. The scene snaps to a talking head mouthing into a mike, floating in front of crime scene tape, the screen crowded with eye-popping graphics. Nearly buried in the background is a sign on the front of a building—MJR Development Group. Staring, Sally's jaw drops as she thumbs the TV's remote, drowning out the background music. Bar chatter quiets as the TV comes up too loud.

At the other end of the bar, a pair of cold eyes hooded by a dove grey Stetson cut to the TV. Catching a glimpse of the latest murder scene, the hardened features twist with disdain, thin lips tightening into a sneer.

The TV booms in the near-empty bar. "… what police are calling a brutal shooting, leaving one person dead and one in a coma."

Jeremy jumps up. "Shit! That's Mike Rodriguez's place!"

Chavez's eyes narrow as they dart around to take in the bar, checking to see who's watching. He talks loud and brash, voice thick with liquor. "Wonder who got it?"

The tall frame beneath the Stetson unfolds, rising off the barstool. Stetson Hat glances up at the TV as a menacing grin creeps across the lower half of his shadowy face. Reaching into his tailored Western suit, Stetson Hat tosses a wad of bills on the bar. The clomp of alligator cowboy boots fails to penetrate the blaring TV's news as Stetson Hat saunters toward the exit unnoticed.

Sally stares at the set. "Wonder if Mr. Whiting knows?"

"Yeah," says Jeremy, not wanting to think about his boss right now. Gary Whiting, the weasel who prefers to be called Managing Partner, not boss. He'd rather have Mike Rodriguez as boss. Big Mike might be an asshole, but at least he knows how to party. He hopes it's not Big Mike that's shot.

Chavez's wide nostrils flare. "Better not be Mike."

"Isn't he your cousin?" asks Sally.

Veins swell in Chavez's long neck and broad forehead. "Yeah. Better not be Mike. I'll kill any bastard who shoots at my family!"

"Just hold on," says Jeremy. "We don't know anything yet."

At the far end of the Chuck Wagon's parking lot, Stetson Hat climbs into his tall F-150 pickup. His coat catches on the door, revealing a holstered pistol in his left armpit. As he fires up the Ford's big V-8, he contemplates his next move.

At WesternAir's Gate B-22 in Sky Harbor's Terminal 4 Gary Whiting slumps in a black plastic hammock chair in a long row of black plastic hammock chairs, his slacks and off-the-rack suit coat crumpled from a long day of abuse. He's jammed between a three-hundred-pound sweating black woman and a palsied wraith of a man who smells like he hasn't bathed in a week. The Valium and Excedrin have worn off, leaving him in a jittery funk, puffy bags under his darting eyes betraying him. His flight to Vegas has been delayed twice. He fumes as he chews on the end of his little finger. He *hates* waiting. And waiting on flight delays are the worst. He should be in the casino right now. They boarded, then after sitting at the gate for fifty-three minutes, de-planed. At least he got a free drink on the plane. First Class isn't good for much else on the short hop to Vegas. According to the most recent gate announcement, they are waiting for a new plane.

The whole time, Whiting's been rolling it over in his mind, chewing on it, worrying it like a squirrel working a nut. *What if Rodriguez is dead?* Best case scenario is that the life insurance pays up and Whiting walks away, scot-free. *What would it take now … to pay everyone off? Probably close to twenty-five mil. Shit. Not much chance of that.* Worst case is that they find out about the numbers. Then the hard-money lenders, possibly Connie Rodriguez and maybe even the police will be gunning for him. *Perfect. Dead or in prison, the same thing really.*

Whiting's cell vibrates, startling him out of his darkening depression. He glances at it and curses under his breath. "Shit." He punches the keypad. "Didn't you get my message?"

His wife's voice comes across in a high-pitched whine. "Did you see the news?"

He glances up at the monitor. "No … why?"

"You don't know?"

"Know what?"

"How could you not know?"

"Shit, Lydia. What are you talking about?"

"Mike's dead and Diane's in a coma. They were shot at Mike's office earlier this evening. You didn't know about it? Weren't you going to meet with him earlier?"

As he hears his wife, he sees images on the overhead monitor of a crime scene on Breaking News, recognizing MJR Development Group's address crawling along the bottom. A tidal wave of fear crashes down, a spastic shudder that dries his mouth and loosens his bowels. Stunned to speechlessness, mouth agape, he struggles to get a grip. *It's true.*

"Know, how would I know?"

"It's on all the channels. How could you miss it?"

"Oh ... yeah ... it's on right now."

"What are we gonna do?"

Absently, he tunes her out. "I'll call you back." Hearing her whine, he ends the call.

The terminal's array of hanging monitors continues to flash Breaking News images at him like laser cannons. He's surrounded. It really is true. He half expects his picture to pop up next to Rodriguez's.

First things first, he needs some privacy. He jumps up, towing his carry-on across the vast expanse of commercial-grade carpet, heading for the men's room. He needs another Valium, maybe two, to calm down, to think. And they're buried in his carry-on. *Fuck!*

Connie Rodriguez paces frantically in her expansive kitchen. The buttery glow of recessed lighting softens hard edges of granite counters and a stone floor. Nestled high in vaulted ceiling planes, skylights collect the emptiness of a dark desert night. Connie's perfect cut whips around her face, hiding mascara runs on her expertly done makeup—her clingy cream-colored satin top stained with tears.

Unconsciously, she smoothes her hips and sucks in her tummy as she paces, never comfortable with her near-perfect figure—a touch on the full side, no matter what she does. She's tried every new diet and every new exercise DVD, nothing really helps. Yet no one would know to look at her that she's pushing thirty-six.

Maria had rushed right over to take the kids. *Thank God!* All Connie could bear to tell them was that there was an accident and she had to go. Now, all alone in her two-point-five mil Tuscan McMansion, she's panicky, at a total loss as to what she should do.

Mike's always told her what to do and she's always hated that. Now, the one time she wishes he would tell her, he's gone! How can he be gone? The police can't be right. They must've made a mistake. Mike would never let anyone get to him. He always kept a loaded nine millimeter in the truck and a .357 Magnum locked in the nightstand. She can't believe it. *No one would dare!*

They told her she could claim his body after the medical examiner was done. She needs to go, to see for herself. She's pretty sure there's enough life insurance, but Mike always took care of those things. She hopes that God is watching over her and the children. She wonders what she'll tell the kids. She wonders which bimbo he was banging. Not surprising he'd get shot with his pants down. She almost suppresses a manic laugh, then breaks down, sobbing. *What am I gonna do?*

Trying to pull herself together, Connie dabs her cheeks with a wad of tissue. She grabs the remote for the kitchen TV while mentally running through a list of people to call. *Can't go there alone.*

Suddenly the flatscreen lights, its speakers pop and she's transfixed, staring at live coverage of a fatal shooting. Her cell beeps with an incoming text. Absently, she checks. It's Brandy, her baby sister, on vacation on Martha's Vineyard, wanting to know if she's watching the news, wanting to know if she's okay.

Connie sighs, succumbing to that sinking feeling in her chest, a wilting deep within, accepting the inevitable. It hasn't been good for several years, but it was once. And no matter how bad it got, no matter how much they'd grown apart, no matter how much they fought, she's always harbored hope, maybe false hope, that it could be good again. But it's over and it hurts. *God's will.*

Sadness and relief wash through her as she realizes that she will get through this, if only for the children's sake. She *has* to get through this.

Thinking Daniel will help, she dials the home number of Mike Junior's martial arts instructor. It's late, but he might still be up. He's always been a big help to Mikey, working him through his issues. In the last year or so he's discreetly been there for her too. Maybe she's kidding herself to think he really cares.

She puts on a brave face as the phone rings.

Daniel's wife, Marcia, answers.

"Connie?"

"Yes."

"OhMyGod, Connie! Are you all right? We were just watching the news …"

"I'll be okay." She is amazed at herself—doing such a good job of keeping it together.

"OhMyGod! I'm so sorry. Do you need me to come over?"

A slight tremor creeps into her voice. "Is Daniel there?"

"Yeah, sure, just a second. You let me know if you need anything."

Connie waits, chewing her bottom lip, reddened crystal blue eyes welling, listening for Daniel, wondering what would happen if Marcia knew about her and Daniel. She can't think about that right now.

"Hey, Connie, I heard. Sorry about Mike. Terrible. You gonna be okay?"

Connie tries to catch herself then blubbers. "Can … you take me … down to the morgue? I need … to see … if it's him."

Daniel Rupert curses to himself. *Shit!* "Hey, Connie, it's gettin' kinda late, sure you don't want to go in the morning?"

"Please, Daniel. I need to see for myself."

Daniel cups the receiver as he turns to Marcia. "Baby, she needs me to take her down to identify the body."

Marcia volunteers. "I'll take her. I know you got an early class."

Daniel backpedals. "I think it would be better if I went. She needs someone to deal with the authorities and I know some of those guys, you know, they're in my classes."

"Yeah, but I could ride down with you."

"Honey, you stay here. It's late and this might take awhile. Besides, you have to go early tomorrow. You know how you are when you don't get enough sleep."

The last thing he needs is Marcia tagging along. Who knows how upset Connie is. And if she were to slip up … No, he's got to keep things under control.

He winks at Marcia. And with a too-tight smile, he drops his hand off the mouthpiece. "No problem. I'm on my way."


The Lion's Den is heating up. Black-light fluorescents sparkle off golden glitter sprayed on flat-black drywall. Day-Glo silhouettes of naked women in suggestive poses shimmer with iridescence, their lioness ears perked and lioness tails about to twitch. In the main showroom sits a colorfully lit hardwood stage with a gleaming chrome stripper's pole dead center. The sound system's subwoofers pound out a hypnotic beat as a long-legged redhead with twin silicone mounds writhes nude on her back near the front of the stage. She pulls her legs high and wide, arching her back to loud whistles and catcalls, all accompanied by a flurry of dollar bills. Behind the stage's front row chairs and the main floor tables, a long black bar hunches against the back wall.

On her break, a sultry Sondra Du saunters up to the low bar, her long blonde mane and custom-built breasts bouncing. She slides her tight over-worked buns up on the barstool next to Lenny.

Lenny Kantor has his back to the action, sipping a club soda. The nature of the job requires him to remain aloof but alert. The dancers, the barmaids, the bouncers, all those who need to know, couldn't mistake him for anything but the boss, king of the cash flow. He watches his iPhone's screen with beady eyes under thick black brows on either side of a pronounced hook nose, picking up bits and pieces of the latest shooting across town. Turns out, his partner's construction company is the headline and he gives a low whistle.

"Whaz up?" Sondra asks.

He gives her a sideways glance and turns back to his iPhone, watching intently.

Sondra waits for his reply. Nobody rushes Lenny.

He taps the screen a couple times. "A shooting at Big Mike's."

"No shit?"

"No shit. Looks like they got him."

She feels a frisson of fear course through her, raising the hairs on the back of her pretty neck. "Whoa, it's gonna hit the fan now."

"Yeah, I think he and Whiting were into Cohen & Company for a chunk of change. And you don't wanna be in too deep to Benny Cohen."

"Shit, wonder what that does to Fellman."

"His bank's got the loan on that deal, huh?"

"Yeah. Wonder if he's gonna havta arm-wrestle Cohen for it?"

Lenny sips his club soda as Sondra ponders the ramifications of Big Mike Rodriguez's early demise. Big Mike still owes her, in more ways than one. And she is planning on it paying off, big time. "If Big Mike's gone, what does that do to the club?"

"Who knows? Maybe I got a new partner."

Sondra's eyes widen. "Hope it's not Cohen."

Lenny shrugs. "Yeah, I guess we'll see." He turns on her with a piercing stare. "Break's over."

Disgusted, Sondra casually slides off the barstool to head backstage. *Shit!* She'll probably never get what Big Mike owes her. Still, she's got other sources of income, just not enough to get out.

# LAST YEAR

### [9:52 AM – Friday, August 21, 2009]

A HOT AND sunny morning. At the curb, large plywood signs blatantly proclaimed premier retail shops, professional offices and luxury lofts available soon. When completed, Sunset Pointe would be a combination of upscale shops and dining with residential lofts above, along with a Class A office complex and an extended stay hotel. For now, the MJR construction trailer was the only structure on the otherwise vacant building site for the newest mixed-use commercial development project in North Phoenix.

A well-dressed little gathering stood around the Sunset Pointe building site, bored with the groundbreaking ceremony, waiting for the formalities to conclude. A semicircle of business associates, friends and family were gathered around Rodriguez and Whiting. Off to the side, a line of limos waited. Their drivers in black uniforms, hats and dark glasses leaned against black fenders, patiently suffering in the bright sunshine.

Standing on bare dirt, Rodriguez and Whiting held a handshake, each with a foot propped on a golden spade, waiting on the photographer. They posed in power suits and striped ties, wearing chrome hard hats and phony smiles, sweating like pigs in the blazing Arizona sun.

Rodriguez hated wearing that monkey suit, usually wouldn't be caught dead in one. They never fit him right, his bulky frame bulging in all the wrong places, like dressing up a silverback gorilla in a rented prom tux. This time, he figured it'd be well worth it with his fifty percent ownership interest as a Managing Member. If he'd known what a spineless sniveler Whiting was going to be, he'd have made it fifty-one percent. No matter, he knew how to work Whiting. Sunset Pointe should be worth thirty mil, easy. He'd make a killing, not to mention the money he'd make as the project's general contractor. Just thinking about it made his smile morph into a wicked grin, heavily creasing coarse features.

Everyone endured the heat, daydreaming about cool limo rides to the executive terminal, a chartered jet and the groundbreaking party in Vegas. Rodriguez savored the moment, thinking about lines of coke and the bottle of Dom Perignon waiting for him in his limo. *Party time!* Too bad Connie would be there. He'd just have to work around it.

At the top of the Tangiers Casino/Hotel, Mike Rodriguez scanned the cavernous penthouse. He'd changed into his Nikes, black Levi's and a purple and orange Suns jersey, more in keeping with his all-around good-guy image.

The penthouse was a study in decadence. A vast expanse of jet-veined marble tile butted up against black-lacquered wainscoting. Ornate patterned wall coverings of scarlet flocking on shiny gold mylar rose to a cathedral ceiling. The domed ceiling was gilded with intricate scrollwork, hung with massive cut-glass chandeliers. And the suite was packed. Must've been fifty, sixty people there, the movers and shakers plus the hangers-on, all guests of Sunset Pointe, LLC. Rodriguez's wide mouth formed a grin, his full lips taut. He was the self-appointed host. *A tough job, but somebody's gotta do it.*

Though the spacious suite was decked out in Vegas Gaudy it was the perfect venue for this crowd. Impressive as shit when you knew what a penthouse suite went for per night. Good thing Whiting got it all comped. At least the little wimp was good for something.

Looking toward the two-story glass with its panoramic view of the glittering Vegas Strip, Rodriguez spotted his wife, her honey hair and supermodel stance unmistakable. Connie was busy chatting up the banker, Fellman. *Good girl.* They'd need to up the balance on that Acquisition/Development loan. Probably need to extend it, too. He watched as Fellman stared at her tits. Can't blame him, everyone stared at Connie's tits, one of her best features. They ought to be. He paid enough for them.

Rodriguez ran his free hand through a thick mane of dark curly hair, his gaze inching across the room like a slow hand sliding up a firm thigh. Off to the side, Diane Telafano leaned up against the bar looking sexy in that low-cut gold lame miniskirt he'd bought for her on their weekend jaunt to La Jolla. He'd catch up with her later.

Glancing up, he saw the encircling marble mezzanine. More guests, with drinks in hand, leaned against the polished brass railing engaged in conversation or looking out over the crowd.

Below, Rodriguez spotted the Lion's Den contingent. Lenny Kantor, dark and brooding. Next to Kantor was the Den's top showgirl, Sondra Du, leaning against one of the foyer's gilded columns. Sondra targeted him with a laser stare, smiling wickedly, her smoldering eyes daring him to come fuck her. He raised his glass and gave her a grin. She'd be busy tonight. He had a couple key clients lined up for her. She'd suck 'em dry in more ways than one. He'd seen a few of the Lion's Den girls circulating. Good thing Lenny did what he was told, made sure there was enough tail tonight for anyone who wanted it.

Across the room, Whiting and his manager Jeremy seemed deep in conversation. Jeremy always made sure Rodriguez and his MJR crew were well taken care of when they showed up at the Chuck Wagon. Never whined about MJR's tab like that idiot, Whiting. Whiting worried too much—too weak, like a little old lady. Rodriguez grinned, knowing he'd never pay up. *Shit, what's a few thousand dollars between partners?*

Rodriguez's gaze cut left to a cluster of attorneys. An extremely well-dressed flock of vultures, draining their drinks and his bank accounts, engaged in casual conversation. Their expensive suits oozed affluence. He hated suits and the people in them, but there was nothing like the right attorney in your corner when you went into battle. Rodriguez learned early on that if you're playing to win, attorneys are a necessary evil. *Shit, they're probably running up the billable hours even now.*

The stately old guy, his main attorney, Hammond Elder chatted away—a full head of fine white hair combed back in a wave, his trademark. Severe in his three-piece pinstripes, he'd managed to get more than a few claims dismissed, but his passion lay on the links. Then there was Sunset Pointe's attorney, Fredrick Marsh, tall, thin, cadaverous with a booming voice like Christopher Lee. Next to Marsh was that cute little legal assistant of his, Teresa Milner. Her ass looked hot in that tight navy skirt. Rodriguez grinned, trying to picture Marsh boning her on that massive cherrywood desk of his. Maybe he'd give the little rabbit a try later. All it takes is a snootful of coke and few shots of tequila to turn the quiet ones into banshees.

Then there was the entitlement team from Swit/Conner. A couple of crafty, well-connected boys. Half their staff used to work for the City. Someone had to wrestle the City's Development Services Department into submission, and these hotshots specialized in the inside moves to take them to the mat. Everyone knew the score. Over the years real estate development had blossomed into one of the City's main sources of revenue, gouging private developers, piling on an additional twenty percent or more to the development costs of new projects. Everyone had their hand out, even the pinheaded, pencil-pushing bureaucrats. And Rodriguez knew how to grease their palms.

As Rodriguez started toward the attorneys, yelling from across the room turned his head. Someone having too good of a time. Over the heads of his guests, he could barely make out the commotion. Damn Trades. Had to invite them, but the rednecks were trouble once they sucked down a few drinks. Pushing through the crowd, he figured he'd head them off.

His loudmouth cousin, Johnny Chavez, roared as he waved his arms, a howling wild man, his black eyes flashing, his wide mouth spread in a big toothy grin. At six-foot-four, he towered over the other subcontractors. All the boys were gathered around Chavez egging him on.

Rodriquez pushed through the crowd and bellowed, "What's all the hollerin' about?"

One of the subs grabbed his arm. "Watch out, Johnny's lit pretty good."

"Hell." Rodriquez twisted away. "Johnny, whatsup?"

Johnny Chavez swung around, looking down into Rodriguez's face. "Hey, cuz. Just in time to get this party started!"

Loud and obnoxious, Chavez had a head start and was letting everyone know about it.

Rodriguez pushed his face up into Johnny's florid features. He grabbed his bicep. "Cool your jets, partner," he said in a low, threatening tone.

Chavez's words slurred. "Partner? Shit, I wish! Hey, where's Diane? Didn' ya bring her?"

"Settle down. She's around somewhere. So what?"

"So what? You need to share, that's so what! I shared her with you, it's the least you could do. Shit, whad am I sayin'? You fuckin' stole her! Hey, I know! How 'bout a gangbang? Share that hot pussy with everyone, ya sonofabitch."

"Hey, watch it. Don't wanna havta toss your ass outta here."

"You and what fuckin' army?"

Rodriguez turned. "Hey Pedro, you an' Stan give me a hand here."

"Sure, Mike."

Rodriguez turned back to Chavez. "Let's get you some fresh air."

Together, they started wrestling Chavez toward the patio's glass doors.

Chavez pushed back, wrenching his big arms free. "Don' need no fuckin' air."

Rodriguez moved in close. "Whadabout some blow to smooth things out?"

Chavez gave him a big rubber-lipped grin. "Hell yeah!"

The four men moved out through the throng of onlookers onto the patio for round two. Mike's coarse features tightened with a sly grin. He knew everyone's buttons and just how to push them. Tonight was his night and he was on top of it, as usual.

# THE E/R

## [12:26 PM – Wednesday, August 25, 2010]

### DREAMING:

*Sonja floats over me just out of reach. She's telling me something of great importance, I'm sure of it. But I can't quite make it out, a low monotonous murmur, droning on, no matter how I strain to hear. Her smile glows, warming me, comforting me and I want to go to her. Her eyes glisten, reassuring me everything will be all right. I try to form the words, to tell her, I'll do whatever she asks.*

*Her radiance lights the way as I follow her into the crystal blue of an ethereal sky. It's a land of light and brilliant colors, of large effortless motions, everything moving in perfect harmony at her beck and call. And I'm exhilarated, tears of joy streaming down my face as I now know this is how it is supposed to be. I'm home.*

*She turns to me, extending her arms, reaching out with loving eyes and a knowing smile. I run to her and we embrace—a giddy dance, like children dancing in a meadow filled with wildflowers on a warm spring day. She tells me this is how it is. Her siren song, a sweet melody. And I bask in its beauty.*

*She hugs me close. "There's more to come, but first you have some bridges to cross," she whispers. "I'll help you. No matter what, don't give up."*

*Her words fade, and I drift off as she fades away—so tired now, just want to rest. All I need is rest. That's all I really need … really … so tired …*

I squint into the too-bright light, surrounded on all sides by white curtains, white pillows, white sheets, a nurse. Or are there two? Dressed all in white. I'd guess I'm still dreaming, if it didn't hurt so much. But the hurting is real. Guts twist in and out of rock-hard knots, head throbs, white-hot shards shoot deep into my swollen brain with every pulse, phosphorescent blue spots scatter across my vision. I'm either awake or in hell. Same thing, really.

And now I'm hearing things, just below the shrill ringing in my ears.

"He's coming around."

"You want to let her know?"

"Mr. Underphal?"

The room spins. Nausea claws at my gut, crawling up the back of my throat. In a cold sweat, spasms seize my thorax in a crushing bear hug as I convulse—the dry heaves. *I must be empty.* Funny I could have that thought in the midst of all this pain, as though I can stand back, outside myself and observe with detached interest. I must've blacked out.


"Lance? Lance? Can you hear me?"

Hmm. Must be Lacey. Is that a hint of concern or annoyance in her voice?

"Lacey?" It comes out in a croak. I try again. "Lacey."

"Yes, Lance, it's me."

"What happened?"

"They had to sedate you. You went into convulsions."

"Oh. No. I mean what am I doin' here?"

"Well. You passed out. They had to carry you out. Good thing there was an ambulance."

"Sorry ... sometimes the migraines ... you know ..."

"Must have been one hell of a migraine"

"Yeah ... still is."

"Well, they say you'll be all right ... and ... uh ... I gotta go. I'll try and stop in tomorrow."

Not sure why I'm disappointed, but I am. Doubt I'll be seeing her tomorrow. Maybe it's just knowing I'm alone. I miss Sonja. She keeps telling me I'm not really alone. But times like these, it sure seems that way. The nurse injects something into my IV and I drift off.

*Dreaming:*

*Sonja is critiquing the photo shoot. I snap the image of a naked babe flat on her back, eyes closed, lips parted in rapture, her honey thighs and calves wrapped around her lover's muscular buttocks, his taut back glistening. As they pant and heave, sweat flies, freezing mid-air in the frame.*

*"Delete, you won't need that one," she says.*

*I hit erase and refocus on a green felt blackjack table. One player against a black-vested Vegas dealer, the crowd is three deep and cheering. High-Roller pumps his fist as Dealer flips him an ace and I click to capture the moment.*

*"Warm, but not the real deal. You can delete that one, too."*

*I'm thinking, Hmm ... won't be much of a shoot at this rate.*

*"No, you'll get it, just keep looking."*

*Something's wrong, I can't get my Canon to focus. A shadowy film, dark and dense, overlays two pictures superimposed—the back of a burgundy leather Chippendale parked in front of a large flatscreen. Arms dangle off the sides, one set of fingers grips the top of an ice-filled tumbler, the other contains a fat cigar wedged between index and middle fingers. Smoke curls lazily up into a haze. And floating just beneath the smoking room scene, blinding lights from a tall pickup, its engine revving. Like a red-misted bull, snorting and pawing, its presence bristles with menace, pumped up and ready to charge with high-beams and running lights ablaze. It grates on me. Weird, the whole thing undulates as though underwater, but crystal clear in detail—too much depth of field. I need to get it into focus.*

Sonja's voice lifts me to wakefulness as though floating into shimmering light. "Close enough for now. We'll resume after you recover."

"Close enough for what?" But she's already gone, cutting me loose to wonder by myself. What am I dealing with here? This damn shooting again. And why me? I don't even *know* these people. Why can't these images, visions, perceptions, whatever the hell they are, just leave me alone? *Shit!*

Ethereal light fades as physical reality sets in, my head thick with impenetrable fog. A dull throbbing grips my skull like a helmet full of fists. I'm whirling from the heavy medication used to tamp down the pain into the tight box I call normal. It's a brand new day—rough as hell. And they are hustling me up and out, discharging me. Probably need the bed for a paying customer, one with better insurance.

I'm still on the nod as I fly down the long corridor in an orderly-powered wheelchair, a hospital-logoed plastic bag with my new prescriptions and personal belongings clutched to my lap. Last I recall, I'm headed for the curb and a cab back to my car.

I fumble my way out of the wheelchair and shuffle toward the cab's rear seat, clutching the door frame for balance. I half fall into the backseat with a sigh of relief. As the cab pulls out of the E/R's loading drive, I give the cabby the last known address of my car. *Shit, wonder if I'll be able drive? No matter … Free at last, free at last …*

# GOING HOME

**[2:38 PM – Wednesday, August 25, 2010]**

I SPOT MY tired old Sentra as the cab pulls up to MJR Development's front gate. A flash of panic. While I was in the hospital, someone dragged my poor car outside the yard and dumped it against the curb. What about my stuff, my camera bag, my Canon? My camera equipment is all I own, the only stuff I've got that's worth a shit. My heart rate slows as I think it through. They probably had to get it out of the yard for security purposes—a crime scene and all. I crawl out of the back seat and prop myself up against the door post waiting at the cabby's window for change. Twenty-eight fuckin' dollars for a ten minute ride and almost all my cash. *Shit!*

The cabby speeds off, spraying gravel. Guess he didn't appreciate the size of the tip. *I gotta tip for him.* He should try lowering his rate, or at least learn English. *Highway fuckin' robbery, piss on 'em.*

Legs are still rubbery as I wobble toward my car. I haven't gone five feet and I'm sweating like a virgin on prom night. It's hotter 'n hell out here, well into triple digits, another day above a hundred and ten. What's that make it, nineteen days in a row? And not even a record for August. They say it's a dry heat. Yeah, well, so is a pizza oven, but you wouldn't want to live in it.

The hellish desert sun illuminates a harsh reality—cracked asphalt and hard baked dirt, all radiating heat and dry as an old bone. Even the tumbleweeds are dried up. Looking through the chain link, I see the yellow crime scene tape shimmer in dead air. All the lights and action are gone—the hollow stillness, ghostly. I glance at the sign and a shudder runs up my spine. It still reads MJR Development Group, nothing's really changed, but it seems sinister, as though fronting for some deadly secret.

How I managed to get dragged into this mess, I still don't know, but it's really starting to piss me off. Yesterday's still a blur, bits and pieces of the crime scene, dull remnants of a nightmarish hospital stay.

Of course, all the tests confirm there's basically nothing wrong with me, just one of those migraines. You'd think with all those expensive diagnostics, they'd be able to find something they could cure, but no. Shit, you should see the bill. Good thing I don't have to pay for it. After all that expensive health care with state-of-the-art medical technology, I'm left with an empty, washed out feeling, still punchy from the residual migraine trauma and heavy pain meds.

I've lived with these damned migraines too long, trying to live my life around them. I've driven myself crazy, trying to identify and avoid those substances and/or behaviors that precede a migraine. Model patient that I was, I had a long list. When I thought I'd spotted the cause, it normally turned out false and I'd have to start all over. *What a load of crap!*

If Sonja hadn't reappeared when she did, I'd have offed myself long ago. She promised me she'd help; that together, we'd get to the heart of the matter; that I could regain some semblance of control over my life. How all this mysticism shit fits in, I don't yet know. I do know there's a correlation; and I still believe that with Sonja's help, I'll get to the bottom of it eventually. So I continue. *Like I have a choice.*

I finally make it to my car and unlock the primer-coated door. I burn my hand on the door handle, pry open the door and am blasted by the escaping heat. The faux-leather driver's seat is so hot it burns my thighs and back through my clothes. The steering wheel is too hot to touch, much less drive. It has to be a hundred and fifty degrees in here. I turn to grab a towel off the back seat, looking for my equipment bag, worried about my camera in this heat. And it's not there. *Shit!* I look frantically, checking the foot wells, under the seats, even the trunk. *It's gone! What did they do with it!?!*

Whipping out my cell, I thumb Lacey's number.

"Lacey! What happened to my shit?"

"What?"

"MY CAMERA!?!"

"Hey, relax, I got it."

"You got it?"

"Yeah, didn't wanna leave it in your car—too hot and it might get ripped off."

"Whoa … okay, okay, thanks. Where are you? I'll come get it."

"You at your car now?"

"Yup."

"Look, why don't you go home, take it easy? I'll bring it to you later."

"Yeah … I guess so."

"Yeah, get some rest."

"Good idea, I'm still a little shaky."

# WAKING UP IN VEGAS

**[2:38 PM – Wednesday, August 25, 2010]**

GARY WHITING GRABS his head, rolls over and pounds the snooze button with his palm. He peers bleary-eyed at the alarm clock's digital display. *Shit!* The suite's blackout shades keep the white-hot afternoon glare at bay, cool and dark inside. The A/C's gentle humming hammers at his head like a thundering locomotive. He can still make the 5:10 flight back to Phoenix. If he could only get up. He rolls back on the super-king bed. Pulling the champagne silk sheets up to his neck, he clutches his skull, his temples pierced by the Devil's own talons. Too much gin and tonic or not enough blow, or is it the other way 'round? The best cure, another lude to sleep it off, but he's got a plane to catch. Besides he's worn out his welcome, at least for this trip—out of funds, he's got to go. Checkout time was an hour and a half ago and the Tangiers will want the room for the next high-rolling sucker pretty damn quick.

He gazes up at the bed's lavish canopy. The comped Player's Suite that looked opulent only last night now seems garish, too extravagant, a hellish reminder of last night's heavy losses. He was up big, nearly forty grand, but gave it all back plus another fifteen K. And trying to recoup his losses, went down another twenty, exhausting his Tangiers Club account on the way south. He ended up signing another note to increase his limit. Might as well, what's he got to lose? His partner is dead and their thirty million dollar mixed-use commercial development project dead along with him. What rotten luck. An all-round shitty twenty or so hours.

He's sick. And knowing it's self-inflicted only makes it worse. His eyes squeeze shut and pop open. The dizziness is too much, turning to nausea curdling in his gut. He propels himself out of bed, stumbling to the marble-tile Roman bath. Bending over, he braces himself against the toilet seat and barks his guts out—strings of yellow bile then nothing, more dry heaves. He curls up on the cold marble, clammy, sweating like a speed freak in a police lineup, limp and wasted as a used condom. He's got to get it together and make that flight. He knows if he gets anywhere near the tables, he'll lose everything. He's got to get out of there. *Hair of the dog, that's what I need, yup.*

After a couple lines he thinks he might be able to keep down some water, a couple Vicodin and a couple Valium.

In the Tangiers limo on the way to McCarran International, he does a couple more lines and a couple more Valium for safe measure, just to get through security and on the plane. *Better.*

Hiding behind his Oakleys, he reclines the first-class seat all the way, dozing off and on for the forty-five-minute flight home. He can't begin to think about who killed Rodriguez or why, not yet. As long as they don't come after *him.* He wonders if Diane will make it—news said she was in a coma. He wonders if she'll get to keep the Bimmer Rodriguez leased for her. He wonders how much she knows.

Connie Rodriguez shuffles to the kitchen island's hand-carved cabinets. Capped with polished black granite, their craftsmanship is of the highest caliber. She ought to know, she handpicked them. Still in the orange XXL Suns jersey she slept in, she scratches her bed-head and eyes the espresso machine. Fumbling with a Southwestern designer cup on the wrought-iron rack, she glances at the time, after 2:30. She must've slept all the way through. Between the antidepressants and sleeping meds, she's numb as a tree stump. At least her au pair, Maria, kept the kids occupied. The Church sent over Father Ambrose for grief counseling. He's working with the children now. Connie will have to face them … just not yet.

She needs to call Hammond Elder and find out where she stands. First coffee and a shower. Half dead from exhaustion, she hopes the coffee helps. Last night was the worst. Daniel was so phony. He hated being there. She couldn't tell if it was her, or the whole scene at the morgue. She can't really think about it. Too depressing. She's having trouble thinking at all. The only thing that keeps her going is deep down, she knows she deserves to be well compensated for the hell Mike's putting her through. *How could he get himself killed? How could he do this to us?* Maybe fate has done them a favor, or maybe *someone* has. She wonders who killed her husband and why. Not that he didn't have enemies. He often told her that people were jealous of his success. However, there could've been other reasons, too—all the women. More than once she had secretly thought about killing him herself. And now, here she is, the Widow Rodriguez. Why should *she* feel guilty?

She can't let herself think about the size of the insurance settlement. She just has to have faith in God's will and that the life insurance will make up for all of it. She'll find a way to get through it. She has to, for the children's sake.

Sondra Du's eyelids flutter open. A sheen of sweat dampens her upper lip, her pits and crotch moist and sticky. She listens to the little A/C's drone, barely keeping August's heat out of the aluminum can of a double-wide. Turning on her side, she spots Naomi's bare brown butt peeking out of the sheets. She smiles and pats Naomi's fine ass. Not only is Naomi a great fuck, she's a real comfort.

Naomi grunts and stirs, then drops back into a purring snore.

Sondra lies back, still smiling. She had a good night last night—a huge crowd at the Lion's Den, probably morbid curiosity about Big Mike. But who cares? They threw lots of dollars at the stage and bought more lap dances than she could count. Counting the gangbang in the van, she must've cleared seven large. If only that were enough for her and Naomi to retire, head south, lie on the beach, maybe the Caribbean.

It's well past 2:30 as Sondra pushes up out of bed. She pads naked through the narrow hall's paper-thin walls toward the tiny bathroom. Scratching her landing strip, she grins thinking of last night. "Rode hard and put away wet," her bull-riding ex-lover used to say. They were just kids then, back when she was wide-eyed and innocent—had she only known. *Shit, gave it away.* She sure missed out on some serious cash. Ah well, she's definitely making up for it now. Last trip to Grand Cayman, she deposited more than seventy-five grand. Her grin tightens to a thin-lipped smirk. Horny men will pay big bucks for a woman with a tight ass, great tits and the skill to use them. And then they continue to pay and pay and pay, just to keep their bimbo wives from finding out—easy scams.

Sondra squeezes into the cramped shower stall. Letting cool water stream over her perfect silicone breasts and flat belly, she thinks about Big Mike, shakes her head and chuckles. He always thought he was *great* in the sack, bragging to anyone who'd listen that *he* didn't have to pay, even though he forked over more dough than most paying customers in tips alone. Then there was Big Mike's cousin Johnny, a real mean bastard with no bucks, at least he was a better fuck. If Big Mike hadn't been the big-tipping boss, she would have charged him double just to listen to all his bullshit. His bragging never let up. Drunk and horny, he would confide all his conquests—women, business, whatever. But he *did* tip well and made her tons of money. Always had rich marks lined up for her—easy scams. She's going to miss that.

She wonders who got to him. Could be anyone. Shit, there's no shortage of people he fucked over—partners, employees, subcontractors, suppliers, lenders. It's rumored he kept a couple small law firms gainfully employed just handling the constant stream of lawsuits. Then there are all the girlfriends, not to mention the wife. *Shit, could be anyone.*


Mr. Benjamin R. Cohen of Cohen & Company struts hurriedly into his expansive office. At his massive, hand-carved mahogany desk, he swings his high-backed executive chair around and slides his plump rear end into the sumptuous Italian leather. Fresh on his mind, Michael J. Rodriguez's demise. He automatically shoots his cuffs to admire the two carat diamond-studded links. Today, their lustrous sparkle fails to improve his mood. His smooth, perfectly primped face barely concealing a scowl. Since funding the loan for Sunset Pointe, the commercial real estate market has imploded, skewing his well-laid plans, forcing him to take a different tack. Rodriguez's passing requires swift and delicate handling, if he's ever going to pull this off and get his money.

Buzzing his personal assistant, Clara, Cohen tells her, "Find Stein and Redman and send them in, pronto."


Charlie Stein's lanky frame climbs into his custom off-road Ford truck. Tossing his dove grey Stetson onto the passenger seat, he grabs his dark glasses off the dash. His alligator cowboy boot pumps the gas pedal. An old habit, left over from his long-haul days. Firing up the silver truck, he mumbles to himself, "Asshole." His boss, Cohen, goes too far—an anal retentive. Everything's under control. No need to overreact. Rodriguez's killing is no big deal. He can handle any repercussions in his sleep. His asshole boss and his precious "investors" will get their money, no problemo.

# THE PHOTOS

**[6:13 PM – Wednesday, August 25, 2010]**

EVEN THOUGH I slept all afternoon, my head's still fuzzy, filled with cotton. I pry myself out of bed and pad barefoot down the hall in my skivvies. My mouth's dry, stomach's rumbling. Early evening and I ought to be hungry, but don't have much of an appetite—remnants of a migraine and heavy meds. I pop open the refrigerator door and stare numbly at bare shelves and vacant bins. A half-empty six-pack, out-of-date cottage cheese, a couple unidentifiable leftovers in crumpled tinfoil, nothing really jumps out at me. Perfect, not much left in the fridge and no appetite, but I scarf down a hard-boiled egg and half a peanut butter sandwich. It'll hold me for now. I wad the paper plate and napkin and toss a hook shot at the over-flowing garbage bin next to the fridge. The ball of used paper products bounces off the stained wall just above the over-full receptacle, hits the trash mound and rolls off, landing on the floor in the company of several other three-point attempts. Definitely need to take out the garbage, but right now I gotta get my gear and I'm feelin' a little rough. I plop my tired ass on the closest stool, eyeing the bottle of pain pills perched on the counter. I snatch up my cell and punch the speed-dial number for Lacey's cell.

"Lacey, hey, when … uh … were you gonna bring my shit over?"

"Well, I can do it tonight if you want."

"Sure, that'd be good. About what time?"

"Well, uh, let's see …"

There's a long muffled pause and I begin to wonder who's she talking to.

Then she comes back on, "I could be there in about an hour, if that's okay?"

"Yeah, sure. I'll see you then."

I hang up, still eyeing the pain pills. I want one, but I don't. My nerves are on edge because they're wearing off. And if I take one, it'll smooth things out. Too bad it doesn't last. Worse yet, when tomorrow comes, I'll be faced with the same decision again only it will be that much harder. I know from long experience with this kinda shit, the longer I wait, the harder it is to face the music. If I had the guts, I'd dump those pills in the toilet and sweat it out. But I know better—need a safety blanket, even if I never touch them. And if a migraine kicks in, they could save me another trip to the ER.

I push off the stool, the pain in every joint sharpened into hot needles—inflammation feeding off raw nerves, probably a combination of old age and the aftereffects of heavy pain meds. I sweep the bottle of pain pills off the counter, clutching them in my fist as I hobble toward the head. Stashing them in the medicine cabinet, I reluctantly turn back to the kitchen. I grab a longneck out of the fridge, twisting off the top as I shuffle for my chair and the remote. Hopefully the beer will take the edge off while I wait for Lacey. Wonder if my gear is okay. Wonder if any of the pictures turned out. Wonder how the fuck I got into this mess. But then, Sonja *did* warn me.


The knocking wakes me. Must be Lacey. Must've dozed off. I struggle to sit up, spilling what's left of my beer. *Shit!* More knocking. "Just a second!" I try wiping the beer off my bare belly with my hands then wipe my hands on my skivvies. Perfect, I look like a near-naked bum on a three-day drunk. I wrap a ragged comforter around me and run my hands through my hair before I reach for the door, figure she can just hand me my shit and split.

It's Lacey, oops! … and Detective Salmon.

*Great, just what I need. What's* he *doing here?* I'm really *not* in the mood for company—not really dressed for it, either. Just want my shit back.

"Hey, Lacey. Detective Salmon." They must be sleeping together.

Lacey hands me my camera bag. "Lance, you all right?" She stands there with Salmon, an exaggerated look of concern on her pretty face, apparently waiting for me to invite them in.

"Yeah, a little shaky, but I'll be okay."

She gently pushes past me. "Can we come in?"

I step back. "Yeah, I guess. Come on in." *This just isn't my night.*

She attempts to mask the mild disgust creeping across her face, wrinkling her smooth features as her forced smile evaporates.

I give them a sheepish grin. "The maid's day off."

Salmon almost cracks a smile as he crosses my pigpen of a living room to sit on a tall stool at the kitchen counter.

Lacey hesitates, looks around then gingerly picks her way toward my ratty couch. I use my couch as an impromptu library and it's buried under newspapers, magazines and various books. She neatly stacks the scattered newspapers in a pile to the side, clearing a small space to sit.

I stand, one hand clasping the comforter closed and the other gripping the camera bag handles. Glancing back and forth between them, I can see it's obviously more than a social visit. Lacey is looking everywhere but at me, and Salmon is looking at Lacey waiting for her to start. My curiosity gets the best of me.

"So, thanks for taking care of my gear. And for bringing it by."

Lacey still won't look at me. "It's no problem. Just wanted to make sure it was safe. I mean, you were ... well, I just thought it would be better if I kept it for you."

Salmon focuses a hard stare on Lacey as her discomfort grows.

I force a smile, gently rocking from heels to toes, waiting for her to spit out whatever it is.

She lifts her eyes tentatively, grins and reddens slightly. "Well, any-way ... I got a look at your pictures." Her tone rises with feigned enthusi-asm. "They're great! We can definitely use a couple with the story. Deadline's day after tomorrow."

She's stalling and she knows I know. I've known since the very first job that the Press's deadline is Fridays. And of course, the day after tomorrow *is* Friday, so what's going on here? Okay, I'll play along. "I haven't seen them yet. Do you wanna take a look and tell me which ones you want?"

Salmon shifts on the stool, losing patience. He turns to me and locks my gaze. "Look, Lance, there's one of your shots I need to ask you about."

"Whaddaya mean?"

"I was there when Lacey scrolled through the photos."

Lacey stares anxiously at Salmon, chewing her lower lip.

*Damn, they* are *sleeping together.* "Yeah, and?"

Salmon's not beating around the bush. "Be easier if we just take a look."

My curiosity runs rampant. "Okay." I move to the counter, set the camera bag down, unzip it and reassemble my Canon with one hand, still holding the comforter closed with the other. Lacey joins us at the counter as we all focus on the LED window on the back of my Canon. I power up and start scrolling through the digital images from the last photo shoot, the murder scene.

There are a few setup shots: clumps of emergency respondents inside crime scene tape backed by the squat industrial building; same scene a bit closer with the well-lit MJR Development sign centered in the frame; a few more bracketing exterior shots. Several shots of the entry, a dark hall, techs in jumpers with their backs to the lens. Not much.

So far, I'm doing pretty good. No adverse reactions, just digital images on a screen. I'm thinking I might get through this, no problem.

First few shots at the office doorway begin to expose the extent of the violence—blood spatter and bullet holes, a broken desk, dark blood stains on mottled grey carpet.

An image flashes through my vision—two bodies sprawled in bloody puddles on the floor, limbs askew like crumpled puppets, a man and a woman, the man in front of the desk, the woman off to the side. I recoil, blinking rapidly.

"You all right?" asks Salmon.

Startled, I glance up at him, "Yeah … fine."

I scroll to the next photo, a composition shot, techs doing their thing, framed by blood-spattered walls and blood-soaked carpeting, color intensity and contrast are good, but it needs to be cropped a bit.

"I like that one," Lacey says.

Salmon glances at me impatiently.

I scroll through the next few photos a little quicker, thinking he'll stop me when he sees what he wants. I feel a slight twinge of pride, thinking that my photos might actually be important to the investigation.

We run through the close-ups. Detail for impact—bullet holes, blood spatter, the caved-in desktop. I glance at Salmon thinking I must be getting close to the end. Nothing. I keep scrolling.

The last picture pops up and I'm staring at images I should recognize, but I'm sure I didn't take this one. It's certainly *not* the murder scene.

"That's it," says Salmon. "Stop there."

"That?"

"Yeah, what's that one?"

"I dunno. I don't recall taking that one."

"Why is it messed up?"

"Looks like a double exposure, but I ..."

"Whose truck is that?"

"I dunno."

Salmon's getting indignant. "You tryin' to tell me, you didn't take that one?"

I'm stumped. "Uh ..."

He raises his voice. "It's your camera, isn't it?"

"Yeah, but I ... uh ..." A dull ache creeps back into my skull. I don't know how this could've happened.

Silence falls like a lead blanket as Salmon gives me a skeptical stare.

The comforter is suddenly hot and heavy, and I break out in a sweat.

Lacey anxiously glances back and forth between us.

I should be trying to explain it, but the only thing I can think of makes no sense and would probably get me committed. Amazing—sometimes I actually know when to shut up.

"Look, I don't care who took it," says Salmon. "All I need to know is whose truck is that."

I glance up at him bewildered, but I keep my mouth shut.

Lacey tries to coax me. "Lance, it could be important."

Another long pause as I think about it. "The truck?"

"Yeah, the truck," says Salmon.

I can't help it, my curiosity is killing me. "Whadabout the truck?"

Salmon turns away, disgusted, like he's dealing with a moron. He gets off the stool, motions to Lacey and heads for the door.

Lacey pops up and follows dutifully.

Salmon pushes the door on his way out. "If you remember anything, get a hold of me."

I try to sound cooperative, helpful even. "Sure thing, Detective."

The door slams and it's not long before the rumble of the Marauder's big V-8 fades in the distance.

I pick up the Canon and pull up the last picture again. It's there: the leather Chippendale, back to the lens; the flatscreen on the far wall; hands dangling off the chair, one suspending an ice-filled tumbler half-filled with coppery liquid, the other nursing a fat cigar. And floating just beneath the surface, a blinding glare of lights obscures a vehicle. At first it appears unearthly, a hovering alien craft. Its lights seem to emanate from several sources. Upon closer inspection, they look like high beams and a bar of running lights across the top—probably a truck. I stare long and hard at the ghostly image from my dream, wondering how 'n hell it wound up in my camera's memory—the TV watching cigar smoker in the armchair superimposed over a rogue pickup truck. Even more baffling, what does it mean?

Sonja chimes in. "You'll find out soon enough."

"Sonja, I can't keep doing this! You're killing me."

"It's a little late now, Bucko."

"Dammit, Sonja!" Yet I know she's already gone and I'm just talking to myself. But then, isn't that what I'm doing anyway? *Shit, I must be fuckin' goofy*.

I begin to wonder if it will ever stop. What a pitiful state of affairs. Nothing like mystic insight and dialogue with the dead to shake one's sanity. How can I avoid these insane episodes? Well, let's see, I could check myself into the nearest mental hospital. That would help. Yeah, great, drugged to oblivion and drooling in my gruel, or possibly shock therapy and bed restraints—that's the life. Who knows, I might get real lucky—a frontal lobotomy and I'd never have to think again. Yeah, psychosurgery, that's the ticket. Do vegetables get migraines? Shit, my cynical side is getting away from me. But then again, it might be worth it if there's no other way to get it to stop. Nah, not really ... Nothing could be *that* bad.

Sonja's voice rings in my head. "Feeling sorry for ourselves again, are we?"

"Well, you can't really blame me."

"Nonsense. You're gonna make it."

"Oh? And just *how* do you propose I do *that?*"

"All you gotta do is see it through to the end."

"Great. More pain, more agony, more visions I don't comprehend."

"Look, I'll help. You can make it. Don't flinch every time you run into a little pain. Keep looking, face it head-on and you'll get the answers."

"Terrific. I've always aspired to masochism."

Sonja's tone softens. "Sorry, my dear. The alternatives are far worse. If you could only see what I see. Looking at it, it's so clear to me, so simple ... It breaks my heart to see you like this, especially when the answers are within your grasp."

I feel a slight tremor of hope. "Tell me what you see. I need to know."

"I couldn't begin to explain. You lack a frame of reference, like trying to explain what the world looks like to a person born blind." She pauses as my heart sinks. "But I'll take a stab at it."

A flicker of hope rekindles as I listen with rapt attention.

Her voice fills me as though I'm an empty cathedral and she is the Light. "Here ..."

I interrupt. "Where's here?"

"Everywhere ... but it's more than that. Language simply lacks the vocabulary to articulate this concept. See what I mean by lacking a frame of reference?"

"I guess ..."

"Yeah, well. I'm doin' my best here."

"No, please, go on."

"It's as though I'm at the center of the universe and the universe is mine."

"That's a little 'out there' for me."

"Okay. Try to get the idea ... Let's say you're driving your car, and instead of the car moving over the road, the road is moving underneath the car. You are stationary. *You* are turning the wheels. *You* are rotating the earth underneath the car's wheels. *You* are causing all motion. In essence, you are the Prime Mover Unmoved of your own universe. Kinda cool, huh?"

"Wow, hard to imagine."

"That's kinda the problem. Believe me, I understand. Probably sounds like bullshit to you. But trust me on this, it's far more real than anything you're experiencing currently."

"I dunno …"

"Not to worry, I gotcha covered."

"What makes you so damn tough?" But I know she's gone again.

Maybe dying in a car crash toughens one up. Maybe it was getting hit by the concrete truck that did it. Of course, she'd been drinking. The problem was the driver of the concrete truck had been drinking more. And now, I'm here alone, wiped out, left with nothing but her voice in my head and a substandard settlement check the fifteenth of every month—seems unlikely that I'll be rotating the Earth anytime soon. I don't know what to believe anymore.

Hard to believe she's still telling me what to do. Harder still, knowing she's right.

# SALMON'S SETUP

## [10:23 AM – Thursday, August 26, 2010]

"THIS IS GARY."

"Mr. Whiting?"

Whiting doesn't recognize the voice, but something about this guy rubs him the wrong way, like a bill collector. His hands start to sweat. "Yeah?"

"Gary Whiting?"

"Yeah, who's this?"

"Mr. Whiting, this is Detective Salmon, Homicide."

*Shit!* He gives a short gasp. Terror flashes through him, standing every hair on end, loosening his bowels. Whiting struggles to pull himself together. "Whaddaya need, Detective?"

"I'm sure by now you've heard about the shooting."

"Yeah ... uh, well, a real tragedy."

"Weren't you and Mr. Rodriguez in business together?"

"Yeah, he was my partner in Sunset Pointe, a commercial real estate development."

"Right, well, we need your cooperation, Mr. Whiting."

"Sure, what can I do?"

"We need you to come down to Homicide."

"What for?" He starts to shake uncontrollably, certain that the Detective can hear the quaver in his voice.

"Well, maybe you can give us some direction on this shooting, some background on Mr. Rodriguez, some ideas on who we should be talking to."

"Well … I would, but … I, uh, have no idea …" Panic crawls up his spine, twisting his guts, clenching his jaws.

"Mr. Whiting, please, we need you to come down to police head-quarters, downtown, Violent Crimes Bureau. How 'bout tomorrow after-noon, say three o'clock?"

"Uh … sure … okay, Violent Crimes Bureau … three o'clock tomorrow."

With the phone connection safely cut, Whiting's fright boils down to indignation. *Why should I have to go see this detective? That detective should make an appointment with me at my office if he has questions.* The more time elapses, the more Whiting screws up his bravado. And he's getting pissed. *A total waste of time. How would I know who shot him?* Then it hits him. What does this detective know? He shakes his head. *Nah, He couldn't possibly know.* No one could, except maybe Mike's bookkeeper and, as it turns out, Lover Boy's last piece of ass. *Nah, she's still in a coma.* The detective couldn't possibly know and he aims to keep it that way. He knows how to handle Diane.


Frank Salmon sneers as he parks the black Marauder in the Phoenix General E/R loading zone, ignoring the no parking signs and red curbing. The Job has its little perks, even if the hours and pay suck.

Checking with reception, he confirms Ms. Diane Telafano's room number in ICU. He knows she's still in a coma, but seeing her will help—gives him a better feel for her chances, what kind of witness she might be. Besides, her doctor wouldn't tell him shit over the phone. Privacy issues.

He's had his fill of doctors and hospitals.

Dwarfed by towering glass as he trudges across the expansive lobby's travertine tile, he grunts to himself. If the medical profession was half as concerned for the welfare of their patients as they were about malpractice liability, people might actually get decent health care. What a concept. But then maybe they have good reason to be worried. He shakes his head. People just need to do their damn job, take a little personal responsibility.

Sure, it's tough. But it'd be a hell of a lot easier if people just did their damn job.

Ms. Telafano looks bad, tubes everywhere and deathly pale—in a deep coma. The ICU nurse said she lost a lot of blood, needed two transfusions, was in emergency surgery for four and a half hours and is not out of the woods yet. One bullet punctured her right lung and ripped through her spinal column on the way out. The other bullet pierced her large intestine— internal bleeding and high risk of sepsis. She has a better than average chance to pull through simply because she's a strong young woman. But her chances for escaping paralysis are not good. It's a shame, she has a whole life ahead of her.

He looks away at the vitals monitor … at the ceiling … at the door to the head. Sometimes this part of the job gets to him. He needs to ask some tough questions, get anything and everything she can remember, the sooner the better, but it'll be hard to be objective. And no matter who he takes down, it won't likely keep her out of a wheelchair. He shakes his head as he turns to leave, bad enough for a young woman in her prime, but anyone on the Job will tell you, the worst are the little kids. Heartbreaking.


Connie Rodriguez lifts the designer handset off the marble vanity on the third ring. "Mrs. Rodriguez?"

"Yes?"

"Mrs. Constance Rodriguez?"

"Connie. Who's this?"

"Connie, my condolences on the loss of your husband. You and I haven't met. I'm Detective Frank Salmon, Phoenix Police, Homicide Division."

Inexplicably, Connie gasps as her fingers go numb and her head starts to buzz. "Uh … well, I'm sorry … thank you. Uh, no, we haven't met … what, what do you want?"

Salmon wonders at her obvious distress—his suspicious nature. "Did I catch you at a bad time?"

"No, well, uh, yes, I mean it's been rough, you know."

"Connie, I understand completely. I can call back another time."

"No, no, it's okay, really. What can I do for you, Detective?"

"I'd like to find a convenient time to drop by, introduce myself, see if there's anything we can do to help."

"Oh, well, that's nice of you to offer, but I'm sure there's nothing … I've already spoken with the police."

"Connie, I know. But it's important I get to know more about your husband. It'll help with the case. When's the best time?"

"Uh, well, if you think it'll help …"

"Thank you. I'm sure it will. How about tomorrow morning, say about ten?"

"Well, uh, I have an appointment with my attorney at ten …"

"Your attorney?"

"Yes, he's the executor for my husband's estate, and …"

"Oh, well then, what about after lunch, say one?"

"Yeah, I should be back by then."

"I'll call before I leave, just to confirm. See you then."

As she hangs up, Connie wonders why she's shaking. She didn't do anything! Why should *she* be nervous? Is that detective *trying* to make her feel guilty? Bewildered, she tries to resume her makeup ritual, still shaking badly. She gives up and throws the mascara, bouncing it off the mirror. Breaking down, she sobs, smearing fresh makeup as she drops her face into her hands.


Salmon pushes back from his beat-up Steelcase, partially reclining in the new ergonomically efficient chair. He longs for his old desk chair. This piece of crap, an OSHA mandate, is hard as nails, uncomfortable as hell. Kicking his feet up on an open corner of his cluttered desk, he switches gears, running through a next-steps list in his head.

The forensics boys have started to feed him scraps. The first forty-eight hours or so are critical in homicide investigations. Nothing much yet, just a few preliminary reports for his crisp new manila folder. If it turns out like a fair number of homicide files, it will be crammed full and dog-eared along with three or four more folders, all jammed full of circumstantial evidence, obscure clues and worthless hunches. They typically end up beat to death, used and reused until the cases are abandoned and the folders boxed and stored on some shelf in an archives warehouse, unsolved. Too bad it's not like TV with all the excitement, glamour and glory instead of the mostly boring, usually frustrating grind. Hell, even when they do bust their asses to nail a perp, half the time the perps walk. Undermanned police forces, liberal courts and a toothless justice system. Sometimes he hates this job, sometimes he doesn't know if the enemy is the perp or the system itself.

Preliminary exam reports show that while there is no evidence of rape, both Rodriguez and Telafano had intercourse around the time of the shooting. No DNA yet, but he's sure they were doing each other. If the wife knows, that kicks her to the top of the motive list with the partner, Whiting. The last number that connected to Rodriguez's cell was Whiting's office number, and at roughly the time of the shooting. He's fairly certain there's a ton of life insurance on Rodriguez. It's a good bet that both Mrs. Rodriguez and Mr. Whiting stand to come away with huge settlements.

Then there are the lenders for Sunset Pointe, First Community Bank and Cohen & Company. A hard-money outfit, Cohen & Company is infamous for its shady dealings. Hanes over in White Collar tells him this guy Cohen is under investigation for racketeering. Seems the clever Mr. Cohen has a sophisticated get-rich-quick scam going full bore. The gist of it, per Hanes, is Cohen milks borrowers and investors for excessive fees until the deal collapses under the debt load. He then forecloses and liquidates the property at auction. Impressive, though teetering on the brink of illegality.

Both the bank and the loan shark, Cohen, likely have completion bonds on the project and life insurance on the principals, Rodriguez and Whiting. One way or another, they always seem to get their money first. Cohen just seems to be a little better at it.

Salmon's learned the hard way. Never overlook the obvious when it comes to motive. Problem here, too many suspects with plenty of motive.

Then there are the images from Rodriguez's cell, curious if not downright chilling. Per their time stamps, they were taken close to the time of the shooting and within a minute of each other. Rodriguez was trying to catch his shooter in the act. The image of a silhouette in the door frame clearly shows muzzle flash. Too bad the glare blots out all of the shooter's features. The other one of a truck is more problematic, too distorted by the glare from its lights to make out any useful features. Looks to be a full-size pickup with running lights, not much to go on. There are literally hundreds of thousands of pickup trucks in the Phoenix area. Virtually untraceable without a license plate.

Normally, he wouldn't think much of it, if it weren't for that pinhead photographer friend of Lacey's. The partial photo of the truck on his camera is close to the photo on Rodriguez's cell, both in likeness and timing. It would be one hell of a coincidence, if he believed in coincidence. But long experience has taught him otherwise, he knows better. Still, it's a big piece that simply doesn't fit.

Lance Underphal. Jeez, where did Lacey find that old fart, anyway? The guy lives in a pigsty and seems to work at looking destitute. Comes to the door wrapped in a wet blanket, stinking of beer with bags under his eyes big enough to embarrass a bloodhound. Still, there's something odd about that guy—knows more than he's saying. His picture of the pickup truck is proof. But proof of what? Does he know the truck, its owner? He's hiding something, Salmon is sure of it.

And Lacey, just thinking of her makes him horny. He needs to give Lacey a call, even if she is a liberal airhead. She loves to chatter away about social injustice and he *hates* small talk, particularly about politics. What a pair they make. However, when he can get her to shut up, she more than makes up for the aggravation—nice tits, a nice ass and she loves to fuck. Probably not a long-term relationship, but then his relationships never are. He recalls her teasing him after a particularly long and arduous roll in the sack. She'd said that he blatantly ignores violent crime and she actively promotes it to the masses—a perfect partnership. He grins, locking his fingers behind his head—and a great sense of irony too. *What a find.*

His thoughts turn back to the two photos of the pickup truck with lights blazing. Lacey made all kinds of excuses for that Lance Underphal character. Apparently, he'd been a fairly successful electrical contractor before the crash of '08. She'd said something about a BK and trying to start over. A little old to be starting over. Now he seems like just another loser, giving it the eccentric artist routine. Lacey claims his photos would be nationally recognized if he wasn't so depressed all the time. Also something about a dead wife, died in a car crash, hit by a drunk driver. And then his health, what with all the migraines. She said she wasn't surprised he couldn't remember anything. She wanted him to give the guy a break, but he isn't buying it. Law of the land, play the hand you're dealt, no whining.

The old fart's picture of the phantom truck is the clincher. Somehow the guy knows something. And he'll get it out of him eventually.

Salmon drops his feet, swivels in his high-tech chair and pulls up to his desk. Time to get back to work. He grabs the phone. *Next.*

"Lion's Den."

"Mr. Kantor there?"

"Who's callin'?"

"Just tell him it's about Mr. Rodriguez."

"Ya mean Big Mike?"

"Look, is he there or not?"

"Hey, don't get your panties in a bunch. I'll check."

Salmon drums his fingers on the scarred desktop, waiting.

"Yeah."

"Mr. Kantor?"

"That's right. Who is this?"

"Detective Salmon, Homicide."

Salmon hears glasses clink, the thump of subwoofers and tinny tweeters in the background as Kantor says nothing. Smiling, he wonders how long Kantor can keep quiet.

"Kantor, ya still with me?"

"Yeah … I'm here."

"So you were Big Mike's partner?"

"That's right."

"Good. I need you to come see me."

"What, Big Mike's partner, that's a crime?"

"Look, do you want to come in or do I send a car to pick you up?"

"Hey, no problem, I'll come see you, Detective."

"Good. Tomorrow, eight a.m., my office, Violent Crimes Bureau." Salmon grins, knowing full well this guy probably hasn't seen eight a.m. since the last time he partied through sunrise. He'll be hatin' life, long about eight tomorrow morning.

Lenny scribbles the time and location on a cocktail napkin, punches "end" and slams the wireless handset on the bar. *Fuckin' asshole.* This detective's gonna be a problem, he can tell. That's fine, he's already done his time and he doesn't plan on doin' any more. This detective can't really do anything, maybe hassle him, but he's survived worse. *Fuckin' asshole.*

# DOUBLE EXPOSURE

## [11:08 AM – Thursday, August 26, 2010]

I STARE AT the flatscreen, my mind numb from too much unreal reality TV and too little sleep. I go through this every time, don't know why this time would be any different. If I could just get my dead ass out of this chair, clean up my act and get to the Circle Jerk, I could have another beer. Maybe if I took a half a pain pill, just to get to the store and back. I could get what I need, make it through the rest of the week without leaving the house. But that would only delay the inevitable and in a few more days, I should be fine. A couple more six-packs ought to see me through.

I tilt up to push out of my ratty recliner and my back goes into spasm. Bright pain radiating down my spine, wrapping my ribs in a vise as I gasp for air. *Shit!* I sit hunched over on the edge of my chair, breathing carefully, trying not to move, waiting for the spasm to pass. It spreads, tying my stomach in knots, clenching my jaws. Doubling up, I slide to the floor, curling into a tight fetal position. My pulse pounds, sweat soaking my T-shirt, tears streaming off my face. I have to relax, think of something else. It's not working, too intense. There's nothing I can do but wait it out. Too bad I turned off the TV. I grit my teeth and lie there trying to breathe, trying to relax.

Eons crawl by and it's still uncomfortable as Hell on a hot day, but the waiting game is beginning to pay off. Had to, couldn't do anything else. The only alternative, to give up and die. Even though death might seem preferable in the moment, I'm still here, at least so far. And as much as I complain about it, when I'm staring down death's ugly maw, I realize just how much I want to live. Fool that I am, I still think I can make something out of this life. Shit, given enough time, who knows? But pushing sixty?

Up close like this, I notice my dirty floor, the grime of neglect. It figures. I think about the cold beers that will make this excursion all worthwhile and I relax a little more.

I think about Sonja. Hand in hand, we meander through a stand of Ponderosa pine into a cool green meadow carpeted with golden California poppies, French lavender, velvety blue lupine, sprinkled with crimson Indian paintbrush. The air, fresh with the aroma of wildflowers and pine, saturated with life-giving oxygen. The sky, a vibrant blue. Does this place really exist?

I think about what she said, about facing up to it. Not sure I want to think about those people, the dead guy, the girl in a coma—the shooter. My Canon's photos reveal more than mere images—turbulent energies, visions of violence. The double exposure, a nightmare imprinted on the Canon's memory chip. How? I need to quiz Lacey, find out what she knows. Salmon must have something that ties the truck into the investigation, otherwise he wouldn't bother. Salmon's never been friendly. I figure he's not the friendly type. Probably wouldn't bother to piss on ya if you were on fire.

I gingerly test my back, attempting to uncurl millimeter by millimeter. Not too bad. Wonder if I can get up. I focus on one move at a time, propping myself up, rolling over, gradually working up to my hands and knees. Armies of angry fire ants crawl under my skin. Muscles twitch as they sting raw nerves. Red-faced and puffing, I stay on all fours for awhile, letting things settle down, cramps unwind. Still too shaky to stand. *Damn.*

How did I ever let myself go this far? Talk about out of shape. I'd laugh if it wasn't so pathetic. Might be easier to just crawl.

I slowly slide on my hands and knees, heading toward a soothing shower. Hot water will help painful joints and muscles.

It's a whole 'nother world down here. I'm coming to appreciate a dog's point of view. My tiny living/kitchen area looks much larger, almost like vaulted ceilings, ha. Broken edges of old linoleum scratch my palms and catch on my knees. The sub-floor's ancient wood creaks differently down here, its dips and ridges more pronounced. The hall's fifties-remodel paneling seems cheesier this close to the floor. And the bathroom floor tile—yikes, stale urine stains everywhere. *What a smell!* How is it I didn't notice all this before? Wonder how much it'd cost me to hire someone. *Too much.* I'll deal with it later.

Pulling myself up and over the rim of the tub, I reach for the faucet knobs, setting the temperature for a long hot shower.

As I wait for the hot water, I pull myself up to lean on the sink. I make the mistake of glancing in the mirror and drop my gaze. Too embarrassing, too painful. I remember what Sonja said and she's there, her voice in the middle of my head.

"Yes, glad you remember."

"You're not serious?"

"Oh, but I am."

"How is looking in the mirror going to help anything? Just going to depress me."

"As I said before, the only way out of all this is to confront it head on. Keep working your way through it and you'll come out the other side."

I glance up at the disheveled image in the mirror. "That's just fuckin' great." But there's no reply. Sonja's long gone.

Now I'm trapped, staring in the mirror at some old codger who doesn't even look like me. *What happened?*

When was the last time I really looked at myself in the mirror? Why bother? Look what I've become—pathetic. It's sobering, that reflection is *not* the way I picture myself, at least not most of the time. Damned mirror has to remind me. If time is the enemy, I lost the war long ago, dead and buried. I drop my gaze to the sink, take a deep breath and try again, raising my eyes to stare that old man in the face.

Eyes are bloodshot but still blue. Large folds of crinkled, darkened skin underneath those bloodshot eyes. Looks like those bags have been there awhile. One eyelid droops more than the other from a jagged scar that starts just below the left eyebrow and twists its way up the forehead. Imagine what I'd look like if I'd lost that knife fight. I remember how it first looked, stitches popping off my forehead like Frankenstein. But over the decades the scar's angry red welt faded. Now its light color and jagged line mostly blend in with the rest of the thick creases across the forehead.

That old break in the nose seems more crooked—a fist fight the first night in county lockup. Only two hits, the big black bastard hit me in the face and I hit the floor. I barely remember the trustees dragging me out of there. I found out later the guy was waiting to go to the joint. He and his partner got life for killing a clerk at a Circle Jerk. They got less than fifty bucks out of the cash drawer. What a waste.

Overall, the nose seems bigger with more bumps. Definitely not my best feature. Neither are the ears. They never did line up, one slightly higher than the other, but now it seems more pronounced. And how did they get so big? *Damn!*

Jowls sag, loose skin hanging off the neck like turkey wattles. Then there's the skin itself, covering the forehead with a mix of liver spots, pink lesions and a few red sores just for good measure, mottled with age. *A lotta hard miles.* I've heard that some age gracefully. Not this face, it's a meltdown.

Hairline? Don't wanna go there. What little hair I have left is thin, brittle and white. What in the hell was Sonja talking about? This is depressing.

I sigh, dropping my gaze back to the basin, wondering if I could get small enough to follow the rest of my life down the drain. I feel it coming, but resolve not to go there. Self-pity, a broken record I've played too often. *That's enough.*

Sonja must have had something in mind here. Back to the business at hand. Screwing up my determination, I lift my eyes to the mirror.

*What am I looking for?* I see myself … well, not really. I see my face—it's just an old face. Where am I, looking out from behind those eyes? I concentrate, staring intently, looking directly into those eyes in the mirror. The edge of my vision shifts as I see my face in the reflection of my eyes, staring at my reflection … in the reflection of my eyes. Suddenly, it tele-scopes, reflections of eyes within eyes, ad infinitum. I'm light-headed, floating, as though cut loose from the physical universe. I'm looking at the back of my eyes, then the back of my head. My perception expands and I see everything, clearly, spherically, three hundred and sixty degrees in every direction. I am no longer trapped in that decaying head. I can see everything, everywhere. *Holy shit!* This must be what she meant. Take a good look.

I turn toward the MJR Development compound, the location of the shooting. It's as though the whole scene is alive, breathing—inhaling, exhaling. It's immersed in a filmy residue, dark, oily and it smells bad. *What really happened here?*

I see them. He's at the desk, bent over her, his designer denims around his thick ankles, his broad hairy back and butt glistening with sweat. She's on her back, legs in the air, bare-ass naked except for that wad of rumpled clothing wrapped around her jiggling waist. *Quite a show.* And it would be innocent enough, but it doesn't feel right, gross and icky, as though they're reveling in it, tacitly violating each other. Each covertly taking advantage of the other. Some sick game of him abusing her and she's slurping it up to use against him. The games people play.

I watch with morbid curiosity, trying to get a handle on whatever it is I'm supposed to glean from all this. I have to laugh. She's not my type, and he certainly isn't. And is there anything more comical than observing a couple run-of-the-mill humans fucking? All that moaning, grunting and sweating, nothing really romantic about it when you're watching a couple of rank amateurs in heat. *Just plain ol' fuckin', a real hoot.*

A cell phone chimes in. At first, the guy (must be Rodriguez) ignores it and keeps on ramming the girl. Must be that Diane Telafano chick. Rodriguez stops thrusting and leans over her, panting and sweating. Must've cum or run out of gas. Her moaning dies down as she lets her legs drop, resting her feet on the desktop. She lets out a deep sigh. The cell starts in again and he pushes back, looking for the cell.

I see him grab the ringing cell.

Rodriguez says, "Damn, Gary. Whaddaya want?"

*Okay. Who is Gary?*

Rodriguez gives a short chuckle, lowers his tone. "I'm kinda in the middle of somethin'."

*Right. Seems like he's bragging to me.*

She sits up, clothes still wadded around her waist. She tries to stand and plops her butt back down. She coos at Rodriguez. "I'm not done with you yet."

Rodriguez gives her a sideways glance, rolling his eyes and grinning, still talking to this Gary person on his cell. "Yeah, like I said, we're kinda in the middle of somethin' here."

Diane giggles and grabs his package.

Still grinning, he tells her, "Stop that." Then to the guy on the phone he says, "She's never done it on the desk before."

Diane laughs. "Do I get overtime for this?"

This breaks him up and now they're both laughing.

Rodriguez talks into his cell. "Hey, don't sweat it. It's almost seven, no one's around, yard gates are locked, lights are off. No one's gonna know."

Diane coos and giggles.

Rodriguez speaks closer into the phone, "That is, as long as you keep your mouth shut."

*Hmm, seems like Rodriguez wants to keep his little romantic liaison quiet. Fat chance. In a few hours the whole world will know.*

I hear an engine rumble as bright light filters through the blinds.

Diane lets out a short yelp. "What was that?"

"Shit!" Rodriguez whispers, "Shit."

I feel more than see a dark presence hovering outside.

Still talking into his cell, Rodriguez says, "Hold on, I think someone's here."

I watch them scramble to get dressed. Rodriguez waddles to the window, grabbing at his pants, to peer through the blinds

Under his breath, Rodriguez says, "Who's that?" He whispers to Diane, "Get your panties on."

Diane whines. "I'm trying."

Rodriguez whispers to himself. "Who is that? How'd he get the truck? Is that ...? I'll get that bastard."

"Gary, hold on, I gotta take a picture with this thing, hold on."

Rodriguez pulls the slats apart and holds up his phone to take a picture. As he turns away, he's talking to himself. "Damn, it's dark ... but I think I got 'em."

He puts the phone back to his head. "Yeah, I'm back, hold on. Gotta check this out."

As the door bursts open, I watch a boiling cloud spit black filth as it forms in the doorway. Enveloped in the turbulent energy is the shifting black shadow of the shooter.

Diane screams as Rodriguez yells, "*You*, you asshole! What the fuck do *you* want!?!"

Muzzle flashes erupt. Ear-splitting gunfire, POP, POP, POP!

Diane screeches, grabbing her head, ducking, jumping, her body twitching and writhing with the impact of the bullets.

I feel the searing slugs tear through her soft tissue as though I'm wearing her ruined flesh. I cry out, flinching from the holes bored into her torso as the wounds well up with blood.

Scrambling to get away, Rodriguez's dive over the desk falls short, collapsing the desk.

I get a glimpse of what he's after—a semi-automatic pistol in the desk's upper right-hand drawer. Even as I grit my teeth I marvel at the vision of a pistol inside a closed desk drawer. *I see it.*

More blinding flashes and ear-ringing pops as bullets thud into his back, neck and head. His grunts come fast with each penetration, turning to deep rattling gasps wet with blood as he slides to the floor.

Like Rodriguez, I'm gasping for air as though drowning in my own blood. I know with a cruel and intimate certainty his wounds are fatal.

Diane's long wail fades as she hits the floor in a lump, grunts and lies still.

I can't get away from either of them—my empathy, too great. Yet, I already know their fate. It's the shooter I need to know. I attempt to reach, to seek out the shooter, but the pain is too much. And as I struggle, it all fades away.

I find myself staring at the wide-eyed visage in the mirror, my head swimming. I stand, shaking, jerking my head from side to side to clear the horror.


I lean against the shower stall, letting hot water run over my head and down my aching back. I could do this forever. Finally, starting to relax. I let my eyes close to take it all in, go with it, drifting away. Behind my eyelids, new images come into view. Arms hanging from the leather Chippendale as though disembodied. I sense an irritation, a grating sensation associated with this person. Negative energy envelopes him like a dark shroud, similar to that at the shooting only deeper, smoother, less intense. He's deeply disturbed, possessed by a self-absorbed wickedness. Ray Charles could see that he's somehow connected to this shooting business, but it's still too obscure. Between this guy, the truck and the impressions of the shooting, my head is spinning. I've got no idea how it's all connected.

Back from the Circle Jerk, cold beer in hand, I sit at the counter and hit the speed-dial number for Lacey's cell. *Gotta find out what she knows.*

"Lacey, it's Lance."

"What's up?"

"Hey, ya know that photo?"

"Which one?"

"You know, the one Salmon's so interested in, the double exposure."

"What about it?"

"Well, uh … why is he so interested?"

"Can't tell you."

"Whaddaya mean?"

"It involves police evidence and he doesn't want anyone to know."

"Yeah, but it's on my camera and I'm workin' this with you. You need to keep me in the loop."

"I dunno. He'd kill me if he found out, and he's my source in the department."

"Seems like he's more than just a source."

"Lance?!"

"Hey, your secret's safe with me. I won't say a word."

"Okay, well, the deal is, they found the guy's phone …"

"What guy?"

"The guy that was killed, Rodriguez."

"Yeah?"

"Yeah, and there were pictures on his phone, one of a truck. Frank thinks it could be the shooter's truck."

"That same truck image that's on my camera?"

"Yeah, as close as he can tell. Spooky, huh?"

"No shit. You have no idea."

"Where did you take that one, anyway?"

"Uh ... I don't really remember."

"Well Frank's pissed. He thinks you're jerking him around."

"Hey, really, I don't remember. If I knew I'd tell him."

Lacey adopts a motherly tone. "Well you need to think about it. Try to remember. It's important."

I'm too old for the lecture I sense is coming. Time to get off. "Yeah, uh ... I'll work on it. Listen, Lacey, I gotta go. Thanks for the info. I'll keep it hush-hush."

"Okay, but really think about it."

Why is it women feel the need to do that? "Yeah. Later." I hang up more confused than before.

# THE RODRIGUEZ
# INTERVIEW

**[12:37 PM – Friday, August 27, 2010]**

AFTER A QUICK meatball sub, Salmon is back behind the wheel of his unmarked Marauder. He heads north for the Rodriguez residence and his next interview. His thoughts turn to the Lion's Den owner/manager as he reruns the earlier interview with Kantor in his head.

Kantor's narrow pasty-white face boasted a large hook nose with dark beady eyes set close together under thick black brows. His black thinning hair crested high on his scalp in a widow's peak, giving him that fresh-from-Transylvania look. He hid his prison-yard muscular build with a round-shouldered slouch, too many nights sitting at the bar. Not surprisingly Kantor was sullen and uncooperative. Salmon was half expecting him to show up with a lawyer. Still, it was more about what he didn't say, the way he reacted to questions, the way he clammed up. Salmon didn't get much, but had some fun rattling Kantor's cage.

Exiting the 101 Loop, Salmon glides the black Mercury to a stop then turns north on Scottsdale Road. The Marauder's supercharged V-8 rumbles as he accelerates up Scottsdale's main artery. It rises gently into North Scottsdale, one of the more affluent suburbs of Phoenix.

Salmon should have seen it coming. Checking Kantor's record before-hand, Salmon knew the guy was an ex-con and streetwise, probably has plenty to hide. However, he drives a Porsche and doesn't own a truck. Yet, it wouldn't surprise him if Kantor was running prostitutes and dealing drugs out of that place. Salmon's convinced that given enough reason, Kantor would be capable of murder. Kantor just didn't seem to have a good enough reason, at least not one Salmon could find. His short take: Kantor is scum but probably not the shooter. He'll have a patrolman drop by the Lion's Den in a couple days with the court order and get Kantor's list of employees, independent contractors and copies of charge card receipts. You never know what will turn up until you dig. Salmon sneers, it's still early, he may find something on Kantor yet.

Turning right on Dynamite Road, Salmon starts scanning the roadside for a monument sign identifying the entrance gate to Desert Pueblos. Houses along here are huge with lots of space in between, mostly in gated communities. Vast open areas of lush desert still support a native ecology. Home to majestic saguaros hundreds of years old, their giant spiny limbs reaching for the desert sky. Coyotes, quail, jackrabbits and rattlesnakes all thrive in this area, protected by city ordinance and largely left alone by their human benefactors. Salmon appreciates this rugged natural beauty, the luxury of wide open desert on the city's fringe—just can't afford to live here. But then few can. It's too bad. Rodriguez was obviously doing all right for himself.

An adobe wall springs up on the right, ambling along the roadside with its twists and dips. Salmon spots bronze lettering on a squat adobe sign that spells out Desert Pueblos. He slows, turning onto the dual-gated drive. A pueblo-style guardhouse perches on the xeriscaped island between gates. The Marauder's wide tires rumble on the pavers as he pulls up to the rustic guardhouse and rolls down his window. A uniformed guard opens a sliding window and smiles. Salmon smiles back. "Rodriguez residence."

"And your name, sir?"

Salmon badges him. "Detective Salmon."

"One moment." The guard ducks back in and picks up a phone.

Salmon waits, watching the guard's lips move and head nod. The guard motions him through as the tall wrought-iron gate slowly swings open.

Salmon drives through on a narrow lane cobbled with rough adobe pavers. To his left, a median separating the other lane, its adobe-walled planters filled with a variety of spiny cacti, twisted greasewood, dusky purple sage and the thorny tangle of blue palo verde trees. He can't help but notice the street, the common grounds, the front yards of the palatial custom homes—everything is immaculate. Not a speck of trash, not even a gum wrapper or cigarette butt anywhere. The upkeep alone must cost a fortune. *So this is how the rich people live.*

The big black Mercury rumbles along at a crawl, barely twenty miles an hour, as Salmon looks for the Rodriguez home. He spots the Rodriguez name in burnished brass letters mounted on a thick pillar—one of two— hand-crafted in dry-stack stone work. The thick stone pillars support a tall stone arch over the drive's entrance. He pulls into the wide circular drive right at one p.m. and parks the Marauder in front of a multilevel Tuscan villa. The exterior walls are done entirely in mortar-free dry-stack stone with a thick tile roof. Impressive. Salmon figures Mrs. Rodriguez is probably sitting pretty. The house alone has got to be worth two to three million, even in the midst of this real estate depression. He wonders if she inherited a big mortgage to go along with it.

Salmon climbs wide stone steps, crosses a stone terrace to more steps, another terrace and finally enters a large, high-ceiling courtyard. An intricate blown glass and wrought-iron chandelier hangs from the ornate stone ceiling. Leaded skylights dapple sunlight on stone tile and lush potted tropicals—large birds of paradise, elephant ear philodendrons, banana palms and other exotics. At the far end of the courtyard stand enormous hand-carved hardwood entry doors bracketed with colorful stained glass sidelights. He glances up and around. Hell, the courtyard is bigger than his whole loft.

She opens the door after the first ring. A tall, curvaceous blonde in tight-fitting cream satin pants and a low-cut black silk top embroidered with black sequins. It's Salmon's first look at Connie Rodriguez. She's a near perfect vision, probably a former super-model turned trophy wife, barely past her prime and hiding it beautifully. Salmon composes himself.

"Mrs. Rodriguez?"

Her flawless face breaks into a slight smile showing perfect brightwhite teeth. "Detective Salmon?"

"Yes." Salmon admires her beauty. The only tell, a faint hint of fear in her crystal blue eyes.

"Please, call me Connie. Come on in."

He pulls the door closed behind him and follows her through the foyer, her shapely rump swaying gently in cream-colored satin.

"Did you find us okay?" she asks.

He grunts an acknowledgement, still marveling at her subdued but sensual gait.

She chatters away nervously as she leads him through the spacious hallway and he begins to realize she may not be that perfect after all. He wonders if she's chatty like this all the time or just nervous. She turns and motions him into a cavernous great room with twenty-foot vaulted ceilings finished in rough-hewn beams and chevron-patterned tongue and groove plank. The entire north wall is glass, floor to ceiling, with a panoramic view of the high desert's mountains. He strides across the hand-cut stone floor to a leather pillow-back sectional. Salmon sinks into the far corner of the comfortable U-shaped couch, leaning back and crossing his legs. He watches as Connie sits at the near corner, straight-backed, on the edge of the cushion, hands folded primly in her lap. She gives him a well-practiced cover-girl smile, doing her best to maintain her composure.

She breaks the awkward silence. "Can I get you anything, something to drink, water, iced tea?"

"No thanks, I'm fine."

Salmon smiles as he watches her. His steady gaze is making her more nervous with every second.

"Well then, Detective, what can I do for you?"

Uncrossing his legs, he leans forward, smiling, holding her in his gaze. "Please, call me Frank."

She starts at his sudden movement, smiling tentatively. "Certainly. What can I do for you?"

He drops his gaze, releasing her, and uses his warmest, most sincere tone. "Before we begin, allow me to offer my condolences on the loss of your husband."

Her shoulders slump as her gaze drops. "Thank you, Detective."

"Please, Frank."

She gives him a weak smile. "Okay, Frank it is."

"Thanks. Again, I'm sorry for your loss. Please accept my apologies for intruding at a time like this. I wouldn't do it if it wasn't important."

Her smile broadens, a bit more relieved. "Thank you, Frank. I appreciate your thoughtfulness."

He keeps her under watch with subtle glances, softening the impact of his gaze, easing her nerves. She's loosening up, dropping her guard, coming around. A bit more and he'll have her where he needs her.

Salmon's gaze wanders around the great room, admiring the luxurious décor. "What a beautiful home you have. And what a view."

Connie looks out at the mountains, wistfully. "Yes, thank you. We've been very fortunate."

"Do you have children?"

Her eyes light. "Yes, we uh … I am very blessed. I have three children, Mike Junior is ten, Brittany is eight and Josh is five."

"That's great. You are a lucky woman. Where are they now?"

"Maria, our au pair, has them. They're busy registering for school."

"Which school district are you in out here?"

"Oh, I'm not sure … we take them to private school, Catholic school, Pope John."

"That's great. A good education is so important."

"I agree."

"Connie, I know this could be distressing for you, but I would be doing you and your family a disservice if I didn't ask these questions."

"It's okay, I understand."

Connie's smartphone chirps and she retrieves it off the coffee table. Glancing at the screen, she taps its face with a ruby fingernail and holds it to her ear. "Hi, Brittany. What is it?"

Adjusting in his seat, Salmon reaches in his shirt pocket and discreetly thumbs his digital microrecorder to voice-activate.

Connie turns her warm smile on him, looking him in the eye as she talks to her daughter, a disarming sparkle in her eye. "Yes, dear, but I'll have to call you back. I'm busy right now." She listens to Brittany's reply. "Okay, bye." She taps her phone and sets it back on the glass tabletop. She shrugs. "Sorry about that. My daughter, Brittany."

"No problem. It's okay if I ask a few questions?"

"Okay."

"Do you know if your husband had any enemies?"

"I don't really know, but he used to tell me that people were jealous of his success, that they hated him for it."

"I'm sure it's all too common. Did he ever tell you about anyone in particular?"

"I dunno. Over the years he might have, but I can't really remember anyone specifically. I mean, he used to get angry with people, people who worked for him, but that's just business."

"I understand. Did he have a lot of people working for him?"

"Well, with the development company, all the other projects and the construction jobs, he had a bunch of people."

"Would it be possible to get a list of his business associates and employees?"

"You'll need to talk to Mr. Elder, but I'm sure it'd be fine."

"Mr. Elder?"

"Yes, he's our attorney."

"Oh. Do you have his number?"

She picks up her smartphone and starts to scroll.

"Connie, please, I'll get that from you later."

She looks up and smiles as she sets her phone down. "Okay."

He watches her closely. "Can you tell me, what was your husband's relationship with Diane Telafano?"

Her eyes narrow, lips tightening as she answers too quickly. "Diane was his bookkeeper."

Salmon drops his gaze. "I see." He pauses then asks, "And how long had she been his bookkeeper?"

She turns away. "Off 'n on, about five years."

"Off and on?"

"Yes, he had to fire her, but then he hired her back."

"He fired her, then rehired her?"

"That's right."

"Can you tell me what happened?"

"Not really. That was my husband's business. I stayed out of it."

"I see." Salmon watches her fidget. Finally, he says, "I'm sorry, I have to ask these questions. Just a few more."

Connie lifts her head with an indignant air.

"Connie, again, I'm sorry to have to ask you … Did your husband have any relationship with Ms. Telafano other than business?"

Her eyes flash as she turns on him. "Are you asking if he was sleeping with her?"

"Please, don't misunderstand me. I'm not insinuating. I just need to know if you were aware of anything out of the ordinary."

Her shoulders slump as she drops her head to stare at the floor. "Yeah … I guess there probably was." She looks up at him with sorrowful eyes. "I guess the wife is always the last to know."

Salmon waits.

She raises her face to the ceiling with a wistful gaze. "I guess it's my own fault for being so naïve." Shaking her head, she lets out a wry little laugh. "What was my first clue, the BMW he leased for her?" Her eyes well up and a tear runs down her perfect cheek. "You know, I'm the one who insisted he fire her. Couldn't help it, I got jealous. He swore there was nothing going on, then the sonofabitch hired her back. He said she was the only one who could do the books. Then the BMW. He said he signed for her because she didn't have any credit. And idiot that I am, I believed him!" She slumps. "Anyway, it's over now."

"Connie, I'm sorry. That's all I have for now."

They stand and Salmon walks over, shakes her hand and heads for the hallway. On his way out, he turns to her. "Oh, by the way, do you know anyone with a full-sized truck?"

Trailing him to the door, she looks up, her curiosity piqued. "Most of the people who work at MJR drive trucks, Detective. Why do you ask?"

"Yeah, construction workers. Guess they do, don't they?"

"Pretty much. Even my husband had a work truck." Connie watches him leave from the entry door, wondering what he thinks of her. With most men she can tell right away, but this detective, she's not so sure. If he was attracted to her, he hid it well.

# LUNCH WITH LACEY

**[12:53 PM – Friday, August 27, 2010]**

DOWNTOWN PHOENIX IS normally hotter 'n hell in late August and today is no exception. Traffic slows to a crawl along Van Buren as I cross Third Street, heading into the heart of Copper Square. My rattle-trap Sentra clunks along monotonously. Wish the damned radio worked. At least the A/C almost keeps it cool. Pioneer Park is empty this time of day. The sidewalks, sweltering. The palms are dry and brittle, the grass burnt and yellowed. It's a hundred and thirteen in the shade, of which there is precious little on this bright scorcher of a day in this so-called desert paradise. The PR people have dubbed it The Valley of the Sun. They're so right, even with dark glasses I squint from the glare. Heat shimmers up from the blistering pavement in sheets, as though someone's got all the subterranean burners turned up past High. I've had it with this heat. Fortunately, it only lasts a couple more months.

As I head for the Chili Bean and my late lunch meeting with Lacey, I wonder about all the crap I've gone through. Seems like the week from hell and it's only been a few days. Hope she's buying. Better be, she made the meeting. Wants to see the crime scene photos again. Good, I need the money. But if I'm honest, there's something more, something else. What does Lacey know? Shit, she's sleeping with the detective, there's gotta be more she's not telling me. If I just knew what Sonja was getting at, maybe I could get shed of this thing. Why should I care who shot who? I don't even know these people.

This is driving me nuts. You could probably make a good argument that it would be a short trip. My sarcasm, boundless. Speaking of driving, there it is, the parking garage on my left.

Sweat beads on my forehead and scalp, already trickling from my pits as I cross Van Buren at the light. The Chili Bean is mid-block on the north side of Van Buren. A short walk, but bright and hot. My wrinkled Polo is getting damp, but not my spirits. I feel hopeful for no particular reason, like I might actually learn something, or at least get a free lunch. I push through the etched-glass door a few minutes late. I scan the public seating for Lacey and see her hand rise as she spots me. She waves me over and I work my way through the crowded tables, heading for her booth.

As I slide in across from her, I give Lacey a silly little grin. Not sure why, really. This alien sense of hope is almost embarrassing. What a dufus.

"Hey, Lace."

"Lance." She gives me a sideways glance. "You okay?"

I settle down and pick up a menu. "Yeah, fine. Whaddaya recommend?"

Lacey's still giving me a curious look. I try to ignore her as I pretend to browse the menu.

She finally turns her attention back to her menu. "The sour cream enchiladas are good."

"Are you buyin'?"

"Don't I always?"

I grin. "Us starving artists appreciate it."

She gives me a smirk while pretending to scrutinize the menu. "Maybe if you got your work some exposure, you wouldn't be starving."

"Yeah, if only …"

She looks up at me earnestly. "No, really. You do good work. With the right exposure, I know it would sell."

"I dunno … maybe … And just how do you do that anyway?"

"Ya need a good agent and a publicist. Have you talked to anyone? Have you even tried?"

I don't want to go there. Last thing I need is another one of Lacey's lectures. "I need to work on my portfolio before I show it to anyone," I mumble.

She shakes her head. "That's crap. You've got plenty of great stuff just lying around."

I know she's just trying to help, but damn. I hide behind the menu and ignore her, hoping the silence will segue to something else. I'm saved by the waitress. She takes our orders and hustles off. The uncomfortable silence resumes. I've gotta say something, even if it's lame. "Anything new on the shootings?"

"Nothin' much. Frank says they're in the grunt-work phase. He's says if they don't nail someone within the first couple days, it turns into a grind."

"He doesn't have any suspects?"

"Yeah. A few, but nothin' solid. Did ya bring the pictures?"

I dig in my jeans for the thumb drive. "Yeah." I slide it across the table to her. "Here ya go."

She picks it up. "Thanks."

"That's everything I got at the scene. Just let me know which ones you wanna use."

"What about the one with the truck?"

I try to be nonchalant. "I didn't put it on there."

"Why not?"

"You can't use that for your story anyway."

"Ya never know. Besides, I thought it was interesting."

"I'll email it to you, if you really want it. Don't mean shit to me."

She gives me a piercing look. "Right."

I figure there's no time like the present. Don't dare back out now. "Besides. I think I've got it figured out."

"Got what figured out?"

"That's the truck the killer used." I watch for her reaction.

"What makes you say that? Just because I told you about Frank?"

"No. Something else."

Her face scrunches up in disbelief. "Bullshit. Just because it looks like the picture on the guy's phone? Frank said it doesn't really mean anything anyway."

Time to plead my case. "No, really. I don't think your detective is being upfront with you. I can't tell you how I know, but I should see Salmon. I think I can help."

"I'm sure Frank will be thrilled." Lacey secretly wonders why Frank was so interested at first then dismissed it out of hand. He never really said. Frank's sneaky that way.

"You said he doesn't have anything solid. It couldn't hurt."

"Well, you've got his number. Give him a call. But don't get your feelings hurt when he laughs his ass off."

"That's why I need you to set it up. He won't believe me."

She shakes her head. "Are you kidding? *I* don't believe you."

"Okay, so what if it's all bullshit? Ya got nothin' to lose. And if it turns out to be something, ya got a great story. C'mon. Just tell him I know who called Rodriguez on his cell during the shooting. That'll get his attention. He'll wanna talk to me then."

I watch her wheels turning as she stares at the ceiling. She can't resist a good story—a true journalist.

She looks back at me. "How do you know that?"

"Like I said, can't tell you now. Maybe later."

Her eyebrows scrunch down and she leans forward, getting into my face. "If I do this and it turns out to be something, you damn well better tell me."

This is getting risky, making me nervous. Hope I can do this without getting into deep shit. "Okay, just hook me up with Salmon."


As I trudge back to the car, I shake my head, disgusted that I can't even remember the three tacos I wolfed down. What good is a free lunch if you don't enjoy it? Anyway, she's going to call me once she sets it up with Salmon.

# THE WHITING INQUISITION

**[3:15 PM – Friday, August 27, 2010]**

KICKED BACK AT his desk, Salmon glances at his watch. Rodriguez's partner has been cooling his jets in the interview room for a good twenty minutes. Should be a ball of nerves by now. Salmon grins as he pushes up out of his chair and ambles across the squad room, headed for his interview with Whiting.

Taking his time, the first stop is the men's room. Next, the observation room adjacent to the interview room where Whiting is parked. It's small, hot and dark with plenty of video and audio recording gear, dark to maximize the two-way mirror. Salmon stands with arms akimbo, watching Whiting. Whiting is anything but nervous, slumped sideways in the metal chair. And those chairs are designed to be as uncomfortable as possible. Whiting's arm is braced on the metal table, hand propping up his head as he gives a big yawn. *Hmm, maybe Whiting's not much of a suspect after all.* But as he watches, Salmon notices little tells—Whiting's eyelids at half-mast and he's yawned three times in the last couple minutes. Whiting doesn't look drunk, so either he hasn't slept or he's on something. Almost looks like he's on the nod. *Could this guy be a junkie?* He's dressed in a cheap charcoal suit, white shirt and a burgundy tie, as conservative as they come. He looks more like a mousy accountant than a rich real estate developer, plain-featured, balding, pale skin, thin and flaccid. Salmon turns for the door. *Might as well get it over with.*

As Salmon enters, Whiting struggles to pull himself upright. Salmon sits down across from Whiting with his back to the two-way mirror. Whiting's eyes follow his every move. He's doing his best to act nonchalant, but Salmon senses a faint tremor just below the surface. Salmon figures it must be drug-induced. Maybe meds, maybe street drugs, who knows? Not that it really matters, the effects are roughly the same. Wherever he gets his drugs, Whiting's definitely on a stimulant-downer cocktail.

Salmon gives him a courtesy smile and extends his hand. "Detective Frank Salmon, Homicide."

"Gary Whiting, Detective." He shakes Salmon's hand briefly.

Salmon notices his grip is quick and firm, a practiced professional, but his hand is cold and clammy. His words are slow but aren't slurred. His voice, weak and tremulous as though he's concerned about his alibi. Assuming he has one. *This guy is under a lotta stress.*

"Thanks for coming down," says Salmon.

Whiting gives a lopsided grin. "No problem. Whaddaya need to know?"

Salmon pierces him with a stare. Time to instill a little fear of God into him. "We need a statement from you regarding your relationship with Mr. Michael J. Rodriguez. And we'll be recording this unless you have some objection."

Whiting pushes back, scooting away from the table, the chair's metal feet screeching on the vinyl floor as he folds his arms in front of his chest. "What if I do?"

Salmon leans in, grinning wickedly. "We're recording anyway. Legally, I just need to inform you."

Whiting's visibly unsettled. "Surely, I'm not a suspect. Or do I need a lawyer?"

"You can have a lawyer present if you wish, your prerogative. But I only have a few questions. Shouldn't take long."

"Hmm." Whiting's eyelids droop as he stares at the metal tabletop, weighing his options. Silence drags on as his frown lengthens.

Salmon finally loses patience. "Your choice, Mr. Whiting. We can re-schedule. Do this another time." Salmon shifts in his chair as though he's getting up to leave.

Whiting's eyes dart down and away. "Uh, well ... I guess it's okay."

Salmon leans back. *I got him now.* He's determined to wake him up, shake him like a terrier killing a rat. "Fine. That'll save us both a lotta time. I just want to confirm a few facts. You mentioned Mr. Rodriguez was your partner."

Whiting relaxes a bit. "Yeah. That's right."

Salmon adopts a matter-of-fact tone. "Tell me about your business relationship."

Whiting's eyes narrow as his lips tighten. "Not much to it, really."

"Just so I can get my facts straight. Background, you know ..."

"Well, we are co-managing members of AZ-Sunset Pointe, LLC. It's an Arizona limited liability company formed to develop the Sunset Pointe multi-use commercial real estate project."

Salmon listens as Whiting slips into a well-rehearsed spiel. It's as though he's about to ask him to invest money. He decides to let Whiting get a little more comfortable. "And when did you and Mr. Rodriguez form this company?"

"We bought the dirt and put the LLC together with investors in January of 2007."

"Almost four years ago."

"Yeah, about that."

"And how's the project doing?" Salmon watches a frisson of doubt flash through Whiting's features.

"Uh, whaddaya mean?"

Salmon pins him, staring directly into his shifty eyes. "I mean, how's it doing?" Whiting's meds must be wearing off, seems his nonchalance is wadding up on him like used toilet paper.

Whiting gives Salmon a furtive grin. "Well, uh ... well you know how it is. Vacancies are at a record high, banks aren't lending, especially for commercial real estate projects. Everyone's having trouble in this economy."

"So I've heard. You and Rodriguez getting along?"

"Sure. No problems. Nothing between us."

Whiting is too obvious, trying too hard to convince him.

"So, no financial difficulties?"

Whiting answers too quickly. "Nothing major."

"I see. How long did you know him?"

"About fifteen years. He started off as a client. I met him when he owned a few franchise quick-lube shops. He wanted to open more shops and needed locations. I found them for him."

"And you decided to partner up on this development deal?"

"Yeah. He had the investors and the general contractor's license. I have the commercial real estate expertise."

"So now your development deal's in trouble …"

"I wouldn't say that."

"What *would* you say? A half-built real estate deal in a shitty economy and a dead partner who just happened to be the general contractor."

"What are you saying?"

"Was Mr. Rodriguez insured?"

"Of course, we couldn't get a bank loan for the project unless both of us were insured. That's routine. What are you insinuating?"

"So Mr. Rodriguez's death benefit pays off a failing project. How convenient."

"Hey, I don't have to listen to this!" There's a tremor in Whiting's voice as it rises nearly an octave.

Salmon gets in his face. "Well listen to this. Your office number is in Rodriguez's cell phone log."

Terror widens Whiting's eyes to a bug-eyed glaze. "So what? We talked all the time. He was my partner!"

Salmon grins to himself. *Time to drop the bomb.* "The time code on that call was the same time as the shooting."

Whiting panics, shouting hysterically. "I've had enough of this! I was on my way to Vegas! I had nothing to do with it! I want my attorney!"

"We're done for now, Mr. Whiting. Make the call. You'll probably need an attorney. Conspiracy is a serious charge. And don't leave town."

Whiting fumbles his way out of the metal chair, deathly pale and shaking, scrambling for the door.

Frank Salmon makes a mental note to pay particular attention to this guy's health and travel records. If he's not top of the suspect list, he's a close second to the Widow Rodriguez. Plenty of motive for both. Hell, who knows, maybe they're in cahoots. He's seen stranger bedfellows with far less to gain. Not much would surprise him anymore.

# BUSINESS LUNCH

### [12:30 PM – Thursday, November 12, 2009]

BIG MIKE RODRIGUEZ pushed through the Chuck Wagon's thick-planked door, leaving the bright sunshine of a mid-November day. Blowing by the "greet and seat" station, he entered the cool darkness of the big dining room. He strolled purposely across the sawdust-littered floor toward his big booth in the back corner, barely noticing the lanky man in a Western-style suit nursing a drink at the far end of the bar. Today's lunch was a two-booth affair. Everyone was already there. He was fashionably late as usual. Some sat with their faces buried in menus. Others were talking among themselves.

Today's invitees in the big booth included: Whiting; their banker, Martin Fellman; the project's attorney, Marsh; their lead entitlement attorney; and Rodriguez's attorney, Hammond Elder, who never missed a free lunch. In the next booth were: the assistant entitlement attorney; the team leader from the City's Development Services Department; the City's head construction inspector; Lenny Kantor, his Lion's Den partner; Whiting's assistant, Jenny; and Marsh's legal secretary, the prim Teresa Milner. Damn, how Rodriguez wanted a piece of her.

Ten feet out and closing, Rodriguez let out a jovial bellow. "Hey, what's goin' on here, ya startin' without me?"

Most grinned, a few chuckled, but they all looked up.

Marsh laughed. "There he is. Now we can start."

Whiting piped in. "If only he'd pick up the tab, we'd be in business."

Rodriguez jabbed back. "If only my partner who owns the joint wasn't so cheap, he'd take care of business and pick up the tab himself."

His cutting remark garnered everything from uncomfortable chuckles to obnoxious belly laughs.

"Scoot over." Rodriguez bulled his way into his booth. He slung his arm over the back, turning to the booth behind him. "How're y'all doin' back there?"

Responses were vacuous and socially correct as Rodriguez turned back to his table, grinning ear to ear.

Small talk ensued as they studied the menus.

Jeremy, the Chuck Wagon's manager, leaned with his back against the bar. At the far end of the bar, that tall guy with the boots and Stetson was back again, becoming a regular. He'd have to stop by and introduce himself, just good business.

Jeremy watched Big Mike slide into his booth and took it as his signal to head over. He needed to put in an appearance, not just because his boss was there, but because these were some of the most influential people who ever graced the Chuck Wagon with their presence. If a guy wanted to get a deal done in The Valley of the Sun, these were the guys who could do it.

Jeremy cranked up a toothy smile as he arrived. "Hi guys, good to see you. Hope you brought your appetites."

Rodriguez glanced up from his menu. "Hey Jeremy, take good care of this crew, will ya?"

Jeremy beamed. "No problem, Mike. I'll send Monica right over."

Rodriguez watched Jeremy turn and hustle off to get their waitress. He glanced around the table, studying each man in turn. He needed to be subtle—needed everyone to buy in.

The food and drinks came: prime rib sliders, jalapeño poppers and loaves of fresh sourdough bread, hot out of the oven. Between mouthfuls, Mike and Gary alternately pushed the project's under-budget, ahead-of-schedule progress. Whiting gave a glowing report, even though conservatively delivered, while Rodriguez shoveled it on. Their guests pretended to listen while smothering racks of baby back ribs in the Chuck Wagon's rich barbeque sauce. Rodriguez and Whiting's bullshit flowed freely, aimed mostly at their lender, while Rodriguez spread it on thick for the City boys.

They needed the City boys to turn the occasional blind eye and hustle things along, needed to make sure the City boys were happy. But Rodriguez knew there would come a time in the not-too-distant future when he'd have them by the short hairs, doing whatever he needed them to do whenever he needed it done, without hesitation.

Lenny Kantor did his best to hide his disdain for all their back-slapping bullshit. He'd never attend one of these things on his own, but Big Mike said "be there," and there he was, bored to tears, awaiting further in-structions. It wasn't until the end, when the plates were cleared, that Kantor's purpose became clear.

Rodriguez stood, making sure he had everyone's attention. "We're having a little get-together to celebrate our good fortune. Lenny Kantor here has graciously offered us his private banquet room at his club, the Lion's Den."

There were some looks and murmurs, but mostly embarrassed grins.

Teresa Milner turned to Jenny, eyebrows raised. "Isn't that a strip club?"

Jenny leaned over and smiled. "It's okay. We'll be in the banquet room, not in the main strip club."

Teresa tried to imagine her boss, the straight-laced Fredrick Marsh, at a strip club and had to suppress a giggle.

Rodriguez kept a close eye on their reactions, mainly concerned with Martin Fellman. Fellman's face squeezed tight, creased with lines while his forehead turned a deep scarlet, looking like someone had just pissed on his Wheaties. "Listen, I know what you're thinking, a gentlemen's club. But listen, the banquet room is private, has its own parking and entrance off at the back, absolutely safe as milk. You could take your mother there, no problem." He kept glancing at Fellman as he talked, gauging his effect.

Fellman loosened up, his sphincter of a face unclenching.

That was close, especially since the whole setup was for Fellman and the City boys. "You'll all be receiving formal but discreet invitations in the mail. Won't they, Jenny?"

Jenny brightened. "That's right, Mr. Rodriguez."

"We'll send cars for each of you," Rodriguez said. "Just RSVP Jenny here and let her know how many in your party. We'll send stretch limos, if you need them. Hope to see you all there."

As the lunch broke up, Rodriguez delayed his goodbye to Fellman until the rest were on their way out. Rodriguez was sure of what he'd seen in Vegas. No matter how he tried to hide it, Fellman had more than a passing interest in those Lion's Den girls, especially Sondra Du. Of course, who wouldn't? Du was a great fuck and looked even better.

Rodriguez pulled Fellman aside. "Look, I understand if this makes you a little uncomfortable."

"It's just that the wife …"

Rodriguez backed off, holding up his hands in mock submission. "Hey, most of the guys feel the same way, but the construction crews love it. It'll be a great time, but I understand if you can't make it. By the way, no one will be bringing their wives. Hope that's okay."

"I often have to do business dinners without her. She'll understand. I'll just skip the part about where it is." Fellman gave him a sheepish grin.

Rodriguez's face broke into a leer. "Great. You're not gonna wanna miss this."

# WAKE UP CALL

**[1:48 PM – Monday, August 30, 2010]**

IT'S BEEN A couple days since the Whiting interview and Salmon's irritability clings to him like a cloud of gnats. He and a couple of uniforms have pored over the leads, adding details, filling in holes, mostly grunt work. And though a clearer picture of the case is taking shape, there's still no significant narrowing of suspects. In fact if anything, the suspect list has grown. Not a good trend.

Hunched at his battle-scarred desk, Salmon mulls over the evidence they've gathered so far. Like a dog chasing its tail, the evidence spins him around in circles, darkening his mood.

His cell beeps, yet he doesn't recognize the number displayed.

"Detective, this is Jenna Haft, the ICU Nurse at Phoenix General."

"Yes, Jenna. What can I do for you?"

"You asked me to call if there was any change in Ms. Telafano's condition."

"What's happening?"

"She's awake."

"Thank you, Jenna. I appreciate it. I'm on my way. Tell her doctor to hold all visitors until I get there."

"That won't be necessary. The only visitor she's had was her mother and she left an hour ago."

"Good, please keep it that way until I get there."

Thirty-seven minutes later Salmon rides a stainless-steel elevator to the hospital's third floor and the intensive care unit. The hospital's subliminal stench flares his nostrils like a stallion on high alert. He hates hospitals—a place you go to die.

Though outwardly cool and calm, Salmon's adrenalin pumps. Telafano's eyewitness account could give him the evidence he needs to button this up. While he's hopeful, he understands most victims of violent crime have trouble remembering much, their accuracy overwhelmed by trauma. It's not unusual for their statements to be sketchy and grossly mistaken, often contributing to the confusion, sometimes leading to false arrests and tainted evidence. Still, you never know. And he needs a break, too many suspects and not enough hard evidence.

Salmon stops at the ICU nurses' station to check in with Nurse Haft. She lets him know in no uncertain terms that Ms. Telafano's condition is still critical, telling him she's in severe pain and grief-stricken, terrified she may be paralyzed for life. To top it off, they've got her on a long laundry list of medications to address her physical damage and mental state. Salmon's beginning to wonder if he's wasted a trip.

Nurse Haft pushes open the door to ICU 3 and follows Salmon in, positioning herself to observe, lips pursed, arms folded across her chest.

Salmon slows, treading softly to Diane Telafano's bedside. She looks bad, hair matted, face puffy and mottled, tubes running everywhere. He can't tell if she's awake. Standing silently, he patiently waits for any sign of consciousness.

Diane groans, turns her head toward him, her eyes, slits.

"Ms. Telafano, I'm Detective Frank Salmon, Phoenix Police."

Salmon waits as she concentrates all her effort to speak.

"Uh ... what?"

"Ms. Telafano, I'm hoping you can help me."

"Help ... what?"

"Can you tell me who shot you?"

Diane's face squeezes shut as tears leak from the corners of her eyes. A deep gasp escapes her throat, breaking down into racking sobs.

Nurse Haft hustles to the side of the bed. "That's all for now, Detective."

Diane lifts a trembling hand to plead between sobs. "No ... wait."

Salmon and Nurse Haft wait expectantly as Diane struggles to get herself under control. Finally, her sobbing subsides. Her breathing, short, choppy, interspersed with hiccups and low moans.

"Sorry ... sorry, I'm ... sorry," she whispers, breathlessly.

Salmon smiles encouragement. "It's okay Ms. Telafano, take your time."

Diane starts again. "I ... dunno. How's, uh ... Michael?"

Salmon turns on Nurse Haft as Haft looks up at him in surprise. "She doesn't know?" he whispers. "No one's told her?"

"Detective, she just regained consciousness. Her doctor saw her for a short time to check on her and go over her chart. It must not have come up."

Salmon slowly turns back to speak quietly. "Ms. Telafano, I'm sorry to have to tell you this ..."

Her eyes widen, lips parting.

"Mr. Rodriquez didn't make it."

Diane's eyes squeeze shut as she turns her head away, lower lip trembling, face turning red.

Salmon watches and waits, half expecting her to get hysterical.

Diane blubbers in her pillow. "I ... I guess ... I knew that."

"I'm sorry. My condolences, Ms. Telafano."

Diane turns her face away. "It must have been her. That bitch."

Salmon's ears perk. "That bitch. You mean ...?"

"Connie. That bitch, Connie."

"Ms. Telafano, are you saying Connie Rodriguez shot you and Mr. Rodriguez?"

"It *must've* been her."

"You saw her?"

"No ... not really ... I didn't see ... too dark and everything ... so fast, but it must've been her. She hates me, hates us, hated Michael for loving me."

"I see." Salmon drops his gaze. Not the hard evidence he's hoping for.

Diane turns back to face him. "You know she was cheating on Michael. And then to accuse him ... that bitch."

He sees this isn't going anywhere and works to get her back on track. "Ms. Telafano, what do you remember about the shooting?"

"It was horrible." She sobs.

Salmon waits as her sobbing eases. Finally, he nudges her. "Anything you can remember will be a big help. Please, Ms. Telafano."

Diane struggles to get a grip. "Uh ... we ... working late at the office ... and then the noise ... and lights. Someone drove up. Michael said ... truck."

Salmon coaxes her. "Tell me about the truck."

"No ... I didn't see it, Michael saw it."

"Okay, what else?"

"The door ... just blew open!" Diane gasps and holds her breath. Her eyes fly open wide, staring off into space.

Salmon sees her distress, then her rapid breathing as she stares wildly at unseen horrors. She seems trapped and he tries coaxing her again. "Okay, go on."

"I ... it's flashing. Loud, exploding ... shooting. Shooting at me!"

Her gasping accelerates, hands jumping, face twitching uncontrollably. "Uh, uh, uh, uh, NO, it burns ... hot, hot, stinging. My ... on fire, my blood. I'm bleeding! NO!"

Alarmed, Nurse Haft forcefully pushes Salmon back from the bedside, hits the call button and works to restrain Diane from pulling all her tubing loose. In a loud controlled tone, she turns to Salmon. "You need to leave. NOW!"

"Sorry." Salmon backs away then turns for the door.


Salmon wheels the rumbling Marauder out of the hospital's parking lot, heading for the traffic light. *Shit.* He's back where he started. No eyewitness to put a face on the shooter. Telafano was really out of it. He wonders if her memory will improve with time. Who knows, once she's over the initial shock and has a chance to recover ... *Hope she'll be all right.*

The light turns green and he accelerates onto the boulevard, headed for the 51 onramp. Distracted, he nearly misses the southbound entrance to the 51, his cell beeping incessantly.

He answers deadpan. "Detective Salmon."

"Hey Frank, it's me."

"Hey Lace, whatsup?"

"Everything all right?"

"Why do you ask?"

"I dunno, you sound a little, uh …"

"Yeah, well … I'm fine. Whaddaya need?"

"Nothing, really. Just checking on you. Seein' if you want me to come over later, make some tacos."

Salmon's surly mood brightens. "That'd be good. I'll pick up a six-pack of Tecate. What time?"

"How 'bout sixish?"

"That'd be good."

"See you then. By the way, you know that photographer, Lance?"

"What about him?"

"Well, you remember that picture of his, with the chair and the truck?"

"Yeah."

"Damndest thing, he changed his mind. Now he wants to meet with you."

Salmon's mood starts to sour. "This better be good. If he jerks me around, he'll be wearing his ass for a hat."

"Hey, no guarantees. He just told me to tell you. It's worth a shot. What have you got to lose?"

"I'll call him, but I'm warnin' ya, if he wastes my time …"

"Hey, don't tell me, tell him. I already know he's out there. See you tonight."

As he clicks off, Salmon quietly chides himself, knowing that crazy photographer will just waste his time. He needs to run a background check on this guy, just in case. *Too curious for my own good. Guess it goes with the territory.* It's a big part of the reason he became a cop in the first place. He smiles to himself. *At least I'll get laid.*

# A WEEK AFTER

**[6:47 PM – Tuesday, August 31, 2010]**

IT'S BEEN A week since the shooting. Gary Whiting slumps over his plate, propping his elbows on their solid oak dining table. Dropping his head into his hands, he lets out a deep sigh. He doesn't see how things could get any worse. The ramifications of his partner's death are swirling around him, pulling him into a pit of desperation.

Connie was barely civil on the phone. All he wanted to do was drop by and express his condolences. It's not like he wanted to sleep with her, just get the lay of the land. But she begged off, suggesting he call Hammond Elder to start working out the business details. She wouldn't even give him a clue as to what to expect. *Not good.*

And why didn't Diane want to see him? He just wanted to drop off some flowers, see how she was doing. Okay, yes, he needs to know what she knows about the project's numbers, but that could wait. *Just trying to get along here, that's all! Shit, what was Rodriguez thinking, boning his bookkeeper?* If she had any idea what he was up to, she could have squeezed him, but good. Who knows, maybe she was. He's got to find out if she's seen the numbers, got to find out what she knows, can't let her squeeze *him* just 'cause Rodriguez couldn't keep his dick in his pants.

Then to have Benny Cohen stop by to introduce himself and his so-called "associates," expressing his regret at "Big Mike's passing." A sure sign that Cohen is playing it close, working the angles, watching his collateral like a hawk, probably after the insurance. He wonders if there's an acceleration clause that would let Cohen default that hard-money loan in the event of Rodriguez's death. Probably, but he can't remember, needs to check the loan documentation. *Shit, that stack of loan docs is two inches thick.*

Cohen is slick and his cohorts, Redman and Stein, are cookie-cutter thugs. That ape Redman looked like a stone-cold killer. And that tall cowboy Stein, all duded out, seemed dangerously bored, like he couldn't wait to hurt someone. Figures they are probably hit men on Cohen's payroll, probably needs them the way *he* does business. Not the kind of guys you fuck with—scary.

And to top it off, there's that dick-head cop and his bullshit insinuations. His attorney, Dalton Payne, suggested retaining a criminal attorney as a precaution. *Shit, just what I need, more legal fees.* So many fucked up scenarios coming together all at once. *Fuck!*

Lydia Whiting watches her husband warily. She moves quietly, careful not to disturb him as she clears the dinner table. He's never been particularly stable, but lately he comes unhinged for no reason at all. Best to avoid provoking him. She doesn't know how long she can tolerate his tirades.

Gary looks up and catches Lydia staring at him like a deer in the headlights. "What the fuck you staring at?"

She watches the blood rise, turning his neck and head crimson. Glancing away, she smirks and turns for the kitchen.

"Hey, where the fuck do you think you're going?!"

Lydia slams the door on her way out. She doesn't need to listen to this shit. She ought to leave the bastard and take him for everything he's got. It would serve him right. Any judge in the country would give it to her for putting up with his abuse. What she ever saw in him ... He's turned into a monster, maybe always been a monster.

Gary picks up his plate and heaves it at her as the door slams shut. The plate explodes against the door and shards scatter.

She hears a plate shatter. *Ooh, what a man ...* That flabby, pasty-white wimp. Naked, he's the most disgusting thing imaginable, about as attractive as a maggot. Yeah, the big-time real estate developer with his off-the-rack suits and his C-class Mercedes. *Who does he think he's fooling?* And that phony smile. He's fooled plenty with that smile, but not her. Never again. Without Rodriguez he'll never make it. At least Rodriguez had balls. She sees right through him. A weak little man, a loser, pissing all their money away at the gambling tables. She's sick of his bullying and she'll get even for every time he's ever hit her.

He hollers at the slammed door. "Fuck you bitch!" His guts churn as he gets up and heads for the stairs. *That bitch!* He could kill her.

It's been less than a week since Cohen read him the Riot Act, yet Stein is tired of shadowing Rodriguez's partner, bored to tears. Parked in his custom Ford 4x4 a couple houses down from Whiting's place, he grumbles to himself as he plays with his 9mm Glock. The gun's cool metal comforting, like a security blanket. This Whiting guy is a real loser, sits in his office all damn day. *What's the point?* Whiting never goes anywhere as close as he can tell. *Fuck it, need some action.*

It's been a week since her husband's murder. Connie still struggles just to get out of bed and start her day. Everyone tells her it will get better. She believes it will, or maybe hope is a better word. Days like today she can't quite believe it. But somehow, she must endure, part of God's plan for her. Mostly lost and confused, she just doesn't know anymore. It's so depressing.

The antidepressant meds her doctor gave her shut her down emotionally. She's feeling fuzzy, flat, blank, unable to remember what she really cares about anymore, leaving her with a dull, distant ache at the center of her soul. When she asked him about it, her doctor said it would take a couple weeks for the meds to reach therapeutic levels and not to worry about her occasional dizzy spells. Hoping he's right, she guesses he should know. She'll just have to muddle through. After all, he is the doctor. But she just couldn't bring herself to ask him about the warning label. Suicide is a sin. She'd never do that.

If she didn't have that lunch date with Marcia, she wouldn't bother getting up. When she agreed, she felt grateful that Marcia cared enough to ask. Now it seems like a grim obligation. To sit for an eternity and smile graciously through yet another misguided smothering of saccharine sympathy. She doesn't think she can take any more. She has half a mind to call Marcia and cancel, but Marcia sounded so concerned and she's already agreed. She guesses that she owes her at least that much. Having an affair with her husband was a thoughtless thing to do. Still, she has to remind herself that like her late husband, Marcia Lago-Rupert's husband is the culprit here. Marcia shouldn't put up with it. Of course, maybe she wouldn't, if she knew. What if that's the real reason Marcia asked her to lunch?

As Connie pushes through the hand-carved wooden door, she sees Marcia waiting in the entry. Marcia greets her with a sympathetic smile and a big hug. Connie stoops slightly to hug Marcia's petite frame. The scent of Marcia's dark curly hair, fragrant.

Marcia chatters away as they follow the hostess to their table, Connie nodding and smiling politely.

At their table, they peruse the menus to festive music of the strolling mariachis. Juanita's Flaming Fajitas not only has the best Mexican food in Scottsdale, but the best traditional Mexican ambiance as well. It's Connie's favorite for Mexican, yet she's having trouble relaxing, getting into the spirit of things. She's really not that hungry and she's gaining weight.

Marcia keeps glancing up at her, worriedly.

Finally the waitress shows up with a pitcher of margaritas and salt-rimmed margarita glasses.

Forcing a smile, Marcia pours for both of them as Connie watches uncomfortably.

Connie works her drink, discreetly sucking it down and pouring another, nodding and smiling at Marcia's idle chatter all the while. After her second margarita, Connie starts to feel better, warm and tingly.

Seeing Connie loosen up, Marcia leans in and in a conspiratorial tone asks, "Have you seen Diane?"

Connie drops her gaze to stare at her fingernails. "No, I guess I should, but …"

Marcia's eyes fill with sympathy. "I hear she's paralyzed, poor thing."

"Yes, well ... they won't know for a while yet."

"Did she say who shot them?"

"No. I guess she didn't get a good look, or doesn't remember or something."

"From what I hear, she had it coming."

Connie sits up straight. "What? How can you say that?"

"From what I hear, well ... I dunno, this is ... awkward." Marcia demurs, "Maybe I shouldn't say anything."

Connie leans in, her curiosity piqued, her defenses slipping further with every sip of potent margarita. "No, it's okay. What?"

"Are you sure it's okay?"

"Uh-huh."

"Well, it's just that ... I heard that Diane Telafano was sleeping around."

"No secret there."

Marcia scrunches her nose in disgust. "Yeah, but with married men?"

Connie's shoulders slump as her gaze drops to her half-empty glass, tears forming at the corners of her eyes. She breathes a deep sigh. "So you heard about Diane and my husband, too."

Marcia crumbles at Connie's distress. "Oh, honey, no ... I didn't mean anything by it, please. It's just that ... well, Daniel said he heard something. And, well I ... you know ... thought you should know."

"Listen, don't worry about it. Seems everyone in town knew about it but me."

"Well, don't feel bad. I think Daniel's been fucking her too."

Connie looks up with wounded surprise. "Daniel?"

"Yeah, I'm afraid so."

"How do you know?"

"Not really sure, but he's fucking someone and it isn't me."

Connie blanches, gripped with panic. She hesitates, pulling herself together. "What makes you think it could be Diane Telafano?"

"I dunno. I mean, I know he knows her. And, well, you know the rumors." Marcia takes a long drink, draining her margarita, then stares directly at Connie, sarcasm filling her voice. "Danny Boy thinks he's a real player, but two can play at that game."

Connie shrinks beneath Marcia's cold stare, fumbling her words. "I guess."

Marcia pours herself another margarita and stares up at the ceiling. Seething, she drops her gaze, staring fiercely at Connie. "If I find out he's been playing around with her, I'll shoot them both and I won't just paralyze her."


Sondra Du surveys the audience at the Lion's Den from stage left. It's a big crowd for a hot Tuesday night—a week since the shootings. They're mostly blue-collar which means mostly singles. Rarely do they toss fives or tens, never hundreds. Too bad. The white-collar types give up the big bucks and faster. But they'll do. She'll just have to make up for it in volume.

Sondra turns to watch Jilly on the big stage, a tall brunette with a perfect set of store-bought tits. Jilly's wild and a bit of a ditz, but she knows how to put on a show. All the white-hot spotlights and colored lasers focus on Jilly as she slides inverted, legs spread wide, down the chromed pole. She's down to her thin black G-string. The last item to go before she wows them nude, picks up the singles littering the stage and trots off. All the horny assholes lined up around the stage rivet their eyes on her, tongues out, panting in anticipation. No one notices Sondra in the shadowy stage entrance, but she's up next and plans on making a killing with this crowd, a rough and rowdy bunch.

Sondra smiles a devious little smile. She's got all the right equipment and she knows it. After all, she's spent a lot of time and money getting it and keeping it that way. All she needs to do is expose it little by little, parade around like she's a nympho in heat and they literally throw money at her. What a gig. *The fools.* Men are such idiots, especially when they're drunk and horny. And they seem to be one or the other or both, nearly all the time. Any girl with a tight ass, a hot pair of bolt-ons and half a brain can lead them around by their cocks like hogs to slaughter. The perfect suckers, easy scams.

For this set, Sondra's a firefighter. Red gumballs flash and sirens scream as she struts out to the pole, center-stage. She's wrapped in a firefighter's bright yellow Kevlar assault coat and topped with a red fire helmet adorned with a traditional shield. Sub-woofers thump and tweeters cry out red-hot rhythms. Burn baby, burn. Sondra prances full circle around the stage, giving everyone a close look at those long, luscious legs. Turning to face the crowd, she grabs fistfuls of yellow Kevlar and pops open her assault coat to reveal bright red firefighting suspenders holding up a yellow Kevlar G-string, her perfect tits poking out between the suspenders' red webbing. Howls erupt and a flurry of singles fly as Sondra pumps and grinds her tight little G-string, inflaming the crowd. Heavy music pulses with mind-numbing intensity. Sondra wriggles out of the assault coat and it hits the hardwood deck revealing her perfect ass, her buns flexing as she struts to the chrome pole. More singles hit the stage accompanied by cat-calls and wolf whistles. Turning at the pole, she pulls her fire hat down low over a wicked-sexy grin. She's got them by the balls and loves it.

Scanning the crowd, she mentally targets two or three of the more affluent patrons. She'll lure them back to her private cubby and serve up lucrative lap dances. She slowly wraps her leg around the pole, hugging it tight to her G-string as though working a giant phallus. Hand on her hat, she gradually leans back into a graceful arch, then flinging off the fire helmet, she shakes out her long blond mane, running the tip of her tongue seductively over parted lips. The tempo and volume ramp up, thundering Jimi Hendrix's "Fire" at trance-inducing levels, sub-woofers shaking the floor. Sondra twirls around the pole, one long silky leg lifted to her shoulder in upright splits, her tiny yellow G-string straining to contain her. Breaking away, she prances out to the stage's edge, popping one then another suspender snap. Red suspenders drop to the stage writhing in an elastic jumble as her slick yellow G-String flies apart and falls away. Planting both spiked heels wide, arms akimbo, she thrusts her naked beauty in the face of all the gaping onlookers, flaunting, teasing them, daring them outright. *Try not to get sucked in.* She knows she's got them and will milk them for every dollar she can get. Another cloud of singles flutters to the stage.

Jimi's soaring electric-plasma guitar riffs cut to the core as Mitch Mitchell's double basses pound eardrums to putty. Sondra works the stage's edge, shaking tits and grinding hips for more singles. Prostrating herself on the hardwood, she slowly spreads her legs then writhes with mock ecstasy in a solo version of the horizontal mambo, her money maker pointed at the crowd. Rolling onto her back, she straightens her legs, pulling them wide, slowly drawing her knees to her shoulders. She stares down through her open legs at a rowdy crew rumbling in from the ultraviolet entrance tunnel. It's Johnny Chavez and his cohorts. She gives a half-smirk. *This oughtta be interesting.* The night's potential take just doubled. Chavez and his crew always have bucks to burn and she knows just how to light their fire.

After her set, Sondra saunters out onto the main floor, winding her way through the crowded tables, hips swaying in see-through lingerie, heading for Johnny Chavez and company. As she passes through the crowd she smiles vacantly, mostly ignoring the leering drunks as they holler, wave money and grab at her. She catches Chavez's eye and his coarse features light up.

Smiling broadly, Chavez slams down his beer, scoots his chair back from the table, twists to face Sondra and opens his muscular arms wide, inviting her onto his lap.

Sondra lets his lustful gaze wander over her body, its liquid heat reflected back at him with her every move. She watches him stare as she expands her chest, inhaling deep, filling her lungs, then a long slow exhale as he's entranced by the rise and fall of her perfect breasts. She slows, lowers her brow and stalks her prey, gliding steadily toward the catch of the day.

Chavez nearly drools in anticipation. Burning desire, a trap of his own making. *Damn, that bitch's hot!* His broad smile twists into a leering grin as he picks up on his crew's raw envy. *They wish.* Maybe he'll let them have sloppy seconds, but she's his—for now.

Looking him dead in the eye, Sondra bends forward to grab his shoulders, pushing her tits into his face to feel his hot breath on her nipples. She slides one long leg over his thighs, easing onto his lap, sliding forward to nudge the erection bulging his fly, grinning at his distress. Teasing them is the best part and she knows how to play that game to the hilt. It's all about control and Johnny has lost his. It's not long before he's following her into her private sound-proof cubby to run his credit card over the limit.

Locked in her cubby with Chavez, Sondra suppresses a chuckle. Chavez is worn out, too much booze and blow, can't get it up. He's panting heavily, his erection long gone. Radiating a crazed feverish look, his eyes roll around in his head, his T-shirt soaked with pungent sweat, dripping wet, large stains in his pits and chest. Still, not bad, she's been at it the better part of two hours and racked up his credit card for all she could get. A tidy sum for a couple hours work. She sneers as she slides off to the side, plopping her tight ass on the black faux-leather divan. She grabs the champagne magnum off the end table, leans her head back and takes a long swig, wiping her mouth on the back of her hand, smacking her lips with pleasure. Turning her gaze to Chavez, she studies him with the satisfaction of a conqueror. He's definitely done.

Chavez props himself up on his elbows. Sweating like a tweaker in a police lineup, his chest heaves as he pants, his face all hangdog. He wonders if he overdid it, maybe having a heart attack. *Shit, can't die now.* He looks over at Sondra Du in disbelief. She's not even breathing heavy. A frisson of rage flashes though him, he wants to fuck her into submission, wear her ass out, teach her a lesson. *Where does she get off?*

Sondra smiles coolly, inserting the blade. "You're not too bad for an old day laborer."

Chavez snarls. "Shit, what would you know about it. Bitch like you never worked a day in your life."

"Yeah, your cousin used to give me that crap, too." She gives him an evil grin, twisting the knife. "Too bad he's not around. Between the two of you, I might get a decent fuck."

Chavez looks away in disgust. "Fuck you, bitch. I'm twice the man that Mike ever was and you know it."

Sondra can hardly stand it, wanting to bleed him out. "They didn't call him Big Mike for nothin'. More than I can say for you."

On the raw edge, Chavez works to laugh it off, doing his best not to let this bitch get to him. "Yeah, well, Big Mike ain't so big now. 'Course maybe that's the kind of stiff you like, the cold ones." Impressing himself, he laughs too loud.

"I can tell you're all broken up about it. You must really miss him."

Chavez roars, explodes off the divan and pounces on her. Straddling her, he pins both arms above her head with one hand and slaps her savagely across the face. How dare she ridicule him! How dare she even mention his dead cousin! Mike was family, his cousin, even if he was a selfish fucking asshole. *No one disses my family and lives!*

Startled and scared, she yelps from the sting then holds still, hoping he'll calm down.

Reddish-purple rage fires his face, veins popping out on his dark forehead as he seethes. "Now whatcha gonna do bitch? I got your ass now!" He slaps her again, harder, nearly knocking her out. Grinning, he grabs her breast, twisting her nipple until she squeals.

She's delirious, blue and white pinpoints of light popping in her blurred vision, trying to keep quiet, trying not to enrage him further, worried about how far he'll go. She's seen his sadistic side before.

Now that he has her pinned, he takes his time inflicting his pleasure, reveling in her fear and agony. He's going to get what he paid for, the way *he* likes to party. She's going to be worth it. It'll be a good time after all.

# THE ARRANGEMENT

**[9:54 AM – Wednesday, September 1, 2010]**

*DREAMING: A COOL moonlit night. A clearing in the trees. She is smiling at me, drifting my way through the mist. She seems familiar. Somehow, somewhere … Shadows crowd the pale light and I can't quite make her out. Wondrous in a wispy sort of way, glowing in the faint moonlight—beautiful, and she seems to know me.*

*Do I know her? I can't seem to remember. And I wish it could be … and I hope … Let it be her.*

*A floating apparition, she's closer, eyes gleaming, just for me. Feels like we've met before, if I could just remember when, where. Yet dark memory's shadows intercede and I can't let myself, don't dare let myself …*

*On and on, eons of moonlit nights drift by on an endless river of time. I've been searching so long, never finding her. Seems like forever, seems like it's too late now.*

*Faint moonlight plays heartless games, so melancholy, so cold. Was it all an illusion, my imagination, swept up in some idyllic fantasy that never could be? A cruel trick of the mind, a lonely heart's defense, rigged to protect from that most wicked of insanities—the barren moonscape of a life alone. What a fool. What have I done?*

*Moonbeams frame her face, their light bathing her beauty in a silvery glow, eyes sparkling, lit with her love. She comes, she reaches out, a gentle touch and I can't resist her. I melt in her embrace and remember … I know love again, I know her again. I've always known her.*

*It's been so long. I won't let her go this time, won't ever lose her. Enveloped in her soul and she in mine, we are one. I break down, weeping, overcome with joy. Sonja holds me, comforts me and whispers, "We will be together again."*

Gasping, I start upright, fully awake, alone in the dark, sobbing un-controllably and not really knowing why, an empty hole in my chest. And nothing—I can't remember. Just another nightmare.

My poor night's sleep leaves me exhausted, cross and inexplicably on the verge of tears. I don't sleep well most nights. I blame it on my favorite scapegoat "getting older" and resign myself to another day. Another ten, twelve-hour trudge through a grey blur that I must endure yet again. Got to find a way through, no more time for self-pity. Maybe some coffee, maybe a long walk off a short pier. Can't help it, my cynical side. Just as well, piers are in short supply in the middle of the desert.

My cell's infernal chirp grates raw nerves. Got to get a new ringtone. *Where is that damn phone, anyway?* I hear it, on the counter somewhere. I push proof sheets, wadded hamburger wrappers, beer bottle caps and other as-sorted detritus around until I spot the little bastard.

"Lance Underphal?"

"Yeah."

"Detective Salmon."

My ears perk up. "Detective. What can I do for you?"

"Ms. Friends tells me you have something for me."

"Ms. Friends?"

"Lacey."

"Oh—right." *Lacey got him to call. Amazing.*

"So, you wanna tell me about it?"

"Be better if I showed ya. When can I stop by?" A long pause. I won-der if my cell dropped the call.

"Detective?"

"Yeah, I'm checkin'. Hold your horses."

"Right."

"This afternoon, four o'clock. Ya know where we're at?"

"Yeah, I'll be there."


Almost four on a scorching Wednesday afternoon, more than a week after the shootings. I shake my head in disbelief as I enter police headquarters in downtown Phoenix. Between passing out at a crime scene, waking up in an emergency room and the splitting headaches, the last several days seem like an eternity of sheer hell. At least the raw nerves and black depression have subsided somewhat. The further out I am from that last pain pill, the more confident and relaxed I feel. Pushing sixty, it's harder to recover.

As I work my way through Security's metal detector, I wonder if Sonja's right, if this is the only way out. I better hurry if I'm going to make it. I'm too old for this shit. Time to get Salmon pointed in the right direction.

The officer at the information desk points me toward the Violent Crimes Bureau. At the reception counter I'm told to wait while they find Detective Salmon. As I squint from the harsh fluorescent light, I find myself mindlessly staring at my shoes and a putty-grey vinyl floor. The floor's generic vinyl sheeting is speckled with something that looks like bits of black olives and red pimento, reminding me of the shitty sub I had for lunch a couple hours ago. My stomach rumbles as I hear my name.

And there he is, tall, lean, severe. "Detective Salmon."

"This way, Underphal."

Salmon seems impatient, distracted, and heads into a maze of off-white corridors at a brisk pace. I hustle to keep up, winding my way close behind, thinking I should be leaving a trail of bread crumbs if I ever want to get out of here. A creeping sensation grows with every step. *I most certainly do want to get out of here, and now!* I've got no business walking into a police station voluntarily. *What the hell was I thinkin'?*

Without a word, the stoic detective directs me into a small interrogation room, metal table in the room's center bolted to the floor, uncomfortable-looking straight-backed metal chairs. Salmon motions me to sit. And sure enough, the chairs are as uncomfortable as they look. I look up at him and smile weakly. He drops into a chair across from me, slapping a manila folder down on the table, staring back with the orbs of a hawk, skepticism painted all over his tight, lean face. He seems like an angry young man—probably in his late thirties, early forties. Unreasoning fear ripples through me. *Holy shit, I could end up in jail!* I attempt another smile.

Aware of my discomfort, Salmon sneers as he opens the file folder. "Before we start, you need to know I did a little checking."

A frisson of panic rips through me. "You're checking on me?"

"Yeah, standard procedure. Looks like you were doing okay until late 2008."

Flush with shame, I drop my gaze. "Yeah. My business tanked with the economy."

"Then filed for Chapter 11 bankruptcy on your electrical contracting company, Pure Power, Inc. That right?"

He's got me. He who asks the questions is in control. *Shit, how do I get out of this?* I tell him, "Yeah."

"Looks like it was converted to a Chapter 7 in August of 2009, that right?"

I grit my teeth. "Yes. I tried everything I could think of to save it."

"Then you and your wife filed for personal bankruptcy ..."

"Uh-huh."

"The accident report says your wife was killed within a few days of your filing. That right?"

A small gasp escapes me as the nightmarish past comes rushing back. I swallow hard, forcing back the hurt and shame. "Yeah."

"Looks like there were hefty settlements from the cement company's liability insurance and your wife's life insurance policy."

My face feels like it's on fire, burning with embarrassment at having to go through all this again. "My wife, Sonja ... bad timing. The BK trustee took all the proceeds, except a small amount I receive from the accident settlement, $1,100 a month."

Salmon glances up from the file to eye me with a dubious look. "Yup, that's what it says here."

I can't believe I'm sitting here listening to this. "What's your point, Detective? Am I a murder suspect now?"

"Lacey Friends thinks you're a good guy, just a little down on your luck. I gotta tell ya, that don't cut it with me. I figure one way or another, a guy makes his own luck."

He's really starting to piss me off. "Thanks for all your poignant compassion and insightful advice, Detective. I'll take it to heart."

Salmon sneers, "Look Underphal, Friends' recommendation and your photo are the only reasons I agreed to see you, so this better be good."

"Yeah, well, trust me on this. I wouldn't be here if I didn't have to."

Salmon's features turn quizzical. "Whaddaya mean?"

I drop my gaze, uncomfortable with his stare. "I dunno. I just, uh, thought I might, uh, have something for you on that shooting. I dunno, maybe it's nothing."

"Look, you're already here wasting my time, so you might as well tell me what's on your mind. Besides, I thought you had something on that photo."

"Well, uh, yes and no. Do you guys ever use psychics to help with investigations?"

Salmon's face bunches up in disgust. "I haven't got all day here, whaddaya got?"

"Well I had this sort of vision, and it uh, had to do with the shooting."

"Shit, you're kidding me. I haven't got time for this. You're a psychic now? And here I thought you were a photographer, or is it an electrician? What the hell was Friends thinking?"

The guy is an asshole and it's really pissing me off. Why did I think I should help him in the first place? "Listen, I came here against my better judgment to give you information that might help with your investigation. Just hear me out and then I'm outta here."

Salmon's eyebrows raise as he sits back, folding his arms across his chest. "Well? I'm listening."

I put my elbows on the table and lean in, looking him in the eye. "That double exposure you asked about, the back of that chair superimposed over a truck. I think I know where the truck fits in."

Salmon just sits there, skepticism furrowing his brow, but at least he's still listening.

"I saw it."

He leans forward, arms unfolding as he grabs the edge of the table. "You saw that truck?"

"Uh, no, not the truck. The shooting, I saw the shooting."

"Yeah, I know you were at the crime scene. Made a scene of your own, getting sick, contaminating the crime scene."

"No! The actual shooting. I saw it! And I know about the truck. The dead guy, he took pictures of a truck with his cell phone, didn't he?"

"Shit! Where did you get that? Did Friends tell you that? How do you know that?"

The words rush out of me. "Like I said, I had a vision. It was the shooting. I saw them fucking on the desk in that office when a truck pulled up. That Rodriguez guy was on his cell phone talking to some guy named Gary. He took a picture through the blinds, said it was a truck. I didn't actually see the truck. Then someone broke in on them and shot them."

Salmon sits stunned, fingers turning white, gripping the table's dull metal edge. I watch and wait, wondering how he's going to react. Finally, after several seconds of dead silence, I can see his wheels start to turn.

"You saw the shooter?"

"Not really, just a silhouette. It was kinda dark, lots of gunfire, lots a blood, kinda hard to see."

His face scrunches with disappointment, dropping his gaze as he lets go of the table. "So how is this supposed to help me?"

"I dunno. Maybe I can give you details."

"Maybe. But the only detail we need is the shooter's ID."

"Sorry, can't help you there. At least, not yet."

"Do you get these visions often?"

"Look, this whole ESP thing is unpredictable, I can't control it. If I could, I'd stop it altogether. Not good for my health, gives me headaches."

"So why are you telling me this?"

I shrug and give him an apologetic smile. "Like I said, thought it might help."

"Yeah, well, maybe." Salmon pushes back, his chair's metal feet screeching on the ugly vinyl, rising up to signal the end of the interview. "Tell you what you do. Write down everything you saw in as much detail as you can and get it to me. Can you do that?"

"Sure. When?"

"Soon as you can."

"Okay."

"And keep in touch. Let me know if you come up with anything else, another vision, whatever."

I brighten up. "Will do."

He moves around the table as I stand. He stops me as I start for the door and shakes my hand.

"Thanks for coming in."

I know his thanks is just matter-of-fact, but I'm relieved, almost elated. I feel better. Maybe I really *can* help. That would be something. Me helping, what a novel idea.

# INTO THE LION'S DEN

### [7:05 PM – Friday, December 4, 2009]

MIKE RODRIGUEZ PUNCHED seven on his cell, speed-dialing his wife. Nine times out of ten it went direct to voicemail, the tenth it normally went to voicemail after three rings. Either way, she never answered his calls anymore. Just as well. He didn't really want to talk to her anyway.

Connie's voicemail picked up.

"Hey babe, 'member I got that subcontractor dinner tonight for Sunset Pointe. Could be a late one. Don't wait up. Luv ya."

Rodriguez tapped his phone off and climbed into his top-of-the-line Ford F-150 4X4, his everyday driver. The epitome of luxury and performance in a big sedan, his Mercedes S65 AMG was his favorite, but his pickup embodied the Big-Shot Contractor image, and image is everything when you're in construction. He had to be one of the good ol' boys if he wanted the subcontractors' respect. Firing up his work truck, he backed out of his private garage, turned for MJR's main gate, heading for the Lion's Den.

It had been a long day: the pain-in-the-ass City inspectors at Sunset Pointe; going over his testimony with Hammond Elder for an upcoming deposition; and checking Diane's numbers for this month's construction draw. He loved his bookkeeper's big tits, loved bending her over the big leather couch in his office, made him hard just thinking about it. Anyway, tonight was all business, everything was set up. As he drove, a broad grin crept across Rodriguez's face. If he was lucky, he might get laid again in the bargain. *Hell, yes!* There might be more to life than hot sex and lots of money, but he wasn't sure what it could be. Rodriguez chuckled as he sped down Deer Valley Road, running late for the big dinner. *So, what's new?* They were lucky he even bothered to show up. *The sonsofbitches.* He started laughing.

Rodriguez slowed the big truck as he pulled into the Lion's Den parking lot. Heading to the private back lot, he wheeled around the side, noticing a silver F-150 4x4 with chrome aftermarket trim. *Nice truck*, he thought as he pulled up to the back lot gate, vaguely wondering where he'd seen that truck before. *Looks familiar, maybe one of the subs.*

The lot attendant waved Rodriguez through, closing the gate behind him. Rodriguez had always told Connie and his priest that he was a silent investor, just helping out a friend in need. However, his silent partnership was anything but. Every dancer, bartender, bouncer, cocktail waitress, cook and dishwasher knew full well who he was, catering to his every whim. And while he got his share of the cash skimmed every week, he was happier about the other perks. All in all, a great investment.

A handful of limos, stretches and custom stretches sprawled across the parking spaces, waiting patiently for return trips. A white super-stretch Hummer stood out against a backdrop of black Town Cars and Escalades. Jenny sent the super-stretch Hummer full of beers and blow to pick up the subcontractors, a nice touch. Rodriguez smirked. Knowing them, they partied all the way there. His private parties at the Lion's Den were renowned amongst the Trades, one of his little tricks. And the day after, while their hangovers kicked them in the conscience, he was quick to remind them that he was looking out for them, making sure their wives and families never found out. He had them by the short hairs. Give them what they weren't supposed to have and they'd follow him anywhere. He smirked again. Almost too easy.

A full thirty minutes late, Rodriguez pulled up to the canopied entrance and jumped out, leaving the door ajar for the attendant. He lumbered across the private entrance's red carpet and through the double hand-carved mahogany doors. Striding across the terrazzo mosaic of a lion's head, he figured everyone must already be there. He paused at the dining room's double doors to gather himself and screw on a big smile. *Party time!*

Pushing through the heavy glass doors, right arm raised in a fist, Rodriguez, at six-foot-two and 235 pounds, looked like an NFL defensive back charging onto the field to start a game. He hadn't changed out of his work clothes, black Levi's, black Nikes and a scarlet Cardinals jersey—just one of the boys. His bad boy/good guy image endeared him to construction crews and scared hell out of his associates, attorneys and competitors. He thoroughly enjoyed his well-deserved reputation for intimidation.

As expected, everyone turned to watch Big Mike's entrance. He shook hands and back-slapped his way around the entire table, expansively re-minding everyone who was putting on the little shindig and insisting that they enjoy themselves.

Once Rodriguez parked at the head of the table, the room's chatter returned to pre-entry levels. He mentally confirmed the roster. All required parties were present: all the Trades including his cousin Johnny Chavez. The City boys were there, too: Development Services, and the department head of Construction Inspections. Tonight would be a night they'd never forget. He'd see to it.

All the attorneys showed, even the staid Fredrick Marsh. Rodriguez shook his head, the balls on these guys. The only profession he knew that would show up to drink his booze, snort his coke, whore around all night, and then try to charge him for it. *What a racket.* His satisfaction came from knowing they'd have to watch his back, no matter what.

A grin crept across his face as he glanced at the table's far end. Whiting and Jenny were next to his cousin Johnny, seated next to Johnny was Martin Fellman, next to him, Teresa Milner. *Great.* Fellman was key. Small and delicate, Fellman looked like a Jewish hobbit next to the six-foot-four Chavez. For a moment, he wondered what they were talking about. Anyway, Sunset Pointe was going to need more funding—he had to pay for that new offshore racer somehow. Plus a bonus, Teresa Milner, his personal project for the evening. It promised to be a pleasurable night.

Sondra Du waited at the kitchen's cafe doors with a half-dozen other girls. They all had the night off to work Big Mike's party. Dinner was about over, most of the food had been cleared and the bikini-clad cocktail waitresses had drinks in everyone's hands. Now the cocktail waitresses stood just inside the kitchen, drink trays at rest, waiting with the dancers. Stupid outfits, tails off the back of their furry bikini bottoms and a pair of ears, Sondra wouldn't be caught dead. But then she wouldn't work for peanuts, either. Most women just didn't get it. But then most women didn't have the right equipment.

Their cue was the end of Big Mike's toast and he'd just started. Sondra couldn't believe how he could go on and on about nothing, verbose and tiresome. She hated men that wouldn't shut up. *Get on with it already.*

She peeked over one of the café doors. The table was full, nearly twenty people, and a couple of them female. *This oughtta be good.*

Sondra scanned the faces, looking for the mark Big Mike set up for her. Probably that fastidious banker-looking dude sitting next to Johnny. She'd find out soon enough.

Slightly amused, she watched Johnny and that banker guy talking. What could they possibly have to talk about? About as far apart as a leper and the Pope. Who knew, maybe Johnny was getting fashion tips. Her attention shifted as Big Mike raised his glass. *Showtime!*


Big Mike sat down to light applause. He had tales of Sunset Pointe's success rippling through his guests, on the tip of everyone's tongue. On cue, cocktail waitresses appeared around the table, taking drink orders. The dancers weren't far behind, hips swaying, tits bouncing as they crossed the terrazzo floor. Wearing G-strings and gauzy see-through tops, they circled seductively, like sharks to blood. Rodriguez grinned as he watched them work. The men were captivated. Jenny and Teresa Milner vacillated between embarrassment and awe.

The dancers took control, teasing their prey with a blend of feigned innocence and lust, creating the perfect illusion, consummate professionals. The men took the bait, hook, line and sinker.

Rodriguez spotted Sondra Du sauntering his way with his usual Grey Goose and Red Bull on the rocks in one hand and his favorite cigar, a lit Montecristo #2 Torpedo, in the other. What a vision. If his father could see him now. At times like these he really missed the ol' fart. *Shit, this is the good life.*

Rodriguez grinned. "Hey baby."

Brushing up against him, she leaned in to set his drink on the table. "Your drink, sir." She pressed her breasts into his shoulder, wrapping her arms around him to suspend the smoldering cigar in front of his lips. "And your cigar, sir."

He grinned, savoring her warm breasts against his shoulder. "Thanks, babe." Grabbing the fat Cuban with his lips, he inhaled then exhaled luxuriously.

She leaned in closer and whispered, "So who's my date?"

He wrapped a meaty forefinger around his cigar, pulling it from his lips. Cigar perched between fingers, he pointed toward the far end of the table. "See that guy next to Johnny?"

"Mr. Conservative?"

"That's our boy, Mr. Martin Fellman."

"What's he do?"

"He's a loan officer—just happens to have the construction loan on Sunset Pointe."

"Hmm. No wonder." Sondra grinned wickedly.

"Yeah, take real good care of him."

"Don't worry, baby. Sondra's got it covered, everything you need."

Rodriguez leaned his massive head back to exhale a series of smoke rings. He eyed Sondra and grinned. "Do I look worried to you?"

Sondra slowly brushed her breasts against the top of his shoulders as she pulled away. Without a backward glance she sauntered off in Fellman's direction.

Rodriguez grinned as he watched her hips sway, her tight ass beckoning. Damn, she was hot, made him hard just watching her. But tonight, he had other fish to fry. He scanned the faces at the long table, a lot of grins, some sheepish, some wolfish, but all eyes were on the girls. Even Jenny and Teresa Milner were watching as the girls pandered to their dates for the evening. Jenny looked nervous, uncomfortable. If he was a betting man, he'd bet she wouldn't make it another half hour. He noticed Teresa glance his direction, then she hurriedly glanced away. *She's mine.* Taking a long drag off his stogie, he calculated how long it would take to have her on her back in his private suite, ankles around her ears. He figured less than an hour. Staring at her, he brought the heat, waiting for her to glance back, knowing she knew he was staring as the color rose in her cheeks.

Teresa clutched her drink, snatched it to her lips and downed the remainder in one long gulp. Her courage fortified, she turned to Rodriguez and smiled. Pink roses in her cheeks deepened to scarlet.

Rodriguez pushed back from the table, stood and began to work his way down the table, chatting up each guest with one eye on Teresa, making sure she saw him headed her direction. If she was going to bolt, she'd do it soon, but not likely. She held fast as he came within striking distance.


Sondra fixed her sultry gaze on Mr. Fellman as she moved in for the kill. She sauntered up to Johnny Chavez, draped an arm on his shoulder and turned to Martin Fellman to show off her tits. Conversation ended abruptly as they turned toward her. Chavez's grin broadened as his leathery complexion flushed. Fellman did his best to stop himself from gawking, concealing it with an indifferent yawn. His charade was too obvious. She had him cold. No one played hard to get with Sondra Du.

While speaking, Sondra stared directly at Fellman. "Well, Johnny, aren't you going to introduce me to your friend?"

Chavez glanced at Fellman. "Would if I knew his name. We just met."

Fellman gave Sondra a cockeyed glance. "Martin Fellman."

Sondra turned coy. "Yes, Mr. Fellman, your reputation precedes you. Didn't I see you in Vegas, at the ground-breaking party?"

Fellman struggled to maintain, his face flush. "Yes, just for the evening. Sunset Pointe is one of our projects. My company provides the financing."

Sondra feigned infatuation. "Hmm. Impressive. Must be fascinating, working with all that money."

Fellman puffed up in spite of himself. "Not much to it, really. It's all about relationships. Sunset Pointe is just one of several accounts we handle in my department. It's actually on the small side for us as far as development projects go."

She ignored Fellman's clumsy attempt to impress and turned back to Chavez. "So what were you boys talking about before I so rudely interrupted?"

Before Chavez could answer, Fellman jumped in. "Mr. Chavez here does all the concrete work for the project. I was about to ask him to take a look at a little side project."

Sondra turned back to Fellman, eyes flirting. "Would you be too offended if I asked you to continue your conversation later? Mr. Rodriguez asked me to dance for you as a favor and I wouldn't want to let him down. Would that be okay?"

Fellman glanced at Chavez, his mouth working soundlessly.

Chavez grinned and gave Fellman a wink.

Without waiting for an answer, Sondra smoothly reached out, took Fellman's hand and slowly pulled him to his feet. She took him in tow, headed for her cubby. Obediently, he plodded along behind, all red-faced and conflicted, embarrassed and excited.


Rodriguez glanced over the top of Teresa's head, watching as one by one, the dancers led their prey away to be slaughtered. Before sunrise they'd all have drunk from the tainted well: the City inspector, boys from the Trades, the entitlement attorneys too, not to mention little ol' Martin Fellman. Of course his cousin didn't count, single, with the morals of an alley cat. The rest were all family men, but all the dirt in the world wouldn't bother Johnny Chavez. Ah well, he had other methods for his notorious cousin. Now, for Miss Milner.

Sondra gazed at Fellman's pale belly fat with mild disgust, his limp nakedness gross in the extreme. Hell, at least she didn't have to fuck him. He lay sprawled on his back, head lolling half off her divan, out like a drag queen at a Gay Pride parade. The weenie took forever to loosen up, three lap dances and a liter of champagne laced with roofies. He never knew what hit him.

Working nude, Sondra set up a tripod next to the black divan and mounted her digital camera. Setting the shutter delay timer for fifteen seconds, she positioned the unconscious Fellman for best effect, slid over the top of him and clicked the camera's button. Dropping back into position, she pulled his face to her breasts and threw a leg over his genitals. She held for the flash then set up the next shot. After a half-dozen poses with the financial genius, she kicked back, satisfied she had all the incriminating photos Rodriguez would ever need.

Having finished ahead of schedule, Sondra contemplated what this little scam of Rodriguez's could be worth. She wriggled into her G-string and tossed the negligee top over her head, thinking Rodriguez wasn't paying her near enough, not for all these great pictures. Stashing the tripod and camera in her locker, she turned back to the unconscious banker with a calculating grin. She decided she'd have to hold back a few choice photos, find a way to cash in on her own, maybe up the price on Big Mike.

# THE ART OF
# PRESCIENCE

**[8:09 PM – Thursday, September 2, 2010]**

I'VE BEEN AT it for hours. My eyes hurt and my head is starting to pound. Wish I hadn't agreed to do this damn write-up for Detective Salmon. I'm no good at writing. I should stick to photography. Not sure I'm much good at that, either. Doubt I could convince anyone, if I was. I've probably talked myself out of more jobs than most photographers ever see. Self-promotion, too close to self-importance, must be one of the seven deadly sins. Or is that pride? Ah well, my writing *does* suck. But for Salmon, how good does it have to be?

Sonja chimes in. "Writing is therapeutic, helps get it out where you can inspect it, objective rather than subjective. Good for ya."

Anymore I cringe whenever she tells me something is good for me. Not sure where this is going, but it doesn't bode well. "What are you prattling on about? This is some scary, gruesome shit. I hate having to write it all down. Why did I agree to do this anyway? Tell me that."

Sonja turns serious. "It's evolving. It's not just the one shooting anymore."

"What does *that* mean?"

"The killer has appetites, and he's growing more confident, thinking he got away with it. If you don't find a way to stop him, he'll kill again."

"He, him—it's a guy?"

"Seems like, yes."

"Should I tell Salmon about this?"

"Just tell Salmon what you know."

"Yeah, but this is important."

"For now, just write."

"Tell me, what else?"

"He's not doing it just for hatred or vengeance; he's into it for the thrill, blood sport, blood lust, whatever you want to call it. If you don't stop him, he'll kill again and again."

"Are you saying that he'll kill again, but it hasn't happened yet?"

"That's the way it seems."

"You don't know?"

"Time doesn't work the same way here—no future, no past. It's all Now. The past is a memory, the future is just potential. And the potential for him to kill again is strong."

"That's just great, so if I can't see who it is in time, there'll be another shooting. Fucking swell." But I can tell she's already gone. *I hate this shit.* What does she expect me to do?

I keep writing. It's getting late and I'm hungry, but I want to finish and get it to Salmon. Let *him* figure it out. But what Sonja said is true, the more I write the clearer it gets. I'm no longer dazed by all the turbulent energy, painful sensations and crazed emotions. It's giving me some objectivity, as though I'm an observer reporting on some sordid little story rather than living it firsthand. The thing I didn't notice before, in the heat of the moment—the shadowy outline of the killer is either a real Amazon of a woman, or a man. It almost has to be a man, just too big. *Sonja's right.*

I stand, stretch and head for the fridge, need a beer to tide me over. Wrenching off the cap, I shuffle back to the counter and my laptop. I take a long pull off my cold beer and rip off a loud belch. A few more swigs and I'm feeling a little better, the pounding in my head softening to a dull throb. *What do I say here?* I've got to give Salmon everything I can think of. Who knows what he thinks is important?

Other feelings, just impressions really, the shooter was gunning for Rodriguez, his intended target. Yet, somehow the killer's rage flared upon discovering the woman, Diane Telafano. I sense his appetite for flesh, the bloodlust Sonja mentioned, releasing all that frustration, like some dark, whole-body orgasm, convulsing at the core—complex and conflicted urges battling to a head. It culminates in roiling hatred, pulling the trigger again and again. I see Sonja's point, he liked it and will do it again. No question, this maniac got off on it.

I pause, wondering whether I should delete that last part. What possible good could it do? What will Salmon make of all this? Probably thinks I'm a crackpot. He might be right. Doesn't matter what he thinks, I need to do this. If it helps his case, fine. If not, well I'm not doing this because I'm altruistic. I'm doing this for my sanity, for me. Writing this up is helping me, anyway. Salmon can go fuck himself if he doesn't like it. I just need to get it all down.

## [5:51 AM – Friday, September 3, 2010]

I can't take any more. Feels like my eyes are bleeding, and I've nodded off at my laptop too many times to count. Can't remember what I wrote. Time to quit. I pry myself off the stool and push up from the kitchen counter. There's some cold coffee dregs in the coffee maker and I dump them into my mug. Swirling the thick black sludge, I stagger through the back door and out into the yard. September. Fall's coming. And along with it, relief from the desert heat. Must be in the low seventies, near perfect this early. As I sip the bitter brew, I gaze at the predawn sky. The purest turquoise I've ever seen, bands of fluffy gold edged with orange and pink off to the east. To the west, a deep crystalline blue glistening with faint pinpoints of starry light as wisps of magenta streak the horizon. Last dawn like this, Sonja and I were out with the Scouts on a weekend backpacking trip, back when I sponsored Troop 28. We watched the sun come up standing in front of our tent, a slight nip in the crisp morning air, my arms wrapped around her to keep her warm. Those were the good times. I miss those days.

I shake my head to chase the memories away, sweet and painful, dead and gone.

As I mull over the last several hours, it occurs to me that Rodriguez's real estate project has taken on the character of an evil entity at the center of a black vortex. I can't look at this anymore. Too much negative energy. I'll finish the write-up after I get some sleep.


Salmon's lanky frame strides through the narrow hall at Violent Crimes, headed for the squad room and his desk. His lean face almost breaks into a smile as he thinks about Lacey and last night. Phew, what a night. The memory of her scent, her taste, still fresh. How could someone so sweet turn so hot and nasty? He doesn't know, but he sure loved it. Ideologies aside, it's enough to make him think she might be a keeper. *Damn, could this be love?*

Sliding into his chair, Salmon fires up his computer. He enters his ID and password, pulling up his case files and email. Time to organize his day and get down to it.

Checking his inbox, he notices a new email from Underphal, the crazy-ass psychic photographer. Ignoring it with a smirk, he scans the rest of his inbox looking for evidence updates on the Rodriguez murder. *Damn, more spam.* His dick would be three feet long if he took them up on all the "enlarge your penis" offers. He still can't believe that with all the technology, they can't stop the creeps that do this, even if they are holed up in Russia. A complete waste of everyone's time. Salmon chuckled, Lacey would call it freedom of speech and want to protect the worthless bastards.

After dumping the junk mail, he's left with a handful of real email. Nothing all that revealing. DNA confirms Rodriguez and Telafano were doing each other, no surprise there. No prints of anyone not already known to be at the scene, no help there. Several slugs recovered from the scene and victims. Shell casings are standard 9mm, Federal brass. Good ballistics from the weapon. Tons of random fibers, hairs and particles, none of which have any real significance yet. As with most physical evidence from a crime scene, it's mostly too vague. Unless and until you have a real suspect to link with the evidence, it's useless. No help, so far.

As far as suspects go, he hasn't managed to shorten the list. The problem is, several people are beneficiaries of large life insurance policies taken out on Mr. Rodriguez. Certainly both Rodriguez's wife and his real estate development partner, Whiting, stand to gain handsomely. Should set them up for life. Then there are all the creditors and lenders with claims that run into the multimillions. And that's just the money motive. More than enough reason to kill. The list of people with reasons to kill Rodriguez has grown exponentially, from business dealings gone bad to jilted lovers. And he's likely to discover more suspects as they sift through the piles of evidence collected through the various warrants and court orders—a daunting task.

Unfortunately, the interviews haven't netted a confession. Not that he thought they would, but one can always get lucky. At this point, unless there are grounds for conspiracy, both the wife and the partner are off the hook, alibis solid—the wife, Connie, home with the kids and Whiting on his way to Vegas. Still, for that amount of money, you could hire someone; and both Connie Rodriguez and Gary Whiting had reason enough to kill him. He's seen people whacked for far less.

The pictures from Rodriguez's cell were a great idea but fall short of providing anything useful, a washed out image of a pickup truck and a dark silhouette of the shooter. Judging from the size, the shooter is well over six feet and probably male. And other than aftermarket running lights, the truck is one of millions. Not much to go on. Then there's Underphal's weird double exposure of the mystery man in a chair and the mystery truck.

What the hell, maybe the crazy photographer's got something. Salmon scrolls back to Underphal's email and opens it. As he reads, he shakes his head. Not sure what he was expecting, but this isn't it. Yet he *did* ask for as much detail as possible. Still, this is some weird shit, talking about black energy fields, rage auras and anger vortexes. The guy must be smokin' something. Shit, even if the crazy bastard really had something, the DA would laugh Salmon out of his office. Either that or have his badge, maybe both. *Not good.*

Salmon reads Underphal's email for the second time, looking for anything that might give him something he can use. Mostly it's a bizarre look at the hypothetical events of the shooting. Still, he has to admit, there's information here that confirms what they've gleaned from forensic test results. Not exactly earth-shattering news. But without the internal police reports, there's no way Underphal could know. Maybe the crazy bastard really is psychic. Unless you ascribe to the theory that even a blind squirrel gets an acorn once in a while. He has to admit, it's definitely an entertaining read. He just doesn't know what to make of it. Maybe keep pumping him for more. *What could it hurt?*

# THE LATEST

**[4:18 PM – Tuesday, September 21, 2010]**

IT'S SLOW AT the Lion's Den. In the main showroom, the Lioness Lair, it's cool and dark with only the black lights' glow bouncing off the phosphorescent nude murals. Iridescent purple highlights shine like rare gems on Formica tabletops and a chrome pole, center stage. The stage itself, unlit on a long break between dancers. Outside it's too bright and hot—a hundred and two degrees and dry as an old bone.

Lenny Kantor hunches at the back bar going over receipts with his day bartender, Hilde, a tall, lean Nordic beauty with high cheekbones, full lips, and wispy white-blond hair down to the top of her full breasts. It's been nearly a month since Big Mike's death. And while there's still the underlying question as to the ultimate disposition of Rodriguez's ownership, it's back to business as usual. As far as Lenny's concerned, Rodriguez's interest could be tied up for years in the estate's probate and it's fine by him, more unreported cash in his pocket. To top it off, he hasn't heard from that asshole detective since the cops picked up the financial records. *Stupid bastards, don't they get it? It's a cash business.* He knew they wouldn't find anything. All that cash and a truly silent partner, it just doesn't get any better.

Sondra Du sits at a small table in the far corner with her lover and roommate Naomi Barr.

Naomi's smooth chocolate skin glows deep purple under the black lights, the whites of her eyes popping like bright-white headlights, a pout on her pretty face. Sulking, she looks down at the moisture rings on the table. "But you said we'd have enough to leave by the end of the year," she protests.

"I know, but Big Mike never paid me," whispers Sondra. "And without him, we don't have the money."

"But I thought you said we almost had enough."

"That's before he got killed, when I thought he was going to pay up."

Glowering, Naomi starts in. "I'm sick of this shit, can't take it anymore. I need to get outta here. Shakin' my ass every night, flashin' my punani for those damn drunks, I'm sick of it! If I never see another stinkin' cock again, it'll be too soon."

Sondra lets her vent, knowing better than to interrupt. "I know. I'm sick of it, too. We'll just have to find another way."

"Shit, we'll be here forever if we have to do it with tips and tricks."

"Yeah, I know. But I got a couple ideas, still have all the pictures, ya know."

"Oh, so now you think you can do it all yourself? Shit, you'll get us both killed! Whaddaya think happened to Big Mike? He didn't exactly die of old age!"

"Just calm down, I'll handle it."

Sondra knows she's about to venture into new and dangerous territory. Who knows, maybe Naomi's right, maybe that's what killed Big Mike. But she's got copies of all the damning photos. And if she plays it right, she'll have more than enough for her and Naomi to get away forever. Hell, if that blowhard backstabbing Rodriguez can do it, she can do it.

It's another hot one. Gary Whiting anxiously pushes aside the Chuck Wagon's solid oak door and rushes into the dining room. He's uncharacteristically late for his business lunch with their lender, First Community Bank's Martin Fellman.

Coming in out of a hundred and two degree heat, the dark interior's cold A/C hits him like a blast of Arctic air. It turns the beading sweat on his forehead and temples icy cold, his pits still clammy with nervous perspiration. A pungent mix of fear and sweat envelop Whiting in a noxious cloud as he hurries toward the booth containing Fellman. He feels a little woozy and thick, his head pounding dully, even after the Excedrin and two Valium he downed before leaving the office. He pastes on a smile and waves to catch Fellman's eye.

Martin Fellman barely notices Whiting as he glances up from his menu. He gives him a short, two-fingered wave, slightly irritated at the man's tardiness. He never really liked Whiting anyway. It was always Rodriguez, that son of a bitch—gained his confidence and turned out to be the biggest confidence man he ever met. The whole thing is a major disaster. Now, with Rodriguez out of the picture, it's all about damage control.

Whiting motions over the waitress and orders an apple martini as he slides into the booth, hoping to smooth his nerves. He grins weakly at Fellman, thinking if he knew the real numbers he'd pull the plug on the whole project, pronto. "How ya doin', Martin? Sorry I'm late."

Fellman sneers, his small features crinkling with mild disgust as he gives a dismissive wave. "That's fine, I just sat down. What do you recommend?"

Whiting can't help but notice the look on Fellman's face which vaguely reminds him of a hairless rodent. Maybe it's the beady little eyes, he's not sure, just something about bankers. He gives Fellman his best-friend look. "Anything barbequed is good. Or how 'bout a mesquite-grilled steak, house specialty?"

"Nah, need something light. How's the chicken Caesar? Think that's what I had last time."

"Yeah. That's good, too."

The waitress shows up with Whiting's martini, takes their lunch orders and scurries off.

After picking at their food in relative silence they push their plates aside.

Fellman wants to get down to business.

Whiting thinks he knows what's coming.

Fellman leans forward, hunkering down on his forearms. "Did you bring the latest reports for the project?"

Whiting's nervous smile tics at the corner of his upper lip and he leans forward a bit too quickly. "Ya know, Martin, I meant to bring those, but I'm still waitin' on the estate. But it's okay, I'm not hiding anything here, I know all the numbers, just tell me whatcha need."

Fellman's brow lowers in a frown. "Gary, you were supposed to have those reports to me last week. Loan Committee wants to know what's going on. We haven't had any reports filed by you guys since Mike's death. Look, these reports are mandatory and it's been more than a month. I know it's been tough with Mike's death and all, but you've got to get me those reports."

"Yeah, I know, I know. Sorry, I'll do my best to get those over to ya. But like you say, what with Mike's death and his bookkeeper still in the hospital, it's been a real mess. I mean, just dealing with his estate ... Well, it's just nuts. Ya gotta give me a little more time."

"Look, I've cut you as much slack as I can. You've got to get me those reports by next week, or it's out of my hands." Fellman tightens his lips and shrugs palms out in a whaddaya-gonna-do gesture.

"Yeah, well, I need to check with the estate's attorney, need their permission to release anything. I'll see what I can do."

As Whiting watches Fellman leave, he feels a tremor in his gut. He can't give him the real numbers. Fellman can't find out about the huge cost overruns, a breach of their loan agreement with First Community Bank, sure as shit. And if he gives him doctored numbers, it's fraud. His stomach gurgles and he figures it must've been the barbeque sauce. He'll have to continue stalling Fellman and the bank. At least until he can work something out. His stomach rumbles as he signals his waitress for another martini. *This is the shits.*

Stein saunters into the Chuck Wagon, brushing past a short guy in a shirt and tie hurrying out. His alligator boots clump up to the bar as Stein scopes the room, spotting Whiting by himself in a booth. He parks his lanky ass on the tall barstool and orders a cold one to kill the time while he waits him out.

Connie Rodriguez stares blankly out her great room's floor-to-ceiling glass. She doesn't really see the desert mountains beyond, but it's another beautiful September day. *Must be Tuesday already. Or is it?* She's lost her train of thought. It used to bother her, but it's been happening a lot lately. So much so that she doesn't really care anymore. She has the sinking feeling it's her anti-depression meds, which don't seem to be helping her depression at all. Yet her doctor keeps assuring her they will work given time. She sure hopes he's right, she needs something. *I wasn't like this before.*

Beyond a dreary drag, her days seem filled with tears. Her doctor keeps telling her it is perfectly understandable to be depressed given all that's happened. But it's not that. She doesn't know *what* it is. Sometimes she just breaks down, crying for no reason. And try as she might, she can't put her finger on why. It can't be Mike's death. What they had together died long before he was killed. And while she's tried to kid herself, it's been mostly a marriage of convenience for the last several years. She pretended not to know about his womanizing. Yet, that has been her excuse for her own occasional indiscretions. It's so frustrating, so hard to even think straight anymore. Sometimes she just doesn't feel she can go on. *It just isn't worth it.*

Today, she's in a particularly black mood. She's meeting Daniel Rupert for their late afternoon rendezvous. Their trysts had gone on monthly for nearly a year prior to Mike's death. She has managed to avoid him since then, too overcome with grief and the adjustments of widowhood, initially. Then, after Marcia's outburst at lunch, she's been petrified, determined to have nothing to do with Daniel, determined to break it off when she got the chance. Not so much out of fear of what Marcia might do if she found out, but out of the misery she's caused. And now she's trapped. Daniel kept asking her, nudging her, cajoling then pleading with her, wanting to know what's wrong until she ran out of excuses. She'll meet him, but she's resolute. It ends today.


Daniel Rupert wheels his black Corvette off Scottsdale Road into the Scottsdale Commons parking garage. He quickly extracts his small wiry frame from the low-slung Corvette with cat-like precision and heads for the elevators that will take him to the promenade level.

As he strides through the afternoon heat toward the Pinnacle Hotel's entrance, he alternately chides and reassures himself. Connie's such a beauty, and now a rich beauty, Big Mike's widow. He should have never gotten involved with her. After all, Big Mike helped with the loan for his Martial Arts Center. It was fate. They'd have never met if his Martial Arts Center wasn't adjacent to the Sunset Pointe site. If it hadn't been for Big Mike's contacts and influence, he'd have lost his dream, a dream that took him his entire career to build, the Rupert Martial Arts Center. He owed Big Mike a lot, but now with Big Mike dead, there's really no reason to pretend. He's always wanted Connie. Who wouldn't? They'd be good together. And he really hadn't intended to mislead her, but he *has* to see her. This is their best chance. He's got to convince her. He knows it'll be good for her. And good for Mikey, too. Mikey is going to need a father figure, someone to set a good example. Besides, who knows what will happen with that bitch Marcia. He's tired of her jealous rage and her whoring around, sleeping with any guy who catches her eye. *The slut.*

At the front desk, he's told the lady is expecting him in Room 2012. Thank God she checked in first, he can't afford to pick up the tab. He rides the hotel elevator to the second floor, pacing, chewing his lower lip. This is it, his chance to really turn his life around. With her by his side and with him taking care of things, there's nothing they can't do. He has to convince her.

Daniel knocks at 2012 then waits. As the door opens, he marvels at her perfection. Dressed simply, in black slacks and a low-cut black silk top, her proportions are that of a golden goddess. At five foot seven, he has to look up into her crystal blue eyes.

As Connie opens the door, she knows this is a mistake. She shouldn't be here. She feels a slight shudder as Daniel's hungry gaze sweeps up her torso and locks on her eyes. Smiling weakly, she motions him in.

"Hi baby. Good to see you," he says.

As he leans in to kiss her, she backs off slightly and turns away, deflecting his advance. "Daniel, we need to talk."

He pulls up short then recovers. "Yes, I know. Thanks for coming." He smiles. "We've got a lot to talk about, don't we?"

She walks past the king-size bed to a round table by the window and sits. Avoiding his eyes, she looks through the filmy curtains at the Scottsdale cityscape. "Yes, we have a lot to talk about," she says softly.

He follows and sits across from her, his concern growing. He can't lose her now. He leans forward, looking up into the beautiful sadness shaping her face. "Listen, I know you must have a lot on your mind. I just needed to see you—to talk things out. Especially with all that's happened. I mean, we haven't been together in almost two months. I really miss you."

She turns toward him, averting her gaze to the table top. "Daniel, things are different now …"

"I know, I know, you've had it rough, I'm sorry. I would have come to you, but I didn't think it would look right. I mean, so soon and all."

"No, it's not that, that's fine. It's just that things have changed. I've got so much to take care of now with Mike gone. I just can't …"

He feels her slipping away and interrupts. "I'm really sorry, Connie. I should have been there for you." *What can I say to get to her?* "It's just that Marcia … Well, listen, you have plenty of troubles of your own. I don't mean to get into this, but …"

Relief floods through her. Without thinking, she sighs at the change of subject. She has to tell him, but she'll come back to that. She looks up to meet his eyes with genuine concern. "What's going on with Marcia?"

He senses the shift, momentum is with him now. He pauses, taking his time. *Have to get this right. Might be my only chance.* He drops his gaze, feigning dejection. "Look … I don't know if I should tell you … but I feel like you're my best friend, the only one I can trust. It's hard to talk about."

She leans forward. "Daniel, it's okay."

"No … no, it's really not. Ya know, she's been pushing me away for so long now. Well, we both know how it is."

Softly, Connie agrees. "Yeah, I guess we'd have never gotten together if we were truly happy. I think about that sometimes."

"That's probably true, but it's gotten worse. She's so open about it now, in my face. She flaunts it right in front of me, going after some of my students and even some of the parents. I mean …"

"Are you saying she's having more than one affair?"

"They hardly seem like affairs. It's more like a contest with her. See how many she can get, see how miserable she can make me." He tentatively extends his hand, slowly sliding it out to the middle of the table.

She reaches, taking his hand in both of hers. "OhMyGod, Daniel ..."

Tears roll down his cheeks. He gently pulls and they lean forward to kiss. She comes out of her chair and around the table, pulling him up into a tender embrace. He kisses her neck. She pulls his face to hers and they kiss passionately. They edge toward the bed, kissing, fondling, pulling off clothing. They slide under the covers and make love, gently at first, then more and more passionately, until he's completely spent. They lie back to stare at the ceiling, sweat slicks drying on their overheated skin.

She can't believe what she's just done. *How am I going to tell him? How am I going to break it off now?*

"Ya know, I still can't believe Marcia was hanging 'round after the classes, chasin' anything with pants," he says.

She is not quite distracted from her thoughts. "Yeah, that's rough."

He continues, his thoughts wandering. "I mean, she was even hanging 'round Mikey for a while there. Made me wonder. Of course, he's too young, but still ... made me wonder. I thought maybe, 'cause Big Mike was pickin' him up."

At first, it only half registers. Then a slow burn creeps up from her core. Her suspicions churn. *Marcia? After Mikey? She some sort of a pervert?* She's heard all the stories—older women going after young boys. She shudders. A child molester with her Mikey? *OhMyGod!* Panic rushes up her spine. Adrenalin surges. Her head and neck flush crimson. She jumps up out of bed, gathers her clothes, throws them on, grabs her purse and bolts for the door. Daniel's saying something, but with the blood rushing in her ears, she can't make it out. She doesn't have time right now. She'll have to deal with him later. *Have to go to Mikey! My son needs me!*

# BIG MIKE AND MIKEY

### [10:17 AM – Saturday, January 23, 2010]

MIKE RODRIGUEZ'S SON beamed up at him. "Thanks, Dad!"

Mike's heart swelled, his eyes welling. He wanted to give his son the things he never had. But not just the things money could buy, like this new dirt bike, the things he never got from *his* dad. He quietly vowed to spend more time with Mikey as he wrapped a meaty arm around his son's shoulders. Mikey was already big for a ten-year-old, looked more like he was twelve or thirteen.

"You're welcome, Mikey. Hope you like it."

"Dad, you kiddin'? I love it! It's great! Can't wait to show Jason and Chad." Mikey stared wide-eyed at the brand new Honda 150cc dirt bike gleaming in the driveway.

"Put it in the garage, for now. We'll take the dirt bikes out later. I'll pick you up from karate class."

"Can Chad and Jason go, too?"

"Sure, why not?"

"Great! I'll see ya after karate."

"You got it."


Rodriguez idled across Sunset Pointe's north parking lot and into the lot next door, parking in front of the Rupert Martial Arts Center. Hopping down out of his 4X4, he went in to watch the tail end of his son's karate class.

Rodriguez stood just inside the door, scanning the main studio. It looked like most martial arts studios, a trophy wall at the back, mirrored side walls and a polished hardwood floor. His son's class was across the floor in the middle of the studio doing drills while the instructor, Daniel Rupert, barked commands.

Rupert amused him, an overcompensating short guy with a complex— too intense. Still, he was a helluva martial arts instructor and good for Mikey. Rodriguez mostly liked him, even though he didn't know shit about running a business.

Rodriguez stood watching his son, thick arms folded across his massive chest. He caught Daniel's wife, Marcia, out of the corner of his eye, heading his way. He couldn't help watching her full chest bouncing as her petite frame pranced along the side wall. All those dark curls and flashing eyes, cute. He grinned. *Sure, I'd do her.*

Marcia Lago-Rupert extended her hand as she approached. "Mr. Rodriguez, what a pleasure. You here to pick up Mikey?"

He enveloped her small hand in his. "Pleasure's mine. And yes, I'm here to pick up Mikey."

She gave his hand a playful squeeze, holding on to it longer than appropriate.

Rodriguez grinned.

She smiled up at him, eyes sparkling. "Mikey's such a great guy. We just love him around here, bright and athletic, catches on fast."

"Thanks, he's a good kid."

"We'd like to see more of him. Got an advanced class coming up the end of next month that'd be perfect for him."

"If he wants. I'm sure it'd be fine."

"Hey, I met your cousin, Johnny Chavez. Quite a guy. He signed up for kenpo."

"Yeah, that's Johnny ..."

"And what about you?"

"Wish I had the time, could sure use the exercise."

"I'd have never guessed. You look like you're in pretty good shape to me."

"Well, I try to get into my gym at least a couple times a week."

"You got your own gym?"

"Yeah, at the shop."

"Wow, I'm impressed."

"Well … it works for me."

"I'd like to see it sometime."

The gleam in her eye gave her away. Amused, he wondered what her husband, Daniel, would think about all this, probably blow a gasket. Still, no reason to turn her down. Hot and sexy, she was definitely his type. "With or without Daniel?"

She blushed crimson, averting her eyes, then looked back to stare hungrily into his. In a hoarse whisper, she said, "Without, of course."

They held each other's gaze for another few moments before she turned away and headed back. He watched her tight little ass wiggle as she pranced off, imagining what she'd be like naked in his private gym. *A helluva workout, no doubt.*

# SWEATING THE DETAILS

**[3:03 AM – Wednesday, October 6, 2010]**

*DREAMING. A NORMAN Rockwell scene from the Dark Side. A weird sort of reverse Americana folded inside out, as though I'm peeking behind the magic curtain—a den, a gentlemen's inner sanctum. Dark and murky, the scene undulates as if underwater. Different, but somehow the same, I've seen all this before. The back of the tall Chippendale upholstered with cordovan leather in a diamond tuck, the chair positioned directly in front of a large flatscreen. At this angle I can see dull images flashing across its face. What's he watching? Doesn't matter. But there must be something to this. Otherwise, why would it keep coming up?*

*There's more. The guy in the burgundy Chippendale, his arms are sleeved in a cuffed smoking jacket. Who wears a red smoking jacket besides Hugh Hefner? A gag gift for a nerd? Maybe that's what it is. On the flatscreen ... a porno ... hmm. The cigar looks expensive as does the crystal tumbler. The coppery liquor on the rocks looks expensive, too. Yet something's not right. The turbidity, dark energies surging, this isn't some private porno diversion. There's something darker at work here.*

I wake soaked in sweat with the dream dancing in my head. It's pitch black. Glancing at the digital clock on the headboard, I notice it's a little after three a.m. I don't sleep all the way through most nights anymore, but this is different. The vision has my mind churning. What does this have to do with a truck? Why the double exposure? Shit, what does this have to do with anything?!

I hear Sonja, faintly with a slight echo, not real clear. "It'll be him …
it's him … him."

"Whaddaya mean, him?" The second I ask, I sense she's already gone.
What is she trying to tell me?

I roll through our last conversation, looking for more. All that crap
about the shooter's appetite to kill again has me spooked. Is this the
shooter or the next victim? I get the feeling this guy's not the shooter. That
leaves next victim. Seems right. Not sure, but it seems right. What if the
double exposure is a premonition? Maybe Red Smoking Jacket is going to
get it next. As I work through the various scenarios, dark swirls and eddies
flow—a pulsing, crackling menace. Looking at it a couple different ways, it
still works. Red Smoking Jacket could be the next victim. Why else would
she be telling me it's him? *Dammit, Sonja, what's the story?*

I hate this shit. It's giving me a headache. Besides, my bladder is ready
to burst. I reach up, turn on my reading light, roll out of the sack and pad
barefoot toward the john. If this guy's in danger, the next target … I need
more details. Regardless, I'll need to get with Salmon on this.


### [9:14 AM – Thursday, October 7, 2010]


Took me two hours to get back to sleep and I wake exhausted and cranky.
It's already after nine. By the time I get my shit semi-together, it's after ten.
With fresh coffee in my mug, I plop down at the counter and open my
laptop. Punching up my email, I see an old read receipt for my write-up to
Salmon, but no reply. Okay. So, what's up? Did he actually read it? He's had
plenty of time for a reply. Maybe he thinks I'm full of shit. That's fine. I'd
like to help, but that's fine. The only problem is the next shooting.
Somehow, I've got to get him to take it seriously. But how?

Sonja's whisper fills my head. "Give him a call."

I fish around, searching through the debris on the countertop, checking for my cell. Gotta be here somewhere. I finally retrieve it and punch in
Salmon's cell off the back of his business card. Gracious of him to give me
his card. A decision he probably already regrets.

"Underphal, whaddaya want?"

"Detective. Did ya get my email?"

"Yup."

"And ...?"

"You've got quite an imagination."

"That's all ya gotta say?"

"Whaddaya want me to say?"

"I dunno, maybe thanks or ..."

"Look, I appreciate you wanting to help here, but so far you're not givin' me anything I can use."

This is going nowhere. Yet, somehow I've got to get through to him, let him know there's going to be another shooting, maybe Mr. Red Smoking Jacket. "I'm doin' my best. Whadabout the killer, anything new?"

"Nothin' all that exciting."

"Can you fill me in?"

"No can do. *You* give *me* info, not the other way 'round."

*I need to go down there.* "Okay ... well, listen, I think I may have something you need to know."

"What?"

"Be better if I came down."

There is a long pause on the other end. Maybe my cell's dropped the call. "Detective?"

"Yeah. Give me a minute. I'm checkin' my schedule."

# FACE TIME

**[1:38 PM – Thursday, October 7, 2010]**

I FIND MYSELF downtown in police headquarters at the Violent Crimes reception desk, waiting, staring at the butt-ugly vinyl floor. Damn, who comes up with these color schemes? No doubt an artistic genius. Slime-grey with dirty bits of black and red. Really?

"Underphal."

Salmon distracts me from my flooring review.

"Detective."

"This way."

I find myself following Salmon into the interrogation room once again.

"Damn, Detective. Is this the best you can do?"

"It's a police station, not the Ritz."

We sit across from each other at the bolted-down metal table in the hard metal chairs. In deference to Steve Martin, I've dubbed these chairs the "cruel chairs." At least I have Salmon's attention.

Salmon gives me a half-hearted grin. "So, whatcha got?"

Now that I'm here and on the spot, I'm not so sure. "Well ... I'm not sure what to say here. I mean ..."

"Look, Underphal, don't jerk me around. I don't have time ..."

"Did you really read my email?"

"I told you—yeah."

"Did you get the part about the killer might kill again?"

"Look, you're wearin' me out here. Just spit it out."

"Okay, but you have to understand, these are impressions, feelings, energy manifestations, not something easily articulated."

"Whatever."

"Yeah, well … since I emailed you that write-up, more details have come to light."

"I'm still listening."

"I think I've found the connection between the guy in the chair and the pickup."

Salmon's giving me a blank stare.

"You know, in that photo …?"

His face still registers zero.

"The picture, the double exposure you asked about when we first met … when you and Lacey came over with my gear …"

I think I see a light come on.

It slowly dawns on Salmon. "Oh, yeah—that one."

"Do you remember that one?"

"Yeah, vaguely."

"Well, the guy in the chair—I got more details and I think I might know what's goin' on."

"And …"

"And well, the guy's wearin' a red smoking jacket, puffin' on a fat cigar, drinkin' expensive liquor and watchin' a porno. A wannabe Player who's really just a nerdy loser. I mean, who wears a red smoking jacket?"

"Go on."

"All right, let's assume for now that the truck belongs to the shooter …"

"Safe assumption, keep going."

"So, it feels like the superimposition of the guy in the chair on top of the shooter's truck is a prediction."

"Yeah?"

"Yeah, the guy in the chair on top of, superimposed over the truck … I think something bad is gonna happen. I think the shooter is goin' after him."

"What makes you think *he's* not the shooter?"

"It's not his truck."

"Why?"

"Doesn't feel right. Feels more like a prediction, more like 'future' than 'past.' Besides, he's wearing a red smoking jacket. He's not a truck guy."

"Okay ... Let's assume for a minute you're right. What do you want *me* to do about it?"

"I dunno. You gotta stop it."

"And exactly how do you expect me to do that?"

*Shit, he's got me there.* "No clue ... I just know we gotta stop the shooter from killing again."

He gives me a condescending smile, slides his chair back and stands up, meeting over. "Well, when you get something to go on, let me know. In the meantime, give me a written description of what you just told me and I'll add it to the file. Best I can do for now. And keep those cards and letters comin'. Who knows, maybe you'll come up with somethin' eventually."

I feel foolish, but he's right. *Time to go.*

# SALMON PUSHES

**[2:30 PM – Monday, October 25, 2010]**

CRUISING IN THE HOV lane on I-17, Salmon's black Marauder purrs like a jungle cat. He likes this car, might even buy it off the motor pool once its duty cycle is up. They don't make 'em anymore. Last of its kind. Of course, it'll be "high-mileage" by then. Still, except for when the Captain had it brand new, it's been his car and he's taken good care of it. The supercharged V-8's rumble really does it for him, reserved, with the promise of horsepower when you really need it.

His thoughts keep coming back to the Rodriguez case. It's been more than two months now and no breakthroughs. Once an open case goes this long, it's rarely solved. Yet, it seems like the answers are sitting right there. His dance card is filling up. More cases every day. Still, he hates to let it go, let a killer get away. Like a dog with a bone, he keeps gnawing on it every chance he gets. Maybe this next interview will help. Diane Telafano had been out of it when he saw her last. Now that she's out of the hospital, maybe she can be more help.

Salmon eases his Marauder over to the right lane and takes the Daisy Mountain Drive exit into Anthem.

Paralyzed from the waist down and in a wheelchair, Diane Telafano moved in with her mother. When he talked to the mother, Diane was asleep, but the mother said it would be all right. After all, she had plenty of time and wasn't going anywhere. The mother sounded bitter. No doubt, she'd find a way to blame him for her daughter's plight.

Pulling up in front of a modest frame and stucco home, he checks the address. It looks ominously similar to every other frame and stucco house on the block and in the rest of the subdivision. For that matter, the entire Anthem Planned Community has that Stepford Wives feel to it. Instead of the warm fuzzies it was designed to elicit, all that gated-community middle-class social veneer gives him the creeps. It might make the homeowners feel safer. But to him, they look more like sheep, scared shitless. *Helluva world.*

The address is right so he shuts off the engine and climbs out. At the front door, he pushes the button. Through the security door he sees the front door open, but can't make out anything through the heavy screen.

"Hello? I'm Detective Salmon."

A dour-looking middle-aged woman emerges from the gloom. She's short and round, black wavy hair salted with grey. Her liver-spotted hand extends on a pudgy forearm to unlock the security door and motion him in.

He extends his card and tries again. "I'm Detective Salmon and you must be ..."

"Angela Telafano."

He musters a smile. "My pleasure, Angela."

Her expression remains stoic. "Wait here. I'll get Diane for you."

He takes a couple steps into the quiet gloom to sit on a brown sofa. In the low nineties outside, it seems warmer in the musty living room, probably only eighty degrees, but it's stuffy, underpinned with a slight air of decay.

As Angela wheels Diane out, he can't help but imagine what she must've been like as a vibrant, attractive young woman. Now, a broken lump of flesh confined to a wheelchair, the lust for life drained away. If he believed in victims, he'd feel sorry for her, not that it would help. He's been around too long, seen too much of what life can do. He knows from long experience in dealing with the criminal elements that people suffer the consequences of their actions and/or inactions. And at the end of the day, they are the *only* ones who ultimately determine their situation, for good or for ill. Life can be a cruel teacher when mistakes are made. Still, it's a shame. No one should have to go through this.

Angela parks Diane in the middle of the room facing Salmon. Without saying a word, she goes to the other end of the sofa and sits.

Diane smiles weakly. "Detective."

"Good to see you out of the hospital."

She hangs her head. "Yeah ... I guess ..."

Salmon is not encouraged. Her speech is slow, eyelids heavy, probably still on a ton of meds. He presses on. "I'm hoping you can help me with a few details. Would it be all right if I ask you a few questions?"

She looks up at her mother. "I dunno. Haven't thought about it much. I guess ..."

He gets out a small pad and pen. "Can you tell me more about Mr. Rodriguez?"

Diane looks down and blushes, then looks at her mother. "Mama, could you please leave us alone for a while?"

Disgruntled, her mother gets up and leaves without a word.

Hunched over, Diane watches her go then turns on Salmon with fire in her eyes. "What? Ya wanna know if I was fuckin' 'im?"

Salmon leans forward. "Look, Diane, I know this is tough ... at the hospital you mentioned Mrs. Rodriguez hated Mr. Rodriguez for loving you ..."

Suddenly confused, she looks away. "Oh ... I said that?"

"Yes."

"Well I ... don't remember. Kinda out of it, I guess."

"I understand. And I'm not accusing you of anything, just need to know more about Mr. Rodriguez. We're working on a theory that the shooter was after him and you got in the way."

She gives a cheerless laugh. "Got in the way all right. Shit." She breaks down into tears and sniffles.

"I just need to know anything you can tell me, the least little thing. Any detail might help."

She composes herself as she sits up. She takes a deep breath. And after a long pause, she starts. "Michael was on the phone with Gary ..."

"Gary Whiting?"

"Yes ... and I remember hearing something, someone pulling up."

"A truck?"

"Don't know. Michael said something about a truck, but I didn't see it."

"Go on."

"Well, Michael was at the window and I heard the door. I keep thinkin' it must've been Connie, but it was dark and I couldn't see. It all happened so fast. All the shooting and the noise, I just don't know."

"Why do you think it was Mrs. Rodriguez?"

"I dunno. I guess she's the only one I can think of who hated us … I dunno."

"You know that Mr. Rodriguez took a photo of the shooter …"

Startled, her voice rises. "He did?"

"Yes."

Her features twist with confusion. "Why didn't you tell me? Who is it?"

"Too dark, we can't make it out. But the figure in the photo is too big, too tall to be Mrs. Rodriguez."

"Are you sure?"

"We are fairly certain the shooter is male, over six foot and two hundred-plus pounds. Anyone come to mind?"

"There's lots of guys that fit that description around MJR."

"Any idea who might have it in for Mr. Rodriguez?"

Diane runs through it, thinking. She remembers something about the way Michael said it, like he knew who it was, like he was pissed. It had to be Connie, just the way he said it, "You! What the fuck do *you* want?" It's all so confused. Maybe she just thought she heard it. She doesn't really know anymore. What difference does it make now? Hopelessly dejected, she answers, "You mean, besides his wife?"

"Yeah, that's right."

"Shit, it could be anybody."

"Exactly what do you mean, anybody?"

"I mean, I did his books. He had me make it look good for the lenders, but it wasn't all that rosy, always robbing Peter to pay Paul."

"Diane, we've gone through some of his financial records. We didn't find much, at least not much that made sense."

"Yeah, well, you wouldn't. Michael liked to keep it that way."

"Could you help us, point us in the right direction?"

"I dunno ... I don't see how diggin' all that up now is gonna help Michael."

"It might help expose the people who did this to you."

Diane's gaze wanders, looking everywhere but at Salmon. Tears form at the corners of her eyes. After a long moment, she drops her gaze to the floor and softly says, "I'll have to think about it."


Heading back on I-17, Salmon lets the Marauder cruise as he replays his encounter with Diane Telafano. She's down and out, buried under heavy medication, spirit crushed. Who could blame her? But if she doesn't find a way to snap out of it, she's got no future at all. Bottom line, he can't tell if she'll ever recover. Right now her chances aren't good. Doesn't look like Mama is helping much, either. It's a shame. She could still manage a productive life if she turns things around. He's seen plenty of people make heroic and meaningful contributions in spite of their handicaps, and in some cases, because of them. Life is hard, but he's seen miracles happen. Can't count them out. Never discount the power of the human spirit. Life is to be lived, no matter what.

Diane hasn't given him much, he doesn't hold out much hope for her to come forward. He'll just have to keep working her. Maybe she'll come around. That comment about Rodriguez's books was interesting. He'll get forensics to go back through them, dig deeper. If necessary, go back for supporting documentation, bank statements, receipts, invoices, deposit slips. Now that he knows there's something there to find, it could be worth it. Who knows where it will lead?

He thinks about what he's got, so far: Rodriguez and Telafano were obviously doin' each other the night of the shooting. Between the DNA and Telafano's admissions, it's a no-brainer. The little blue Bimmer she drove, parked at her apartment, leased to MJR Development indicates that the relationship was more than casual office sex, at least for Telafano. Maybe there's more than meets the eye with the wife, Connie. Maybe she's not as innocent as she lets on, that blonde air-head routine just an act. Certainly, she had the most to gain. Get rid of a cheating husband and cash in on the life insurance. Conspiracy? Did she hire someone? Can't rule it out, at least not yet. He wonders how she'll react to a warrant for more of Rodriguez's financial records. He'll contact her directly rather than through the attorney, see how she handles it.

Then there's that weenie of a partner, Whiting. Probably doesn't have the guts to kill a fly. Still, a multimillion-dollar real estate development project going south and Whiting with everything on the line. Plus there's that big life insurance policy. He'll make more off Rodriguez's death than he could ever hope to make as Rodriguez's partner. And the boy is a mess, chronic gambler and pill-popper, could go off the deep end at any time. Another conspiracy candidate? Possibly. Can't rule him out, either. In-depth financials from Rodriguez might shed some light on their development deal as well. He'll sweat Whiting, let him know he's after more financial records, see if he cracks. It's a long list of suspects after that. And if it's Conspiracy, the shooter was no pro. For one thing, a pro wouldn't leave a possible witness like Telafano. Like Telafano said, could be anybody, a loan shark or a jilted lover, no easy way to know. He shakes his head. It'd be simpler if this Rodriguez character hadn't made so many enemies. He needs a break. This case is getting colder by the day.

# CLOSER TO HOME

**[12:13 PM – Wednesday, February 17, 2010]**

A BLUSTERY DAY at MJR Development as Big Mike Rodriguez jumped into his S65 AMG. He squealed the tires heading out of his private garage, the AMG's six-liter twin-turbo V-12 roaring to life. Mildly annoyed, Rodriguez bunched his jaw muscles into rock-hard balls as he grumbled to himself, hustling the powerful Mercedes down Deer Valley Road toward Seventh Street, the freeway and his twelve o'clock lunch appointment. Late again and he couldn't care less, just another hand-holding session with his loser partner, Whiting. *Let him wait.* Good thing Whiting was buying or he might not show at all. Big Mike grinned, creasing the dark shadows of coarse stubble and acne scars on his thick cheeks, feeling a little better about the time he'd have to waste on his lame partner.

The Mercedes told him he had an incoming call from Whiting. His grin withered to a frown. *Figures.*

"Yeah Gary, what is it?"

"Are we still on for lunch?"

He hated this. The guy *always* called to check on him when he was running late. *What a whiner.* "Yeah, I'm on my way. Be there in a few." He punched the end-call button before Whiting could reply and gunned the big black Mercedes up the on-ramp. Hitting eighty-five on entry, he blew by slower traffic, headed for Scottsdale and Whiting's Chuck Wagon Steak & Ribs restaurant.

Gary Whiting listened to dead air as he held his cell phone to his ear, unsure whether the call got dropped or Rodriguez hung up on him. Didn't matter, he was on his way. Pissed him off though. Rodriguez was always late, no matter what. This lunch, no big deal, but what worried him was when Rodriguez showed up late for important meetings with investors or lenders. Whiting couldn't understand it. At least Rodriguez was consistent, a half-hour late for everything, could almost set your watch by it. It got to the point where he'd tell Rodriguez a meeting was a half-hour earlier just to get him to show up on time. It was so bad that it was a running joke around the MJR shop. They called it "Rodriguez Time."

Rodriguez spotted Whiting in his favorite booth. He sauntered through clumps of sawdust, scattering it in swirls across the Chuck Wagon's stained concrete floor. As he crossed the dining room, his wide mouth stretched into a broad smile, waving at Jeremy Gott and Sally, the bartender. Rodriguez parked in his booth across from Whiting, giving him a curt nod.

"Gary."

"Glad you could make it," Whiting said sarcastically.

Rodriguez lowered his thick brow and grinned wickedly. "Look, fucker, good thing you're buyin' or I wouldn't be here at all."

Whiting grinned, his eyes flicking with apprehension. He could never tell if Rodriguez was kidding when he said shit like that.

A smiling Jeremy Gott appeared at their booth, ready to serve. "Gentlemen, the waitress is on her way. Need anything from the bar?"

"Grey Goose and Red Bull," said Rodriguez.

"Apple martini for me."

The waitress took their lunch orders as Jeremy hustled off to put in their drink requests.

Rodriguez sneered. Whiting looked like he was already three sheets to the wind, probably had a couple martinis before Rodriguez arrived. Whiting always had that stupid-ass grin on his face lit or sober, didn't much matter. At least he was consistent.

"First Community emailed the loan docs this morning," said Whiting. "I forwarded them to you. Did you see them?"

"I saw the email but didn't open it. I'll get to it later. You review 'em?"

Whiting nodded yes.

"What's the bottom line?"

"There's a bunch of crap in there, but we were expecting that. Did you say anything to Fellman about personal guarantees?"

"Just that we won't do it."

"Well, that's not *quite* right."

"Whaddaya mean?"

"Well, there are some carve-outs, but we're personally guaranteeing the construction loan. But the personal guarantees drop off once it converts to a permanent loan."

"Shit, that's not what we agreed. I'm not doin' that!"

"Then what do we do? It's too late, we can't get financing anywhere else. We don't have time. Besides, no one else is gonna loan us that much, we've already tried."

"Fuck, Gary, don'tcha think I know that? We already broke ground. The off-sites are nearly done. I gotta have that first draw within the next couple weeks or I'm screwed. I used my money. I gotta get it back."

"Yeah, I know."

"Besides, there's those hard-money guys ..."

Gary shook his head and held up his hands to stop. "Don't even go there."

"Did ya send the loan docs over to our attorney?"

"Yeah, I copied Marsh when I forwarded the loan docs to you."

"What did *he* say?"

"Haven't heard back."

"Shit, Gary. Don't make me take this on. I've got enough on my plate with the construction. If I've gotta do this, you're gonna forfeit your fee."

"Mike, I'm on it. Marsh has only had it a couple hours."

Rodriguez pounded his hand on the table, rattling the table settings.

Heads at the bar turned as the Chuck Wagon went dead silent.

Whiting's jaw dropped, speechless.

Rodriguez lowered his voice to a menacing tone. "Gary. Don't make me wait for my money. I need that draw, even if I have to go over and straighten Fellman out myself."

Rodriguez pried himself out of the booth, threw his napkin in the middle of the table and stomped off. Meeting over.

Whiting sat stunned, trying to stop trembling. He'd always known Rodriguez was a hothead. Convinced he'd just witnessed the tip of the iceberg, it scared him shitless.


Rodriguez fumed as he sped up Scottsdale Road. His wimp of a partner couldn't get shit done and it was pissing him off. Now he'd have to call Marsh and find out for himself. He wondered why he ever took Whiting on. *Shit!* As usual, he'd have to do everything himself. And he already had too much on his plate. He decided to stop at the house, get a quick shower and a change of clothes then get back to the shop. He had work to do.

As the door rolled up, Rodriguez whipped the S65 into his four-car garage. He jumped out as the door rolled down. He hustled through the side door headed for the master bedroom suite. His wife, Connie, was sitting at her vanity as he crossed to his walk-in closet.

To her surprise, Connie saw Mike whiz by. "Hi, dear. What are *you* doing home?"

Rodriguez rustled through his closet. "Been out on a jobsite. Have to grab a shower and get back to work. Got a draw request to finish this afternoon."

Connie's face flushed with rage. She jumped up and stormed over to his side of the master bath. "So you're meeting with that little bookkeeper of yours?"

Rodriguez couldn't believe it. "Shit, Connie. Now? You wanna fight about this, now?! You know I've gotta work with her if I'm gonna get shit done. She's my bookkeeper, for Chrissakes. We've already discussed all this!"

"You're fucking her again, aren't you?!"

"What the fuck are you talkin' about?! I never fucked her!"

"You are! You're fucking her again! I can tell!"

"You crazy bitch. Snap out of it!"

"You asshole, you don't care about me, about the kids, just your little bookkeeper whore!"

Losing it, Rodriguez turned and grabbed his wife. He cocked his fist to punch her, but stopped short. Enraged, he picked her up, holding her in front of him, his thick arms outstretched. With giant strides he carried her out of the master bath, across the bedroom to the four-poster and threw her on top of their bed. *That's it!*

He skipped the shower and stomped out, headed for the garage.

Connie scrambled to her feet, shaking, the creamy skin of her face blotchy, flecks of spittle flying from her lips as she screamed at Rodriguez's back. "I swear if I catch you with her, I'll kill you! You hear me?! I'll kill you!!!"

Without turning or breaking stride Rodriguez held a meaty fist up over his shoulder, middle finger extended.

# TURNING UP
# THE HEAT

**[9:48 AM – Thursday, October 28, 2010]**

A GRUMPY DETECTIVE Salmon drops into his ergonomically challenged chair, plopping a fat accordion file onto his beat-up desktop. The accordion file contains several manila folders stuffed with reports relating to the Rodriguez case. Their sheer girth represents hundreds of man-hours. Frustrating. He hates the ones that go cold. In Homicide, it means a killer on the loose and justice undone, a particularly bitter state of affairs. It goes against his nature, a constant irritation, like a burr in his hiking boot. It's the unsolved cases that wear him out. His mood sours, he drinks more, sleeps less and work is a grind. It's times like these that he hates his job— makes him want to move on to the next case. But he's been on the Job long enough to know, it would only get worse. Probably why he's considered good at what he does. He needs to take the bull by the horns, there's a killer running loose. *Time to get busy and solve this bitch kitty.*

Salmon pulls the well-used suspect list out of a dog-eared file, picks up the phone and dials the first number.

"Mrs. Rodriguez, this is Detective Salmon."

A long silence ensues as Salmon waits for Connie Rodriquez to respond.

Her voice is quiet, her tone timid. "Yes, what is it, Detective?"

"We've uncovered new evidence in your late husband's case."

"Yes?"

"We'll need additional financial records, both business and personal."

"For a moment, I thought you were gonna say you caught the killer."

Curious. Not what he expected. "We think we're headed in the right direction, but no arrests yet."

"I really don't deal with this kind of thing, Detective. That's why I have my attorney. Please, just call him. You still have his number?" She sounds distant, distracted.

"I'm sure we do, Mrs. Rodriguez. Should I arrange your interview with him, as well?"

"Oh … you need to see me again?"

"Yes, I'll need to see you after we go through the records."

"Well, I guess … if Hammond says it's okay."

After Salmon hangs up he digests the exchange with the Widow Rodriguez. Odd on a few different levels, but his overall impression is that she couldn't care less. Not that it's an indication of guilt or innocence, it could go either way. He's seen it before. Some criminals get careless, go into a sort of selective amnesia then become aloof, as though their crime has nothing to do with them.

He'll have a uniform serve the warrant and pick up the additional records. Once Forensics has gone through them with a fine-tooth comb, he'll call her attorney to arrange the interview.

Salmon turns back to his suspect list and dials the next number. He listens as it rings through to voicemail. He leaves a message at Whiting's office to return his call, hangs up and tries Whiting's cell.

"Detective, you callin' me 'cause you caught the killer?" Whiting sounds smug or loaded, maybe both.

Time to rattle Whiting's cage. "I'm calling, Mr. Whiting, because we'll need more detailed financial records. I'm sending …" Salmon realizes he's talking to thin air. The line's dead. Whiting hung up. *Hmm, maybe I'm on to something.* Either that or his cell dropped the call. He tries Whiting's cell again. This time it goes straight to voicemail. He leaves a curt message to return the call, important police business, etc., etc.

As he puts down the receiver, a twinge of elation zips through him. He might actually be getting somewhere. He's eager to get those records. Diane

Telafano inadvertently pointed him in the right direction. He can smell it, fresh blood. He can't wait to get Whiting into the hot seat.

# ANOTHER SUNNY DAY

**[10:05 AM – Thursday, October 28, 2010]**

CONNIE RODRIGUEZ LEANS against the kitchen island's black granite counter. She wonders why she no longer takes any joy in it. The kitchen used to be her sanctuary, a friends and family crossroads, a warm and comfortable gathering place. She used to love spending her quiet moments here. Her creation, her domain, replete with all the high-tech appliances and creature comforts *Architectural Digest* could envision for the perfect kitchen. Somehow she's lost that joy, that sense of accomplishment. She seems to have lost a lot, lately.

The call from that detective has Connie distracted. She stares absently at the phone as if she's forgotten something important. She wonders why they haven't found the killer, but that's not what she really needs to worry about now. This whole situation with Mikey has her unnerved, eating at her like a malignancy. She can't bear the thought of Mikey molested by that evil bitch, Marcia, despite Mikey's continual denial. He's emphatic that nothing happened. She's talked to Father Ambrose about it, but he seemed reluctant to get involved or give advice. Perhaps because the Church has had its share of difficulty with pedophilia. Father Ambrose mentioned that he'd refer her to someone more qualified.

What hurts Connie most is Mikey's attitude. If only she could get him to see somebody, get some counseling, or just open up. He's been more distant since his father's death, which is understandable. However, since this thing with Marcia came up, he's been sullen and hostile. She feels she's losing him. Breaks her heart. Vacillating between despair and panic, she feels she's not only losing touch with her children, but with everything. She's been praying desperately, believing it must be God's will, but this is not how it's supposed to be. She doesn't know how much more she can take.

Gary Whiting leans heavily on the sink, hanging his head, wondering if he's really done puking. Acidy bile burns his throat, his mouth and the back of his nose. Cold sweat pours off his forehead and soaks his pits. He's too sick to notice the acrid stench of vomit permeating the little restroom. Strings of bile run down the front of the toilet bowl. Unidentifiable chunks of break-fast swim in slime on the ceramic tile next to it. He turns the water on full as he bends over, scooping up the cool water with trembling hands to rinse out his vile mouth. His head spins as he gags then chokes on nothing, swallowing hard, his stomach void of contents. He wonders if anyone is listening, the office restroom walls, paper thin, the door, hollow. He's heard the girls complain, embarrassed to be heard when peeing or flushing. He always mocked their modesty. Now he has a unique appreciation for their complaints. How many of his office staff heard him in here retching his guts out?

It's been one hell of a morning. After he hung up on that detective, he knew it was over. They're coming to get *all* of the Sunset Pointe financial records. That means they'll get them from Connie for MJR, too. If they really dig, they're going find out, and then Rodriguez won't be the only one who's dead. He's not so worried about the cops. Hell, jail is the least of his worries. It's those hard-money loan sharks. If they find out, he's a dead man. The thought makes him gag. His stomach lurches up his throat, trying to come out his gaping mouth in a hoarse croak as he trembles all over. *Gotta get that insurance settlement money and fast.*

Whiting fishes around in his front pockets for his pills and his coke vial. He's needs to get it together. He pops two Valium and a Vicodin with water from the faucet, tossing his head back to swallow. He concentrates, trying not to shake as he taps the lip of his coke vial on the top of his fist, pale flesh between his thumb and forefinger. *Just need a taste.* His nostrils burn and his eyes water as he snorts the crystalline powder. He fumbles the coke and pills back in his pockets then sits heavily on the toilet lid, waiting for sweet relief.

*How did it go so wrong?* They had it made. Money in the bank. Sunset Pointe was a sure-fire winner. It was his lottery ticket, his big score, financial freedom. And now he's fighting for his life. Everything he owns or ever will own is on the line. He should never have let Rodriguez talk him into that loan. For that matter, should've never let Rodriguez sign the checks. *Shit! Where did all the money go?* Will he ever really know? Rodriguez gave him all those explanations for use of funds, but he'd be damned if he could see it. He could never get a straight answer out of him and he didn't dare press him. Rodriguez was way too scary when he got mad. *Shit! Millions of dollars, gone!* Hell, if Rodriguez hadn't bit the big one, he'd probably have sucked Sunset Pointe dry before Whiting realized it. *Good thing someone killed him. A* wry smile crosses his face. *Too bad they didn't do it sooner.*

Whiting does a once around. His stomach has gone numb and the cold sweats have subsided. He breathes a sigh of relief. Everything is smoothing out, settling down, loosening up. His tremors have melted away along with the hammering in his skull. He grabs the edge of the sink and cautiously pulls himself upright, keeping a hand on the sink to steady himself as the dizziness passes. *Gonna be all right.* He knows it's tight, but he still has a little credit left at the Tangiers Casino. *Time to get the hell outta Dodge.* He'll leave his wife a voicemail on his way to Sky Harbor.

Whiting wheels his Mercedes-Lite out onto Greenway, heading west for the 51, on his way to the airport. He fails to notice the silver F-150 4x4 pulling out to follow him. Behind the tall truck's wheel, a pair of dark glasses sits beneath the brim of a grey Stetson, a sneer plastered on thin lips.

Subwoofers thump in the cool darkness of the Lion's Den main showroom. The dim glow of plastic sconces throws a dirty-yellow wash along the flat black wall behind the bar—black lights reflecting off the Day-Glo nudes haze the room with a purplish glow. It's midafternoon and the stage is empty and dark. A few die-hards crouch along the bar working on their watered-down two-drink minimums, waiting for the action to begin. At the far end, Lenny Kantor, the Den's sole owner de facto, hunches over the black-lacquered bar nursing a Bud Lite.

Swinging her hips through the empty tables, Sondra Du spots Kantor at the bar, just the man she wants to see. If she's going to make this pictures-for-cash scam work, she's going to need some muscle. She slides onto the barstool next to Kantor and leans her elbows on the bar, pushing her ample breasts up and out. Looking directly at Kantor, she smiles, waiting for him to acknowledge her presence.

Kantor is an enigma. She's never been able to get a handle on what makes him tick. He's the owner/manager of a strip club with the hottest women in town. Yet as far as she knows, he's never shown interest in any of the girls, strictly business. Dressing room gossip has it he's gay, but she's not so sure. A couple of the gay bouncers are Naomi's close friends. She's certain she would have heard something by now. And looking for leverage, she's asked around. She knows he did a stretch in the joint and she's heard that like here in the streets, sex is power—power to control, power to manipulate, power to dominate. Who knows, maybe in the joint he was punked to the point of no return. Strange though, he looks big enough and acts tough enough to survive it. Still, she figures it is possible for too much sexual abuse to ruin anyone, certainly enough to jade you, something of which she has intimate knowledge.

Tired of Kantor ignoring her, Sondra decides to warm him up. "Hey, Lenny."

Without turning from his beer, Kantor mumbles, "What?"

"I need some ideas on something."

"Yeah, and …?"

"Well, I've got this friend …"

"That's a shocker."

Sondra ignores his sarcasm. "Well, she's owed some money and the guy that owes her is tryin' to stiff her."

"So why ya askin' me? Hire a lawyer."

"No, it's uh … not that kinda money. Ya know what I mean?"

"Yeah. Ya need an enforcer."

"Yeah. I guess. Do ya know anyone?"

"Yeah, but they're not cheap."

"Yeah? How much?"

"Depends ... how much we talkin' about?"

"It's a chunk of change, why?"

"They're gonna want a percentage."

"Yeah? What kinda percentage?"

"Figure forty, fifty percent, depending."

"Wow ... that much." Sondra hadn't figured on having to give up that much of the take.

Kantor takes a sip of his beer. "Yeah, that's about it."

She runs numbers and scenarios through her head. "So ... do you know someone?"

"Yeah, I can get ya a couple numbers."

"Thanks, Lenny, you're a peach."

Pushing away from the bar, Sondra slides off the barstool, turns and heads for the dressing room. This is where it gets tricky. Anyone with enough muscle to make this little scam of hers work could just as easily turn on her and keep all the cash, or worse.

# RATTLING CAGES

**[9:15 AM – Wednesday, November 17, 2010]**

IT'S FIFTEEN MINUTES past the interview times for both Mrs. Rodriguez and Mr. Whiting. Tall and trim in his off-the-rack charcoal suit, Detective Frank Salmon stands behind a uniformed security officer, a young black woman named Taneesa Clark. At the monitor console in the dimly lit security kiosk, she sits at attention. Leaning forward, he rests his hands on the back corner of the console to better scrutinize the bank of monitors. He senses her new recruit nerves and gets a slight whiff of perspiration, a delicate spicy aroma. And underneath, there's something else, just a faint hint. She's recently had sex or has just started her period, he's not sure which. He realizes he could do something to put her at ease, but leaves her rigidly at attention.

Salmon watches one particular screen with mild interest. It reveals a wide-angle view of the Violent Crimes waiting area. Mr. Whiting has yet to arrive, but the attractive Mrs. Rodriguez showed up a few minutes early. She's accompanied by her aged attorney, Hammond Elder. Decked out in a tailored three-piece pinstripe, Mr. Elder is making calls on his cell—his toe impatiently tapping the floor in a tasseled slip-on. Mrs. Rodriguez sits slightly slumped as though exhausted. Pretty head lowered, staring blankly at the floor, she seems lost in introspection. As Salmon continues to study her, he notes there's nothing all that revealing.

Salmon watches as Jacob Silverman, Mr. Whiting's attorney, nervously hustles into the waiting area with Whiting plodding along behind. Mrs.

Rodriguez jerks up, startled. Elder's eyes roll to take in Silverman and Whiting as his creased lips move in front of his phone. Silverman gives Elder a sideways glance as he quickly walks toward reception. Whiting looks loaded, barely noticing Mrs. Rodriguez as he follows Silverman to the reception counter.

Salmon set it up so he could watch their reactions when they ran into each other. He wasn't sure what to expect, but he hasn't seen much so far. He wishes he could hear them, but it's only a security camera, no microphone. *Ah well, time to rattle some cages.*

Salmon straightens up. "Thank you, Officer Clark."

Taneesa turns to give the detective a tentative smile. "You're welcome, sir."

As Salmon strides toward the Violent Crimes waiting area, he decides to take Mrs. Rodriguez first and let Whiting cool his jets. Whiting seems like a better suspect anyway. And making him wait an hour or so might be enough to crank him up, especially since he's paying that criminal lawyer by the hour.

Salmon strides to the middle of the waiting area to get everyone's attention. He looks at Elder and Mrs. Rodriguez. "You, come with me." He turns on Silverman and Whiting. "Wait here."

As Connie and her attorney rise, Salmon turns his back, heading for the interrogation rooms. Out of the corner of his eye, he catches Silverman's gaping stare. He almost expects Silverman to say something, but it doesn't come and Salmon doesn't wait.

Salmon holds the door to IR-1 as Elder and Mrs. Rodriguez pass through. He breathes her subtle fragrance as she brushes past. She's as gorgeous as he remembers, but somehow more frail, as though her ordeal has beaten her down. Salmon gestures for them to take seats on the other side of the scarred metal table. They sit facing the two-way mirror. Salmon sits across from Mrs. Rodriguez with the stately Elder off to his right. He makes eye contact, first with Elder then Mrs. Rodriguez, holding her timid gaze. She squirms, averting her crystal blue eyes.

Elder, noticing her discomfort, tries to engage him. "Detective Salmon, we're here today as a courtesy, to help you with your investigation. Mrs. Rodriguez intends to cooperate fully ..."

Salmon turns on the attorney, interrupting him in mid-sentence. "Is that why *you're* here, to see that she's cooperating fully?"

Elder sits up straight, his lined face a rigid mask, put off by the detective's brusque remark. "Have it your way, Detective. I'm here to see that my client's legal rights are not violated."

"I'm sure you are." Salmon turns back to Connie. "Well, then, let's get started. As always, I need to make you aware that this interview will be recorded—both audio and visual. Any objections?"

Connie turns to Elder with a blank look. Elder nods a full head of white hair to assure her he's got it under control.

"Any questions?" says Salmon.

Connie looks to Elder. Elder shakes his head no.

"Fine, we'll continue on." Salmon turns to Mrs. Rodriguez. "As you're probably aware, Forensics has been reconstructing your late husband's financial records in an effort to give us a better understanding of the circumstances surrounding his murder."

Connie faces the detective's penetrating glare, eyes slightly downcast, listening.

Hammond Elder remains stoic, taking it all in.

"It appears as though your husband ran several companies with dual sets of books. Records indicate he had a pattern of falsifying construction loan draws on several projects. He padded costs and skimmed the excess for personal gain, funneling the funds into various other businesses and fictitious entity accounts."

Elder drops his gaze to interlaced fingers, his hands resting on the scarred metal table.

Connie attempts to suppress a look of surprise as it creeps across her features.

"In addition to defrauding lenders, your husband embezzled funds from business partnerships and filed false tax returns, both state and federal, which constitutes criminal tax evasion. He was a busy boy." Salmon pauses for effect, waiting for either Mrs. Rodriguez or her attorney to say something.

Connie wonders, *What is God's purpose in all this? Has Mike managed to completely ruin our lives from the grave? How could he have kept all this hidden from me? Why hasn't Hammond told me about any of this?* She turns to her attorney in dismay.

Elder continues to look down at his hands, waiting for the detective to continue.

"And while we're sure his lenders, business partners, and the IRS will take a keen interest in our findings, we're more interested in his killer's motives." Salmon pauses as he watches Mrs. Rodriguez's expression change.

Recognition lights Connie's face in a slow burn. *If Hammond won't say anything, I sure as hell will!* Her voice erupts in a high-pitched scream. "HOW DARE YOU SIT THERE AND ACCUSE MY HUSBAND! HOW DARE YOU ..."

Elder tries to interrupt. "Connie ..."

She balls her fists and pounds on the table. "HOW DARE YOU!" Her face reddens as her eyes water.

Salmon sits passively, watching intently as Mrs. Rodriguez rants. He's finally hit a hot button. Maybe now he can get at the truth.

Elder leans toward her, placing a hand on her shoulder. "Connie, please!"

She throws off Elder's hand, and with her mouth gaping, stares wide-eyed at the detective. She's at a loss. Panic crawls through her gut as she turns back to her attorney. *Did I blow it, give myself away?* Her eyes plead for her attorney to bail her out. Her instinct tells her to get up and run out of there as fast as she can.

Elder sees a look of panic overtake his client. He firmly grabs her shoulder to hold her in place. He knew Mike Rodriguez operated in the grey areas, but he had no idea it was this bad. He silently questions whether the predatory detective has been completely honest or has embellished the facts for his own purposes. He quickly wonders about his client's culpability in all this. He'll need to calm her, get her to shut up, if he's going to get her out of there without getting arrested. He gives Connie a penetrating glare.

Connie catches the warning flash in her attorney's eyes and slumps back. Avoiding the detective's invasive stare, she wonders how her attorney is going to handle all this. After all, it really is his problem not hers, that's why she pays him all those exorbitant fees.

Elder turns to Salmon, formulating his tactics as he speaks. "Detective, my client has come here of her own volition. Your accusations against her dead husband are outrageous. Instead of badgering my client about her dead husband's alleged business practices, you should be out finding his killer."

Connie consoles herself. This really has nothing to do with her. She hasn't done anything wrong, unless you consider marrying a womanizing thug a crime. *Now that the bastard's dead, not my problem.*

Salmon leans forward, getting into Elder's face. "Mr., uh … Elder, is it?"

Elder's eyes narrow. "That's right."

"Well, counselor, I will do whatever it takes to get to the truth of the matter. And the truth is, a man was murdered and your client has as much or more motive than any suspect in the case. And ninety-nine percent of the time, the one with the motive, the most obvious suspect, turns out to be the guilty party."

Connie's features turn to stone with the realization that she's just been accused of murdering her husband. Her world collapses as she drops into a tailspin, running all the horrifying scenarios. *I'll be arrested, there'll be a trial, it'll be on the news, everyone will know. I'll be humiliated, my reputation ruined, my children wrenched away from me by the state.* And to end up in prison, or put to death by lethal injection, it's too much. It's all over. Her life is over. *Can this truly be God's will?* She drops her head in her hands as her life force drains away, on the verge of passing out.

Clipping his words, Elder confronts Salmon. "If you have an arrest warrant, charge my client now. Otherwise, this interview is over."

Salmon leans back in resignation. "Not yet, counselor. We'll let you know."

Elder stands, leans over to help his client up and ushers her out of IR-1.

Salmon grunts in disgust. He's fairly sure that if the attorney hadn't stopped her, Mrs. Rodriguez would have confessed. Maybe not to murder, but he's seen it all before. Her range of emotions were classic, clear indications of guilt. He pushes up out of the metal chair. At least he's making progress. He heads out of IR-1 and down the hall to retrieve the next suspect, Whiting.

Salmon strides into the Violent Crimes waiting area, scanning the room for Whiting and his attorney. He spots Whiting slumped in a plastic chair against the far wall, but no Silverman. *Hmm, maybe Whiting released his attorney, maybe Silverman couldn't wait.* A predatory grin creeps across Salmon's face. *Be great to interrogate Whiting alone.*

Whiting can barely focus, but some inner warning system lets him know that the fuzzy outline headed directly for him is that asshole detective.

Salmon crosses the waiting room, heading for Whiting. "Ready?"

Whiting gives him a quizzical half-lidded gaze. "Yeah ... sure thing." He leans forward to grab the seat's edge, propping himself up. The wait obviously hasn't done anything to snap Whiting out of it.

"Where's your attorney?"

Whiting struggles to stand. "Dunno ... he was just here."

Salmon grabs Whiting's upper arm and points him toward the hallway. Maybe he should just arrest him now for public intoxication. "Well, he's not here now."

"Humph ... lemme call."

Whiting reaches into his coat pocket to retrieve his smartphone just as Silverman dashes back into the waiting area.

Salmon holds his disappointment in check. *Damn, almost.* He lets Silverman follow his client. From behind, he notices Silverman's stilted pace and Whiting's weaving gait. Silverman looks to be equal parts annoyed and embarrassed by his client's condition. Whiting is definitely loaded. *This oughtta be interesting.*

Salmon herds them into IR-1, facing them toward the two-way mirror, in position for the cameras and mikes. Dropping into a chair across from them, he's ready to start.

Salmon takes his time, studying each of them in turn, watching for little tells.

Silverman, what a piece of work, small, nerdish, in a constant state of agitation. One of those driven-to-succeed types, wearing his suit out from the inside. Probably obsessed with a law career for the money. Thinks he's dressing the part, high-dollar name brands at a discount. Problem is that his clothes are ill-fitting, too loose on his scrawny little frame and rumpled like he slept in them. And wearing brown wingtips with a navy suit and a red and silver striped power tie. *Damn.* Even Salmon knows better than to go out in public looking like that. He needs to watch out for this guy. *Probably a crack attorney.*

Then there's Mr. Whiting. The man's a basket case. He's balding, but otherwise lacking any clear-cut masculinity, his amorphous shape defined by thin arms and legs and a flabby midsection. He dresses immaculately if conservatively. Everything matches, on the surface he's the whole package, the plain-featured conservative business executive, desperate for respectability. Though not high-dollar names, his grey suit and white shirt look tailored. His tie, a conservative burgundy pattern—almost looks money. But the man's a dead giveaway, the slack features, drooping lids, blotchy skin, the phony smile with a nervous tic. And the real tell, the eyes, bloodshot, glazed, at half mast, nearly obscuring the stark terror hidden within. This man's hitting it hard, wasted, hoping no one will notice. If there's anything worth knowing, Salmon will find it.

"Gentlemen, before we get started it is my duty to inform you that today's interview will be recorded, both audio and visual. Any issues with that, you need to let me know now."

Silverman cuts a sideways glance at Whiting then focuses on Salmon. "And if we do have any issues?"

Salmon frowns at Silverman, unwilling to play his little game. "Counselor, I'm sure you're aware of your options here. Are we going to do this or not?"

Silverman leans back, looking at Salmon with conceit. "You may continue for now, Detective. I'll let you know if I decide otherwise."

Salmon tightens his lips into a thin line, refraining from rolling his eyes. Dismissing Silverman out of hand, he turns to Whiting.

"Mr. Whiting, you understand you're being recorded?"

Gazing languidly at the two-way mirror on the far wall, Whiting does his best to appear nonchalant. "Yeah, no problem."

"Okay then, Mr. Whiting. I'm gonna tell you the same thing I told Mrs. Rodriguez."

"Which is what?"

"Well, for starters, it appears that Mr. Rodriguez was ripping you off." Salmon sees Whiting's eyes flicker for just an instant before dropping back to half-mast.

"No, Detective. I think you got it wrong. It wasn't like that."

Silverman watches the exchange like a hawk.

"I see. So you approved all those padded draw requests for the construction loan?"

A slight tremor races through Whiting's features as his face bunches up in disgust. "What are ya talkin' about? Those draw requests weren't padded. Everyone knew construction costs were going up. The bank approved them."

Silverman interrupts. "Detective, what are you doing? I thought this interview was about Mr. Rodriguez's murder. It's all we've agreed to discuss, nothing more."

Salmon completely ignores Silverman. "Mr. Whiting, if you prefer, I'll show you the material receipts and subcontractor billings and then you can explain why they don't add up to the draw amounts submitted to First Community Bank."

Salmon watches the color rise in Whiting's face, the facial tic firing rapidly. Whiting's on edge, about to go nuclear. Just another little push …

Silverman picks up on it, too. "All right, Detective. That's enough." Turning to Whiting, he says, "We're not putting up with this." Silverman noisily scrapes his chair on the vinyl as he stands to leave.

Whiting looks dazed but relieved and scrambles to his feet, working to steady himself.

Salmon takes one last swing. "You know, Mr. Whiting, there's a law against public intoxication. Maybe I should just take you downstairs to a holding cell."

As he grabs for the back of the chair, Whiting starts shaking, beads of sweat rolling down his forehead, the color drained from his face. Pale and pasty, he's on the verge of passing out.

Silverman jumps in. "Just a minute here, my client is under a physician's care and on medication."

It's over. Salmon pushes back his chair to stand, turning on Silverman. "Yeah, he looks like he needs a doctor. Get him outta here." Hands on his hips, Salmon watches in disgust as they shuffle out of IR-1 and head down the hall. *Shoulda nailed him.*

# SEEING THINGS

**[3:05 AM – Monday, February 21, 2011]**

I REACH FOR my reading light, pulling the chain. The cramped little bedroom bursts into light. I squeeze my bleary eyes shut, waiting for them to adjust. Glancing at the digital clock, I notice it's three in the morning ... again. This is the third night in a row. Sonja calls them premonitions, I call them nightmares. Whatever they are, I can't keep waking up like this. *Dammit!*

My head swims as I struggle out of bed and stumble toward the bathroom. I sway in front of the toilet, trying to piss. Giving up, I drop the toilet seat and plop down.

"Dearest Lance, you need to get a grip." Sonja's voice, sweet and clear, penetrates my skull only half startling me.

I'm simply too exhausted to care. "Now what?"

"Tell me what you're thinking."

"Thinking? I'm too damn tired to be thinking, thinking I need some sleep, that's what I'm thinking."

"Don't get pissy."

"Well, I *am* on the can, here. Pissy seems appropriate."

"You know what I mean, smartass."

"Yeah, yeah. Can we discuss this some other time? Really can't think right now."

"Suit yourself, but you realize that you're not likely to get any sleep until you handle this."

"So why didn't you tell me this the first night?"

"You weren't ready."

"Oh, but now that I'm completely exhausted from sleep deprivation, I'm ready? Perfect."

"Lance, this is important. You can't just blow this off, it won't work."

"Fuck. Just shoot me now."

I can tell she's gone, bugged out, leaving me holding the bag. And why the hell is she always right? Infuriating, but I guess there's no getting away from it.

Sitting bare-assed on the toilet with my elbows on my knees and my head in my hands, I try to think. And if this position doesn't inspire deep thought, nothing will.

It isn't thinking, really, more like scanning scenes of a half-finished documentary. I keep rerunning short clips of obscure images, over and over, trying to deduce the subject, the storyline, anything that makes sense. Pieces of dreams. What's it all mean? *Probably don't mean shit.*

*Okay, concentrate, before the headache gets to be too much.* Images swim behind a murky curtain, just out of view. If I can focus ... *There ... what the hell is that?*

It's that truck from the double exposure, the shooter's pickup. The image shimmers, becoming clearer the more I concentrate. It's light-colored, maybe white or silver. Looks like a late-model Ford, maybe an F-150, custom—big, like one of those off-road jobs with a lift kit and lots of chrome. Big fat tires on custom wheels and a roll bar sporting a half-dozen running lights. It has one of those extended cabs, a crew cab or super cab, something like that. *Hmm, this is new.*

There's more. Over there ... a woman writhing naked on the floor in the throes of passion. She's hot and she's putting on quite a show. The shimmering truck with lights ablaze pounces on top of the nude dancer, then dissipates into a fine mist and evaporates. The dancer lies still as I rotate over her. She's dead, her eye sockets black holes, her flesh decaying in fast-forward. Darkening fields of negative energy eddy in whorls around her rotting body, obscuring it, absorbing it into its blackness. The image fades.

The message is clear. The killer kills again. My headache eases up a bit and I start to relax as the pain releases.

The only question is when. Has it already happened, or is it happening now ... or is it about to happen? I don't know. Infuriating, yet it's a significant piece of information. How can I get it across to Salmon? He'll probably blow it off as more psychic bullshit. Shit, maybe Lacey would know. After all, she's sleeping with the guy. Need to update her anyway. Whew ... after I get some sleep.

# DRIVE-THRU

**[5:51 PM – Monday, February 21, 2011]**

SUNSET'S BRILLIANT BLAZE radiates out of the desert hill's dark silhouette. The smoldering reddish-golden glow fades to wisps of pink, magenta and lavender as it dissipates into a steel grey sky above. Below, pairs of wide concrete ribbons stretch east, west and south as Loop 101 transitions to the 51. Streaks of bright headlights flow north against rivers of red taillights rushing south, streaming into dusk's coming gloom.

Southbound, the silver F-150 exits the 51 at Shea Boulevard. It's been following a black Corvette for several miles. The 4X4 picked up the Corvette's trail as it left the Rupert Martial Arts Center about an hour ago. Following it to the Lion's Den Gentlemen's Club, the tall off-road truck idled at the corner as the Corvette picked up a passenger. The lumbering truck stayed close on its tail as the sleek Corvette looped back onto the freeway.

Rupert's Corvette turns left on Shea Boulevard, the pickup hot on his bumper pushing a yellow light. Annoyed by the tailgating truck, Rupert guns the Corvette's big V-8 and rockets up the road a few hundred feet. He gives his current squeeze a quick glance to see if she's noticed the Corvette's impressive acceleration. Glancing in his rearview mirror, he sees that damn truck right on his ass again. His blood rises, turning his face and neck a ruddy red. *I need to ditch this asshole.*

Rupert notices a Jack-in-the-Crack drive-thru burger stand on the corner up ahead. He switches the Corvette's suspension setting to Sport, downshifts and punches it. The back tires break loose as the V-8 roars, smoke billowing out of the back wheel wells. The Corvette leaves the truck behind in a trailing cloud of tire smoke. As he eases off the throttle, Rupert sees that damn truck gaining ground fast, must be doing at least seventy in a thirty-five mile-an-hour zone. *This asshole is really asking for it.*

The Jack-in-the-Crack's drive-thru exit comes up fast on his right, no one in the queue. Rupert whips the wheel and darts into the drive-thru going the wrong way. As the Corvette zips past the service window, Rupert hears the truck lock its brakes.

The 4X4's big off-road tires screech as it slides past the drive-thru exit. The truck lurches violently as it turns hard, bouncing into the Jack-in-the-Crack's parking lot.

The Corvette dives through the curved end of the drive-thru, sliding out its entry into the parking lot. Rupert slams on the brakes, screeching to a stop, confronted head-on by the big 4X4. Petrified, Jilly sits speechless. Rupert furiously slams the gearshift into neutral and yanks the hand brake, leaving the Corvette to rumble at idle. *Enough! Time to teach this road-rage asshole a lesson!*

Rupert elbows open the door and jumps out in one fluid motion, cat-like, ready for action. The truck's driver door is opening as Rupert rounds the Corvette's door. A hand and arm extend through the truck's window. *What the hell?*

Rupert sees the semi-automatic too late. The pistol jumps in the shooter's hand. He sees the muzzle flash. As the bullet slams into his chest, he hears the gun pop. He doesn't see the second muzzle flash as the 9mm slug punches into his forehead. Rupert watches his body crumple out from under him and he's gone.

A wide-rimmed cowboy hat and wraparound dark glasses obscure the shooter as he grins at the private joke. *Never show up for a gun fight empty-handed.*

The shooter moves around the door and saunters over to the Corvette. He aims through the windshield at Jilly, the silly stripper sitting there frozen like a rabbit caught in the headlights. He squeezes off two more shots, watching the stupid bitch's head slam back against the headrest. He waits to see if she's done. Jilly slumps forward, dead. *That was fun, time to go.*

The truck door slams shut. The engine revs and all four tires squeal as the tall Ford truck backs suddenly, then lurches forward around the idling Corvette. It shoots over the curb, through the desert landscaping, crushing oleanders and spraying crushed granite in its wake. Spinning its fat off-road tires across the sidewalk, it leaves twin trails of black rubber as it bounces into the street.

The Jack-in-the-Crack's shift manager, an older couple finishing their fries, and a few assorted bystanders stare dumbfounded, as a big off-road truck, lights ablaze, roars off towards the freeway.

# ON CALL

**[10:08 PM – Monday, February 21, 2011]**

THE STOVE LIGHT'S yellow haze sticks to the grimy kitchen wall like grease. Brown glass of empty longnecks, an overflowing garbage can and a debris-strewn counter hunker in ocher shadows. The reek of rancid garbage, stale beer, dirty socks and unwashed armpits permeates the little two-bedroom, one-bath rental.

Deep snoring emanates from the tiny living area adjoining the pigsty of a kitchen. Suddenly, an obnoxious cellphone erupts.

*Asleep. And from the depths I hear ... what? What is that? Sounds awful, a bird-like cry, a giant raptor. Makes my skin crawl. Some prehistoric predator's keening, a sort of signal, sonically searching for prey. It's hunting. It's hunting for me, looking for something to eat. Getting closer, growing louder. Gotta get away!*

Gasping, I start awake, lurching upright in my broken-down recliner. It's taken me hours and several beers to finally get to sleep. And now, in the middle of the night, some asshole decides to call. What luck, and after several nights of little or no sleep, perfect. *Where's that damn phone?*

I hobble over to the counter, my joints creaking. I fumble for the cell. Guided by its shrieking din, I retrieve it from under a dog-eared magazine.

"Yeah, who's this?"

"Lance, it's me, Lacey."

"Shit, Lace, it's the middle of the night. Whaddaya want?"

"Lance, it's only a little after ten."

"Like I said, middle of the night."

"I need some photos, you gonna make it?"

"Tell me about it."

"Got an inside tip. A shooting over on Shea and the 51. Two people dead."

It hits me with a tingling rush and I feel all my hair standing on end. Spooky, like tiptoeing through a graveyard at midnight under a full moon.

"Lance, ya still with me?"

"Yeah, I'm here … Who got killed?"

"Dunno. Ya gonna do it or not?"

"Yeah, sure, gimme the address."

After hanging up, I drag my tired ass into the funky kitchen. I grab a dirty coffee mug off the counter and slosh the dregs into the sink. I pour yesterday morning's stale coffee from the cold pot. A whiff of overripe garbage assaults my nostrils on my way out of my sparkling kitchen. Wrinkling my nose, I muse, *One of these days I need to clean up my act.* I grimace as I chug the bitter brew in two gulps, heading for the shower.

Hands against the shower wall, I lean into the steamy spray. I let the hot water stream over my aching body. Too old and too little sleep make for a bad combo, but the hot water helps. I think about things as I try to find spots that don't hurt. Overall, I've been doing pretty damn good lately. Only four major migraines in the last couple months. And I managed to reduce the painkillers to only half a pill. Only two painkillers total, a new personal best. Of course, my housekeeping skills could use some work. Fuck it, I'm not expecting company anyway. What I really need is money. Then I could hire someone. For that matter, if I had some money I could find a better place to live and move out of this shithole. First, I need the money. Time to get to work.


As I rattle down Shea Boulevard in my derelict Sentra, I see the lights of the news choppers in a dark sky. They circle slowly over an intersection a block or so down. I'm nearly there. Seems like déjà vu all over again. I can't shake this sinking feeling in the pit of my stomach. *What if it's her, the naked dancer?*

All those sleepless nights. I have a bad feeling about this. Don't think I can do this. Maybe I should turn around, call Lacey, tell her I'm not going to make it. *Shit, I'm here.*

Crime scene tape is strung across the parking lot entrance, triggering the surreal vision unfolding before me. I'm feeling faint, like I'm not really here, not really anywhere. Suddenly it's hard to control myself, arms numb and tingly, legs rubbery, guts loose and watery.

I slow and pull past the burger stand's parking lot, turning the corner. There are emergency vehicles and cop cars everywhere. I slide the Sentra in between a cop car and a tow truck. Quickly pulling to the curb, I throw open the door, thinking I'm going to lose the contents of my stomach. I thrust my head out the door and lean over, just in case, barely holding it down, lovely. Finally, I unclench, tilt back into my seat and close the creaky car door. My head pounds like it's getting hammered by Thor himself. This is not starting off well. I should call Lacey.

I jump at the loud chirp from my cell. Staring at the caller ID through watery eyes, I see it's Lacey. This is embarrassing.

"Lance, where the hell *are* you?"

"I'm here, but I don't think I'm gonna make it."

"What the hell are you talkin' about? You gotta make it! It's too late to get anyone else. I gotta have pictures!"

"Yeah, yeah. I know, I know ..."

"Whaddya mean you're here? Where *are* you?"

"In my car, on the street, next to the wrecker."

"Oh ... I don't see you ... but get your ass over here, we're waiting on ya."

"Right. On my way." *I hate this shit.*

I push the car door open, grab the door frame and pull myself out. I hesitate as nausea crawls up the back of my throat, dizziness spinning my head. Taking it slowly, I turn sideways. I hold on to the door frame, caught on the verge of a convulsion. *Shit, where's my gear?*

Eventually I manage to stretch to the curb and pull myself out. Leaning on the car, I slowly crabwalk along the top of the curb to the trunk and get my photo gear.

I'm sweating profusely as I gingerly weave my way through the emergency vehicles. Lacey must be over there somewhere. *What the hell am I doing here?*

Wiping my watering eyes on the back of my arm, I duck under the yellow crime scene tape. As I crane my neck looking for Lacey, a uniformed officer cuts me off. He grabs my upper arm, turns me around and forcibly escorts me back outside the crime scene perimeter while asking me my business. I show him my media badge as I tell him I'm a news photographer and that I'm authorized to be here. He listens sternly, incredulity skewing his features. I keep after him to check, and finally, as a more or less professional courtesy, he radios in. More clipped dialogue and police radio code transmit before he tells me to wait. I do my best not to fidget, but I hurt and stink of sickly sweat. I'd be more embarrassed if my head wasn't pounding like a Howitzer on a battle line.

Despite all the lights and action, the night is cool and dark. A faint autumn breeze evaporates the sweat on my clammy skin, giving me the chills. There's a sinister aura permeating this place, grim odors, murky shadows, the look and feel of violent death. And it makes my skin crawl. Don't know how long I can take this.

Head sticking up above the crowd, Detective Salmon heads my way. For the first time in several long minutes, I pull my thoughts away from my discomfort and direct it to the morbid scene surrounding me. Maybe *he* can get me out of this.

Salmon strides up with Lacey in tow and dismisses the uniform. Catching wind of me, he wrinkles his nose. "Damn, Underphal. Ever hear of a shower?"

Lacey pulls up short, a look of dismay stretching her face. "Lance, you all right?"

Now, I really *am* embarrassed. "No, uh, I'm fine, just got a little sick on the way over."

Salmon turns and walks off without another word.

Lacey just stands there, shell-shocked.

From the look of her, I must be in worse shape than I realize. "Maybe I should just go."

Lacey snaps out of it. "No, no, let's get the pictures, only take a minute, then you can go." She starts working her way through the throng of official personnel, clearing a path.

I follow at a slight distance, trying my best not to offend. Nearing the south end of the burger stand, the crowd parts and I'm facing a black Corvette with the driver's door wide open. A tape outline blocking a dead body's position makes me wince, a dark stain on the concrete. Spiderweb cracks in the passenger-side windshield radiate out from two bullet holes. A hellish scene steeped in the stench of death.

I act quickly, trying not to think about it. The pounding in my head ratchets up a couple notches while my ears ring like a fire alarm. I glance at the Corvette's empty passenger seat, a black leather bucket smeared with thick black bloodstains. Hollow eye sockets, stringy hair, the bloody blue-black face of a dead young woman flash through my vision. I'm overcome with surprise, shock and a palpable anguish at suddenly finding myself in this state. Then I realize it's her, her last thoughts and emotions still hanging suspended in time. Her electric shock and raw terror still fresh, thick with her turmoil at suddenly finding herself a killer's victim.

Setting down my gear bag, I drop to one knee, stare at my trembling hands and shakily assemble my camera, afraid to look up, afraid of what I'll see.

I feel him behind me. His manic stare, boring holes through the back of my skull. Under a big cowboy hat and wraparound dark glasses a leering grin twists his face as he sights down the semi-automatic. He oozes blood-lust, feeding an insatiable hunger to inflict pain, gorging himself on the putrid flesh of his victim's terror. I don't dare look behind me to see if my vision is real.

My guts clench and I bite back the bile rising in my throat, swallowing hard. I set my camera lens on autofocus and my shutter release on automatic. My guts roil as sweat pours out of me like toxic waste. Reeling, I'm determined not to throw up. I stand too quickly and a bout of dizziness makes me pay. I steady myself and turn back to the Corvette. Squeezing off three frames at a time, rapid-fire, I work my way around the scene. Done, I dump my camera in my gear bag, heft it onto my shoulder and start for my car.

Lacey sees me and trots my way, hollering. "Lance, you get everything?"

I wave her off and yell back. "Yeah. Got it all. Call you tomorrow."

I duck under crime scene tape, heading for the relative safety of my old Sentra. A tiny glint of relief begins to pulse through damaged tissue at the prospect of escape. I drive mindlessly to a dump of a rental house I call home and the sanctity of my reclusive existence. *Shit, what a night.*

# THE TRUCK

**[3:10 PM – Tuesday, February 22, 2011]**

BARGAIN-BASEMENT CURTAINS, torn and threadbare, flutter with the faint breeze. Fragrances of a warm afternoon waft through the dimness of the cluttered little bedroom, refreshing the stale air with the mellow winter haze of Central Phoenix. A fly drones in erratic spirals, its atonal buzz counterpoint to the dissonance of background traffic. Adrift in the doldrums, the day floats in small circles, quietly murmuring nothing to no one.

I finally wake up, my head thick from the pain pill (a whole one) and all the beers. When I roll over to check the time I get a little queasy. Pinpricks of sharp pain light up my nerves like a swarm of fire ants. It's late afternoon. Even though I've slept all the way through, I'm exhausted. I have the remnants of a migraine faintly throbbing in swollen brain tissue. My stomach feels like it's been tortured by a CIA interrogator. *It's going to be a great day. Shit.*

After a long hot shower and a cold beer, I'm feeling slightly better. Better than last night. Last night was a bitch, one of the worst. At least it's behind me. Yeah, much better. So good, in fact, that I can almost think about what to do next.

I grab another cold one for moral support and rummage around in my gear bag. I assemble my Canon and turn it on to review last night's photos. As I thumb through the digital images, it starts to come back to me. *I saw this! I knew this would happen! That woman and that guy didn't have to die!* I should've warned somebody, Salmon, at least. Maybe he could've done something to stop the killer. Maybe it's too late, but he needs to know.

Unplugging my cell from the charger, I power it up and scroll through recently dialed numbers. Spotting Salmon's number, I punch send.

"Underphal. Feeling better?"

"Yeah, somewhat. Got a minute?"

"Whaddaya need?"

"Well, I was just curious, about the murders …"

"Yeah, so am I," he says.

"Do you have any leads?"

"We have some eyewitnesses, but too soon to tell."

"I think I might have somethin' for ya. Just not sure if it's these murders or something else."

"Whaddaya got?"

"I've been having this vision."

"Look, I'm up to my armpits in a double homicide, can this wait?"

"Yeah, sure, but let me just ask a couple questions, then I'll let you go. Was one of the victims a nude dancer or a stripper?" I wait for Salmon to say something. Maybe my cell dropped the call. "Detective, ya still there?"

"Yeah, I'm here, just thinking. Was there a stripper in your vision?"

"Yup."

"The female vic was a dancer at the Lion's Den, a strip club in North Phoenix."

"Yeah, I know the place. Okay, what about the truck? Was the killer driving an off-road 4X4 truck with running lights?"

"Shit, was that part of your vision, too?"

"Yeah. It's the same Ford pickup as the Rodriguez murder."

"You say it's a Ford?"

"Yeah. A customized F-150 with an extended cab."

"Hmm … Can't be sure, but a couple eyewitnesses described a silver off-road truck."

"So it could be the same truck."

"Could be."

"Detective, I had this vision three nights in a row before your double homicide."

A long silence ensues as Salmon mulls it over. "Why didn't you call me?"

He's got me. Guilt floods my guts. *I knew I shoulda called.* "Well, I uh, thought about it ... but wasn't sure what to say. I mean, at the time it didn't seem like I had anything concrete and I didn't want to waste your time and ..." This sounds lame, even while I'm saying it. I give up and tell him, "Shit, I dunno."

There's another lengthy pause on Salmon's side of the call. "Think you can identify that truck?"

"Maybe. I can give it a try."

"How long will it take you to get down here?"

*Shit, he would want to do this now.* Even though I'm better, I still feel like shit, weak and achy, but I gotta do this. "Uh, well I uh, haven't eaten or anything ... give me a couple hours."

"Okay, get your ass down here. I'll get it set up."


There's an aluminum sign announcing the Violent Crimes Bureau on the wide entry door. It's propped open and I turn into the harsh glare of the reception area. Typical government décor, so bland it numbs the senses. It has less life than photos I've taken of the dead. Wonder what kind of human being would design this. *Glad I don't work here.*

I announce myself at the reception counter and Salmon shows up in short order to escort me back. I dutifully follow him through the rat maze. He ducks into a smallish dimly-lit office and I'm right behind. Across the desk is a young woman with dark hair and thick glasses. There's an oversized monitor set to the far side of her gunmetal desk.

"Lance, this is Officer Latham." Salmon motions for me to take a seat.

I smile and nod as I sit down across from her.

"Among her many talents, Officer Latham is our digital sketch artist."

Officer Latham grins and blushes.

I smile and nod.

"I want you to describe that truck to her, with as much detail as possible."

Officer Latham looks at me expectantly.

"Any questions?" he asks.

"No, I've got it."

Latham wags her head no.

Salmon turns to Latham. "Call me when you're done." He gives me a sideways glance as he exits into the hall.

Staring back at Officer Latham, I suddenly feel uncomfortable, stuffed into the close office sitting across from a strange woman in a police uniform—a female police officer who, so far, hasn't said a word.

Latham smiles sheepishly. "Lance, is it?"

I'm eager to work through an awkward moment. "Yes, Lance. And what should I call you?"

"Elizabeth's fine."

"Okay, Elizabeth. How does this work?"

She adjusts the monitor's angle to make sure I can see. "Let's start with the basics. It's a pickup truck, right?"

Elizabeth works the mouse and the large monitor lights, displaying a generic truck in a 3-D setting. It sits at an oblique angle from a point of view that looks down slightly on the roof, hood and left front fender.

"Right. It's silver."

"Okay. Dark silver or bright silver?"

"Bright silver."

She clicks the mouse and paints the truck bright metallic silver.

"It's a Ford F-150."

"Do you know the model?"

"Model?"

"F-150s come in several variations. Is it a regular cab, super cab or super crew?"

"Not sure."

She shows me each cab variation.

"It's a super cab."

She updates the image. "Do you know what year?"

"Dunno. Late model."

She clicks through recent model years until I spot it.

"It's that one. I can tell by the grill."

"That's 2009–2010." She locks in the update.

I sit back and study the image—too generic. "It's a 4X4."

She makes the change, but it's still too generic.

"I can rotate the view," she says.

"Okay."

I continue to study it as the bright silver 4X4 rotates. "Tires are different, taller, wider, like off-road tires ..."

She works the mouse. "How about wheels?"

"Yeah, the wheels are different, maybe custom, for the oversized tires."

"Okay." She opens a small widow and starts a slideshow displaying custom wheels and tires.

I catch a glimpse of something that looks familiar. "There."

She stops the slide show.

"Nope, go back a couple."

She scrolls back and stops.

"Yeah. Try that one."

She updates the truck with new wheels and tires.

I stare at the truck. We're getting closer. "It's still not tall enough."

She clicks her mouse. "I'll lift it." The image updates with the metallic silver F-150 sitting tall on its polished custom wheels and oversized off-road tires.

"Yeah, that's better. Okay ... it had some lights on top of a roll bar, a chrome roll bar."

"What shape are the lights?"

"Round."

"How many?"

"Try six."

I watch as Elizabeth pastes a chrome roll bar into the 4X4's bed then adds six large KC running lights across the top. I shudder, a quick spasm of recognition. I tell her, "Chrome tubing on the sides just below the doors."

"Nerf bars?"

"I dunno. What are nerf bars?"

Just below the doors she adds large chrome tubing, like steps. Its diameter and look match the chrome roll bar. They curve in slightly at the ends to meet the bodywork.

"Yeah, that's it. Now it had something like that, another chrome bar, sticking up from the bumper in front of the grill."

"A bull bar."

"If you say so."

She pastes a bent piece of chrome tubing up from the bumper, in front of the grill. Looks like you could ram something with it and not get a scratch.

"Wow ... yeah, I uh ..." It hits me, washing over me like a thundering wave. The digital image comes alive. It's eerie as though animated by evil— a killer's weapon. I've never really seen this vehicle, but it's unmistakable. I know it cold. And I can't take my eyes off of it.

Sonja whispers inside my head. "It's the one."

In the distance, I hear Elizabeth. She's on the phone. No. Maybe she's asking me something.

I seem to be saying, "No, I don't see a license plate ... Wait, yes, in the back ... but it's got something on it, smeared on it, like mud."

Detective Salmon is asking me something. Am I sure?

I hear myself say, "Yes, this is the killer's truck. Has to be."

The detective seems to be ushering me out, thanking me for my help. It's all vague, dreamlike, as though I can't quite wake up. I tell him I need to get home, get some sleep.


Striding briskly back down the hall, Detective Salmon absently wonders whether he should have had someone drive Underphal home. The old guy seemed out of it, probably just needs to get some sleep. He turns into Officer Latham's tiny office. Leaning on the desk to get a closer view of the mystery truck, he lets his gaze wander over the details.

"He seemed pretty positive about it," says Latham

He stares at the silver off-road F-150 gleaming on the monitor. "Yeah, for what it's worth."

Pulling up, he directs his steely gaze at Latham. "Print out about a dozen of these for me, will ya?"

"Sure, Detective. When do you need them?"

"Now's fine. Bring them to my desk." He turns into the hall.

"Right away, sir."

Detective Salmon grabs the manila file folder containing the printouts off his desk. Leaning back, he crosses his long legs, planting a heel on the desk's corner. He glances through the 8.5 X 11 digital images, all high-quality glossy pictures. There are several views, oblique, front, side and back. Looks like the real thing. He tosses the sheaf of prints onto the scarred desktop.

This guy Underphal is something else. He can't quite figure him out. Most of the time ol' Lance looks and smells like a homeless drunk, used up and kicked to the curb by life, just another victim. Salmon's seen plenty of them, the dregs of society, on the dole, worthless to themselves and everybody else. Unlike the violent criminal element—a pack of jackals in a feeding frenzy, actively tearing civilization apart—the derelict element's crimes are more subtle and more devastating. Victims. Nothing drains the spirit, the élan vital of a people like its victims, an insidious parasitic gnawing on the very soul of its host until both host and parasite succumb.

Salmon chuckles thinking how Lacey would jump to the defense of victims everywhere, their would-be champion. She's a peach, a real keeper. And she may be naïve, but he loves that quality about her, her bright shining ambition to save the world, exposing all society's ills with crack investigative reporting. Hell, he'd be satisfied if he saw any justice at all—a rare occurrence in these hard times.

Interesting that Lacey had brought Underphal into the picture. And who knows, maybe ol' Lance might do some good, after all. The old fart's an enigma, a most unlikely psychic. But then that whole psychic shit is unlikely to start with. He can't be sure. No doubt there's something there, far more than just coincidence could allow, but damn …

Salmon recalls his first brush with the supernatural. He was ten, at Grandma's funeral. Grandma always protected him, even against his dad when she had to. He loved her. But at the side of her open casket, he saw a corpse for the first time. He knew it wasn't her. He jumped when he heard her voice, thought he saw her lips move as she spoke to him, but not really. Though ghostly, her soothing tone reassured him. She told him what a good boy he was, that everything would be all right and she'd see him again, then she told him goodbye. He'll never forget it, a sublime sense of warmth and peace, and he still misses her.

Breaking out of his melancholy, Salmon collects the printouts off the top of his desk and thoughtfully shuffles through them again. Amazing that Underphal could give such a detailed description of the vehicle. It's as though he'd seen it in person. *So this is it, the mystery truck.* He wonders if ol' Lance really got it right. Only one way to tell, he has to see for himself.

# BUSINESS AS USUAL

**[12:23 PM – Tuesday, March 9, 2010]**

BIG MIKE RODRIGUEZ stomped into his private garage, exasperated. His bone-headed cousin was hanging around waiting for a check and he had to run to another meeting. *Fuck him, Johnny can wait all damn day.* He'd sign the check when he got around to it. That fucker was always trying to get into his back pocket, always wanting money—a real moocher, always had been, even when they were kids.

Flinging open the Mercedes' door, Rodriguez cursed to himself. *Shit!* He thought he had Fellman under control, but Martin Fellman had been whining more than ever. *Fellman can shove that damned loan committee up his narrow little ass.* As Rodriguez wheeled the powerful S65 AMG out into the yard, he checked the time. *Shit, late again. This emergency meeting shit has gotta stop.* He wondered what that little weasel had up his sleeve. Rodriguez's face broke into a broad grin. Doesn't matter, he's holding all the cards, or in Fellman's case all the pictures. *The little lech.*

As Rodriguez accelerated up the on-ramp, the V-12's twin turbos spooled up with an exotic whine. As much as he loved the Mercedes' prestige, he loved its performance, smooth and quiet. For a big sedan, the thing hauled ass, a real blast to drive. He had to keep a lid on it though. He already had one speeding ticket this month. As he shot on to the 101 Loop, he backed off, letting the AMG coast, his speed dropping to a more reasonable seventy-five. That was the problem with all this great German engineering in the US, no autobahn.

The autobahn. Rodriguez smiled as he recalled their trip to Stuttgart. Best decision he ever made, to take delivery of his new Mercedes at the European factory, the Sindelfingen Delivery Center. What a difference from Phoenix, all the trees, lush forest greenery and snow-covered peaks. Then there were the quaint Old World villages paved with cobblestones, the stunning castles right out of a fairy tale, the winding Alpine roads. And yes, the autobahn, big stretches with no speed limits. He remembered Mikey, how thrilled he was when they were doing a hundred and sixty plus on the autobahn outside of Munich. Mikey rode shotgun. Rodriguez had picked the Black Forest/Alps tour package and Mikey loved it. Brittany and Josh were a little too young. Brittany, absorbed with her iPod. Josh, entranced by his Game Boy. Connie hated high speeds, did nothing but scare her. Otherwise she was mostly bored with their European driving experience—not enough shopping. But it was the best week he'd ever spent. It was worth it just to see the constant ear-to-ear grin on Mikey's face.

Rodriguez was still harboring fond thoughts of Mikey when he pushed through the Chuck Wagon's heavy door. The dim dining area snapped him back to reality. He needed to make this short. That hot little Marcia Rupert was coming by the shop this afternoon—another workout in his private gym. A leer crept across his coarse features as Rodriguez envisioned Marcia naked with her knees pulled up on either side of those luscious tits.

He spotted Fellman on the far side of the dining area, raising his hand with a quick wave. He slid in across from Fellman, giving him a deadpan stare. Fellman's eyes darted away. Fellman looked smaller than usual, like he'd shrunk. His color was bad, ashen grey. His folded hands betrayed a slight tremor—a tic twitched at the corner of his left eye. And while Rodriguez expected to intimidate him, Fellman's agitation was over the top. Warily, he made a mental note to keep a close eye on this boy.

"What's up Martin?"

Fellman turned and fumbled with his briefcase on the seat next to him. Finally, he pulled out a manila folder. He pulled out copies of construction draw request forms and spread them out between them. Hunching his shoulders, he drew his head down like a snapping turtle, a devious look sparking his beady eyes.

Fellman started in, talking too fast, like a nervous old woman. "Mike, you've got to do a better job on these. Not enough detail, explanation, they don't match up. I can't get these approved this way."

Rodriguez pulled up, towering over the little banker. "Whoa, Martin, what the hell are you talkin' about? We did these the way we always do them."

"They're incomplete, not enough detail."

"You approved the last draw request ..."

"Yeah, I know, but I shouldn't have. Underwriting's all over me."

Rodriguez picked up the draw requests. He knew full well what was eating Fellman, but he thumbed through them, as though studying them closely. Problem was, Fellman was right, they were vague. Hell, they needed to be vague to cover the discrepancies. Rodriguez and Telafano had worked long hours (with a few breaks for recreational sex) to make sure they covered MJR's tracks. Hell, it worked before.

Rodriguez leaned forward, set down the draw requests and glared at Fellman. "You need to approve these. I need the money. If you need more detail, I'll get my bookkeeper to get you what you need. Just let her know. But you need to get me paid."

Fellman hung his head and looked down to study the backs of his hands for a long moment. "Mike, you'll need to redo these and resubmit. I can't do this for you anymore," he said sheepishly.

Blood rose in Rodriguez's face. *Steady now.* Holding himself in, he waited for the initial flash of rage to pass. His fury roiled unspoken as he forced himself to be patient. *The little prick—I could break him in half. Who the fuck does he think he is? No one fucks with my money.*

Daring a quick glance at Rodriguez, Fellman's stomach turned queasy. Rage colored Rodriguez's face a deep scarlet, veins popping out of his thick neck and Neanderthal forehead—a terrifying specter. He half expected the big man to throw a punch. Curiously, the ruddy red faded and a placid look smoothed Rodriguez's features. Relief coursed through Fellman's veins. He exhaled, not realizing until that moment that he'd been holding his breath. Confident he'd dodged a bullet, Fellman figured the worst was over.

Gathering himself, Rodriguez eased back, thinking it through. After several moments, he hunched forward and looked expectantly at Fellman. "Martin, I thought we were friends."

Fellman fidgeted, but kept his head down. He looked at his hands, saying nothing, figuring that if he just kept quiet long enough, Rodriguez would eventually give up and go away.

Rodriguez kept his focus, waiting for Fellman to respond. Several awkward moments crawled by. "Martin, look, we need to help each other out, here. I told you I'd cover for ya. Didn't I cover for ya? Now I need you to do this thing for me."

Confused, Fellman looked up at Rodriguez. "Cover for me?"

"Yeah, you know ..."

"Whaddaya mean, cover for me?"

"Damn. You're kidding, right?"

"What?" As the question escaped his mouth, it hit him. Stark terror shot though every cell in Fellman's body. *He wouldn't ... would he?*

Rodriguez watched as Fellman unraveled. "Look, Martin, I told you I'd cover for ya. That hooker was expensive. Those pictures cost more than we thought."

Fellman collapsed in on himself like shattering funhouse mirrors, raining splinters of sharp glass from all sides. He'd already paid for those pictures, already burned them. Hadn't Rodriguez given him the originals? A deep sinking sensation took hold. Suddenly weak, he was on the verge of passing out. He knew now what Rodriguez meant. He thought after that incident at the Lion's Den, Rodriguez was just taking care of things, helping out a business associate in trouble. How naïve. His life had been ruined in that moment and he hadn't recognized it. He now knew, he'd been set up. Rodriguez was blackmailing him. A common criminal, a thug, a gangster masquerading as a real estate developer. He should've known, should've seen it coming. *Shit, it's over. What am I gonna do?* With a weak voice, Fellman said, "Okay, uh ... I'll think of something."

"Thanks, Martin. When can I expect the draw?"

Fellman's head spun, eyes darting around as he scrambled, trying to think it through, trying to recover. Rodriguez had him, pulling the strings like he was his own personal puppet. "Give me a couple days."

Rodriguez gunned the big Mercedes, a wide grin tattooed on his face like the cat that ate the canary. Back on the freeway, Rodriguez broke out into a loud laugh. *I got him.* He owned that little weasel. He was laughing so hard, his face turned a deep crimson. Fellman just lost big time, another punk-ass bitch, another little minion in Rodriguez's back pocket to cater to his every whim. *Cha-ching!* He couldn't stop laughing. Hysterical, Rodriguez wiped at the tears with the palm of his hand, trying to keep his vision clear enough to drive. It was hilarious. Rodriguez loved winning and the most satisfying win was when he crushed the competition. Now that he had his little lender back in line, it was time to celebrate with that horny little housewife, Marcia Rupert.

Marcia, what a find, wild yet discreet, the perfect combo. Discreet because she was married to a martial arts black belt with a short-man complex. And wild? *Damn.* Horny as a pack of she-wolves in heat and hardwired for kink. *What a find.* A bit dicey having her come to the shop with Diane there. His excuse? They were discussing Mikey's progress with his karate lessons. Not sure how long it would hold, but so far his hot-blooded bookkeeper had bought it. *What's Diane gonna do, quit?*

As the garage door slid closed, he noticed the door to his private gym open a crack. Odd, as he always kept it locked. Maybe one of his staff let Marcia in. He hoped Diane hadn't seen her. Marcia was probably waiting for him, all wet and naked. He bounced out of the Mercedes all fired up, heading for the gym.

Built out at one end of his personal garage stall, his gym was a thousand square feet of mirrored walls and ceilings, chrome weight stations parked on black rubberized floor mats, chrome lift benches upholstered in black Alcantara—dumbbells, barbells and weight plates all chrome. It had its own redwood sauna, Italian marble steam room, whirlpool therapy tub, professional massage table, white marble shower and dressing room, perfect for today's busy commercial real estate entrepreneur.

As Rodriguez entered, he saw light through the door to the back room, illuminating the darkened workout area. A cool fluorescent glow bounced off the surrounding mirrors and lit the chrome weights and workout stations like tricked out choppers at a custom bike show. He heard giggling over the bubbling rush of the therapy tub and grinned. Marcia must be ready and waiting. He started to get hard.

Rodriguez stopped cold as the therapy tub came into view. The tub's swirling water had more than one occupant. Leaned back against the tub's edge, breasts high out of the water, Marcia had her eyes closed and mouth open, moaning in rapture. The back of some guy's head worked between Marcia's legs in a frenzy, long matted hair bobbing on the roiling water.

It only took Rodriguez a split-second. "What the fuck is going on?!" he bellowed.

Marcia's eyes popped open as her mouth slammed shut.

Johnny Chavez jumped up and jerked around to face Rodriguez, water streaming from his long wet hair and torso. His face reddened with startled embarrassment. But he quickly recovered, eyes narrowing as an impish grin split his face. Chavez spread his arms, extending his hands palms up as though he greeted a long lost friend. "Hey, Cuz, you're just in time. Come on in."

Rage rippled through Rodriguez, blood pumping, adrenaline surging.

Marcia sank to her neck in the tub's froth. Her wide eyes blinked rapidly, darting back and forth between Johnny and Big Mike. The two giants faced off, Johnny naked, attempting to blow it off while Big Mike looked ready to paw the ground. Johnny told her Big Mike wouldn't mind, that they'd done threesomes before and it turned Big Mike on, said his cousin knew all about her and Johnny. *OhMyGod! The lying asshole!* And if these two monsters tore into each other. *Oh My God!*

"What the fuck are you doing here?!" he yelled. "Get the fuck outta here!"

Chavez stood still, arms stretched wide, seemingly unaffected by Rodriguez's fury. "Hey, come on. We're all friends here."

"Don't fuck with me, Johnny! Get the fuck out, NOW!"

"Hey man, we were just waiting for you."

"OUT! Get OUT! Get the fuck out before I throw you out!"

Chavez seethed. "Hey man, ya don't have to get shitty. Just havin' some fun."

Rodriguez's jaw clenched. "Just get the fuck outta here."

Chavez reluctantly sloshed out of the tub, muscles coiled with tension, trying to decide if he should take his cousin down.

Rodriguez stood with his feet apart, arms akimbo, resisting the urge.

Without taking his eyes off his cousin, Chavez slowly stepped out of the tub, grabbed a towel off the rack, and deliberately took his time drying off. He continued to glare at his cousin as he slowly picked up his jeans, slid them on one leg at a time and zipped his fly.

Rodriguez's patience wore thin as he watched his cousin bait him. Just like when they were kids, Johnny was jealous of him, always trying to piss him off. And it was working.

Grabbing his boots in one hand, Chavez picked up his Western shirt with the other hand and tossed it over his shoulder as he stood tall in defiance. "Hey man, I was just waiting for you to get back. I need my check."

Marcia thought Big Mike's head would explode. Veins popped out on his neck and forehead as his face purpled with rage.

It took everything Rodriguez had to keep from jumping his asshole cousin. "You'll get your fucking check when I get around to it. Now get the fuck outta here!"

Chavez bristled but said nothing as he forcefully brushed by Rodriguez on his way out.

As he heard the gym door slam shut, Rodriguez fixed his gaze on that little whore, Marcia.

Marcia inched up out of the turbulent water, her eyes turned seductively toward Big Mike. The water ran off her ample breasts as she slowly exposed them. She watched his eyes fix on her breasts. It was working.

Titillation made Rodriguez hesitate, just for a moment. Then he turned on her. "You little slut—get out and stay out! Don't ever come around here again! And stay the fuck away from my son!" Before he gave in to his urge to grudge fuck her, Rodriguez turned and stomped out.

# TRACKING
# THE TRUCK

**[1:23 PM – Tuesday, March 8, 2011]**

WAXY PALM FRONDS clack in a faint breeze. Tall palms line the city's boulevards framed by an azure blue sky. It's a beautiful winter's day in the Valley of the Sun, seventy-two degrees with clear skies, warm and sunny. You can't beat the winter weather in Phoenix. It's why people keep coming. Regardless of grim employment prospects and one of the worst real estate markets in the US, they just keep coming. Growth is one of Phoenix's major industries even when it's negative growth. One out of every three Valley homeowners is upside down, their mortgage balance exceeding the market value of their home. Foreclosures are at epidemic proportions. Newer housing developments and condo projects throughout the Valley stand largely vacant. Homes are boarded up, as though their owners died in some massive viral plague—their deserted rooms testament to the savage oppression thrust upon their hapless occupants during what is arguably an economic depression. Regardless of how the media tries to spin it, local residents are having the toughest time in their multi-generational memory. Only the oldest Phoenicians tell tales of the Great Depression for comparison. For everyone else, it's the worst ever.

And along with hard times comes more crime. Job security remains a non-issue for Salmon. He's got the job as long as he wants it even though the City is considering more layoffs. But today is a beautiful winter's day in the Valley of the Sun and today he likes his job more than most. It's a good day to be Detective Frank Salmon.

He grins as he glides down Central Avenue in the unmarked Marauder. The big black Mercury's V-8 purrs in the background as he contemplates the latest evidence in what the media dubbed "the Drive-thru Murders." It feels good, like he's on the verge of a real breakthrough—back in the game.

Salmon just left Mr. and Mrs. Madison's little cinderblock ranch-style off of 32nd Street, the elderly couple at the drive-thru burger stand the evening of the homicides, and the last of his eyewitness interviews. Both agreed, the silver Ford truck in the digital renderings was the truck they saw leaving the scene. The burger stand's shift manager had also identified the truck without hesitation—same for the four other eyewitnesses. Unfortunately nobody could remember a plate number, not even a partial. At least they all positively ID'd the truck. Not perfect, but it would have to do.

As he sits at a red light, the sleek light-rail slides by, its burnished metal shell gleaming in the sun. He rolls down his window to savor the balmy breeze, fresh air recharging his senses. He marvels at how little hesitation the eyewitnesses exhibited when he spread the pictures in front of them. He has to give ol' Lance his due. Amazing detail, as though he'd taken a picture. Maybe his photography background helps explain the details. But the image, itself ... *how did he do that?* Salmon shakes his head. Pretty good, especially considering he's never actually seen the truck. Now all Salmon has to do is find the damn truck.

Salmon scrolls the dialed numbers on his smartphone until he recognizes Lance's cell. He hits send.

"Yeah?"

Underphal sounds rough, like Salmon woke him up.

"Detective Salmon."

"Hey, Detective. What can I do for ya?"

"Just wanted to let you know, we've verified the truck's description with the eyewitnesses and it's a match."

"Good to know. Thanks."

"It'd be a big help if you had anything on the license plate, anything at all."

"Like I said, couldn't make it out, like it was covered with mud or something."

"Yeah, I was afraid you'd say that. Our shooter's covering his tracks. You have anything more on the shooter?"

"Nah, not really. Mostly impressions. Like I said, so far just a tall guy in a big cowboy hat and dark glasses with a semi-automatic pistol. It's definitely the same guy, though."

"As the Rodriguez shootings?"

"Yup, same guy."

"Okay, well … you call me if you get anything. Don't wait."

"Right. Got it, Detective. Will do."


As I end the call, I roll over and sit up on the edge of my sagging mattress, scratching my bed head. Salmon's call buoyed my spirits somehow, like I'm doing something useful. The afternoon breeze stirs the cheap curtains, fresh air filling my nostrils as I breathe a sigh of relief.

Shit, must be important if Salmon's asking *me*. Call him if I get anything, that's a switch. Feels good for a change. Should have *something* to show for all this brain damage. Guess I can still get something right. 'Bout time.

I lean on the stained bathroom sink and lift my face to glance in the water-spotted mirror. Still the same ol' handsome devil, lots of hard miles and mostly used up, but tons of potential. *Yeah, right … Look atcha—whadda bum. Sonja's fulla shit. This introspection-in-the-mirror thing isn't helping.*

Sonja's voice fills my head. "Full of shit?"

"Yeah, you heard me, fulla shit."

"Look, Bozo. Your attitude sucks."

"So what's new?"

"That's the problem, not much. Now pull your head out of your ass and get this straight."

I hang my head, face reddening, resistance building to the lecture I know is coming. *Why does she always do this to me?*

"I don't give a fuck about what you think of yourself. It's not even vaguely important."

*Great. She's on one of her tirades.*

"And if I waited for you to get your shit together, your dead corpse would be stinking up the place long before anything happens. You're pissing me off! Whether you think it's important or not, whether you feel you're up to it or not, whether you're uncomfortable or not—like it or not, you've got a job to do. And whether it's a blessing or a curse, you just happen to possess the skills, talent and ability to pull it off. Use your gifts and contribute something useful, make something out of your pitiful existence, or fail to use them and be damned. Only you—only your attitude determines whether your abilities are, in fact, a blessing or a curse. Now knock it off and take a good look!"

Smarting, my face burns with her words. I want to snap at her, but what can I say? Besides, I know she's already gone. *Take a good look, she says. Whaddaya think I've been doin'? Give me a fucking break!*

Sheepishly, I look up into the mirror. What the fuck am I doin'? It's not my fault. I don't have to take this shit from her.

Sounds good, might even look good on paper, but I know that dog won't hunt. This is for me to do, nobody else. Not even Sonja can pull my ass out of the fire if I fuck this up. I look at that old man in the mirror and realize I'm out of time, out of second chances, it's now or never—time to suck it up, get my shit together and do something, even if it's wrong. *Hell, what've I got to lose?*


Bleary-eyed from staring into the mirror, I turn away. Seems like I've been doing this for hours and it's not working. *Figures, when I really want to do it, I can't.*

I find myself at the kitchen counter staring into my empty coffee mug wondering if my chance is gone, wondering if I ever really had a chance.

Tired of dwelling on what might have been, I grab my gear bag off the floor and heft it onto the counter. I pull out my Canon and fire it up, watching the LCD as it boots. I start back through the images from the drive-thru photo shoot. Automatically scrolling with the slide-show setting, I absently glance at the crime scene images as each exposure blooms then fades. My vision blurs, maybe from all that time in front of the mirror. I wipe my watering eyes with the back of my hands, trying to focus. Pictures float free from the LCD. These are not from the crime scene. *What am I looking at?*

Out of the swirling murk a high-back armchair emerges. The leather Chippendale. Why am I not surprised. I squint, trying to bring it into focus. There are those arms dangling off the armrests decked out in Hef's smoking jacket, red velvet sleeves with black satin cuffs. This is not the drive-thru victim, Rupert. This guy is still alive. Hovering just below the Chippendale scene, the silver 4X4 coalesces into view. Same vision, different day. Red Smoking Jacket is not the victim. I still get the feeling that he's not the shooter, but that he's in on it somehow. Maybe Red Smoking Jacket is the brains behind the shooter, not sure, but they are definitely connected, their dark energies colliding like thunderheads, vaporous serpents writhing and coiling to spark and rumble.

The more I look, the more the images envelop me. I'm determined not to flinch, to get everything I can, every detail, trusting that what I see are symbols—symbols from which truths will emerge. Yet, I don't really know what I'm doing or how I'm doing it. My thoughts swirl—thick, like mud in a blender. My head swims, bordering on vertigo. Getting dark, hard to see.


I come to in an awkward pile on the floor, the toppled barstool lying next to me. Must've passed out. Everything hurts, but the large knot on my head hurts the worst. It throbs away, like an alien trying to hammer its way out of my skull. I reach to touch it and find a sticky mess in my hair. Looking at my fingertips I discover coagulating blood, thick and dark. I've been out for a while.

I struggle to a sitting position. I've got to let Salmon know he's looking for two men.


Soft rays from the winter sun filter through police headquarters' gun-slot windows. High in the southern sky the distant sun blazes in benign serenity, spreading warmth and light. Its evil summer twin isn't due back for several weeks. The multi-story concrete box that houses police headquarters squats squarely on the corner of Washington and Seventh Avenue, impervious to the elements both natural and human.

High in its upper entrails, Salmon sits hunched over his battered desk studying reports from his juniors. Oblivious to the harsh glare and incessant hum from the fluorescents overhead, he squirms in his ergonomically correct chair, poring over the latest results.

Salmon's crew has been at it for days with little to show for it. Not surprising given the assignment—find *the* silver F-150 4X4. After the Valley-wide press conference and release of the truck's description to the media, they had to tackle it head-on. The enormity of the task began to sink in once they came to grips with the fact that the Ford F-150 is the best-selling truck in the US. Narrowing it down to only those registered in the Phoenix Metro area (a best guess) and only 2009-2010 silver super-cab 4X4s, it still left them tracking down several hundred vehicles. Salmon's crew is using old-fashioned detective work to visually inspect the vehicles, checking for the modifications that distinguish the suspect truck from all the other silver Ford pickups in the Valley. They slowly drive by the registration addresses, sometimes knocking on doors and looking in garages— slow freight. Unfortunately, they don't have much else to go on. Finding the truck is their best option.

Looking up from the stack of reports, he yawns. They've whittled away at the list, down to the last couple hundred and still nothing. He hopes like hell the vehicle is registered locally.

Salmon leans back in his stiff chair and stretches, thinking back to the call he received the other day from his derelict photographer. The guy is a basket case. At first he thought Underphal was drunk, speech slurred, almost incomprehensible. Finally, he got it out of him, the guy fell and cracked his skull. When Salmon sent Lacey over to check on him, she called an ambulance and they hustled him off to the nearest emergency room. The doctors diagnosed him with a concussion, bandaged him up, and kept him overnight for observation. The old fart looked like day-old dog shit when Salmon stopped by Phoenix General later that same night. If he didn't know better, he'd swear ol' Lance was medicated, but they don't give painkillers to head injuries for fear of them slipping into a coma. Wide-eyed, bordering on delirium, Underphal recounted his latest vision.

The idea of a conspiracy, a hired killer, wasn't new. Salmon had pursued that line exhaustively during the Rodriguez investigation but came up cold. Now Underphal insists that the drive-thru killer and Rodriguez's killer are one and the same and that the killer has an accomplice. Salmon wonders if he should reconsider. However, that leads him directly to the question of whether or not there's a connection between Rodriguez, Rupert and the stripper, or whether the shootings were just random acts by a killer for hire, or whether there are two completely unrelated murders with different shooters and different silver trucks and Underphal is full of shit. Baffling. If it's one shooter, he isn't a pro. Amateurish elements show up in both shootings. Still, whether by accident or design, he's managed to cover his tracks so far. They need to find that truck. Either that or ol' Underphal needs to have clearer visions. Better find that truck.

# HARD MONEY
# THE HARD WAY

**[2:09 PM – Thursday, March 10, 2011]**

DINGY POOLS OF light interrupt the shadows behind the long black bar. A vibrant ultraviolet glow glistens off the chrome stripper's pole, center stage. The Lion's Den showroom tables are vacant, the stage empty and dark. The state-of-the-art sound system lies dormant, its screaming tweeters and thunderous subwoofers on pause, quietly waiting to accompany the next nude dancer's troll for cash.

Lenny Kantor slouches against the bar, mainly bored. Last night's haul is counted and secure, all the beer and liquor restocked for this evening's show, nothing left to do but scowl at the lazy help and wait. A smirk lifts Lenny's gash of a mouth. He's awash in cash. Last night's take was higher than usual—way higher. He guesses maybe he can afford a little boredom. As he lifts the fizzing club soda to his thin lips, he watches three new customers filter in. A short pear-shaped guy in an expensive suit, bracketed by two more suits, a walking fire plug and a lanky twist of barbwire dressed like a gentleman rancher. Thinking he should recognize these guys, Kantor squints. He can't make out their faces in the dim light, but they look like trouble. They saunter to the middle of the empty showroom and take a table. Sitting backs to the bar, they face the dark stage as though expecting the show to start. *Who are these guys?*

Sondra Du works her way across the showroom, weaving through the empty tables on her way to the bar. She feigns a smile as she slides up on a barstool next to Kantor. Kantor seems transfixed, staring intently at the only occupied table in the room. Turning to get a better look, she sees the trio of newcomers facing the stage.

Sondra turns back to Lenny. "Little early for a show …"

Kantor keeps his eyes on the three at the table. "Yeah."

"Who are they?"

"Not sure."

Sondra turns to gaze at the three early birds, her curiosity piqued. "So why are you staring at them?"

Kantor gives her a disgusted look. "What?"

"Who are they?"

"Like I said, not sure. What's it to you?"

"Hey, man, you're the one staring." She watches Kantor for an answer until it's obvious he's ignoring her. She drops it and moves on. "Shame about Jilly, huh?"

"Stupid whore. Had it comin'. She knew the rules. I warned her, no fuckin' the customers, but she didn't listen and now she's dead. Don't ever let me catch you fuckin' the customers. I'll bounce your ass right outta here. We got rules for a reason."

Sondra turns away, biting her tongue. She wants to scream at him. *Heartless bastard!* Still, she knows better than to say anything. Jilly was a friend and to be shot to death in her boyfriend's car was tragic. Especially since her boyfriend turned out to be married. Typical for Jilly. Jilly was her own worst enemy, made her own bad luck. Still, it was a shame.

A long cold silence ensues as Sondra stares at the three new customers, thinking she should go over, take their money and fuck all three of them just to show Kantor. *What an asshole.*

Kantor's eyes narrow as he turns his gaze back to the newcomers, mumbling to himself. "Turn around, lemme get a look at ya."

Sondra glances back at Kantor. "Who are you talkin' to?"

Kantor ignores her. And as if catering to his command, the tall wiry guy in the Western duds pushes back from the table, stands, and heads for the bar. Kantor mumbles under his breath. "I know that guy. One of Cohen's men."

"Cohen?"

"Yup."

"The loan shark?"

"That's them."

"Whadda they doin' here?"

"Fuck if I know. A lap dance?"

Kantor and Sondra watch as the tall guy clumps toward the bar in his Stetson and alligator-hide cowboy boots. He leans on the bar and beckons to the bartender. The hired gun's head turns in their direction, hat pulled low shading an angular face. Too dim to make out his features, but his eyes gleam with a hard intensity. Focusing on Sondra, a faint leer crosses his lips exposing even teeth. He turns back to wait on the bartender.

Kantor takes the measure of the gunslinger wannabe. One of Cohen's toughs, but in a scrape he could take him. It's been awhile since Rodriguez bit the big one, but Rodriguez was into Cohen for some serious cash. *Too late to collect now, fuckball.* Out of the side of his mouth, Kantor quietly says to Sondra, "Maybe you should find out what they're doin' here."

She cocks her eyes at him, giving him a suspicious look. "You want me to give'm a lap dance?"

They watch as Cohen's henchman gives the bartender drink instructions and heads back to his table.

"Sure, whatever. See what they're up to."

Sondra studies the three mystery men as Allison, the dark-haired cocktail waitress, delivers their drinks. Something about these guys bugs her. "Just make sure Jesse's close, in case I need him."

Kantor figures Jesse is overkill. A six-foot-eight, three-hundred-ten pound black belt with a concealed weapon permit. But what the hell, if it makes her feel better. "He's up front. I'll get'm. Get your ass to work."

Sondra rolls her eyes as she pushes off the barstool and sashays toward their table. As she approaches, she overhears their conversation. She can't make out much, just bits and pieces—Rodriguez, Whiting, and something about Sunset Pointe. She glides by and turns in to face all three, letting her exposed curves interrupt their discussion.

The tall country gentleman slumps in the chair to her left, hunger in his cold gaze as his greedy eyes ravish her body.

Seated in the center, the baby-faced man feigns innocence, almost believable except for the dead shark eyes. Well-groomed and graying at the temples, his thinning dark hair caps his smooth-skinned features. Plump shapelessness and the expensive suit betray his pampered lifestyle. Cold, aloof, as though he could easily ignore her altogether. He oozes money, obviously the kingpin, Mr. Cohen himself, no doubt.

The stone-faced man to the right sits rigid as carved granite, his beady black eyes burning a hole straight through her. His thick torso looks crammed into his ill-fitting suit like ten pounds of ground beef stuffed into a five-pound bag. She'd guess Italian from the dark complexion, except for the hair, too straight, like an Asian. His head shaved around the back and sides, military style with a thick shock of straight black hair bristling from the crown.

Tough customers, but she's worked tougher.

Easing into her pouty little smile, Sondra lets her gaze wander across each man's face in turn, her seductive look lingering as she makes eye contact. She sways up to their table, puts her hands on the table's edge and leans down, locking her elbows to push her ample breasts up and out. The tiny string top barely contains her, enhancing her cleavage, exposing thin crescents of pink at the top of her nipples. She cocks her head letting her blond locks slide over one eye and smiles seductively at Cohen. "You gentlemen need something to go with those drinks?"

Stetson Hat grins hungrily. "Whaddaya got in mind, sweetheart?"

Without taking her eyes off Cohen, Sondra replies. "Whatever you want."

"Not likely," says Stetson, eyeing her like a barracuda.

She gives Stetson an enticing glance. "You'd be surprised what money can buy. How 'bout we start with a private dance?"

"How much that gonna cost?"

Sondra teases, rolling her hips as she leans from side to side. "Probably can't afford it if you have to ask."

Stetson looks at his boss questioningly.

Cohen gives him a slight nod. "Don't be too long."

Stetson unfolds out of the chair to clump along behind Sondra as she winds her way back to her private cubby.

She guides him to the divan.

Stetson drops into the black faux leather, slouching with legs splayed and arms draped along the back, leering up at her.

"Haven't seen you 'round here before. What's your name?"

"Stein, what's yours?"

"Just call me Sondra. Gotta first name, Stein?"

"Yeah, Charlie."

"Okay, Charlie. A hundred bucks to start. What kinda music you like?" Sondra turns to the stereo.

He digs in his front pocket, pulls out a money clip, peels off a bill and leans forward to hand her a hundred. "Got any Rascal Flatts?"

She daintily lifts the hundred from his outstretched fingers. "Sure, I can do that." She turns back to the stereo to fiddle with the buttons. "What brings you gentlemen to the Lion's Den?" She turns for his answer.

"You gonna talk or you gonna dance?"

"Just being friendly."

"So shut up and be friendly." Hostility flashes from his eyes.

She sees it's going nowhere and turns back to the stereo. *Get it over with, get this animal outta here.*


Diffused light spills from skylights perched high in the kitchen's vaulted ceiling. The midday radiance paints polished stone surfaces with a vibrant sheen, reflecting gleaming star points off brushed metal appliances, stainless steel basins and polished fixtures.

Connie Rodriguez leans against the island counter, a half-filled earthenware mug nestled in her hands. She's lost in a daydream she can't quite remember. She turns her face up to break the spell, her fine features bathed in soft natural light from above. *Oh, yes.* Now she remembers, she came in to freshen her coffee.

She jumps, nearly dropping her coffee mug as the designer phone next to the fridge clamors for her attention. Setting the mug on the counter she steps to the phone, lifting the handset to her ear. "Yes?"

She hears a smooth male tenor speaking quietly, closely, as though standing right next to her.

"Mrs. Rodriguez, my name is Benjamin Cohen. You don't know me, but I was a friend of your late husband. My condolences."

Connie's not sure how to respond. It's been several months since Mike's death. *Why would someone wait until now to call? And how did he get this number?* She's had all the numbers changed to avoid the constant harassment from solicitors and Mike's creditors. "Uh ... Thank you."

"Mrs. Rodriguez, the reason for my call is not personal. I had business arrangements with your husband that I need to discuss with you and wanted to wait until it was more appropriate."

Well practiced, Connie knows exactly how to handle these types of calls. "I'm sorry—Mr. Cone, is it?"

"Cohen."

"Mr. Cohen, sorry. Anyway, I don't handle the business side of the estate. You'll need to talk to our attorney, Mr. Elder. I can give you his number ..."

"No, that's quite all right, I have his number. Sorry to disturb you."

Connie gives a slight shiver as goose flesh erupts, raising all the hair on her body. Something about that voice ... She shakes her head to banish the eerie feeling as she hangs up.

It's mild and sunny, the kind of winter day Phoenix is famous for. The mirrored glass spires of Camelback Towers glisten in the sun's warm rays. Glimmering light bounces off the surrounding mirrored office buildings, lighting up bright patches of passing traffic on the prestigious Camelback Corridor below.

Seated at his broad teak desk, Hammond Elder gazes out the floor-to-ceiling glass of his twenty-fifth floor corner office, lost in thought. Fluffy white clouds dot a pastel blue sky. Perfect weather for a round of golf. He debates whether he can get away with cancelling his two o'clock in favor of an afternoon on the back nine at the Phoenician. The Phoenician's owners are clients and he has free access to the renowned resort course any time he chooses. Fortunately, his clubs are at the ready in the trunk of his seven series Bimmer, downstairs. All he needs is someone to join him on the links.

Hammond's intercom startles him out of his reverie.

"Mr. Cohen and his associates are in Conference Room Two, Mr. Elder."

"Thanks, Doris. I'm on my way."

Hammond shakes his head. *Two o'clock already. Must be slipping.* There was a time he'd be teed up by now. He stiffly works his way out of his executive chair with a groan and grabs his coat off the rack by the door. Slipping into his tailored charcoal coat and straightening his silk tie, he heads down the hall to Conference Room Two, dreading yet another confrontation with yet another unhappy business associate of the late Mr. Rodriguez. If he's lucky, he can keep this short and still get over to the Phoenician before the afternoon is out.

As Hammond Elder enters the conference room, he makes a quick assessment of Cohen and his associates. All three sets of eyes are on him, taking their own measure. The three men sit on the far side of the long conference table facing the door. First is an angular man slouched down in the high-back conference chair, a tall guy's bad habit. He's dressed in a Western-cut sportcoat, Western shirt with a bolo tie and a Stetson hat. With his hat pulled low over surly eyes, he reminds Hammond of a petty criminal with something to prove—the most dangerous kind.

Hammond extends his hand. "Hammond Elder."

Reluctantly, the man sits forward to shake Elder's hand. "Charlie Stein."

Hammond releases Stein's hand, gives a quick nod and shifts his gaze to the second man. This guy looks ex-military, like he's seen too much action. The thousand yard stare, probably nobody home, and if there is, you don't want to know about it. Dark and thick, he sits like a stone, his too-tight, ill-fitting suit and his crisp military hair, a paradox.

Hammond leans across the table to extend his hand. "Hammond Elder."

A big meaty fist extends to grasp Elder's hand in an iron grip. His low voice filled with quiet menace. "Noel Redman."

Hammond withdraws his smarting hand and moves to the third man. He's taking it all in with a thinly veiled air of arrogance. The man's facial features are those of a cherub, but the eyes are cold and dead giving him the countenance of an evil doll disguised as a businessman. He wears an expensive suit and tie, neat and trim, though flaccid rolls of flesh reveal a certain overindulgence.

Adopting a thin smile, the devil doll pushes a small well-manicured hand at Elder. "Mr. Elder, Benjamin Cohen, a pleasure."

As he shakes the cool limp hand, Elder cringes and smiles politely. "Mr. Cohen, the pleasure is mine." Elder slides into a chair across from Cohen. "What can I do for you gentlemen?"

Cohen's snake eyes bore into Elder as he sits forward, a thin smile fixed upon his lips. "As I mentioned on the phone, I was referred to you by Mrs. Rodriguez. She tells me you're handling the business affairs of the Rodriguez estate."

Elder leans back, lines in his cheeks tightening as his lips purse. "I'm the executor of the Rodriguez estate, yes."

Cohen's eyes gleam. "Then you must be familiar with the Sunset Pointe project."

Elder steeples his fingers. "Yes, somewhat."

"As you may know, my investors hold a deed of trust on that project which is technically in default."

"I don't get involved with the day-to-day operations. Mr. Whiting, the other managing member, is the project's manager."

"I'm aware of Mr. Whiting's role and we are in contact. However, the technical default still exists."

"What is the nature of the default?"

"Mr. Rodriguez's untimely death creates a breach allowing for acceleration of the loan balance. And since my investors took this loan on the strength of Mr. Rodriguez, they are concerned about their collateral. I'm sure you can see their point."

"Have you addressed this issue with Mr. Whiting?"

"Yes. He tells us that the project is tied up in probate, and until it's released, he is powerless to resolve this issue."

"Is the project current on its debt service payments?"

Cohen leans back without releasing Elder from his cold stare. "Yes, so far."

Elder purses his lips as his forehead furrows in thought. *What's he after?* He lets the pause linger. "So the concern is not whether or not the project can pay, is that correct?"

"At this point, it's been several months since Rodriguez's death. My investors are concerned."

Elder seizes the opportunity to wrap it up and head for the Phoenician. "We appreciate your patience. But please understand that estates of this size and complexity are not quickly resolved. Let me assure you Mr. Cohen, your collateral is as good as ever. We'll do our best to resolve it as soon as possible."

Cohen slowly leans forward, resting his forearms on the table's polished surface, his thin smile evaporating, his eyes glistening with menace. "I'm sure you are aware that with changing market conditions, the project's value is not what it once was. If we are to continue this relationship, the investors will require additional collateral."

Elder eyes his opponent. *This guy isn't goin' away.* He contemplates his next move before speaking. "Mr. Cohen, I'm sure your investors can appreciate the fact that we can't control market conditions. And until the estate clears probate, no material changes will take place. Perhaps after the estate is settled, additional collateral discussions could be appropriate."

Cohen's eyes take on a predatory sheen. "I'm afraid that's not good enough, counselor. My investors are not inclined to wait in line with all of the estate's creditors. It would be unfortunate for all involved, if other measures had to be taken in order to secure the debt. I strongly urge you not to put us in that position."

Clenching his jaws, Elder stiffly stands and glares at Cohen. "I don't respond well to threats. This meeting is over." He strides to the door, abruptly leaving Conference Room Two.

Cohen scrutinizes Elder, swiveling his chair to watch the aged lawyer's hasty exit. He's not entirely satisfied that his message was taken seriously. Fortunately, he's still collecting the loan's default fees, a tidy monthly sum. Otherwise … Well, the old coot doesn't know how lucky he is.

A light breeze stirs the lush sissoo trees, their branches swaying gently, leaves aflutter. A pale blue winter sky peeks through the courtyard's luxuriant foliage, its soft light dappling the red clay pavers. A noisy cactus wren squawks as he bustles from branch to branch. Languid radiance at long angles, purveyor of a balmy seventy-six degrees, the late afternoon sun washing glass and stucco in golden hues. Another idyllic day in the Valley of the Sun.

Encased in the office's white stucco and mirrored glass, Gary Whiting is oblivious to the day's serene beauty. Slumped forward at his desk, gripping his aching head in trembling hands, he grinds his teeth as he waits for the Oxy to kill a ferocious headache. Hung over from another losing jaunt to Vegas, he's been suffering all day from the ill effects of too much blow and too many Valium. The migraine began tightening its thick coils around noon, sinking its fangs into tender brain tissue about an hour ago. It's been a shitty day and he's been hiding in his office for the duration, but it's almost over.

Whiting furiously rubs his temples as he ignores the flashing intercom call light on his phone console. He took the Oxy at four fifteen, about fifteen minutes ago. And if he can survive until it kicks in, he'll be fine. Seems like an eternity.

At first he's not sure. Is someone knocking at his office door or is that just the pounding in his skull? No, someone's knocking. *What the fuck?* He tries to ignore it, but there it is again. "What?"

He barely hears the meek voice from the other side of his door. "Mr. Whiting?"

Whiting can't believe it. *Shit!* "What is it, Jenny?"

The door opens a crack and Jenny sticks her head through. "There are some gentlemen here to see you."

*What the hell?* He can't think, but he's sure he doesn't have any appointments. "Who is it?"

"Mr. Cohen and his associates."

Panic flashes through Whiting like lightning, its power surging through the stabbing migraine. *Shit! Shit! Shit! Not now!*

Jenny continues to wait expectantly. "Mr. Whiting?"

*Shit! What to do?* He can't very well tell Cohen to fuck off, come back later. *Shit!* His head spins, he needs time. "Tell them I'm on a call. Ask them to wait in the conference room. I'll be there in a few minutes."

"Okay, I'll tell them." Jenny eases the door shut.

Whiting fusses with the Valium's bottle cap as he fumes. *Maybe Cohen will get tired of waiting. What's he want anyway? It's not like he has an appointment. What does he expect? Maybe he'll just go away.* Shakily, he pops the Valium and reaches for his water, wondering if he should take another Oxy. Glancing at his watch, he feels the migraine loosen its vise-like grip as the Oxy starts to work. *Pull it together.*

Whiting sees his intercom light blink. *Maybe Cohen left. Maybe he decided not to wait.* Desperately hopeful, he reaches for the handset.

"They're in the conference room, Mr. Whiting."

"Okay, I'll be there in a minute." Whiting exhales heavily as he hangs up.

He leans back, closes his bloodshot eyes and rubs his throbbing temples, trying to relax, trying to dissolve the lingering pain. *Fucking asshole. Let the fucker wait.*

Whiting opens his eyes with a start, wondering how long he's been out. The intercom light blinks as he attempts to get his bearings. *Shit!* He picks up the handset and punches the intercom button. "Jenny?"

"They're still waiting, Mr. Whiting. Mr. Cohen wants to know how long you'll be."

"Tell him I'm on my way." Whiting rocks forward as he restores the handset to its cradle. He grabs his water, his mouth suddenly dry. His palms sweat as his heart pounds, thudding in his chest. He struggles to pull it together, the room whirling around him in slow motion. He concentrates on breathing deep regular breaths as the Oxy melts the fiery shards of pain into puddles of cool release. *I can do this.* Pulling himself out of his chair, he tentatively heads for the conference room, wobbling on rubbery legs.

Lids at half mast, sweat beading on his pallid forehead, Whiting is unaware of the disgusted frown that darkens Cohen's features.

Cohen glances at his watch, noticing it's well after five. He's been waiting the better part of an hour. And for what? Whiting's clearly out of it.

It'll be a short conversation if he can figure out how to get this guy's attention.

Whiting gives a stuporous grin as he fumbles into a chair, trying desperately not to slur his words. "You'll hav'ta excuse me. Not feelin' too good."

Cohen's fairly certain they're the last ones left in the building and decides to wake this fool up. "There *is* no excuse for you," he spits. "You're an incompetent fool, and without Rodriguez, a liability. My investors want their money and they want it now." He nods at Charlie Stein. "Mr. Stein, why don't you show Mr. Whiting here what we do with liabilities." He gives Stein a wink, as Stein unfolds his lanky limbs and rises out of his chair.

Stein ambles around the table to tower over Whiting, reaching inside his Western sportcoat to unholster a matte-black Glock 9mm. He cocks the pistol and shoves the muzzle into Whiting's cheek.

Whiting's eyes fly open, jaw dropping in shock as a surge of adrenalin hits his system, temporarily snapping him out of his drug-induced daze.

Cohen rises, straightening his tie, shooting his cuffs, his diamond cufflinks sparkling in the fluorescent light. He fixes Whiting with a penetrating glare. "You will make whatever arrangements you need to make to pay us off in full. Be prepared to deliver funds upon my request, or suffer the consequences." Cohen casually heads for the door. "I'll be in touch."

The burly Noel Redman stands to follow while Stein reholsters his Glock.

Whiting sits in his empty conference room, shaking in the spreading wetness of his own urine, reeling with fear and the poisonous effects of the drugs.

# WORKING THE CLUES

**[7:48 PM – Tuesday, March 15, 2011]**

THE EVENING AIR is cool and still. The sky, the deepest midnight blue. Floating high to the east, a crescent moon caressed by wispy clouds of gunmetal grey. The aluminum skin of the diner's travel-trailer shell reflects the faint moon glow, shimmering with highlights from the red neon sign on the pole high above.

Frank Salmon pushes through the diner's double doors, working a toothpick between his molars as he heads for the parking lot. One of his faves. A throwback, like Elvis or the Platters. Not that he was around during the fifties, but he remembers his parents' stories. Great food. And what a great chocolate malt, old fashioned, rich with malt, like when he was a kid. His mom used to take him out to the Orbit Drive-in just outside the city limits on Grand Avenue. A taste of nostalgia for her and a real treat for him. The old Orbit was torn down years ago, swallowed up in the inevitable urban creep, all industrial buildings now. *A lotta years ... Mom's gone now, too.*

Salmon saunters across the parking lot toward his waiting Marauder. *Back to work.* He does his best to keep the overtime to a minimum. With all the City's budget cuts, it's usually a bitch getting OT approved, but Homicide has priority. He needs to act quickly if there's any chance of making arrests that will stick. And the media value of solving a high-profile homicide while it's still fresh in the minds of the voting public is not lost on City officials. OT should be no problem tonight.

Easing the big black Mercury onto the boulevard, Salmon heads for I-17 and the Lion's Den. He intends to do more in-depth interviews with the help, find out as much as he can on the second drive-thru homicide vic, Janice Parkson aka Jilly.

As Salmon cruises north, his mind churns, running through the evidence so far, trying new combinations—a crazy jigsaw puzzle. Linking the drive-thru case to the Rodriguez case makes sense in some ways. In others, it's a complicated mess. The too coincidental connections: the married Rupert dating a stripper from Rodriguez's strip club; plus, it turns out Rupert was the junior Rodriguez's martial arts instructor. Almost incestuous, it stinks. Besides, he never buys coincidence as an explanation for anything. Could be just a jealous wife, if the drive-thru perp weren't male. *A killer for hire?* Could it really be the same killer, using the same truck as the Rodriguez homicide? If it weren't for Underphal, would he even be considering such a scenario? Hard to know, but when he looks at it from that angle, the evidence tends to align. Too bad ballistics weren't more conclusive.

Still a lot of big holes in the puzzle. Fortunately, by their very nature, criminals are stupid and always make stupid mistakes, as if they *want* to get caught. All he has to do is discover their mistakes—sometimes, a monumental task, especially with limited resources and very little time. *Damn budget cuts.* He sighs as he exits I-17.

The distant city lights glow in Salmon's rearview mirror. Ahead, a tiny cluster of colored lights pales against the empty desert's impenetrable darkness. As he approaches, more details come into view. A gaudy Vegas-style sign blinks and flashes golden ribbons of light in the shape of a full-maned lion's head. Above and below, thick bold letters spell out Lion's Den Gentlemen's Club in bright red neon.

It's a working weeknight, still early, yet the parking lot is jammed with redneck trucks and yuppie sport sedans. While Salmon understands the attraction, he's embarrassed for the male species. Foolishly wasting their hard-earned money on the biggest come-on known to Man makes his brothers look weak and stupid. He considers their lack of restraint a genetic flaw, requiring only a modest amount of personal discipline to overcome.

Pulling to the backside of the lot, Salmon finds a spot, parking against a tall fence. He locks up the Marauder and heads to the main entrance.

Just outside the city limits, the Lion's Den stands alone at the edge of a sparsely developed industrial park. Records show that the Rodriguez Family Trust owns the land and improvements, leasing the building to a shell corporation set up as an Arizona limited liability company, named MJR Holdings, LLC. The shell corp, MJR Holdings, has only one managing member. Its managing member turns out to be another shell corp, a Nevada LLC with a fictitious entity name of Rampart Holdings, LLC. It had Rodriguez, himself, as a shadow member and his attorney, Elder, as statutory agent. Apparently, Rampart Holdings, LLC leases the property to Lion's Den Entertainment, set up as another Nevada LLC. Rampart Holdings, LLC also holds a controlling interest in Lion's Den Entertainment. Quite a tidy piece of legal maneuvering, effectively creating ownership obscurity. Not all that unusual for a strip joint.

To discover this, Salmon had to go outside the department to an private contractor. He hired one of his old Navy buddies, an ex-SEAL named Jake Jacobs, who runs a private investigation firm named Two Jakes PI. And he dearly loves his work. Jake uncovered the camouflaged paper trail in no time. *Ain't technology grand.* From Social Security numbers and bank account numbers to private medical records and sealed court documents, his buddy Jake can usually find anything on anyone without a court order or a warrant, no restrictions, extremely handy and mostly legal. The rule of thumb is: The more illegal the activity, the more difficult to prove culpability. Thorough due diligence is the key to successful prosecution. It's all there, if you're willing to dig.

Salmon's been to the Lion's Den before, a few years back on another homicide investigation. There have been some changes to the tall stucco building. A dark red canopy adorned with golden lion heads, a red carpeted sidewalk, ornate entry doors that mimic a lion's cage. He smirks. *What a rip-off.*

The low-frequency thump of subwoofers penetrates the walls, rattling the studs and buzzing the stucco. He falls into line behind three boisterous junior-exec types, clean cut with white shirt sleeves rolled up and ties loosened. Probably drive desks all day, too soft and pudgy around the middle.

Two steroid-soaked weightlifters bracket the red velvet-roped entry, mostly for show. They stand like Herculean statues, their arrogant disregard for the incoming clientele clamped on their faces in a permanent mask, beefy torsos and thick necks bulging out of too-tight Lion's Den T-shirts. They check IDs with their big MagLite flashlights, as much a weapon as a flashlight. Salmon ought to know, he's used his own department-issue flashlight in more than one skirmish.

He digs into his sportcoat and pulls his leather badge/ID wallet. He fixes his gaze on the muscle-bound kid to his left, staring him in the eye. "Detective Salmon. Homicide."

"Ya know it's a twenty dollar cover and a two-drink minimum."

"Police business. I'm investigating a homicide."

Musclebound gives him attitude. "Sorry, dude. Still a twenty dollar cover and a two-drink minimum. No one gets their rocks off for free."

"Get your manager out here."

Without taking his eyes off Salmon, Musclebound pulls a two-way radio off his belt and asks for Jesse. Apparently Jesse is on his way. Musclebound re-clips the radio, still locked eye-to-eye with Salmon.

Salmon waits without breaking eye contact, casually wondering why Musclebound hadn't called Kantor. Whatever. He'll wait for Jesse and work his way up to Kantor, if he has to. Anyway, this bouncer guy is big, no taller than Salmon, but probably has him by fifty or sixty pounds. Still, he figures he can take him, if it comes to that. In Salmon's experience, all that bulk restricts range of motion and slows them down. *All show and no go.*

One of the iron-barred doors opens and a huge black man in a dark suit strides up to tower over the two bouncers. Salmon looks him up and down and whistles to himself. *Must be Jesse.* This guy Jesse is enormous, at least six-foot-eight and no less than three hundred pounds.

Jesse glances at Musclebound who nods in Salmon's direction. Jesse's gaze shifts to Salmon. "Can I help you?"

Looking up, Salmon flashes his badge. "Detective Salmon, Homicide."

"What can I do for you, Detective?"

"I'm investigating a double homicide. One of the victims, Janice Parkson, worked here. Just need to ask you and your staff a few questions."

Jesse's face scrunches. "Janice, who?"

"Parkson. You probably knew her as Jilly."

"Oh, right. Jilly. Follow me."

Jesse turns and heads for the entry.

Salmon pushes past the bouncers, following the ebony giant into the Lion's Den.

As Jesse opens the door, a thunderous pulsing rolls out to envelop them. A cashier's window protrudes from the wall just inside to the right. Jesse walks past the window to a door labeled "PRIVATE."

Salmon takes it all in as Jesse digs for his keys. Glass cases on the far wall promote upcoming attractions, posters of nude beauties in suggestive poses. He stands looking at the beginning of a tight winding corridor, a curved ceiling rounding to curved walls, rough stucco, finished to look like a cave. The throbbing beat pours out of the tunnel, blasting like the mouth of a megaphone.

Jesse yells over the amplified roar as he opens the door. "Come on in."

Salmon slides by as Jesse hits the lights. He pulls the door tight muffling the booming racket to dull thuds, the obnoxious soundtrack absorbed by thick sound-deadened walls. Jesse rounds the desk and sits in a swivel chair, motioning for Salmon to take a seat. Salmon pulls out the cheap folding chair and sits, casually crossing his legs.

Jesse leans down to meet Salmon's eyes, resting his large forearms on the desk. "We were all sorry to hear about Jilly, Detective. What do you want to know?"

Salmon extracts a small notepad and pen, less intimidating than his microrecorder which is set on voice-activate in his top pocket. "You don't mind if I take notes?"

Jesse spreads his hands. "Guess not."

"You're the manager?"

"More or less."

"And your name?"

"Jesse Orton."

Salmon makes a note. "How well did you know Jilly?"

"Not very well."

Salmon looks up from his notepad. "And you're the manager?"

"Look, I don't have much to do with the girls. That's up to the boss."

"And who's the boss?"

"That would be Mr. Kantor, the owner."

"Lenny Kantor?"

"That's right."

"But you *did* know Jilly."

"Yeah, a little."

"Tell me about her."

"Not much to tell. Like most of the girls, I guess. Does her thing and she's outta here."

"What's your impression? Was she friendly?"

"Yeah. Maybe too friendly."

"Whaddaya mean?"

"Well, she used to push it with the customers."

"Piss 'em off, what?"

"Nah, just come on a little too strong, lead 'm on. Girls here aren't allowed to date the customers—house rules."

Salmon glances back down at this notepad. "I see." He pauses for a moment then lifts his gaze to Jesse's. "Did you like her personally?"

"Okay, I guess. A little too wild for my tastes."

"Did you know this guy she was with, Daniel Rupert?"

"Yeah, a little. Used to instruct at his studio for a short time a few years back. Seen him pick her up a few times, is all."

Salmon makes a note. "So you're into martial arts."

"Tenth degree. Been instructing for several years now."

"Impressive. You knew Rodriguez?"

"Big Mike?"

"Yeah, Big Mike."

"Everybody knew Big Mike."

"So I've heard. Did he hang around here much?"

"He was a regular, a high roller, big tipper, big parties in the private showroom, the works. Think he was part owner. Nice guy, hated to see 'm go that way."

"Did you ever see Rupert with Big Mike?"

"Nah."

"Whaddabout Jilly?"

"Big Mike?"

"Yeah."

"Big Mike knew all the girls."

"Did he ever get too friendly with Jilly?"

"Nah. She'd have loved it, though."

"Why ya say that?"

"Jilly was always on the lookout for the guys with bucks."

Salmon scribbles. "Got it, thanks." He looks up and smiles at Jesse. "Okay. That's about all the questions I have for now. Would you get Mr. Kantor for me?"

"Sure. It'll be a few minutes. The boss is pretty busy this time of night."

"Just tell 'm it's me and not to keep me waiting."

"Right." Jesse rises to leave. The music floods in as the door opens. He ducks through, damping out the soundtrack as he shuts the door behind him.

Thinking back through Jesse's answers, Salmon wonders about the Rupert/Rodriguez connections. The more he digs, the more oddities come to light involving those two. How well did Rodriguez really know Jilly? How well did Rodriguez know Rupert? It deserves further investigation. He glances at his watch. *Where's that asshole, Kantor?*

Looking around, he inspects the bank of blank security monitors on a cheap credenza behind the rickety little desk. Jesse's job is obviously more security-oriented than managerial. He wonders what those monitors would show if they were switched on. As he contemplates whether to explore the idea, the soundtrack goes to ten as the door cracks open.

Lenny Kantor crosses to the desk and sits to glare at Salmon.

Salmon returns the glare. "Glad you could finally make it."

Slouching down in the chair, Kantor cocks it sideways, his shoulders hunched, a foul grimace on his pallid features. Hook nose, dark beady eyes and widow's peak complete Kantor's visage of the undead. His thin lips curl in a snarl. "Whaddaya want?"

Salmon grins at Kantor's discomfort. "Not much, just need to ask your employees a few questions?"

Kantor squirms in his chair. "What for?"

"Ya know Lenny, I don't really hafta tell ya. You can start by getting me a list of all your employees at the time Janice Parkson was employed here."

Kantor's frown deepens. "You gotta warrant?"

Salmon sits up, getting in Kantor's face. "You know I can get one, if you want to play it that way. Then I'll drag your sorry ass and every one of your employees down to Violent Crimes and run you all through a meat grinder."

Kantor holds up his hands. "No, no. No need to get shitty, Detective. I'll cooperate, just hold on." He slips out of the chair. "Jesse will get ya what ya need."

"Don't make me wait."

Salmon watches like a hawk as Kantor slinks out of the shabby little office.


The scrawny cocktail waitress with overdone implants and too many tattoos, a foul-mouthed little bitch named Heather, leaves the cramped and dingy room. Her hostile attitude follows her out the sound-deadened door like a black cloud. Salmon leans back in the tattered chair behind Jesse's cheesy little desk, exhaling exhaustion. The constant pounding rhythms echo in his ears like a boom-box stuck on Play. It's after midnight, several hours of mostly bullshit. Thankfully, he's down to his last interview, having questioned nearly every employee for tonight's shift. One to go and he's beat. Jesse brought him a Red Bull earlier. There's still half a can, but it's warm and flat. He needs a fresh one to get him through this last session. *What I really need is to get outta here. Go home. Get some sleep.*

Jesse's huge head ducks through the doorway. "Ready?"

Salmon looks up with bloodshot eyes. "Who's next?"

"Sondra. She's the last one."

"Great, send her in. And could ya get me another Red Bull?"

"Comin' up."

Salmon closes his eyes, just for a minute. The sudden jump in the soundtrack's volume startles him awake, his head jerking forward as his eyes fly open. Closing the door behind her, an attractive, well-endowed blonde swishes into the tiny room. Draped in a sheer silvery little top and sporting a small glittering G-string, she leans too far forward to hand him a sweating can of Red Bull.

Salmon's eyes wander to her too-perfect breasts as he reaches for the Red Bull. "Thanks."

She smiles coyly. "Sorry to wake you."

He shakes his head, slightly embarrassed as he pops the Red Bull's top. "No, it's okay. Sleep is overrated." He takes a long swig of the frosty elixir, his senses coming back to life.

She sits primly in stark contrast to her lack of clothing, crossing her legs in the folding chair, smiling patiently.

Salmon's head begins to clear as the caffeine hits his grumbling stomach. He smiles back. "It's been a long night. You must be Sandra."

"It's Sondra," she says with a pouty little smile.

"Right ... Sondra. Just a few questions, Sondra, and I'll let you get outta here."

"Okay."

"I appreciate your cooperation. Are ya comfortable? Maybe you should put something on."

"No, I'm fine." She arches her back, pulling back her shoulders to push her breasts out and up. "Why, is this bothering you?" Her sensuous lips curl into a Cheshire grin as her eyes sparkle with mischief.

Salmon refuses to be distracted, denying her the upper hand. "You *are* a little underdressed for a police interview, but that's fine." *What the hell, might keep me awake.* He gathers up his notepad and pen. "You knew Jilly?"

Sondra's gaze drops as she slumps in the chair. "Yeah. Too bad about Jilly."

"Were you friends?"

"I knew her, but we weren't close or anything."

"Tell me what she was like."

"Oh, I dunno, kinda wild and crazy, but kinda sad."

"Whaddaya mean?"

"Well, she was always looking for love—you know, Mr. Right. Kinda tough in this profession." She sighs wistfully.

"I see what you mean."

"It caused her a lotta grief."

"Like what?"

"Oh, you know, partyin' with the customers, that sorta thing."

"That how she met her boyfriend?"

"Not sure, maybe. Which one?"

"The guy she was with when she was shot, Daniel Rupert."

"Dunno."

"Whaddaya know about Rupert?"

A wicked little grin curls Sondra's lips. "He's dead."

"Besides that."

"Not much. Seen him around is all."

"Jilly ever say anything to you about Rupert?"

"She seemed pretty excited about him. But she was always like that, at first."

"So this was nothing new?"

"Not really, she was just kiddin' herself. I mean, the guy was married. We'd seen it all before."

"Hmm." Salmon looks down to add a note. Finished, he looks up, pausing to gather his thoughts. "What about Jilly's other boyfriend?"

"Which one?"

"Big Mike."

Sondra pulls back, indignant. "What? Where did you hear that?"

"Just heard they were an item."

"Not Big Mike. Someone's strokin' you, big time."

"Hmm." Salmon rubs his chin then takes another swallow of Red Bull. "But she knew Big Mike."

"Hell, everybody knew Big Mike."

"And Jilly never went out with him?"

"Hell if I know, not my job to babysit, but they were never an item."

"You knew Big Mike, too, then?"

"Sure, who didn't?"

"And you'd know if they were an item."

Sondra sneers at the idea. "Shit, everyone knows everything around here."

"Huh, I heard you were tight with Big Mike."

"Damn, someone's really pumpin' you fulla shit."

"A professional hazard, I'm afraid."

"Who told you that?"

"I heard it a couple times tonight."

"Yeah, well, this place is like that. They'll make up shit just for somethin' to say."

"So how well *did* you know Big Mike?"

"Like all the girls, I guess. A big tipper, so we did our best."

"And I'll bet your best is pretty damn good."

Sondra smiles coyly.

Salmon takes a different tack. "Did any of the girls ever date him?"

"Shit, who knows?"

"Whaddabout you?"

"Nah, I don't date the customers."

"Even if they're big tippers?"

Salmon sees the slow burn in her blue eyes, he's finally getting to her.

"Look, I don't care what you heard. I already told you, I don't date the customers. It's against the rules. Are we done here?"

Salmon's lips twist. Tough cookie—too bad. "Yeah, I guess for now."


It's after one in the morning when Salmon glides the big Mercury down I-17, heading home to a comfortable bed. Still buzzing from the Red Bull, Salmon's mind works overtime, thoughts churning, rehashing the night's interviews. Bouncers, bartenders, cocktail waitresses and strippers, consummate bullshit artists all—what they inferred was more important than what they actually said. It was worth the trip.

Underneath all the canned answers and bogus lines, a few clues reluctantly came to light. It's obvious that Jilly had a problem keeping her hands off the customers which is a big no-no. Apparently, Jilly and Rupert were just getting started. No one openly admitted that Rupert and Rodriguez were more than casual acquaintances, but there are too many coincidences. He'll have to pull that string from a few different directions. *How close was Rupert to Mike Junior? What about Connie Rodriguez?* And the way everyone denied knowing much about Big Mike makes Salmon doubly suspicious.

They all maintained he was just another big tipper. No one but Jesse even mentioned he owned the joint.

A lot of questions whirl through Salmon's thoughts as he struggles to connect the dots. *For that matter, what about Rupert's wife?* In her statement, she claimed she didn't know Jilly. No one asked her about Rodriguez, no reason to until now. *How well did Mrs. Rupert know the Rodriguezes?*

Tons of blanks to be filled in. Salmon resolves to get on it first thing tomorrow. He thinks back to the employees' reticence, almost as though they were coached. Not that surprising. Everyone closes ranks when it comes to the cops. Makes for an interesting and often frustrating game of cat and mouse.

All the employees were tight-lipped, but none more so than the stripper, Sondra. Of all the employees interviewed, she said the least. Which to Salmon's way of looking at it, reveals the most. She has the most to hide. Her physical beauty is the kind every man wishes his wife or girlfriend possessed. Yet, buried beneath those implausibly perfect looks and behind all that simmering sensuality a cool, calculating manipulator pulls all the strings—a maneater, a real pro. *What a way to make a livin'.*

As Salmon wears down, his thoughts wander back to all that sumptuous flesh. Luckily he's headed home to a warm bed and a hot live-in girlfriend. A thoughtful smile lights his tired features. He and Lacey agreed to live together a while ago. She moved in a couple months back. It's been great, one of his better moves. His smile widens as he shakes his head. *Ain't love grand.*

# BACK AT THE DRIVE-THRU

**[8:48 AM – Thursday, March 17, 2011]**

I COME AWAKE easy in the quiet comfort of my little bedroom. The sun's been up awhile now. I lie relaxed, breathing deep. The cool breeze ruffling the faded curtains smells fresh and clean. I smile to myself. I've slept all the way through, hardly any aches and pains, a rarity for me. The knot on my skull has dwindled down to a small sore spot, hardly noticeable unless I press on it. When I wake like this, I can almost believe life is good again, reminiscent of younger days with Sonja. I stretch and yawn, lazily enjoying the simple pleasures of quiet moments alone. Feels good to get away from all the crap, all the drudgery of daily existence. I could stay like this all day.

My mind wanders as I stare through the ceiling. What would life be like if I had some say in the matter, I wonder. I envy those people who seem to have control over their lives, confident and purposeful. How did they get that way? Were they born with it? Is it genetic, did they have the right parents, or what? I recall marveling at Sonja's bright shiny air of confidence. It's what drew me to her when we first met. I know life with me wore her down. But in spite of all the losses life heaped upon us, she always had that glimmer of hope, that seed of certainty that I came to rely on so heavily. I still miss her—miss her every day.

"I'm still here."

I feel Sonja's presence intimately, as though we are one, in the same place, together in time. It *is* a comfort, although just not the same. "Maybe in theory, but not in the flesh."

"Feeling sorry for yourself again?"

"If I don't do it, who will?"

"Nice."

"It's a tough job, but somebody's gotta do it."

"Boy, you're really feelin' your oats this morning."

"Hey, it's not often I get to smile for no reason."

"Yeah, I've noticed. We're gonna change all that."

"You mean I'm done smiling, don't you?"

"No. I mean you'll have plenty of reason to smile."

"Promises, promises ..."

"First, you've got some work to do."

"I knew there was a catch."

"Enough with the snappy banter, listen up."

"I'm all ears. Well, almost, except for the fleshy part in the middle which is actually a nose ..."

"Okay, I *got* it. Now pay attention."

"Right."

"Okay, remember when I had you look in the mirror?"

"Yeah. Hated it."

"This time you can stay right here, but I need you to focus."

"Okay."

"I want you to put your full attention on the time you spent at that crime scene."

"Which one?"

"The most recent one, at that burger stand where the two people were murdered in the drive-thru."

"Actually, it was in the parking lot, but ..."

"No, that's good, continue. What do you see?"

What a miserable night that was. And now, she wants me to go back? *I hate this shit.*

Sonja's voice reverberates in my head. "I can hear you."

Great, all of the drawbacks and none of the benefits ... *what a bitch.*

"I can still hear you."

"Of course you can." There's no getting away from it, she's got me cornered. "Alrighty then, what did you want me to do?"

"Your full attention on the murder scene. Tell me what you see."

"Right." I close my eyes and think back. At first nothing but a dark blurry haze accompanied by a sickly sense of unease. No, it's more like dread. *I really hate this shit.*

"I got it. Keep looking."

"Do I have to describe it to you, or can you just read my thoughts, save me the time?"

"It'd be better if you tell me as you go. Helps clarify it for you."

"Right." I push myself to remember that night. If I recall, I was feeling shitty before I even got there—a harbinger of things to come. My stomach starts to gurgle and my head thickens. So much for my peaceful morning in bed. "It's late at night—I see the news choppers."

"Go on."

"I don't want to do this."

"Do it anyway."

"No, that's what I was thinking, 'I don't want to do this.'"

"I gotcha. Keep going."

"Lacey had called me. Needed pictures of the murder scene."

"Good. What else?"

"I was wondering if it was related to the recurring nightmare, the one about the stripper and the truck."

"You mean, you were wondering that at the time."

"Yeah."

"Good. Okay, what else?"

Images start to coalesce: a big cop blocking me, Salmon and Lacey, the crowd of emergency workers milling around in the parking lot, the whole thing making me dizzy.

"You're doin' good. Keep goin'."

Sonja's calm tone reassures me and I press on.

More ghostly images unfurl, shimmering into view. I'm in a clearing, in the parking lot. A dark mass of energy twists and writhes before me.

Embedded in the roiling mass sits a black Corvette barely visible in the turbulence. "I see the car."

"Whose car?"

"The dead guy's."

"All right. What else do you see?"

An indistinct outline forms on blood-stained concrete next to the car. Gradually, he comes into focus. He's small and wiry, eyes wide in a death stare. His image shimmers as he blinks with surprise, his mouth moving soundlessly like a carp out of water. There's nothing I can do for him now.

I tell Sonja, "The guy ... lying next to the car. He's surprised. Didn't know he was dead at first, then didn't know what to do."

Clear and soft, Sonja says, "Been there ..."

Someone's in the car ... behind the bullet shattered windshield ... I can't quite see through the squirming shadows. I squint hard to get a better view. She's tightly wrapped in dirty swirling layers of cold dark energy, at the center of her own hellish little tornado. Her mouth gapes, her eyes roll in their sockets, walleyed and unseeing, her nostrils flaring with rapid puffs of panic. I desperately want to throw her a safety line, pull her out of the abyss, but I can't reach her. She's long gone.

I try to articulate for Sonja. "The girl in the passenger seat ... she's worse than dead. It drove her insane. She's unreachable."

Sonja whispers as though the dead girl might hear her, "There's nothing you can do for her now. She must find her own way. Don't dwell on it, move on."

I pull myself away, tentatively letting go, reaching out with my mind to feel around in the churning murk. He's in here ... the killer. He's always been here, right behind me, watching me with that malevolent leer. It's as though he's laughing at me, knowing that I know he's here and there's nothing I can do about it. But it's more than that. His laugh is hectic and shrill, more a cackle—the glee of insanity. He's driven by an insatiable hunger for his victims' raw death throes, overconfident in his clever concealment, foolishly believing in his delusion of supreme power. I sense the danger at gut level. His presence makes my skin crawl and I want to get away, before he finds me, before he kills me. Yet I must find a way to stop him, to bring him down.

"Sonja, he's in here with me," I whisper. "What do I do?"

"See without being seen," she whispers. "Find out more. Knowledge is power. At the end of the day, there's really nothing he can do to you."

I move for cover, holing up in a pocket of bunched up shadows, gathering them around me like dark blankets of invisibility. He can't see me. I feel Sonja, she's got my back and I settle in. I peer out to spy on him. He's lost me, unaware that I watch covertly from the cover of darkness.

As I watch, I marvel at the oddity of all this, as physically, I haven't really gone anywhere. This is a way different universe, on its own wavelength, with its own laws that I don't even pretend to comprehend. Sonja has only given me hints and glimpses of this ethereal, otherworldly reality. It seems to exist outside or maybe even surrounding our collectively known universe, that physical universe that we all call day-to-day living. Where she is seems surreal—beautiful and serene. She reigns supreme, as though she's naturally all-knowing, all-powerful, effortless omnipotence, completely self-assured and at ease. It gives her a presence, a radiance more potent than anything I ever experienced when she was alive. And I've come to trust her implicitly. Yet, more often than not, she reveals just enough to leave me guessing. Then there's the killer enveloped in a buzzing, crackling darkness. All I can do is cope with it as best I can and take her word for it.

I carefully scrutinize this maniacal murderer, a conflicted mass of compulsions, driven to kill his fellow human beings, slaking his twisted desires—bizarre in the extreme. I just don't understand how someone can end up like this, but there he is. Other images shimmer into view, a collection of visual memories, snapshots from the back of his mind. Two I recognize instantly: the silver truck; and the high-backed Chippendale cradling the mystery man in the red smoking jacket. A heavy sense of déjà vu grips me at my core. Then there's the nagging feeling that I know … *What is it?*

"I think I know that guy," I whisper.

"The killer?"

"No, the guy in the chair."

"Who is it?"

"I think it's the other guy he killed, Rodriguez."

"You think it's Michael Rodriguez …"

"Yes, no ... Wait, that can't be right. I mean the guy in the smoking jacket is the guy that had Rodriguez killed ... but now it seems like it's Rodriguez. And what's that got to do with the truck? There's something about that truck."

The images swirl and eddy like dust devils on a hot desert day. I can't take it. "This is giving me a headache. I don't get it."

"Just ignore it, keep going, you'll get it."

My vision fades as I reel with confusion, my head thickening with pulsing heat. Suddenly, it's all black and closing in fast.

# MORE MONEY

**[11:48 AM – Friday, March 26, 2010]**

THE DESERT AIR was clear and crisp, a whiff of spring in the light breeze. Powder blue skies stretched from horizon to horizon, a bright shining sun gleaming in the late morning sky. It would be plenty hot soon enough, but today was another gorgeous March day in the Valley of the Sun.

Rodriguez wheeled his work truck into his garage, back from his morning rounds at the MJR jobsites. He had just enough time to check in with Diane and head out to his lunch meeting. He jumped out of his 4X4, heading for the back door of his private office. Rodriguez hung the truck keys on the key rack on the way in, grabbing the Mercedes remote and stuffing it in his pocket.

Diane waited for him on the other side of his massive desk with the inner door closed. She'd maneuvered herself into more than just his bookkeeper and mistress. She also interfaced with the rest of his administrative staff as his executive assistant.

Rodriguez preferred having one person as his gal Friday, handling all the paperwork. It helped cut down on the bullshit. He hated paperwork. No patience for it. And as long as he kept her satisfied, he felt he could trust her.

"Hey babe." He handed her a manila folder stuffed with the week's time sheets and subcontractor invoices from the jobsites. "Here ya go."

Her hazel eyes sparkled, taking the fat folder and handing him an envelope. "Thanks, Michael. Here's your tickets and parking pass for tonight. I got the extra tickets from Gary, like you asked."

"That's great, babe."

"Gary isn't using his. Guess he's going to Vegas."

Rodriguez shook his head. "That sonofabitch is always in Vegas. All that money for season tickets and he hardly ever makes a game. That's good though, Mikey'll love it."

"Who's playing?"

"Suns 'n Lakers. Extra tickets are for Mikey's friends. He doesn't know yet. Didn't want to say anything until we got the tickets." Rodriguez pointed at the folder in Diane's hand. "Take care of those for me. Gotta run."

Diane smiled. "Sure. You meeting with Mr. Cohen?"

As the AMG Mercedes accelerated out of the MJR yard, Rodriguez punched voice-activation. The S65's androgynous computer announced it was ready for his command.

"Dial Mikey."

"Dialing Mikey."

His son's cell phone rang. The kids were on spring break, should be no trouble reaching him.

"Hi, Son. Whatcha up to?"

"Just hangin' with Chad and Jason."

"Why don't you ask them if they're busy tonight."

"Sure, whassup?"

"Got extra Suns tickets for 'em, if they want to go."

"You're kidding! That's great! Hold on."

Rodriguez's smile broadened. He loved surprising his son. He got so excited.

Mikey came back on, bubbling with enthusiasm. "Yeah, sure! They can go! Thanks, Dad!"

"Okay. I'll call you after my lunch meeting and we'll work it out."

Still grinning, Rodriguez ended the call. He could hardly wait. Tonight would be great. Rodriguez cranked the volume, bobbing his head to the music as the Mercedes whisked him toward the Chuck Wagon and his lunch with Cohen & Company.

Rodriguez heard about the hard-money lenders from Goodson, one of their entitlement attorneys. The buzz was these guys had tons of private money to loan on real estate projects and funded fast. Just what he needed. Goodson added that Cohen was a piece of work, not just your typical loan shark. He went on to say he'd heard Cohen rarely funded the full amount of the loans he closed—said he had a nasty habit of defaulting borrowers and foreclosing. Goodson figured the guy was a snake. But what the hell, Rodriguez figured he could handle Cohen, no problem. Besides, Sunset Pointe was taking too long to finish. The extended stay hotel had been de-layed indefinitely. Plus the ongoing hassle with the City and slow pre-leasing was rapidly sucking all the cash out of MJR Development. Along with everything else, the project's cost overruns and funding delays from Fellman cramped his style. It boiled down to the fact that too many eggs in one basket made him uncomfortable.

Rodriguez had a couple sweet deals he wanted in on. He knew these guys doing smaller real estate flipping scams. With very little down they could easily double his money by buying cheap, securing new financing and cashing out. Plus it added assets to his balance sheet, increasing his net worth, giving him more borrowing power—perfect.

He'd go for the kill. Cohen & Company should get him the money he needed, pronto. He'd put up his equity in Sunset Pointe and make sure his attorneys covered his ass. What could Cohen do? Of course he'd need Fellman to get him past the secondary financing prohibition clauses in the First Community loan. Fellman would whine about it, but he'd do it. Fellman had no choice.

Rodriguez grinned as he drummed on the wheel in time to the music. Things were lining up. *Money in the bank.* It was going to be a good day.

Thirty minutes late, Rodriguez pushed through the Chuck Wagon's thick oak door. He hustled across the dining room, kicking his size twelve crosstrainers through the sawdust. He'd called ahead to make sure Cohen would wait for him. Cohen had sounded a little aloof, but agreed.

Striding up to his booth, Rodriguez saw three guys working on their lunches. A tall drink of water in a Stetson Carson sat at one end, a frosty glass of lager tipped to his lips. The guy looked vaguely familiar. The way it hung loose on his lanky frame, he suspected the guy's Western jacket concealed a shoulder holster. In the booth's center sat a plump, pear-shaped little man dressed to the nines. His fleshy boyish cheeks vigorously chewed a bite of steak. A stocky bulldog of a man in a suit two sizes too small crouched at the other end of the booth nursing an iced tea. *Hmm, what kinda lenders are these guys?*

Rodriguez grinned. "Gentlemen. Enjoying your lunch?"

The slick little fat boy looked up at Rodriguez while he chewed.

"Mike Rodriguez." He waited expectantly for the men to introduce themselves.

Fat Boy swallowed, set down his silverware, extended a small hand, giving Rodriguez a sly little grin. "Benjamin Cohen, nice to finally meet you."

Ignoring Cohen's little jab, Rodriguez took Cohen's soft little hand, careful not to crush it. "Lemme grab a chair and I'll join you."

From the nearest table, Rodriguez hefted a chair in one hand, swung it around to face the booth and sat. The other two men hadn't said anything, so Rodriguez pressed the issue. He reached a hand to the stone-faced bulldog and repeated himself. "Mike Rodriguez."

Bulldog grabbed his hand in a vise-like grip. "Noel Redman." Releasing his grip, he sullenly turned back to his iced tea.

Rodriguez turned to the cowboy, extending his hand. "Mike Rodriguez."

The cowboy gave him a sneer and took his hand with a firm shake. "Charlie Stein."

Rodriguez turned to catch the waitress. "Ginger, gimme a barbeque pulled pork and a Diet Coke."

"Coming right up, Mr. Rodriguez."

Rodriguez turned back to find Cohen sizing him up, Cohen's eyes glistening like a predator. "Our attorney tells me your company is lending on development projects. A rarity these days."

Cohen slowly cut a bite of steak, popped it in his mouth and methodically chewed as he casually watched Rodriguez.

Rodriguez waited. *What's he playing at?*

Cohen took his sweet time. Finally, he swallowed and smiled. "My investors always have money for the right people and projects."

Rodriguez sat forward. "Tell me about your loan programs."

Cohen casually took a drink of water, slowly set it down and carefully licked his lips as he delicately dabbed at the corners of his mouth with his napkin. Setting his napkin by the side of his plate, he leaned back. "We tailor our loans to meet our customers' needs. Tell me a little bit about what you're looking for."

*This guy* is *a snake. Okay, Game on.* Rodriguez leaned back, not wanting to appear too eager. *First order of business, let 'em know who's boss.* "We haven't really decided if we want to borrow any more against our project. Kinda testin' the water."

Cohen grinned. "Well then, tell me a little bit about your project."

"We have a little mixed-use commercial project at the southwest corner of 40th Street and Union Hills, right off the 51."

"Great location. Is that your Sunset Pointe project?"

Cohen's interest perked him up. "That's right. You familiar with Sunset Pointe?"

"I make it my business to know."

"It's a combination of upscale shops and dining with residential lofts above, along with a Class 'A' office complex and an extended stay hotel. A little over a hundred thousand square feet."

"Sounds like a winner. What else can you tell me?"

"Gimme your card and I'll have my assistant email you a brochure."

Cohen flashed his diamond cufflinks as he extracted a business card and handed it over to Rodriguez.

"Thanks. I'll get it over to you this afternoon."

"I'll look for it. How much do you think you're going to want?"

"Haven't really decided yet. We already have a construction loan with a permanent take-out commitment for twenty-two five. Anything we did would have to be on top of that."

"We do that all the time. How much would you want on a second?"

"Another seven point five ought to do it."

Cohen smiled broadly. "No problem, consider it done."

Rodriguez sat back. Cohen was moving too fast, making him suspicious. Another seven and a half million and the combined financing would exceed the project's appraised value by a fair chunk. "I'll need to know terms and I guess you'll want my financials before we go further."

"I'll email you a commitment letter with terms. And don't worry about financials, just a formality. We know you're good for it."

This guy was way too slick, but a quick seven and a half million made Rodriguez ignore any misgivings.

"Our investors always make money, whatever it takes," said Cohen. "It's my job to make sure they get their return on investment, one way or another."

Rodriguez guardedly eyed the two thugs on either side of Cohen. Cohen's veiled threat was not lost on Rodriguez, but he simply couldn't resist that much easy money. Besides, he knew it would be no problem paying it off once they completed construction. Once he saw the terms, he knew he'd go ahead. Didn't much matter, he'd already made his decision. *Just gimme the money.*

# BLIND LEADING THE BLIND

**[1:51 PM – Thursday, March 17, 2011]**

THIN FLOWERED CURTAINS flutter, puffed by light gusts through the window screen—the background traffic noise, a dull hum. How long have I been out? I let the sounds drift through the darkness before I pry open my crusty lids. Flat on my back, right where I started, only this time it's with a thick head and aching bones. Feels like I've been run over by a bus. Not the kind of day I had in mind. These visions are driving me nuts. Why can't I get them outta my head? Why do I bother with all this paranormal bullshit? If only I could stop. Why can't Sonja just leave me alone? All I wanna be is a photographer. I'm only kidding myself. I can't tell shit from those visions. How could I possibly know who the killers are? *Damn it! Now what?*

I can tell before she speaks, Sonja's back. "You need to tell Detective Salmon."

"Tell him what? That I've gone nuts? I'm sure he already suspects."

"Just tell him what you saw."

"Great, but I don't really know *what* I saw. Besides, I already told him there are two killers: the one doing the shooting; and the one in the chair telling him who to shoot. And now, you want me to tell him we're back to one killer because the guy in the chair might be Rodriguez? Fat chance, he'll blow me off as a crackpot. Hell, I wouldn't blame him at this point."

I pause to catch my breath. Sonja isn't answering, she's already gone.

I struggle to sit up on the side of my bed, head in hands, elbows on my knees. I've got to sort this out, think it through, make some sort of sense out of it. I rehash this morning's visions: the dead guy, Rupert sprawled on the concrete in his own blood; the lifeless, mindless stripper, bullet holes gaping, spirit trapped in madness; and the killer, his maniacal delusion, his bloodlust. Then there are the superimposed images: the diamond-tuck cordovan leather on the back of the Chippendale; hands protruding from the sleeves of a red smoking jacket, a cigar in one and a drink in the other; the flatscreen alive with the writhing flesh of some porno. And floating beneath the surface is the monster truck with the promise of more deaths to come. My head spins as I try to grasp the meaning of it all. It's too much. Better to concentrate on the little things, the details. Maybe help the detective figure it out. *Shit, who knows?*

My head pounds as I struggle to my feet and head for the john, off to a rocky start. *A piss and some coffee, then I'll call.*


I grab my cell off the counter, pull up the detective's number and tap Call. As I listen to his phone ring, I wonder just what in the hell I'm going to say.

"What can I do for ya, Lance?" Salmon's tone is unaffected as usual.

I grab my raw nerves by the throat and squeeze, struggling to gain control. "You told me to call if I got anything, even if it seemed like nothing."

"Right. Whaddaya got?"

"Well ... not really sure yet. Can you tell me if you've found a connection between these drive-thru murders and the Rodriguez case?"

"Nothing solid, but the vics *did* know each other."

"What, Rupert knew Rodriguez?"

"Yup. And Janice Parkson, the other vic, worked at Rodriguez's strip club."

Bolts of bright light flash behind my eyes. "Wow, no wonder ..."

"No wonder what?"

"It's been confusing. Impressions from both murder cases all jumbled, like it's an ongoing saga instead of separate cases." Kaleidoscopes of bright colors pinwheel through my vision and spin away.

"So ya got anything for me?"

I pause to get my bearings. "It still seems like a conspiracy of some sort. Not sure how Rodriguez fits into it, but he's more than just a victim. And this psycho killer thinks he's invincible, getting ready to kill again."

"Anything else?"

"Can't be sure, but it seems like Rodriguez, Rupert and Janice Parkson knew their killer. Are you checking for friends, family and acquaintances?"

"Workin' on it. Can you give me any details?"

Then it occurs to me. "Do you know if Rodriguez smoked cigars?"

"Why would that be important?"

"Can't be sure, but that image of the cigar smoker in the chair keeps haunting me. That and that damned truck. Any luck finding that truck?"

"Not so far."

"I'm *sure* it's the killer's truck. If you can find it you've got him nailed."

"May take awhile. You got any idea how many late-model Ford F-150 trucks are registered in Arizona? And for all we know, that truck may not even be registered here. A plate, even a partial would be a huge help."

"Sorry, it's obscured. I think the killer did it intentionally." There's silence on the line as I try hard to think what else could be important. "Do you know if Rodriguez has a high-backed armchair with the back done in diamond-tuck burgundy-colored leather?"

"How the hell would I know that?"

"I dunno, you're the detective."

"Yeah, well, why would I even care?"

"One of the guys you're looking for is the guy in the picture."

"Which picture?"

"The double exposure of the chair superimposed over the killer's truck. The guy has a den or smoking room with a flatscreen and that chair. He also wears a red smoking jacket, smokes cigars, drinks liquor, and watches porn."

"Great, that narrows it down."

"You asked for details. I'm doin' my best here." Frustration rises to a low boil.

"What about the killer, the guy pullin' the trigger?"

"I dunno, a big guy, could be a cowboy or just uses it as a disguise, he's gotta grey cowboy hat, boots and a black semi-automatic."

"Terrific, probably more grey cowboy hats in Arizona than there are F-150s."

Exasperation gets the best of me. "Look, I dunno what to tell ya. It's all I've got!"

"Easy there, just keep doin' what you're doin'." Salmon's tone is calm, reassuring. "Maybe something useful will come to you. Never know."

I disconnect, head whirling like a dervish, disappointed that I don't know any more than when I called, disgusted that the killer still runs loose, discouraged that I'm not much help. *Fuck it, I'm going back to bed.*

# HITTING THE BRICKS

**[3:08 PM – Thursday, March 17, 2011]**

THE AFTERNOON SUN cuts through the gun-slot window behind Salmon's metal desk, running a narrow swath of bright glare diagonally across his cluttered desktop. He leans back, digesting Underphal's call. It's uncanny how Underphal's description of the killer matches eyewitness accounts. Amazingly, the guy's right. Although by now, he should be used to it. Too bad he isn't coming up with anything useful. Still, it helps confirm evidence and point the investigation in new directions.

Connections between Rodriguez and the drive-thru vics, there's bound to be something else. He wonders if the truck will pull things together. Leaning forward, he opens the fat file. He picks the most recent report on the elusive F-150. A lot of legwork. Hundreds of silver late-model F-150s checked and eliminated. Several near misses. His special truck detail is roughly three-quarters of the way through the list without a hit. There's still a strong possibility that they'll get to the end of the list without finding it. He tosses the report back into the open file. He needs another angle, just in case. *Time to hit the bricks.*

Salmon's Mercury rumbles out of the police parking garage, heading for the I-10 onramp. Squinting at the afternoon glare, he drops the visor. Three-thirty p.m. and it's officially rush hour, traffic snarling bumper to bumper, exhaust fumes watering his eyes. He plugs Mrs. Rupert's address into his computer as he sits in gridlock. Directions to her home in northwest Phoenix pop up on his monitor.

Stuck at the on-ramp, Salmon mentally runs through the file notes on Marcia Lago-Rupert. Daniel Rupert's murder should be an open and shut case. All the usual indicators point to Marcia Lago-Rupert as the prime suspect, the jealous wife in the midst of a messy divorce. And yet, her alibi seems airtight. The field interviews give the impression the Ruperts were sleeping around and fighting about it. Domestic disturbance reports seem to bear that out. There had been three calls to the local substation within the last four months from nosy neighbors. The reports described run-of-the-mill domestic bouts, yelling and screaming, slamming doors, smashed houseware, broken furniture, etc. Yet, no physical abuse had been reported by the officers on the scene.

According to those interviewed, Mr. Rupert had more than one transgression against Mrs. Rupert. Besides the Parkson woman, the homicide statements mention a history of womanizing. The same statements accuse Mrs. Rupert of her own varied and numerous indiscretions. However so far, there's no hard evidence Mrs. Rupert has been involved with other men. Seems simple enough, enraged wife kills cheating husband, a no-brainer.

The only problem with that scenario is her alibi. Mrs. Rupert happened to be working late the evening of her husband's murder. As co-owner of their martial arts studio, she handled the administrative duties and was working with their bookkeeper in their office at the time. The bookkeeper corroborated her story. It's almost too convenient. Was it staged? But if *she* hadn't arranged the killings, then who? To date there are no other potential suspects, nothing but dead ends. He may not be able to prove it yet, but Salmon would bet a month's salary it was her.

Once on the freeway, Salmon pushes the Marauder to the HOV lane. He flashes past a sea of red brake lights crawling along the northbound lanes. Some asshole cuts him off, trying to maneuver into the carpool lane. Salmon blips his siren and lights. The guy in an Escalade panics and slows down to pull over. Salmon speeds past. Nearing the Northern Avenue exit, he starts to work his way across the plugged lanes. Traffic's a bitch and his patience wears thin. It reminds him of his early days as a uniform. Traffic duty, a thankless job. Of course, Homicide is often no better.

Salmon slows as he turns off Northern into an older neighborhood. Mature date palms rise thirty-forty feet into the bright afternoon sky, lining the narrow side streets like alien sentries. A typical Phoenix subdivision, every house is one of three elevations, cookie-cutter in the extreme. Most of the houses are dated but well-kept, their ranch-style slump block facades and pitched shingle roofs showing their age.

He pulls the unmarked Marauder to the curb in front of Rupert's address, sees the Lexus SUV in the driveway and figures she's home. Turning the microrecorder to voice-activate, he drops it into his shirt pocket. He logs out, turns off the ignition and slides out of the car. He didn't call ahead, didn't want to give her time to put up her guard. As he strides up the driveway, he notices the front window drapes move. *Someone's home.* At the front door, he rings the bell and out of the corner of his eye, catches the drapes swishing again. He waits a few moments and when no one answers, rings the bell again. He waits awhile longer. *Hmm, someone's hiding.* Tired of the little charade, he pounds the door with his fist. "Police, open up."

The door whips open partway to reveal a small well-built woman with dark curly hair and flashing green eyes. "Sorry, Officer. I was just getting dressed."

Incredulous, Salmon puts a formal edge in his voice. "It's Detective, actually. Detective Salmon, Homicide. You Marcia Lago-Rupert?"

She feigns sheepishness, her eyes downcast. "Sorry, Detective. Yes. What can I do for you?"

"I have a few questions for you. Mind if I come in?"

She swings the door wide and steps aside to let him in. "No, not at all."

As he walks into the tiled entry, she smiles up at him. "You must be here about my husband, Daniel."

"That's right. Sorry for your loss."

She waves an arm toward a couch in the living room to his left.

As he moves across the thick carpet to the couch, she follows behind chattering away. "Thank you, Detective Salmon. You're very kind. It's been extremely difficult for me since Daniel's death. I've been so busy I really haven't had much of a chance to grieve. What with the all the funeral arrangements and everything and keeping the studio going, I mean, I just haven't had time ... our pastor says ..."

As he turns and sits, he gives her a half-hearted smile and interrupts. "I'm sure it's been difficult. I just have a few questions, won't take much of your time."

She sits in a velour armchair across from him, smiling expectantly with the faintest hint of sensuality. Under different circumstances, he'd swear she's flirting. He's seen people behave in a great many quirky and unpredictable ways, reacting strangely to the violent death of a family member. It never ceases to amaze him. Yet in this case, it hardly seems she's overcome with grief.

Salmon leans forward, resting his elbows on his knees, fixing her with a penetrating gaze. "Mrs. Rupert, do you know if your husband knew a Michael J. Rodriguez?"

A quick snap of fear darts through her eyes and settles into a quizzical look. "Well, uh, let's see ... Of course, his son, Mikey, was one of Daniel's students."

He drops his gaze at her obvious dodge, pausing for effect. He lifts his eyes to reengage her. "How 'bout other than the son's classes?"

She averts her eyes to the ceiling as though seriously contemplating his question. She answers too quickly, eyes darting, looking everywhere but at him. "Well, I know Daniel asked him for business advice on occasion. Mr. Rodriguez was developing the land next to our studio, you know. Daniel said he was a smart man and very helpful ... and ..."

"I see."

Stepping on her mid-sentence, Salmon shuts her up, holding the silence to sweat her. She fidgets, bouncing a knee and knotting her fingers, still avoiding his stare.

"And how well did *you* know Big Mike?" he asks.

She sits upright emitting a short gasp. "Oh, uh ... not hardly at all, not really. I mean I knew who he was of course, but didn't really *know* him. I uh, know his wife, Connie. I mean we are friends because of her son taking classes and all. We see each other occasionally, for lunch and stuff, just to get together. Terrible about her husband. Daniel and I really liked ..."

"Mrs. Rupert ..."

"Uh ... yes?"

"That's fine, Mrs. Rupert. Let me make sure I've got this straight. You didn't know Big Mike at all?"

"Yes, that's right. He was Daniel's friend. Connie was—is my friend, didn't really know him."

"I see." Salmon looks down at the carpet to give her time to compose herself. He purses his lips, casually raising his glance. "Mrs. Rodriguez ever confide in you, say anything about her husband's murder or the woman he was with at the time of his death?"

Salmon watches her eyes flick around the room. Tiny beads of perspiration form on her upper lip and forehead as she wrings her hands. After a few moments she seems to calm herself. She leans in, eyes askance as though about to share a confidence.

"Well, Connie was devastated, of course. I mean her husband shot dead, and then, with another woman, you can just imagine, poor thing ..."

Salmon wonders where in the world this woman is coming from, describing the same scenario as her husband's homicide. *How bizarre.* Maybe she is still in shock or too heavily medicated. *Damn!*

"Excuse me. Mrs. Rupert ..." He waits for her to shut up before continuing. "Do you know Diane Telafano?"

"Who? Oh, uh, the woman that was shot with Mr. Rodriguez, oh yes. No, I don't know her. But Connie told me that she'd done it before. Slept with her husband, I mean. But I ..."

"Right, well ... thank you very much Mrs. Rupert." Salmon pushes off the couch. "I'll be in touch if I have any other questions."

As he moves toward the door, she follows, chattering incessantly. *No wonder her husband was playing around.* He smiles stiffly and turns away, tuning her out, glad to get away from the psycho bitch from hell.

It's late afternoon and traffic worsens, the freeways reduced to parking lots, everybody edgy, in a hurry to get home and going nowhere fast. Surface streets aren't much better, long lines of frowning motorists at every light. Salmon checks the traffic reports and wheels the big Mercury out onto Northern heading east. Every day nerves fray, road rage rearing its ugly head. And it's always worse during peak hours. Over the years he's had his share of homicides from irate drivers killing each other—stupid and senseless. He'd avoid the rush hour traffic if he could, but he wants to get to the Rodriguez home yet today, hopefully catch Connie Rodriguez before her crazy-ass friend Marcia calls.

Methodically making his way through the stop-and-go traffic, Salmon ponders the implications of Marcia Lago-Rupert's behavior. It's never much of a challenge to know when people are lying. The trick is finding out what they're hiding, or if they're hiding anything at all. Some people are compulsive liars, apparently lying with no real agenda or nothing better to do. Hard to tell what Mrs. Rupert is hiding, obviously lying through her teeth. If nothing else, her body language would give her away. She's hiding something, but did she kill him?

Wondering if she's clever enough to arrange her husband's murder, Salmon waits behind a line of cars for the next light. He can't get over her bizarre mannerisms and her eerie little story about poor Connie Rodriguez. And the compulsive yammering. Could hardly shut the bitch up. *If she's not bug-shit crazy, she's damn close.*

Salmon turns east onto Dynamite, looking for the gated entrance to Desert Pueblos. At the adobe guardhouse, he's kept waiting while the uniformed security guard has a lengthy discussion with the Rodriguez house. Apparently, his unscheduled visit is going over like a lead balloon. Finally, he's waved through and eases the Marauder up the adobe-paved lane. He pulls through the Rodriguez home's massive stone archway, across the broad circular drive and parks at the base of the terraced steps. As he closes the car door, he sees Connie Rodriguez standing just inside the entry courtyard, ready to intercept him. Salmon waves politely and ascends the stone steps.

"Mrs. Rodriguez. Thanks for seeing me on short notice."

Connie waits until they're face to face. The thin veneer of makeup over Connie's cover-girl features fails to mask her anxiety. "Detective Salmon, this is a bit unexpected. Is there any way we can reschedule? I have another engagement in a half hour."

"My apologies for not notifying you in advance. However, this is an ongoing homicide investigation. It can't wait."

Connie's face reddens as her mouth opens and shuts with a slight spluttering sound.

Salmon fixes her with a severe look while he waits.

Connie drops her face, eyes downcast, shoulders slumping slightly. "Let me make a couple calls." She turns to head into the house.

"No problem." Salmon follows her elegant sway through the lush courtyard.

She pauses in the cavernous entry hall to grab a smartphone off a rough-hewn console. She turns to Salmon at the great room's sunken entry and motions him in. "Please excuse me while I make a call."

Salmon nods and steps into the great room. He ambles across the thick-pile carpet to the floor-to-ceiling glass. While he waits, he admires the panoramic view, the setting sun painting an opulent desert sky: a panoply of gleaming golds, brilliant oranges, reds and purples.

In the window's reflection Salmon sees her enter. He turns and catches her with a measured gaze, checking her mood. Avoiding his eyes, she crosses to the leather couch and sits. He strides to the couch and sits facing her.

"Thank you for your cooperation, Mrs. Rodriguez. Again, my apologies for interrupting your busy schedule. Unfortunately, this can't wait."

"I understand, Detective. What is it?"

"I assume you're aware that Daniel Rupert has been murdered."

Connie's face crumples with grief. Tears forming in the corners of her crystal blue eyes, she wipes at her cheeks with the back of her hand and takes a deep ragged breath.

More of a reaction than Salmon was expecting and he zeroes in. "You knew Daniel Rupert well?"

She struggles to compose herself. "Sorry." Wiping her cheeks again, she then dabs at corners of her eyes with her fingertips. "No, not well. It's just that it's overwhelming ... my husband and then Daniel. When's the nightmare end?"

Salmon waits silently. "We're doin' our best Mrs. Rodriguez. That's why I'm here now."

"Sorry."

"It's okay. Please, tell me what you can about Daniel Rupert. I understand he was your son's karate instructor ..."

"Yes, that's right. But I pulled Michael Junior out of those classes a few weeks ago."

"I see. And why was that?"

He observes her hesitation, as she searches for an answer.

"Personal reasons."

"I see. I'm sure you had your son's best interests at heart. And did you ever see Daniel Rupert in any other context, I mean, besides being your son's karate instructor?"

Her look turns thoughtful. "Because of my son's classes, we got to be friends."

"You and Daniel Rupert."

"Yes, and Marcia and my husband, too."

"You were all friends."

"Not close, but we knew them. My husband helped Daniel with his business. His studio is right next door to one of my husband's developments."

"Yes, of course. Your husband was friends with Daniel. And you, you are friends with Marcia?"

"We used to be friendly, go to lunch and stuff, but not close. I haven't seen her since my son quit going, since before Daniel—Mr. Rupert's death."

"I see." Salmon pauses, wanting to ease past her defenses. "How'd your son do in karate?"

Connie smiles wistfully. "He was doin' great, hated to quit, could hardly pull him away." She shakes her head as she recollects.

Salmon gives her a moment. "Please, don't think me indelicate, but this may be important. Can you tell me more about your decision to pull your son out of karate?"

Her face scrunches into a frown, brow deeply furrowed.

He watches her carefully, giving her time to open up.

After a lengthy pause, she replies, "It didn't have anything to do with his instructor, Mr. Rupert."

"Uh huh ..."

"It really was more about Marcia."

"Marcia?"

"Yeah, she uh … How can I say this? … I was concerned about her behavior … in front of my son."

"Please, help me understand."

"Well, we're good Christians … and I, uh … was concerned about her morals."

"And what caused you to be concerned?"

"I'd heard that she was having trouble with her marriage."

"What kinda trouble?"

"Well, I dunno exactly—like she'd made a pass at one of the students. I just got worried, didn't want Mikey exposed to that sort of thing."

"I understand completely. Don't blame you a bit. Anything else?"

"We were at lunch one day and I remember her telling me that she suspected her husband was having an affair."

"Did she give you any more details?"

"Just that she thought it might be—oh my God, I can't believe I'm saying this—Diane Telafano."

"Your husband's bookkeeper?"

"Yeah, I don't know if it's true. Marcia was angry, said she'd kill her if she found out it was her."

"Kill Ms. Telafano?"

"Like I said, she was angry. I don't know if it's true."

Salmon leans forward. "Connie, please. You can tell me. Did Marcia molest your son?"

Connie drops her face in her hands, sobbing. "God help me, I don't know. I just don't know."

Salmon reaches out and rests a hand on her shoulder. Inside, he's running rampant with possibilities as more pieces to the puzzle fall into place.

# INTERVIEW WITH
# A HOMEWRECKER

**[8:28 AM – Friday, March 18, 2011]**

A LIGHT HAZE, fresh after a pre-dawn shower. The blustery sky clearing to azure blue, filled with puffy clouds, shafts of sunlight shining through, bathing the desert floor in a warm glow. New shoots glisten emerald with dew, greening suburban yards. Plants blossoming, birds singing with the promise of spring. Cool and brisk, an invigorating scent magically transforms the senses, lingering humidity charging the desert air with life. A brand new day and a beautiful spring morning in the Valley of the Sun.

Draining his coffee mug, Salmon turns away from the balcony railing, savoring the crisp morning air before stepping through the slider. He parks the mug on the counter and heads for the door, ready for another sunny day.

Salmon unconsciously whistles an upbeat tune as he climbs into his Mercury. He's never felt better. He and Lacey are hitting it off, getting along great. And making love in the morning is a great way to start the day. He can barely contain himself.

Cruising on I-17, headed for Anthem, Salmon revisits all the clues from yesterday's interviews with Marcia Lago-Rupert and Connie Rodriguez. The new leads excite him, driving him to push hard before the trail fades. These newly exposed relationships put a fresh spin on all the evidence collected, so far. Rupert and his wife, Rodriguez and his wife, all seem to have Diane Telafano in common. He's confident Ms. Telafano will shed valuable light on his investigations.

Exiting on Daisy Mountain Drive, Salmon wheels the big Marauder through Anthem. The sacred sameness, all frame and stucco cookie cutters—hypnotic. He wonders how the middle class lives. Do they go through life in a trance, every day a monotony of work, wife and kids? He cringes at conjured images of human slaves, little more than meat robots preprogrammed to fatalistically trudge through life in lockstep. He shakes his head to clear the sordid pictures from his mind. *A brave new world.*

Salmon raps sharply on the screened security door. He's batting a thousand with his tactic of showing up unannounced, figuring the odds are better with Telafano. He stands waiting for several moments then knocks again and rings the bell. Behind the security screen the front door slowly opens part way. He can't make out who's in the shadows, obscured by the screen, but he suspects it's Angela Telafano.

"Mrs. Telafano?"

Without a word, a liver-spotted claw reaches out to open the screen door. The dour middle-aged mother gives him a stern look. "You again. What do you want?"

Salmon attempts a smile. "Mrs. Telafano, is Diane available? I need to speak with her. Urgent police business."

She mumbles as she moves aside to let him in. "Does it ever stop with you people?"

Salmon ignores her and moves to the stained couch.

Mrs. Telafano disappears down the hall.

As he sits, Salmon takes in his surroundings—the living room, close with heavy ornate drapes pulled against the light as though hiding in a shadowy tomb. His nose crinkles at the faint odor of decay permeating the musty air, reminiscent of shut-ins. A particularly oppressive atmosphere given the fresh clean air outside. He adjusts his frame of mind to ignore the assault on his senses and focus on the job before him. *Got a couple cases to solve here.*

Diane Telafano slowly wheels herself in. Haggard and pale, she looks beaten down, physical deterioration setting in, flaccid flesh, atrophied limbs, thick torso, bent spine, dark circles under her eyes. A sour chemical smell of medicine, rancid flesh and stale sweat surrounds her in an odorous cloud.

Salmon sees it in her half-closed eyes, she's succumbed to the hopelessness that overwhelms so many young paraplegics, realizing a normal, healthy life has escaped them. Violent death is one thing, but to be entombed in your own flesh seems the worst sort of hell. Her life gone in a muzzle flash, a modern-day tragedy. It's the reason he embarked on a career in law enforcement, to prevent such tragedies from occurring in the first place. Seeing her like this is difficult, tough to cope. He struggles, his bright new day sucked away, absorbed by the rotting gloom of the Telafano house. He hangs his head for an instant, clearing his mind before he tackles the grim task at hand. He reminds himself. *Sympathy doesn't help anyone.*

Diane comes to a stop across from him, cocking her wheelchair at an angle. "Hello, Detective."

Leaning forward, bracing his elbows on his knees, Salmon smiles politely. "Ms. Telafano. Thanks for seeing me this morning."

Distant and somber, she gives him a detached gaze. "Not doing anything else."

"I just have a few questions for you, this morning. Help clear up a couple things for our investigations."

She slowly nods.

"I assume you're aware of the recent homicides. Two victims were killed in a fast-food drive-thru in north Phoenix."

"Saw it on the news."

"Ms. Telafano, did you know Daniel Rupert?" As he asks, he scrutinizes her closely, looking for any sign of recognition.

Her vacant eyes turn toward the drapes, her features deadpan. "Knew of him."

He wonders if her emotions are as lifeless as her legs. "How 'bout the other victim, Janice Parkson?"

"No."

"Some people knew her as Jilly ..."

"No." Her eyes wander back to Salmon's face. "Why are you asking *me?*"

"Do you know a Marcia Lago-Rupert, the victim's wife?"

A wry smile crosses her lips as she gazes at the floor. "No, not really."

He'll need to penetrate her apathy if he's going to have any chance of gaining her confidence. Otherwise, her stonewalling will result in another dead end. Not what he came for.

He opens up to her. "Look, Ms. Telafano, I know this must be difficult for you. I am truly, very sorry, but I wouldn't be here if it wasn't important. You can't know how helpful you've been. Your contributions have helped fill important gaps in the Rodriguez case, a case that I'm still actively working. We ... I really need your help here—you can do a good thing."

She looks up, eyes glistening with tears. "I don't know what you want me to do."

"This will be painful, but I've got to let you know ... Mrs. Rodriguez claims you knew Daniel Rupert well, perhaps even intimately."

Diane's face twists with rage. "That bitch! She's still trying to get me! Hasn't she done enough?" She drops her face into her hands, sobbing.

Angela Telafano scurries into the room to glare at Salmon.

Seeing her mother, Diane chokes back her sobbing. "It's okay, Mother, it's okay, please."

Scowling, Angela Telafano stalks from the room.

"Sorry, I know how you feel about Mrs. Rodriguez. Where do you think she might've gotten such an idea."

Diane sniffles. "She hates me, she tried to kill me. Why don't you ask Marcia Rupert?"

"Ask her what?"

"About that bitch, Connie."

"What about her?"

"I'm sure she hates Marcia, too."

"Why would she hate Mrs. Rupert?"

"That little slut was fucking Michael."

"Michael Rodriguez?"

Overcome, Diane breaks down, weeping uncontrollably, her breath coming in short gasps. Angela rushes to her side. Salmon watches for a moment as Angela tries to console her. He carefully rises, excuses himself and heads for the door.

# BACK IN
# THE SADDLE

**[11:19 AM – Thursday, March 24, 2011]**

IT'S BEEN AN interesting few days, parked in my broken down recliner, sucking beer from longnecks like it's mother's milk, glued to the
mind-numbing flatscreen—life on the Dark Side. Things have settled down
a little and I'm back to my more or less normal routine, furiously avoiding
reality at the altar of the so-called average American's latest religion, Reality
TV. Now that I'm not bombarded on every side by bizarre ailments, I'm
putting things into perspective between commercial breaks with Dr. Phil
and Oprah. After lengthy deliberation and occasional inebriation, I've deftly
determined Sonja is right. This psychic shit—I need to look at it as an opportunity. I might actually accomplish something good here. Just too bad it
isn't more practical. It'd be great if I could pick the winning Powerball
numbers. I'd be on a beach somewhere in the Caribbean sipping a margarita
with Jimmy Buffet, lose some weight, get a tan. Who knows, maybe I could
get him to do a ringtone for my cell, introduce me to a couple of those
beach bunnies. It'd be nice to be a winner for a change. Yet, here I am,
alone in this dump, well below the poverty line, twiddling my thumbs while
hoping I don't get slammed by another episode. Like I said, more or less
normal, wallowing in self-pity like a hippo in a mud bog.

    I need to get off my dead ass and do something, anything, even if it's
wrong. So far, my life has been pretty much a waste. This could quite

possibly be the last best chance I have. And regardless of how painful, I need to see it through—do my best to make sure that monster doesn't kill again. *Okay. So what do I do?*

"Take pictures." Sonja's voice rings clear.

"What?"

"You're a photographer. Take pictures."

"Of what?"

"Just get your gear and go. You'll find something to shoot."

As I formulate yet another highly intelligent question to further clarify these mysterious instructions, I realize she's already gone. *Great.*

I pry myself out of my ratty recliner, joints stiff and achy, muscles sore from too much sitting. Inspired by the prospect of a real live adventure, I hobble off to the shower.

The hot water soothes my aching bones, restoring circulation to my broken down body. Eyes closed, I let the spray run down my neck and spine as I contemplate a destination. *Where to go?*

Feeling and smelling considerably better, I hoist my gear bag off the counter and head out. As I back out of the carport, I realize I've got a decision to make.

On Glenrosa, I head east to 24th Street with no idea where I'm going, thinking it will come to me at any moment. Then it hits me, I don't have to decide, just improvise. Like a Miles Davis jam, I'll go with it. And it feels right.

While grinning at my new-found freedom, I realize I'm heading for the MJR Development compound. I need a cover story if I'm going to get in. Grabbing my cell, I speed-dial Lacey's number.

"Lacey. Need your help with somethin'."

"What is it?"

"I'm headed for MJR Development. Want to do a follow-up shoot. Need you to back me on this."

"Sure, use your media badge, I gotcha covered. And I want to see the photos."

"Done deal."

Blue skies and bright sunshine, a warm spring day in the low seventies, perfect Phoenix weather and the kind of day that buoys the spirit. I hand crank the driver's side window down to savor the clean fresh air as I chug along. No radio, so I bask in the road noise, wind in my hair. Almost takes me back to the late sixties. A rumbling Harley chopper between my thighs, bare arms dangling from ape hangers, wind whipping though my leather vest, bug carcasses stuck to my shades, a cute girl's arms wrapped tight around my trim waist—those were the days. I wonder, if I'd known it then, would I have enjoyed it more, been more in the moment? *Damn, I was stupid.*

I snap out of my reverie as I turn into the MJR compound.

The hair on my neck and arms rises as I pull into an empty parking spot. Something's happening, intensely tingling, a violation, as though I've stumbled over the top of a sidewalk grate and hot sewer gases are blowing up my skirt. I sit for a moment, working to get my bearings, searching for the source. Suddenly I realize I'm sitting in the exact same spot as the murderer's truck. My head jerks as a shiver runs down my spine. I take a deep breath to shake it off.

I rummage through my gear bag for the camera body and a lens, doing my best to ignore the lingering unease. I twist the lens onto the camera, set it next to me and paw through the bag for the media badge. The unease festers, as though someone's watching. Like a raunchy fart in an elevator, I can't get rid of it, just keeps hanging around. I consider moving to another parking space and dismiss the idea as ridiculous. Can't let it get the upper hand or I'm dead before I start. *Fuck it, I'm goin' in.*

Camera in hand, I swing open the front door. And mustering up my most professional manner, I stride, businesslike, to the reception counter.

A pleasantly plump young woman with straight auburn hair, hazel eyes and cute smile looks up to greet me. "Can I help you."

I offer a friendly smile and dig in my pocket for the media badge. "Yes, my name is Lance Underphal. I'm with the *Valley Free Press*." I hold out the media badge for her inspection.

She looks it over and looks back up at me, duly impressed. It must be working. "Yes. What can I do for you Mr. Underphal?"

She's prettier than I first noticed. In a subtle way, she's growing on me.

"I'm here to do a photo shoot. Take a few pictures for a follow-up story we're doing on the shooting tragedy."

It dawns on her. "Oh … uh, okay. Just a minute." She bounces up and scurries off through a door at the back, leaving me to wait at the counter.

I do my best to be patient, but I've never been much good at waiting. Killing time, I wander around the reception area, looking at expensively framed, full-color architectural renderings of shopping centers, office buildings and industrial complexes. The projects are labeled with unimaginative names such as The Shops at Desert Ridge, Arrowhead Plaza, Deer Valley Corporate Center. *What a yawn.* It's bad enough that they build these things, but then to memorialize them like they're works of art—atrocious. I remember back in the day when I helped build these outhouses. And if you've got to do it, might as well be proud of it. Although I know all too well, it's all about the money. Boy, when I'm bored my cynicism runs rampant.

"Mr. Underphal?"

"Yes?"

A small thin woman with a pinched face in her late forties/early fifties stands next to the receptionist.

The receptionist opens her hand toward the woman. "This is Ms. Conroy. She'll help you."

A tight smile creases Ms. Conroy's features. "Please follow me, Mr. Underphal." She moves efficiently around the counter and heads off down a wide hall at a brisk pace.

I follow Ms. Conroy, hustling to keep up. The woman has all the charm of a Doberman bitch in heat. I don't have to be psychic to sense this isn't going to go well.

She turns into an office near the end of the hall. Crossing the room, she motions for me to sit in one of the chairs facing an oak executive desk as she takes the seat behind. Donning a rigid smile, she leans forward, propping her elbows on the desktop, interlocking her fingers. "How can we help you, Mr. Underphal?"

Used to be I actually had some charm. But now, who knows? Dusting off my decrepit powers of persuasion, I give her my best ice-thawing smile in a lame attempt to warm her up for the bullshit I'm about to spoon feed her. "I'm with the *Valley Free Press* and we're doing a follow-up story on the tragic shooting here last summer—a human interest piece, to show how the people affected survive and go on with their lives. I just need a few quick photos to round out the piece. I'll do my best not to disturb anyone and be gone before you know it."

Her unblinking stare never wavers, boring a hole through my feigned bravado. "Mr. Underphal, I doubt that's possible under the circumstances. As you may or may not know, the Rodriguez estate owns the majority interest in MJR Development Group, LLC. And I have been appointed by the estate's executor to oversee operations at MJR until the estate is resolved. I'm certain that the executor would frown on any publicity during this delicate time." She gives me a smug little smile.

I lean back in the stiff little side chair, deterred for the moment, then gather my thoughts for a second volley. "Ms. Conroy, the story will run whether you cooperate or not. It would be unfortunate if the only photos that ran with the story were of a gruesome shooting. Probably not the business image the executor wants portrayed for MJR Development."

She breaks her stare, flicking her eyes to the side, contemplating my threat, weighing her options. It's like watching a lizard distracted from stalking a beetle by a diving raven's shadow. It's her nature, she's going to run for cover.

She turns her icy smile back to me and punches the intercom. Without taking her eyes off me, she summons Melba to her office.

Melba turns out to be the pretty receptionist, who is instructed to show me around.

I smile graciously and depart with Melba, a winner.

I follow Melba around as she drones on about what department is where and whose office is whose. I stop at each point of interest and dutifully snap an obligatory photo or two. At first I don't notice the faint hum building in my head, more like a pesky gnat that you swat at without really seeing. As we continue the tour, the hum grows louder, now accompanied by an irritating buzz. We're outside now. She's showing me the heavy equipment yard, the buzzing hum in my head drowning out her words. I'm shooting pictures indiscriminately, hoping somehow I'll get what I need and sort it out later. The buzzing hum mutates to a crackling roar, the back of my head beginning to pound.

I find myself in a large garage, stark white walls and grey floor, immaculate. Ghostly images shimmer in front of my aching eyes, a human outline crawling with shiny little worms of raw energy. Beneath the roaring in my head I hear Melba say something about Rodriguez and personal vehicles. I catch a glimpse of a big black Mercedes sedan, its lustrous obsidian paint polished to a mirror finish, but it's the vehicle next to it that calls to me. I'm drawn to the tail end of a tall pickup truck, its shiny chrome bumper and bright silver tailgate hit me like a quick jab to the jaw. A gleaming chrome roll bar with chrome running lights mounted on top, the fat off-road tires, the glistening metallic silver flanks, they shimmer, telescoping in and out, vibrating with a malevolent aura. This is the truck, the killer's truck. The truck that's been haunting me since that first digital image. It's right here, in this garage. *I found it!*

I switch the camera to motor drive and depress the shutter button, sweeping the area like I'm firing an Uzi, determined to ID the monstrous truck and catch the energy manifestations as digital images. This must be why I'm here, but I'm almost too sick to tell. *Can this be real? Is that truck really there?*

My voice trembles as I try not to talk too loud, my words drowned out by the thunderous roar rolling through my skull. "Is this a company truck?"

Melba says something about it belonging to the late Mr. Rodriguez, but I can barely hear her over the din in my head. I'm just relieved that she sees it. I crab my way around the big Ford F-150, camera to my face, firing the shutter in bursts of three frames per second, shooting every detail, not taking any chances.

Finished but half delirious, I turn away from the truck, attempting to regain control of my senses. My distress must be obvious, judging from Melba's reaction. I tell her I need to go. Melba heads for a door across the garage and I follow her into a hall as the cacophony swirling around in my skull begins to dissipate. I'm way past done. Can't take any more. Yet the pictures—these seeds of accomplishment—give me an underlying sense of satisfaction I haven't felt since I was a kid. *Wait 'til Salmon gets a load of this!*

# CHASING WILD GEESE

## [9:35 AM – Friday, March 25, 2011]

SALMON EYES OFFICER Denton, giving him the once over. He can't believe what just came out of Denton's mouth. "Ya wanna give me that again?"

Denton's eyes widen with the realization that he's about to get raked over the coals. Why, he's not sure. "It's like I told you, Detective. We eliminated the F-150 registered to MJR Development based on the fact that Rodriguez was the vic, therefore not a suspect—couldn't be the truck we're lookin' for."

As he listens to Denton's explanation again, Salmon's face reddens, veins bulging on his neck and forehead.

Salmon purses his lips, running through Denton's logic, trying to calm himself. He can almost see how they missed it. Scary, it almost makes sense. Yet, potentially the most important piece of evidence had been sitting right under their noses the entire time. Infuriating.

Salmon can't turn loose. Nothing pisses him off like incompetence. It's tough enough to solve complex crimes when you do everything right. Incompetence makes it damn near impossible. And this is clearly a case of gross incompetence.

"Officer Denton, who gave you authority to eliminate the Rodriguez vehicle without a physical inspection?"

Denton shrinks into the chair, averting his eyes as though suddenly interested in the clutter on Salmon's scarred desktop.

Salmon doesn't wait for his answer. "Of course you realize that the Rodriguez vehicle perfectly matches the description of the suspect vehicle."

Denton's face flushes with embarrassment as he looks down at his hands and nods, yes.

"Matches every detail. Make, model, year, color, aftermarket trim." He yells as he slams his fist on his desk. "EVERY FUCKING DETAIL!"

Denton jumps then cringes as he hangs his head.

"You could have cost us the CASE! If we hadn't caught a lucky break, we'd have NEVER found that damn truck!"

Denton begins to wonder how long the tirade will go on.

Salmon looks off across the room and lets out a deep sigh. He leans back in his chair, drumming his fingers on his desk as he decides what to do.

Turning back to Denton, Salmon furrows his brow. "I oughtta write you up for this, but I'm gonna give you a chance to redeem yourself here."

Denton raises his head with a hopeful look. "Thanks. Anything you say, sir."

Salmon points a finger at Denton. "The Rodriguez vehicle was impounded by Forensics last night. Who knows how long it'll sit there until they get to it. I want you down there to babysit this thing, personally. Push it through. See that every hair, every fiber, every microscopic particle is thoroughly examined as potential evidence, then bring the findings to me. And don't quit until they've got it all. You understand me?"

Denton pops up, stands at attention and salutes. "Yes, sir. Thank you, sir." He turns on a heel and hustles off.

Salmon watches Denton go, wondering how good a lead the Rodriguez truck really is. He thinks about Lance Underphal and shakes his head. *How in the hell did he find it?* Obviously, someone has been using the Rodriguez truck as an escape vehicle. It's not stolen. Or if it was, it was returned and not reported. For now, it gives him more questions than answers, a situation he intends to remedy shortly.

# FIRST DAY OF
# SUMMER

**[5:27 AM – Monday, June 21, 2010]**

A FAINT BAND of gold stretched along the jagged eastern horizon, turquoise fading into cornflower blue, then slate grey—remnants of night, darkening the predawn sky with faint starlight. Cool and dry, a slightly spicy scent of creosote hung in the still desert air. At the first hint of daylight, a vast expanse of raw desert owned by the Arizona State Land Trust began coming to life.

Just north of the 101 Loop, Big Mike Rodriguez sipped his Starbucks' double Espresso Macchiato as he rolled his work truck down the power line access road. He let it crawl over the rough terrain in four-wheel drive, easing into the early morning light. Potholes, ruts, rocks and sand scarred the dirt road, and the Ford's off-road suspension was perfectly suited for the chore. Riding shotgun, Mikey chattered away with his best buds, Chad and Jason in the back seat. Strapped in the bed, the dirt bikes rode ready for action, along with the gas cans, helmets and gear. They crept along, heading for one of Rodriguez's all time faves, a place he'd dubbed Saguaro City.

Tall saguaros appeared out of the gathering light, rising fifty/sixty feet off the desert floor, their spiny arms twisted up to the sky, like silent sentries waiting for the return of alien craft. It never ceased to amaze Rodriguez how so much valuable land could sit undeveloped in one of the city's richest areas. Still, what a treat to have a huge desert playground virtually at his doorstep. As he pulled up a wash to park, he marveled at the majestic desert. Must have been that way for centuries.

Rodriguez stepped down from the tall pickup, surveying the lush desert. Mottled grey in the thin light, thickets of thorny brush crouched between fingers of rocky terrain. Clumps of creosote spread twisted profusions of spidery limbs toward the coming light. Here and there, ancient ironwoods stood sentry against the glowing sky, their snaking branches clustered with grey-green leaves, clinging like scraggly beards. Leafy cottonwoods lined the arroyo, tap roots sunk deep, feeling their way to precious water. Off by themselves, jumping cholla huddled together, bristling with ultra-sharp needles, spreading their colony inch by inch, through centuries of heat and drought. Smatterings of other cacti clung to the dusty earth as though dropped from the sky to fend for themselves. And the band of mighty saguaros towered over it all, thick as thieves cutting up the spoils in their desert hideout.

Stretching his stiff back, Rodriguez wondered what it must have been like in the pioneer days. No power lines, no contrails, no planes droning overhead. An empty sky void of every manmade object, only the sun and moon, the hawks and buzzards, and the occasional cloud. Long stretches of baking hot desert without water. But to be the first to see it … The harsh beauty must have been both cathartic and captivating. He figured he would have made a good pioneer—good survival instincts. *They must've had guts.*

The boys dropped the tailgate and slid the ramp into position. Rodriguez jumped up into the bed and started unhooking bungee cords from frame rails and handlebars. Once the dirt bikes were unloaded, Rodriguez and the boys suited up—knee and elbow pads, leathers, tall knee-high motocross boots, helmets and gloves.

As Rodriguez headed for the truck's cab, he heard Mikey holler, "Dad!" Then the buzz of an angry rattler. He sprinted around the other side of the truck. *Mikey!* He pulled up short. Just out from the rear tire, the rattler sat coiled, ready to strike, its forked tongue flicking, its rattles vibrating at the end of its erect tail. Had he parked his truck another foot to the side, he'd have run it over. Mikey and Jason stood frozen, staring wide-eyed at the rattler. They were far enough away, but Chad stood too close, trembling like a leaf, petrified, not knowing whether to hold still or bolt.

"Don't move, Chad. I've got it." As Rodriguez inched toward the big diamondback, the rattler turned on him, its rattles buzzing louder, raising its head and cocking its neck to strike. In one swift pounce Rodriguez planted his foot on the rattler's neck, but not before the rattler struck the shin plate of his motocross boot, leaving a trail of venom. He had the rattler pinned, its head writhing, mouth wide, fangs extended, spasmodically striking the side of his boot. Balancing carefully, Rodriguez stomped on the rattler's head. Heart pounding in his throat, he motioned Chad back. He stood still, waiting until he was sure it was dead. Making sure all the boys were safe, he jumped back to leave the dead snake at a distance, just in case. Satisfied it wasn't going anywhere, Rodriguez moved to the truck bed, grabbed a shovel and hacked off the snake's head.

As he threw the shovel into the truck bed, his hands shook, remnants of an adrenalin rush. In the driver's door pocket, he found his Spyderco folding knife. He quickly marched back around to the dead rattler. Opening the blade, he knelt and grabbed the rattler's coon-striped tail. With one quick slice from the razor-sharp blade, he severed the rattles. A fitting souvenir for a close call. He held the rattles up and gave them a shake. *No one threatens my kid, you sonofabitch.*

Eyes wide, Chad stared in awe at Mr. Rodriguez. Likewise, a newfound respect for Mr. Rodriguez shone in Jason's eyes.

Grinning, Rodriguez shook the rattles again. Admiration sparkled in his son's eyes. It was uplifting to see his son's adulation, washing away the last little residue of rage. Tears welled, Rodriguez's vision blurring at the thought of his son.


What a great morning. Rodriguez and the boys tore it up in the desert, giving the dirt bikes a real workout. On the way back, the boys couldn't stop talking about Chad's close call and Mr. Rodriguez stomping the rattler to death. He beamed as he sped for the MJR yard. Time enough to shower, change and make it to the loan closing, no problem.

Rodriguez whipped into his private garage and braking hard, squealed the big off-road tires to a stop. When he'd called in, Diane said she needed to see him. Jumping out of the cab, he hustled to the office still dressed in his motocross pants and boots. His sweat-stained T-shirt stunk from hard exertion and motorcycle fumes, his face and thick black hair streaked with sweat and dust. He planned on checking in with Diane and hitting the shower.

Diane stood waiting for him as he charged into his office, her face screwed up in an angry frown.

Rodriguez pushed past her around the desk and dropped into his chair, taking a load off. He cocked his head with an inquisitive look. "What's up, babe?"

Diane's face turned red as she stared at her hands. "I know what's goin' on," she said, voice soft and trembling.

Rodriguez's eyes narrowed. "Okay ... you wanna fill me in?"

Diane raised her head, eyes flashing with rage. "Your little whore left you a message!"

Rodriguez bolted upright in his chair. "What?! What the fuck are you talkin' about?!"

Diane crossed her arms, her voice ratcheting up. "That little whore Marcia is what I'm *talkin'* about!"

Rodriguez hefted himself out of his chair and moved back around the desk. "What the fuck has Marcia Rupert got to do with anything?"

"I know you've been fuckin' her!"

"Where the fuck did you get *that* idea!?!"

"Johnny told me!!!"

Rodriguez turned crimson, veins popping on his neck and forehead. "Fuckin' Chavez, that sonofabitch!" He tried to laugh it off. "You believe Chavez?"

Tears streamed down her cheeks. "He said he was in the therapy tub with you and her, in front of the whole office, bragged about it!" She screamed up into his face, pounding his chest with both fists. "How could you?!"

"You stupid bitch! You don't know what the fuck you're talkin' about! He's a fucking LIAR!" Losing it, Rodriguez reared back and slapped her hard across the face.

Diane gasped, reeling from the blow, fear shining in her eyes like a trapped rabbit.

He bit his lower lip as his shoulders slumped. In that instant Rodriguez realized he hit her way too hard and that it was Chavez he should be hitting, not Diane. *Dammit!*

Diane cowered, her trembling hands covering her reddening face, sobbing hysterically.

He moved to comfort her and she fought against him until he gently smothered her in his embrace. She broke down weeping, burying her face in his chest. He held her, rocking gently, soothing her, whispering "I'm sorry, I'm sorry," letting her cry it out. Thinking the whole time, *That fucking Chavez* ...


Headed to the loan closing at Cohen & Company, Rodriguez stepped into the elevator still thinking about his dickhead cousin. It took him nearly a half hour to calm Diane and convince her Chavez was full of shit. Having dated Chavez, it didn't take her long to remember what an asshole he was. He punched the third floor button and stepped back, shifting his Zero Halliburton briefcase to both hands.

A dark-haired beauty sat behind the ultra-modern reception desk, headset on, efficiently directing the incoming calls. Rodriguez leaned an elbow on the tinted glass countertop waiting for her to break free.

She glanced up, a sparkle in her eyes, giving him a seductive smile as she thanked the caller. "May I help you?"

Rodriguez loved flirts. *Nothing like a sweet young thing giving you the eye.* He held her gaze with a practiced look that openly encouraged her, letting the moment linger, waiting until she was about to break eye contact. "I'm Michael Rodriguez. I'm here to see Mr. Cohen."

Her cheeks flushed as she dropped her gaze, punching buttons on the phone console.

"Mr. Cohen? Mr. Rodriguez is here." She glanced up, smiling coyly. "Mr. Cohen will be right out."

"Thanks. And what's your name?"

"Jenette, Jenette Asher."

Rodriguez's smile broadened. "Thanks, Jenette."

Jenette blushed as she picked up a call.

Through double glass doors, Rodriguez saw the plump little Cohen approaching.

He was immaculately dressed, an expensive three-piece suit, tie straight, not a hair out of place. He pushed open a glass door, cursorily greeted Rodriguez and invited him to follow.

"That receptionist of yours is cute."

"Yes, she is, isn't she? She's new, only been with us a few weeks."

Cohen turned into a conference room with Rodriguez at his heel.

Rodriguez grinned. "Looks like a keeper."

Cohen just smiled coolly as he took a seat on the far side of the long teak table.

Rodriguez grabbed a chair and laid his briefcase on the tabletop.

All business, Cohen punched a button and picked up the receiver. "Alice? You want to join us in the conference room?" He turned to Rodriguez. "Alice is on her way, she's our closing officer and a notary."

Rodriguez opened his briefcase, pulled out a thick stack of documents and set them down on the table, resting both hands on the top of the pile. "Great. I've got everything right here, ready to go."

Cohen cocked his head, giving him a wry little grin. "Mr. Whiting won't be joining us?"

Rodriguez leaned forward, smiling smugly. "No need, I have full authority to execute on behalf of Sunset Pointe, LLC."

An obese woman with a jovial grin bustled into the conference room to sit next to Cohen. She looked to be in her late thirties, too much make-up inexpertly applied, frosted blonde hair in disarray. She smiled openly, doing her best to lean across the table and extend her hand to Rodriguez, the table's edge creasing her bulging abdomen. "Hi, I'm Alice."

Rodriguez gently took her hand. "Mike Rodriguez, nice to meet you."

Cohen gave terse instructions to Alice to examine all loan docs for completeness and extract the signature pages for execution. Once executed by Rodriguez and Cohen, she was to notarize and re-compile the pages, making sure they had two compete sets.

Rodriguez pushed the stack of documents across the table to Alice and she expertly started in.

Cohen studiously watched Alice work, quietly avoiding eye contact with Rodriguez.

Rodriguez watched intently, eyes shifting from Alice to Cohen and back to Alice.

Alice slid the various signature pages back across to Rodriguez.

Pulling a platinum Montblanc from his briefcase, Rodriguez began signing the pages with a flourish. He then slid the pages over to Cohen in one effortless motion.

Cohen pulled a gold Cross ballpoint from his inside jacket pocket and efficiently scribbled away, sliding individual pages back to Alice as he finished.

Alice asked to see Rodriguez's ID and had him sign her notary log. She then diligently applied her signature and notary seal to each signature page and put the documents back in order. Looking up, she smiled. "All done." She pushed one set of loan documents back across to Rodriguez. "Thank you, Mr. Rodriguez." Pushing away from the table, she stood, gathered up her document set and with a wide rolling gait, exited the conference room.

Rodriguez carefully watched Cohen as he withdrew a windowed business envelope from his inside jacket pocket and slid it across to Rodriguez. Rodriguez picked up the envelope, examining the name on the check, Sunset Pointe, LLC. Pulling the check from the envelope, he beamed as he read the amount—seven million five hundred thousand an no/100 dollars. *Perfect.* Rodriguez casually tossed the check into his briefcase along with the loan docs. As he stood to leave, Rodriguez smiled broadly, extending a meaty hand to Cohen. "Thanks, Benjamin, a pleasure doin' business with ya."

Cohen limply took his hand with an insincere smile. "The pleasure is all ours. Sunset Pointe is a gem. Best of luck to you, Mike."

At a First Community teller's window, Rodriguez opened his briefcase on the counter. He grabbed the loan proceeds check, flipped it over and endorsed the back to MJR Development Group, LLC. He grinned and winked at the mousey little teller as she looked at his ID and the proceeds check in awe. She entered the deposit, robotically thanked him and gave him his receipt. He threw the receipt in his briefcase and headed for the car, smiling ear to ear. *SEVEN AND A HALF MILLION DOLLARS! YES!*

Low on the horizon, the sun's blaze shimmered with heat, scorching the June sky—the first day of summer coming to an end. Radiance from the demon sun flowed like volcanic magma, molten gold flaring to velvet rose. The devil's own furnace couldn't have been more hellishly alluring. On the surface, beautiful to behold but blinding to the eye that looked too long, much like Rodriguez's idyllic lifestyle.

Rodriguez gunned the Mercedes, blasting through late day traffic, eager to celebrate his latest coup—seven-point-five mil. He'd been spreading the word, working his hands-free cell non-stop—a loan-closing party at the Lion's Den.

Rodriguez left a voicemail for Connie, he had a subcontractor dinner, he'd be late, don't wait up. He told Diane a similar tale, an obligatory boys-night-out with the subs, but the dozen long-stemmed roses he'd had delivered earlier had the desired effect. She sounded almost grateful when he promised to take her out to dinner tomorrow night.

Pulling into the Den's private lot, Rodriguez laughed, ready to party. He left his AMG idling for the valet, hopped out and trotted to the private rear entrance, laughingly known as the "back door" by his inner circle. He grinned, figuring to get into more than one back door tonight.

Rodriguez loved this place, more pussy than he could handle, no matter how hard he tried. And he'd tried hard, several times. Here, money talked and he could indulge in any carnal pleasure he desired—do whatever he wanted, to whomever he wanted with impunity. He paid the girls well and they never gave him any shit, the perfect working relationship. Shallow, yes, but great fun. And when it was over everybody went home happy, no attachments, no emotional baggage. Everyone knew him as the wealthy real estate developer, a big spender, hard partier, generous to a fault and all-around good guy. If it wasn't for Mikey, Brittany and Josh, he'd probably live here.

Through the hand-carved doors, Rodriguez hustled across the inlaid terrazzo, headed for the Manager's Suite, a fast shower and a quick change of clothes.

He'd conveniently added the Manager's Suite to the project's "Scope of Work" when he bought in, forcing Kantor to hire MJR's construction arm to handle the extensive renovations. One of several "special conditions" to Rodriguez's investment.

Kantor was in no position to object. On the verge of bankruptcy, Kantor let Rodriguez dictate terms for a large cash infusion. Though Kantor knew Rodriguez was shafting him, it was better than the alternative.

Rodriguez knew he'd cut a sweet deal, getting controlling interest of the Lion's Den along with all the unwritten perks in the bargain. Turned out to be a real cash cow. He received large chunks of unreported cash every week as his take. Terrific foresight on Rodriguez's part and very profitable, not to mention his own private playpen.

Toweling off, Rodriguez mentally scrolled through a list of the Den's dancers—mouthwatering, as though perusing a menu of sweet and exotic fare. He figured he'd start with a few appetizers, a Grey Goose and Red Bull, a cigar, maybe a couple lines to get things rolling.

Pushing through the glass double doors, Rodriguez headed for the private dining room's bar. The big room was empty except for the bar help: the bartender, and a couple cocktail waitresses. Leaning on the narrow little bar, Rodriguez ordered his usual and Jack the bartender expertly delivered. He took a sip and lit up. Taking a long leisurely pull on his cigar, he puffed a couple smoke rings and smiled.

"Hey, Jack, get Sondra back here, will ya?"

"Sure, Mr. Rodriguez." Jack picked up the phone and relayed the message. "Sondra's on her way."

Sondra Du took the shortcut through the kitchen. She pushed through the swinging door and sauntered up to Big Mike.

Rodriguez grinned. Sondra was not only the hottest looking dancer in the joint, but a great fuck, his fave.

Sondra gave him a impish smile and a hug. "Hey, congratulations."

Rodriguez inhaled her fragrance, her soft flesh pressing against his groin as he pulled her to him. "Thanks, babe. Ready to party?"

Pulling away, she gave him a sly grin. "Anytime you are."

"Great. Got this guy showin' up tonight. Want you to hook him up. He's my kid's karate instructor and I want to show him a good time. Who ya got?"

"Wild or gentle?"

"How 'bout wild?"

"Jilly's as wild as they come and she's always lookin' to try somebody new."

"Great, set it up."

"You got it."

"And I got money to burn. Want to do somethin' extra special with ya."

"How 'bout I ask Naomi to join us? We'll put on a show. You can dive in anytime."

Exotic images raised his pulse, a warm thickening in his groin. Naomi was hot and dark, as sexy as they come and a perfect counterpoint to the voluptuous creamy-blond Sondra. His eyes sparkled as he licked his lips. "Mmm, let's do it."


The Den's gate attendant waved the black Corvette through. As he wheeled up to the rear entrance, Rupert's nerves crackled with raw excitement. A dark red canopy adorned with the Lion's Den logo extended to a valet station. Below the scalloped canopy, a red carpeted walk led up to hand-carved mahogany doors, golden lion's head logos everywhere. Impressive, Big Mike had done it again: all the right contacts and inside access to the most exclusive strip club in town. He'd heard rumors about the notorious "back door" at the Lion's Den, but didn't know anyone who'd been there. And there he was, about to go in as Big Mike's guest.

Barely able to contain himself, Rupert popped out of the car and left the Corvette in park for the valet. He couldn't help wondering what Connie thought of her husband's involvement in all this. That is, if she new. And what would she think if she knew he was here as her husband's guest? How ironic. Still, their little affair had been mostly superficial through no fault of his own. Even though Rupert wanted a more meaningful relationship,

Connie wouldn't commit to anything other than the monthly clandestine rendezvous, staying inaccessible and distant more often than not. Given Connie's attitude, he was well within his rights to explore all options. He needed a night out. Nothing wrong with a little adult entertainment with the boys. Plus, what Connie didn't know couldn't hurt her, right? His wife, Marcia, never entered his mind.

Bounding up the red carpet, Rupert rushed through a thick mahogany door. Crossing the inlaid floor, he entered the private dining room. Several men milled around with drinks in hand. Rupert worked his way through the crowd, finally spotting Big Mike at the bar. Well over six foot and built like an immense fireplug, his Big Mike moniker was well deserved. He remembered Marcia once said Big Mike had rugged good looks and a certain animal magnetism. Hell, Marcia probably would've fucked him if she had half a chance. Big Mike, olive skinned and hirsute with thick black hair, a low Neanderthal forehead and the makings of a mono-brow perched over his thick nose, Rupert could definitely see the "animal" and the "rugged" parts. More like werewolf, when he really thought about it. He figured women were probably more attracted to his loud gregarious manner, his fat wallet and his "big-spender" style. Nothing impresses like confidence with the coin to back it up. At the bar next to Big Mike stood the most voluptuous creature Rupert had ever seen. Blonde and curvaceous, her stunning looks almost made him drool.

Before Rupert made it to the bar, Rodriguez spotted him. "Hey Daniel, get your ass over here!"

Rupert grinned as he approached, his eyes drawn to the luscious blonde. "Mike, thanks for inviting me."

Sondra smiled seductively.

"Hey, just wait 'til ya see what I have lined up for you." Rodriguez looked at Sondra and nodded.

Rupert's eyes darted between Big Mike and the hot blonde. "Yeah?"

"This is Sondra and she's got someone she wants you to meet." Rodriguez turned to Sondra. "Go get her, babe."

Eagerly awaiting Sondra's return, Rupert's head buzzed, barely hearing a word Big Mike said.

As Rupert scanned the crowd, he noticed Sondra shouldering her way through with a tall, well-built brunette in tow.

Sondra stopped in front of Rupert pulling the brunette up next to her. The brunette's smooth delicate features and too perfect breasts complemented her long luscious legs and narrow waist, giving her the allure of a supermodel. Her big dark eyes focused on Rupert, glistening with raw hunger—hypnotic. With a sly grin, Sondra gazed directly at Rupert while speaking to the brunette. "Jilly, this is a friend of Big Mike's." She turned to Jilly, winked and turned back to Rupert. "What's your name?"

"Daniel, Daniel Rupert," he stuttered.

"Daniel, this is Jilly." Sondra slitted her eyes, cocked her head and pointed her finger at Rupert. "You be nice to Jilly."

With a delicious smile, Jilly reached out to Rupert. "Let's go somewhere private."

Grinning like an idiot, Rupert let her lead him off.


Needing a breather and another vial of coke, Rodriguez threw on some clothes and stumbled out of Sondra's private cubby. Sondra and Naomi stayed behind, lounging languidly, naked limbs entwined on the divan. There were still several people partying in the dining room. Naked dancers, lines of coke and half finished drinks adorned the long dining table. Electronic dance music pulsed as they congregated in small clusters, hooting at the dancers and laughing too loud. Rodriguez headed for the bar. Jack always had an extra vial or two. Might as well get a couple more cigars, a couple Viagra and another magnum of champagne while he was at it.

Rodriguez stopped and turned as he heard someone shout his name from across the room, that asshole cousin of his. Adrenalin surged in a burst of rage. Blood boiling, he charged across the room to let Chavez have it.

Well lit and teetering, Chavez saw his cousin headed his way. He grinned and held up his drink in salute.

Fuming, Rodriguez slapped the drink out of Chavez's hand and growled through clenched teeth. "What the fuck do you think you're doing?"

Bewildered, Chavez held up his hands. "Whaddaya talkin' about?"

Rodriguez started poking Chavez in the chest with his index finger. "Are you a fucking moron? Braggin' about fuckin' Marcia in my therapy tub in front of my office staff? Tellin' them I was in on it? And in front of Diane? What the fuck's the matter with you?"

"Hey, man. Don't get your panties in a twist. Just havin' a little fun."

Rodriguez seethed as he continued to poke Chavez in the chest. "Look, asshole. Marcia's old man is a friend of mine. In fact, he's here to-night. Last thing I need is for him to find out I was porkin' his old lady. And you fucked things up with Diane, big time! If I ever catch you doin' anything like that again, I'll cut your balls off and ram them down your throat! Got me, Cuz?!"

Chavez's face turned beet red, wide nostrils flaring, features twisting into an ugly snarl. He slapped Rodriguez's finger away. "Yeah, I gotcha, all right. Now get the fuck outta my face!" Before Rodriguez could react, Chavez turned and stormed out of the building.

Rodriguez turned back for the bar, mumbling under his breath. "Fuckin' asshole ..."

# HEATING UP

**[10:46 AM – Thursday, April 7, 2011]**

WHILE THE CALENDAR still reads spring, it's full-on summer outside. Gary Whiting winds his way down the 51 headed for his attorney's office in the Camelback Corridor. He can hardly believe it's April and it's already this hot. The outside temperature reads ninety-three degrees and he's sweating profusely even though he has the Mercedes' A/C cranked down to sixty-five. The A/C, not doing much for his nervous perspiration.

Back a couple of car-lengths in the middle lane, a tall F-150 4X4 cruises in sync with Whiting's Baby Benz. Self-absorbed, Whiting fails to notice the silver and chrome-trimmed pickup following him through the Dreamy Draw.

Woozy from pills and jacked up on coke, his fingers tap the steering wheel in time to the music, his thoughts racing with anxiety. Like most parts of the country, the local commercial real estate market is worse than bad. Valuations dropped off a cliff and left him holding the bag, thirty million in combined debt on a project that's only worth about ten. To make matters worse, their pre-leasing for Sunset Pointe is dismal, falling far short of projections. Fellman at First Community Bank made it clear that they're out of time. And Whiting didn't dare think about Cohen and his goons. They should've never done the second mortgage with Cohen. *Fucking Rodriguez!* His skin crawls at the thought of Cohen's last warning. Knowing the day is coming when Cohen will demand his money makes Whiting's stomach clench and sharp pains shoot behind his eyes. *Fucking Rodriguez!* So far he hasn't figured out where all the money went. With Diane disabled and all the books and records tied up in the Rodriguez estate, he's screwed. *Fucking Rodriguez! If he wasn't already dead, I'd kill him!*

It'd be different if he could get his hands on the insurance money. He'd pay off Cohen. But it's all tied up in probate. From time to time he still wonders who killed Rodriguez. He used to think it was Connie. Now he wonders if it was Cohen and his crew. Especially since Rodriguez's death put the loan in default, triggering the acceleration clause. Cohen can now legally demand full payment of the outstanding loan balance. Doesn't really matter anymore. He's screwed no matter who killed Rodriguez. And if he doesn't do something about Cohen, he'll be just as dead as Rodriguez. *Fucking Rodriguez!*


Whiting is ushered into the glass-walled conference room at Murphy, Payne & O'Connor by Dalton Payne's personal assistant. Dalton and a younger man in a suit and tie are talking and smiling as though casually discussing the significance of their golf handicaps. As he enters, Dalton Payne rises to shake his hand. The other man rises and introduces himself as Bernard Worth. They all sit, Payne and Worth across the table from Whiting. Whiting grins suspiciously, wondering how much the new guy, Worth, is going to cost him. Dalton Payne has been Whiting's attorney for more than five years because he's good, not because he's inexpensive.

Payne slouches in his chair. "Based on our discussions, I've asked Bernie to sit in today. He's an expert in corporate bankruptcy."

As the word "bankruptcy" hits Whiting, he goes numb. He sees Dalton's lips move and sees Worth's lips move, a vague mumbling of legalese. As the banalities drone on, he feels more and more disconnected, like he could pass out. *Bankruptcy … Cohen will kill me.*


Stein pulls off his sunglasses as he enters the parking garage. Tossing his hat into the passenger seat, he bounds out of the truck and trots to the elevator. He catches a glimpse of Whiting in the lobby as he slides between elevator doors. Watching the indicator lights, he notes two stops—fourth and fifth floors. He ambles across to the building directory, noting the law firm of Murphy, Payne & O'Connor. It's Whiting's attorney. That's all he needs. Alligator boots clomping with his long stride, Stein heads back to the truck.


North Scottsdale's desert warms up in the late morning sun, coming alive with chittering chipmunks, cooing doves and the plaintive call of quail searching for their mates. A lizard skitters across heated rocks, stopping to bob in time to its primordial rhythms. The creosotes and palo verde wave their flowering branches in the gusty breeze, clear blue skies and bright sunshine above. It promises to be another spring day in the nineties.

Connie Rodriguez lies in her large four-poster bed, thick drapes drawn on the floor-to-ceiling windows in her cavernous master suite. Lately she's been having difficulty getting up and starting her day, her energy having dwindled to nothing, gripped with a grinding anxiety, unable to sleep more than a few hours a night. And when she finally makes it out of bed, she's shuffling through her days zombie-like, drained, exhausted. She wonders how it ever managed to get so bad. This is not how she envisioned her life. She's tried everything, yet here she is.

Father Ambrose suggested prayer and a psychiatrist, telling her that his grief counseling only went so far. Her doctor keeps insisting on increasing her antidepressants although he did give her a referral to a psychiatrist. On her first visit with the psychiatrist, he assured her she was on the right path with her medication, and that there's no cure for depression, just a lifelong battle to manage the symptoms. How depressing.

Is this really what God intends for her? Her eyes well with tears. She cries softly, wondering if it will ever end. It isn't worth it anymore, she just wants it all to go away, wants it to be over.


An early afternoon breeze buzzes the window screen over Sondra Du's bed, warm air filling the doublewide's small bedroom with the fragrant aroma of spring. All her creases and folds are sticky with sweat, the afternoon heat creeping up past her comfort level. She stirs from a dreamless sleep, rolls onto her back, spread eagle. Eyelids flutter as she yawns. *Time to get up.*

Padding naked down the narrow hall, she scratches crotch stubble. A shower and shave, get beautified for tonight's action. Shaving, waxing, such a pain in the ass, literally. She grins—the price of beauty—knowing she'll be well paid for all that buttery smooth skin. Turning on the shower, she twists to the sink and briskly brushes her teeth. She twists back to the shower, tests the water and ducks into the cramped shower stall.

As she soaps herself, she runs through a list of the things she needs to do. Naomi should be back from the grocery store soon. Besides her wax and nails appointment later, she needs to get the ball rolling with Fellman. *He needs to pay up.* She's thought of several ways to do it, but keeps coming back to the simplest, most lucrative way—do it herself. She grins. *After all, what's the little weenie gonna do, call the cops?* She'll call Fellman after her shower.

At Fellman's insistence, Sondra agreed to meet him in one of Sky Harbor's long-term parking garages. Even though the lingering exhaust is intense, cars are sparse on the fifth level, hardly any traffic. Probably why he picked it. She's been there for almost fifteen minutes, waiting in the heat and fumes. She seethes at the inconvenience, leaning on the rear fender of her little yellow Porsche Boxster S. She's jittery, the inherent risks gnawing at the back of her mind. In her purse she has copies of the photos as promised, along with a canister of pepper spray and a small nickel-plated .25 caliber semi-auto. She doesn't really think Fellman will give her any trouble, but she's prepared.

A golden E-Class Mercedes sweeps up the ramp and swerves into the empty space next to the Boxster, chirping the tires as it stops. Fellman furtively steps out and rounds the back of the Mercedes. His head swivels and eyes dart, looking to see if he's been set up. This is his worst nightmare, a tiny indiscretion gone very wrong. He wonders how he'll ever get out of this mess, figuring she'll eventually bleed him dry. Turning to the slutty blonde, a nervous tremor cracks his voice. "You have the pictures?"

Sondra smirks. "You got the cash?"

"I've got a cashier's check, made out to cash. Twenty-five thousand dollars, just like you said."

"I told you cash! I can't cash a cashier's check, you fucking idiot! I'd have to use ID! I need cash!"

"Okay, okay. I've got it in the car. Hold on."

Sondra watches as he scurries to the far side of the Mercedes, realizing that he has just attempted to set her up. *The fucker!*

Fellman comes back with a cheap briefcase and hands it to her.

Sondra opens it on the Boxster's deck lid. She stares at the stacks of rubber-banded hundreds. She grabs and fans each stack, counting, looking for marked bills and tracking devices.

"Please hurry," he says, his voice weak and shaky.

Satisfied, she closes the case and tosses it into the Boxster. She turns back to Fellman as he stands hunched, wringing his hands. Pawing through her purse, she makes sure he sees the pistol before extracting the envelope full of pictures. She hands Fellman the envelope and stands back, arms akimbo.

Fellman carefully opens the envelope and peeks at each photo, grimacing and shaking his head as he shifts through the lot. Suspiciously, he peers up at Sondra. "Are these all of them?"

"Yup."

"You don't have any copies?"

"I have a disk copy of the files as backup."

Fellman trembles. "What!?! You told me I'd get all of them! That's not part of the deal! I want that disk!"

"Fuck you, Fellman. I'm keepin' the disk for insurance. Don't worry, it's in a safe deposit box and will never see the light of day as long as you don't give me any trouble."

"Shit! Shit! Shit! You can't do this!" he whines. "That wasn't part of the deal!"

Sondra turns to get in her Boxster. "Tough shit, Fellman. Deal with it!"

Sondra winds her engine and backs out, barely missing Fellman. Flashing him a wicked grin, she screeches off down the exit ramp.

Jeremy Gott hunches over his smallish desk in his cramped office in back of the Chuck Wagon's kitchen, scanning the weekly sales numbers. Down again this week, the Chuck Wagon's numbers are abysmal. Forty percent drop in gross sales for the last calendar year and this year isn't looking any better. It continues to lose money every month no matter what Jeremy does to stop the bleeding. He's cut food costs, payroll, even negotiated a temporary rent reduction, and still the numbers plummet. And to top it off, they're headed into the slow summer season.

Over the past few weeks, he's had to let a number of his best people go, from barmaids to cooks. Of course, it doesn't help that Whiting is feeding gambling and drug habits. Worse, the last couple times Jeremy called, he caught Whiting at the tables in Vegas. And when he saw Whiting earlier in the week, he seemed on the verge of a full-blown panic attack, all wild-eyed, pale and sweaty. With Whiting at the helm, it's a wonder the Chuck Wagon is still open. Too bad Big Mike isn't around anymore. Between his extravagant lunch meetings and his cohorts adopting the Chuck Wagon as their watering hole, Big Mike generated a ton of business—well worth the huge tab he ran. The man was a mover and a shaker.

Jeremy gets up to get out on the floor, do a walk-around, greet some customers, anything to get his mind off his predicament. As he pushes through the kitchen door, he notices the dining area is nearly empty and there are only a handful of regulars at the bar. As Jeremy props himself up on a barstool, he scans down the long bar. At the far end, the mystery man. He makes a mental note to go over and introduce himself to the tall gentleman in the grey Stetson and alligator boots. The guy is getting to be a regular customer, and in this economy a regular is gold. But there's something about that guy. Isn't he the same guy he saw in the booth with Big Mike? Jeremy catches himself staring, drops his gaze and turns back to the bar.

# INNER VISIONS

### [2:53 AM – Friday, April 8, 2011]

## *DREAMING:*

*Cool moonlight reluctantly gives up its ghostly illumination—a frail scene wavering on the border of illusion under its lunar spell. Barren desert, deathly still as though lying in wait for its next victim. A weathered dirt road disappearing into darkness, the only road out.*

*Going nowhere on a dusty trail to nothing. Bone-weary of this search, a trek of tears, gone on so long. Seems all I've ever done, all I'll ever do, is search. And for what?*

*There was purpose once, but long ago. Despair is all that's left. Distant longing, faintest desire, a pale glimmer of what might have been, ground down to nothing, hopes crushed under Time's hobnail boots, turning dreams to dust.*

*Quit the constant plodding, mindlessly marching ever downward, steep spirals sinking into oblivion. Rest … for just a little while. So tired. Resigned to the truth of it, I've lost. All gone … gone away.*

*Darkness hints at cosmic secrets yet to be revealed. Just another lie? Dragging me down? Sucking me into its smothering embrace?*

My eyes open and I'm staring at the dingy ceiling, gripped with anxiety, my head throbbing. Feels like I've been beaten with a lead pipe. I haven't woke up feeling this shitty in a while. Something's not right. It's an odd way to perceive premonitions—random aches, phantom pains—but I'm finally getting the hang of it. Where is this shit coming from?

I lie still, nerves tingling all over, like tiny pinpricks from hordes of nano-mites. Looking at it for what it is, helps. Nothing but psychic phenomena. I repeat it like a mantra. It can't really hurt me, or can it? I've never really asked. "Sonja?"

"Only lack of understanding can hurt you." Sonja's words fill my mind, putting me more at ease.

"Must be a lot I don't know."

"At least you're learning. Don't stop now. You know too much to quit. I don't want to worry you, but if you try to quit now, it could get worse."

"Great, how lucky can I get?"

"You've made good progress, but there's more to do. Get through this and a lot of questions get answered, a lot of doors open."

"Feels like someone keeps slamming them in my face."

She ignores my sarcasm, or maybe she's simply had enough. All I know for sure is that she's no longer around and the bizarre symptoms are back stronger than before.

I focus on the ceiling's texture, like greyish cottage cheese frozen in time well past the "sell by" date, accumulating dust. I wonder how is it that dust particles cling to all those inverted little peaks and valleys. Patterns form, daisy chains of little textured storm clouds whirl and eddy, pulsing before my eyes. I shut my eyes to will it away. Yet the images continue, mutating into dirty ice cream, melting, oozing. Gobs of sticky grey matter dripping from an undulating ceiling. Eyes open or closed, it all looks the same. Viscous slime puddles all around me. Blobs drop with sickly wet plops, lumping together into gelatinous mounds of pulsing putrid flesh. There's an energy at work here, taking on a life of its own. Or should I say death? Looks more like death to me.

One of the more pronounced grey lumps grows into a mound of putty-like tissue, reaching up to its birthmother, the ceiling, to stand erect. A form, an outline, a female shape materializes. As it wavers before me, I attempt to glean its meaning. The featureless female refines her shape, her movement. Hips sway as lips part on a corpse that in life must have been a real beauty. I'm entranced with the transformation taking place, knowing full well that it's only psychic phenomena, a supernatural form of media. The method to the madness, communication of the unseen, using visual symbols—its cryptic meaning, yet to be deciphered.

By the time I understand, it's all too obvious. Hell, even Ray Charles could see this woman is a stripper. A dead stripper. Not the stripper I saw at the drive-thru, but the same one as that earlier premonition.

The dead stripper prances around the pole.

She's the premonition I had just before the drive-thru killings.

The dancing corpse grabs the pole with both hands and kicks up both long grey legs with a flourish.

I'm obviously on the right track. Before, I'd rushed to conclusions, assuming the stripper in my visions was the same one as the dead stripper in the Corvette, but no. There's no Corvette in this one. It's not her.

Particles pop into view and shimmer, coalescing into a custom off-road pickup.

The nude necromancer releases the stripper's pole and hits the floor, revealing all, writhing in mock-ecstasy, her tale nearing its end.

The tall truck runs its fat tires over her prostrate form unceremoniously, returning it to the goo it came from, leaving me with only one logical conclusion.

The killer isn't done killing.

# PHANTOM F-150

**[10:14 AM – Friday, April 8, 2011]**

OFFICER DENTON WALKS briskly through the maze of corridors leading to Homicide's squad room. Clamped in his hand is the manila folder containing a printout of Forensics' report on the Rodriguez vehicle. As the corridor empties out into the squad room, Denton's heart rate jumps at the prospect of Detective Salmon's wrath. Denton quickly crosses the room to stand in front of Salmon's desk.

Kicked back on the phone, Salmon pulls his feet off the corner of his desk, sits up, and gives Denton a side glance as he continues his phone conversation. Denton remains at attention, waiting for Salmon. After a few moments Salmon ends the call, motioning Denton to take a chair. "Whaddaya got for me, Denton?"

Denton offers the folder to Salmon. "Sir, here's Forensics' report on the Rodriguez vehicle."

Salmon removes a thick sheaf of paper and begins to scan the pages. "What did they find?"

"I made sure they went over it with a fine-tooth comb. I even got them to recheck it. There's a lot of potential evidence there, sir."

"Anything concrete?"

"It's mostly consistent with what you'd expect, dirt, hair, fibers, dead skin, plant cellulose, fast food remnants, plenty of stains—a ton of shit. Rodriguez also had a 9mm and a knife. The concealed weapons permit was in the glove box. Ballistics says it's probably not the same 9mm used in any of the shootings."

"Any blood?"

"Yeah, but it's reptile blood, and a couple of snake scales, consistent with the set of rattlesnake rattles in the console."

A wry smile crosses Salmon's face. "Figures. More than a few people thought Rodriguez was a snake. Guess we got proof. Nothin' else though, huh?"

"Nothing that would tie the vehicle to any of the murders."

"Once we start making arrests we'll have somethin' to work with. Thanks, Officer. Good work. Here's what I need you to do. Get with whoever's in charge over at MJR Development Group and find out who had access to that truck."

"Will do, sir. Their attorney was already asking when we're gonna return the vehicle."

"I can't see any reason to keep it, if Forensics is done."

"I'll let them know they can pick it up and I'll get you what you need."

"Good. Get on it and get back to me."

"Consider it done, sir." Denton stands and heads back the way he came.


As Salmon peruses the forensics report, he thinks about the wild set of circumstances that led them to Rodriguez's truck. He hasn't heard from ol' Lance in a while and wonders what he's up to.

Salmon's cell chimes with an incoming call. Seeing it's Underphal, he grins. "Damn, you must be psychic!"

"What?"

"I was just thinkin' about you."

Underphal's face screws up at Salmon's humor. "Cute, Detective."

"So why did ya call?"

"I had another vision—a premonition. Thought you should know about it."

"Hmm, let's hear it."

"Don't know if you remember, but just before the drive-thru murders I had a premonition about a stripper getting killed."

"Yeah, vaguely. Good call."

"Yeah, well as it turns out, it wasn't the right stripper."

"Whaddaya mean?"

"I had the premonition again. The killer's got another stripper in his sights."

"You're sure?"

"Sure as I can be. You know how it works."

"Yeah, well … thanks for the tip. Anything specific?"

"Not really. Just that I think it's the same guy, but I can't really tell ya about the stripper."

"Hey, you're doin' good. Let me know if you get anything else."

"Yep, I'll let you know."


Salmon's gears turn as he conjures ways to use Lance's info. After thinking for a couple minutes, the light comes on and he punches Denton's number into his cell.

"It's Salmon. You talk to MJR's lawyer about that truck?"

"Sir, I just got back to my desk and was gonna call …"

"Does that vehicle have any anti-theft?"

"Yeah, Lojack."

"Great. When you talk to their lawyer, tell him you want them to re-store the truck to the same location as though it never left. And that we have reason to believe that someone may attempt to steal it. Tell him not to worry as we'll track it with the Lojack."

"Uh, sure thing, Detective."

"If he gives ya any trouble, call me. And let me know as soon as you've got the names of people with access to that vehicle."

Heat simmers in Salmon's eyes as he clicks off.

# HARD LUCK

**[4:41 PM – Friday, April 8, 2011]**

GARY WHITING WATCHES the caller ID on his desk phone. The little LCD screen reads "Cohen & Co." The screen goes dark when the ringing finally stops. This is the third time today Whiting has let a Cohen call go to voicemail. Whiting pulls out his pencil drawer, gingerly lifts out a small mirror with four lines of crystalline powder and sets it in front of him. Digging in his pocket for his money clip, he thinks about what he's going to say when he returns Cohen's call. Pulling off a hundred dollar bill, he begins talking himself into a rational explanation as to why they can't pay off Cohen's loan. He rolls the hundred into a tight straw and bends his face over the mirror, holding the makeshift straw to his right nostril. Pressing his left nostril closed, he quickly snorts all four lines of coke. He tilts his head back, gasping, eyes watering from the four-alarm fire he's just ignited in his sinuses. A tidal wave of euphoria sweeps through his head, neck, shoulders, torso, and out to his extremities, warming his genitals with a burning kiss of desire. Setting down the hundred, he grabs his package and feels the bulge. He smiles to himself. *Ready for that slime ball Cohen now.*

Blood pressure through the roof, Whiting vibrates away in his tall executive chair. He licks his lips incessantly, sniffling his runny nose, eyes round as saucers. He dials and holds the handset to his ear as it rings Cohen's extension.

Benjamin Cohen leans in to pick up the phone. "Hello?"

A cocky grin is plastered all over Whiting's sweaty face. "Mr. Cohen, Gary Whiting returning your call."

Cohen's shark-like eyes light up. His tone is low, threatening. "Mr. Whiting, I've been trying to reach you all day. You had me worried. I was afraid you might be avoiding me. You're not avoiding me are you, Mr. Whiting?"

The not-so-veiled threat grates on Whiting and he comes unglued. "Listen, Cohen, I told you before, the damn estate has got this all tied up— GET OFF MY BACK!"

Cohen holds the handset away from his ear, his jaw clenching to control his rage. He brings the phone back to his ear. "Mr. Whiting, I don't think you fully appreciate the gravity of your situation. You WILL pay me, one way or another, of that you can be sure." Without waiting for a response, Cohen slams the handset into its cradle. *That's it!* Cohen picks up his cell and speed-dials Charlie Stein's number.

Whiting yells at the dead phone. "Shit! Shit, Shit, Shit!" He slams the phone down, seething. Fired by cocaine, his mind races with various scenarios of getting even. He mumbles to himself as the dramas play out in his head, dangerous scenes flickering at the speed of light. "What's that fat little fuck gonna do? He can't do anything to me. I don't owe him any money, Rodriguez owes him the money. I didn't sign anything. That fat little fuck. Who does he think he is?"

As scenes rush through his head, it gets worse, more violent, with him becoming the victim instead of the victor. Visions of him shot in an alley, bleeding to death with no one around to help. In an instant he sees the gun pointed at his head, hears the explosion, feels the muzzle flash on his temple as the bullet penetrates his skull, blowing his head apart like a rotten cantaloupe. *Gotta get outta here!*

Fumbling in his pencil drawer for his Valium, he trembles at the prospect of his sudden and painful demise at the hands of Cohen & Company. He punches up the WesternAir website and books the next flight for Vegas.

### [12:07 PM – Saturday, April 9, 2011]

The HVAC system quietly pumps oxygenated air at a constant seventy-two degrees. Bells clang and colored lights flash like an arcade full of pinball machines in a crazy cosmic carnival. Watered-down drinks sit two deep at the elbow of every player, twenty-four/seven. There's not a clock or an outside window to be found. Could be noon, could be midnight in the Tangiers main casino, no way to tell.

Gary Whiting's concentration fizzes and skips, darting around like bait fish in a bucket. He's been up all night, working his way through every dealer at every table, looking for a winner, losing at them all. Hammered, he sits slumped at a high-limit Blackjack table as the dealer tosses him a second card—two of clubs. With the king of spades in hand, he flicks the table top. "Hit me," he mumbles. Ten of hearts—bust. As he tosses the king face up, the dealer scrapes away another thousand dollars in chips. Whiting's luck is still shit. Can't catch a break. Nothing but bad luck since he arrived. Downing the last of his watered-down vodka tonic, he wonders, *How long has it been?* He needs something to change his luck. Maybe another little toot to smooth things out, sharpen his wits.

Pushing away from the table, Whiting staggers off to the men's room near the Tower One elevators. Glancing at the mirror over the men's room sink, he ignores the red nose, blotchy cheeks, and cold sweat beading on clammy flesh. All he sees is that hunted look in those bloodshot eyes. Fears of Cohen & Company flare up. Running his index finger and thumb under the water, he dabs at his nostrils, snorting the moisture to help relieve his swollen sinuses. Figures he's safe here, Cohen's thugs will never find him. He tilts his head back to let the cocaine residue drain down the back of his raw throat. Time to change his luck and get back to the tables. At least he can forget about Cohen while he's at the tables.

Furtively glancing around, Whiting makes sure he's alone. He retrieves the little vial of coke from his front pocket and unscrews the cap. Tapping out a healthy pile of crystalline powder, he snorts the coke deep into his left nostril. He repeats the process and sucks another large pile of cocaine up his right nostril. He pinches his nose shut. Inhaling deeply as he releases his nostrils, he pulls the white powder deeper into his sinus cavities. The effort makes him dizzy, the room fading to grey momentarily, pulsing blue-white lights spotting his vision. Hanging onto the counter, he blinks rapidly trying to clear the electric blue spots from his eyes. His vision gradually clears. And as he refocuses, he notices something warm and wet on his lips. He swipes at his upper lip with the back of his hand. Looking at his hand, he's puzzled by the red smear. He glances up into the mirror to see blood pouring from his nose, down his chin and draining on to his blood-soaked shirt. Panicky and light-headed, he turns to grab a handful of paper towels to stanch the bleeding. As he reaches out, his arm and shoulder explode with sharp pain. Stabbing pain flashes down his shoulder into his back and wraps around his ribcage like a giant python squeezing the life out of him. His eyes roll back in his head as he loses consciousness, dropping to the floor in a quivering heap, spittle leaking from the corner of his gaping mouth.


Whiting hears the murmur of voices, the squeak of rubber soles on lino-leum, the clink of metal utensils in stainless steel trays, the pneumatic whoosh of doors. He blinks rapidly at the too-bright light as he tries to open his eyes. Everything's white: white ceiling, white curtains, white lights, white sheets. He hears a calm male voice speaking to him in an East Indian accent.

"How are you feeling?"

Whiting tries to answer and it comes out as a hoarse croak.

He tries again and manages a raspy, "Where am I?"

"Las Vegas General Hospital, Intensive Care Unit. How are you feeling?"

"Not sure yet. What happened?"

"I'm Dr. Shamala. You've had a heart attack brought on by a drug overdose."

"Heart attack?!"

"Please, Mr. Whiting, calm yourself. You are still in a very delicate condition."

Whiting lets the news sink in. It explains a lot, like why he feels so shitty. Everything hurts. Must've been run over by a bulldozer. "Am I gonna be okay?"

"You should recover given proper treatment and if you stay off the drugs."

"How long before I can leave?"

Dr. Shamala gives a light chuckle and lightly pats his shoulder. "Oh, don't worry about that now. Just relax and take it easy. We'll work on getting you back on your feet before long."

"Thanks, Doc," he mumbles. Cringing, he turns his head aside as the doctor exits.

# KEEP ON TRUCKIN'

## [6:15 PM – Monday, April 11, 2011]

IT'S EARLY EVENING, the sun just above the western horizon—the day's built-up heat starting to dissipate. Detective Salmon glides the big black Marauder up Central Avenue on the short ride home. Hell, he'd walk if it wasn't so damn hot. It's been a long day, but he feels good about it, like he actually accomplished something. He spent the better part of the afternoon setting up a surveillance team and working out the logistics for monitoring the truck's Lojack device. If Underphal's prediction is right, they'll be all over it.

As his cell phone buzzes, he punches talk and puts it to his ear.

"Detective Salmon, it's Officer Denton, sorry to call you after hours."

"No problem, Officer. Whaddaya got for me?"

"Got that list you asked for."

"People with access to the truck?"

"Right. Seems Rodriguez was a generous guy."

"Whaddaya mean?"

"Well, according to the MJR vehicle maintenance people, Rodriguez lent that truck to almost everyone. Most of his subs used it at one time or another, any MJR employee that needed a truck, even his neighbors. Helluva list ..."

Salmon's mood sours. "Damn."

"Too bad the killer didn't use Rodriguez's Mercedes. Hell, he wouldn't even let his wife drive the Mercedes. Well, anyway, it's gonna take a while.

We're starting with their vehicle maintenance people, more specifically, the two main guys, a Rodney Stearns and a Timothy Jackson. We're checking the databases for priors and prints now."

"Let me know when you have somethin'."

### [9:28 AM – Tuesday, April 12, 2011]

Clear morning light fills the squad room, the gun-slot windows bathing the floor, the walls, and the used up metal furniture in its golden rays. Salmon throws the reports across his cluttered desk in frustration. Nothing has turned up on either of the MJR vehicle maintenance men. No criminal records and no forensics matches for either crime scene. They don't even fit the description, one short and stocky, the other average height and too thin. Nothing to tie them in as real suspects. That only leaves another fifty or so potential truck users to go. *What a pisser!*

He lets it simmer, sorting through it in his head. Maybe there's a faster way to shorten the list.

His lips tighten to a thin line as it dawns on him. There are at least two people who could possibly shed some light on this. Jumping up, he grabs his cell and dials Rodriguez's widow as he heads out. It's still ringing as he steps on the elevator. The doors close as he punches the parking garage button. His cell drops the call as the elevator drops down the shaft. *Shit!*

He redials Connie Rodriguez's number as he hustles out of the elevator toward his dormant Mercury. It finally rings through to voicemail. He leaves a curt message, letting her know he's on his way without really telling her why. Important police business.

The Mercury Marauder roars up I-17 pushing eighty. As Salmon approaches the 101 Loop interchange, he tries Connie's number again. Back to her voicemail. He decides to try Diane Telafano instead.

After reaching Diane's mother, Salmon speeds through the interchange heading north on the I-17 to Anthem and the Telafano residence. He'll catch up with the Widow Rodriguez later.

# MURDEROUS WORK

### [9:51 AM – Tuesday, April 12, 2011]

SPRAWLED IN MY broken-down recliner, I stare numbly at the flatscreen waiting for the secrets of the universe to be revealed. If the secrets aren't forthcoming, perhaps I'll get lucky and drift off. That would be good since I haven't slept in days. I'd like to blame it on old age, but it's getting increasingly difficult to get that old hound to hunt. Problem is, the onslaught of cryptic info pouring through my head in the form of prescient visions. Is it morning yet? Must be, nothing but infomercials, home shopping and reruns. There's no getting away from it, no relief.

If I could do anything else ... I can't eat and I'm out of beers. Stuck in my chair, my head reeling and my stomach in knots, I'm exhausted well past the point of no return. Not likely I'll ever sleep again. *Shit!* I'd yell at Sonja, but she's all I've got. And if she goes, it's over. Besides, she'd just ignore me or worse, yell back. I don't think I can take it anymore. *Shit!*

This latest bout is more confusing than any of them. Almost unrelated, not sure what it means other than she's in trouble. And it's taken me several hours just to figure out who "she" is. She's driving that damn truck, taking it over a cliff's edge into a pool of blood. As she sinks, the truck disintegrates around her, evaporating in the bloody murk. The music comes up and her husband waltzes in to take her in his arms. They dance and swirl downward, ever sinking as the music plays, the Tennessee Waltz echoing in the background. *I remember the night ...*

I reach for my cell and autodial Salmon.

"What can I do for ya, Underphal?"

"It's Rodriguez's wife ..."

"What about her?"

"I saw her. It came to me. She's in trouble"

"Whaddaya mean, she's in trouble?"

"Not sure exactly. A vision. She was dancing."

"Dancing, I see. And she's in trouble, how?"

"You know that song, the Tennessee Waltz?"

"Yeah, kinda."

"She was dancing to that song, the Tennessee Waltz ... with her dead husband."

Salmon automatically rolls his eyes then catches himself and thinks about it. "Yeah, well. I've been trying to reach her. Got to see her later anyway. I'll call her again."

"Thanks, Detective. I appreciate it. It'll make me feel better"

# NO TIME FOR GOODBYES

**[10:19 AM – Tuesday, April 12, 2011]**

CONNIE RODRIGUEZ LIES naked and alone in her sculptured marble tub, staring at the inlaid vaulted ceiling, tears leaking from her puffy face. The water's surface, still as a breathless night, smooth as a polished mirror, surrounds her in its liquid embrace. Her half-empty wine glass sits on the tub's deck next to an empty bottle of Merlot. Next to the bottle lies a razor-sharp paring knife from her custom kitchen. The very kitchen she helped design, right down to the selection of professional culinary knives that sit on her polished granite counter.

Drifting away, Connie listlessly wanders back through all the little things that led her here, confirming she's right, out of options, that there's no other way. How many times has she attempted to wean herself off the antidepressants? Every time she thought she was going to finally make it, really do it this time, the gnawing anxiety ground her will down to nothing. Unable to sleep, exhaustion fueled her constant headaches, then the nausea and the agony in her muscles and joints. *And OhMyGod, the whirling—the brain zaps.* Each time she tried to stop she had to go back on the meds to function at all, back on the very poison that led her to this precipice in the first place—diabolically insidious, a perfectly crafted trap.

Her crystal-blue eyes drain as she cries herself out, feeling the tears dry on swollen cheeks. Her pampered skin stretched tight, salt from the dried tears itching. A wry grin almost lifts the pretty mouth as she wonders, *Where's my doctor now?*

She'd watched herself split into people she didn't recognize, detached and zombie-like on the outside, a raving lunatic on the inside. Her life wasn't that much worse at first, but everything kept going wrong, leaving her drowning in regret for things she wasn't even sure she'd done, the house, the business, the estate, and most of all, the children.

Maybe she hadn't tried hard enough. Maybe she didn't have the guts, have what it takes to be a good Christian, a good person. How many times has she asked the Lord for guidance? She's lost count, but her prayers remain unanswered. She tried and tried and it's come down to this. The only way out.

The warm bathwater turns a thin pink and then a dingy yellowish red as blood leaks from her ruined wrists. She doesn't hear her smartphone ringing on her vanity.

She's feeling light-headed as the room starts to fade. Soon it'll all be over. Her only regret, she didn't think to say goodbye. And now it's too late. She wonders if God will damn her soul. She doubts that God cares. She can't expect them to understand, but she hopes the children will be all right. Too weak to think about it anymore, she's slipping away.

# TOUGH DUTY

**[10:27 AM – Tuesday, April 12, 2011]**

AS SALMON PULLS up in front of the Telafano home, he cringes, recalling Diane's breakdown. He glances at the nondescript tract house. This is the part of the job he hates, moments like these. He knew when Diane's mother answered the phone that this would be tough duty. He'll have to stir up more bad memories, cause more anguish in a life that already has more than its share. Regrettable, but he's got a job to do.

He flashes a forced smile. Without a word Angela Telafano glares at him as she lets him in, her stare full of daggers. Ah well, if looks could kill, he'd have been dead and buried long ago. Guess he can't really blame her. He resigns himself to the task at hand, moving to the couch as Mrs. Telafano leaves to fetch Diane.

Diane gives him a sad little smile as she slowly wheels up to face him. "Back for more dirt are we, Detective?"

Her sarcasm is almost poignant. Yet he knows deep down, no one has a right to be bitter. Besides, it never helps. He tightens his lips, mustering his resolve. "Diane, I really do appreciate everything you're doing. It may not seem like it to you, but it's making a big difference."

Diane nods, resigning herself to his presence.

"Please do your best to remember—who at MJR had access to Mr. Rodriguez's vehicles?"

She cocks her head, thinking. "You mean Michael's Mercedes or his work truck?"

"Specifically, the silver F-150."

"Yeah, that'd be his work truck. He lent it to almost anyone who wanted it. Kept it in his private garage with the Mercedes. Keys on the wall next to the door." She thinks about it for a few moments. "Even though they were registered to the company, they were his personal vehicles. The maintenance crew took care of them, anyone could borrow the work truck, but Michael was the only one who drove the Mercedes."

Salmon leans forward. "Think you could help us narrow it down to the most frequent users?"

"I don't know, Detective."

"We've already checked out the vehicle maintenance staff. Anyone else come to mind?" Salmon pulls out his note pad and pen.

"Did you try the subs?"

"We've got a list. Maybe if you'd look it over, to make sure we're not leaving anyone out." He puts his note pad and pen away.

"Yeah, I guess."

"Okay, I'll have someone drop by with the list."

"I really don't want to see anyone. Could you email it to me?"

"Sure, whatever you need." Salmon rises to leave. "And thank you."

Diane smiles weakly as she watches the tall detective depart.


Headed south on the I-17, Salmon guns the Mercury, pushing it to eighty. Telafano didn't help much, but it's a start. He'll get Denton on it then head over to North Scottsdale to see if Mrs. Rodriguez has anything for him. He calls Denton.

"Denton, I need you to email that list of subs to Diane Telafano for verification."

"Will do, sir."

Easing off to seventy-five, Salmon takes the Loop 101 exit east, heading for Scottsdale and the Rodriguez residence. As he merges into traffic, Salmon redials Connie Rodriguez. After several rings, it goes to voicemail and he leaves another message, letting her know he's on his way.

Salmon pulls up to the Desert Pueblos guard house. Recognizing the guard, he flashes a smile and his ID. Curiously, the guard opens the gate and waves him through without calling the Rodriguez residence. Maybe she heard his message, maybe she's expected him.

A surge of adrenalin flashes through him as he idles up to the Rodriguez's stone arch entrance. Two Scottsdale police cruisers, a Metro Fire EMT unit, and a Southwest ambulance crowd the circular drive, red and blue lights flashing. *What the hell?*

Salmon slots his Marauder between the two cruisers, logs off and jumps out. Spotting a uniform at the top of the stairs, he trots up. The uniform is a trim female with close-cropped red hair, in starched blues. She gives him a quick nod, a serious look chiseled on her young features. He pulls his ID, extending it for her inspection as he mounts the last stair.

She looks at his badge. "What can I do for you, Detective?"

Salmon glances at her brass nameplate. "Officer Nelson, what's the story?"

"An 11-45," she replies matter-of-factly.

"Attempted suicide? Who?"

"A Mrs. Rodriguez. EMT boys are trying to stabilize her now. Chopper's on its way."

"Thanks."

He pushes past Nelson and rushes through the entry courtyard into the Rodriguez home. Hearing a commotion, he turns left and sprints through a broad hallway into a huge master suite. Another uniform stands in the master suite. He's herding a short woman and three children toward the tall double doors. The officer has his hands full, trying to calm the frantic woman and children. Salmon hears the roar of the approaching chopper as he strides into the master bath. Underphal's words ring in his ears. *"I saw her . . . she's in trouble."* Three EMTs crouch next to a pale body, working furiously, their backs to Salmon. He bites his lower lip. He could have acted sooner, taken Underphal at his word. *How did Underphal know?* The EMTs coordinate a lift, hefting the slack flesh onto a gurney, then lifting as the wheels drop and lock. Using gauze tape, they quickly but gently secure the naked body to the padded surface. Salmon watches intently, sees the heavily bandaged wrists, the IV tubes and bags as they cover her with a blanket, belt it down and wheel her out, rushing for the chopper.

An EMT lags behind to collect their gear. His boyish face is deceiving, too young for such heavy responsibility. Salmon catches his eye as he looks up from a first aid case. "She gonna make it?"

The boy shakes his head. "She's lost a lotta blood. We did everything we could. It'll be close, if she makes it at all." Grabbing a large first responder bag in one hand and a medical kit in the other, the young EMT trudges out of the master bath to leave Salmon standing there alone.

Salmon takes it all in. The imported tile smeared with blood, wet and slippery. Pinkish water beaded into little puddles. The luxurious tub filled to overflowing, its brackish water dark reddish-brown with blood and excreta, the gut-wrenching stench overpowering.

*What a waste.* Death photos of Marilyn Monroe flash through his mind. A frigid shiver runs up Salmon's spine, raising every hair on his body in goose flesh. He exhales deeply to gather himself then turns away.

As Salmon hustles out of the Rodriguez home, Underphal's words replay in his head. *"She was dancing …with her dead husband."* He keeps thinking, *Should have been here sooner.*

# HEAD BANGIN'

**[11:59 AM – Tuesday, April 12, 2011]**

SLEEP DEPRIVATION IS a bitch. Cloistered in this dump of a rental, I lost count somewhere around five days. Best I've managed is a couple hours here and there when I passed out in my recliner. I smell bad, haven't changed or showered in a week, rank as hell. Truth be told, I haven't been outta this chair except to hit the head and grab another brew-ski for about that long. Too dizzy when I attempt to stand, my head pounding like a sheet metal shop working overtime. The first couple days I thought it'd pass. But now, it seems unreal, getting worse, as though it will go on forever. I'm long past the point of caring. Too bad the beer doesn't help the stream of visions barreling through my head—like an infomercial from hell on that cursed flatscreen. If only I could turn it off.

Are they real or hallucinations? Eyes open or closed, it all looks the same. Visions of the dead. I don't really know these dead people, but the dead are the dead, a constant reminder of those I've lost … mostly my wife. When all those around you are dead, the tragedy isn't that they're gone. The real tragedy is that you're still here, left behind to face what's left of your life without them. Times like these, I long for the promise of peace that death offers. If only …

I miss my wife, miss her warmth, the sweet scent of her skin when we embraced, the gentle fragrance of her hair. I miss Sonja. Don't know how much more I can take.

"Feeling sorry for ourselves again?" Sonja's words are close and clear, like she's speaking from inside. I feel her as much as I hear her, her thoughts emanating at my very core.

I'm put off by her callousness. *Who is she to tell me how I feel? I'm the one suffering here!* "I don't know where you think you get off, but this is bullshit! I'm dying here and all you can do is make snide remarks? This is TOTAL BULLSHIT! I need you to help me! Do something! Anything! WHAT THE FUCK?!"

Sonja's tone warms, reassuring. "Easy there cowboy, you've got work to do—*we've* got work to do. Not to worry, we'll get through it together."

I start to relax, the pulsing thunder in my brain easing ever so slightly. It's a start. And right now, I'll take anything I can get.

"Now focus. Know that what you're experiencing is simply communication. Communication in a different form. You're perceiving information from another plane of consciousness no less real than the material world. It's yours to use. But the more you resist, the more you flinch and turn away, the more difficult it becomes, the less control you have and the more overwhelming it will be. Remember, it's just communication."

I try to wrap my wits around what she's saying—communication, communication from another world ... I don't know. "Seems like I was doin' so good before. Somehow I lost it."

"Like anything else, it takes practice. You can't quit now. You've gone too far down this path to turn back. You have to see it through. Back off now and it'll drive you insane. And don't think for an instant that you can get out of it by dying. That will only make things worse. It won't go away."

Her words conflict me, giving me a spark of hope and yet at the same time terrifying me. *What if I can't do it? What if I fail?*

I screw up my courage, determined to get through it somehow. "Don't leave me. I need you."

"You can handle it. Trust me. I'm here. I won't let you fail." Sonja's voice resonates within me, comforting me, shoring me up.

I feel her here with me, backing me up, part of me, inside me, giving me strength. I think I can do this.

I relax, stop trying to hold it all at bay and just let it flow. A violent shudder runs through me, and then it's gone. The pounding in my head subsides a bit more. The cramps, the muscle spasms, all the tension melts away and I'm left raw and naked, wide open, ready to experience anything. I check for Sonja, making sure she's still here.

"You can do this. Just take a look."

Eyes closed, I look around. It's dark and thick as though shrouded in dense fog. The impenetrable billows shift and pulse as if alive and breathing. Faint pinpoints of light appear through the turbidity. As they approach, I see they're headlights with a row of day-bright running lights above, their beams searching through the murk. My heart pounds, my pulse races. I sense it. I know what's coming. *It's that damn truck.*

The lights grow closer as they hunt back and forth through the thick fog. Sweeping in my direction, they turn on me, blindingly bright, lighting up the fog like spotlights at a Hollywood premiere. I'm entranced, caught in the 4X4's lights, exposed to view. As the tall pickup sits idling, I can almost make out the shiny grill, the chrome bull bar. But there's a blank spot where the windshield should be. *Who's driving that damn thing?*

I work my way around to the driver's door and peer up at the dark glass. The driver's window slides down with a hum. From the dark cab, a mottled grey face stares at me with a death's head grin. In spite of the desiccated flesh, I know this face. It's the dead guy, Rodriguez.

I see the door swing open on the far side of the cab. I back away, uncertain. Fishing around for Sonja's presence, I feel her warm glow, constant, as though this is all routine, and I'm reassured. I work my way around the front of the monster truck to the passenger door, climbing up and in. As I squirm into the big leather captain's chair, the door swings shut, cloaking me in darkness.

There's an edge to the air in here, a palpable energy and I'm electrified with the tension. I look in the driver's direction. A set of teeth glow in a Cheshire's grin, then disappear. I feel the truck roll forward. *Communication, my ass!*

I look around, straining to see, but there's nothing. It's so dark I can't see my hand in front of my face. I lower my hand to my lap and stare straight ahead, unsure what to do next.

A small disturbance in the blackness. Is there something there, or am I trying so hard that I'm hallucinating?

"It'll clear up, keep looking," says Sonja.

The disturbance spreads, forming the outline of the windshield. It intensifies, crawling with fat worms of dark energy, writhing as though feeding on each other, vibrating with crackling light. At first, ever so faint, taking on a dark glow like molten lava seeping up through the fissures, the forming mass burns. The glowing mass brightens to red-orange, then yellow, finally radiating white-hot heat. The white-hot mass burns off, leaving a perfectly clear view of the dissipating fog outside.

I glance to the side to see Rodriguez staring straight ahead, hands at two and ten on the wheel. I want to ask where we're going, but it doesn't really matter. I'm along for the ride.

We pick up speed as the fog thins. The driving lights illuminate a winding dirt road. The dirt road is little more than tire tracks carved into the desert floor, rough and weathered, full of stones and ruts. Rodriguez guns the engine, pushing our speed past anything close to reasonable. We barrel down the narrow track, bouncing, sliding, pitching side to side, the fat tires spraying dirt and rocks as they break traction. I hang on as we fly out of a dip. As we slam down, I see a man running up ahead, his back illuminated in the glare.

Rodriguez speeds up, laughing maniacally. Just before we run him down, the man turns and stumbles. I see his face clearly as the chrome bull bar slams into him. His head smacks the dirt like a ripe melon and he's gone.

I keep telling myself it's only communication. But is it communication about something that's already happened, or something about to happen? I can't tell. And who was that guy? I haven't seen him before. I glance at Rodriguez. He's laughing hysterically.

Rodriguez turns to me, still laughing. "One down, two to go."

I muster a little courage. "Who was that?"

Tears stream down Rodriguez's grey-mottled cheeks, he's laughing so hard. "Death's a bitch, ain't it?" More laughing. "Can you believe it? That genius was my partner!"

Somehow I need to check out of this nightmare and warn Salmon. *Sonja?*

## [2:01 PM – Tuesday, April 12, 2011]

Still dazed from all the new meds and weak from his heart attack, Gary Whiting shuffles slowly through the Tangiers' main casino, headed for the bank of elevators and his room. It's been three days since he ended up in the hospital. He's lucky the Tangiers held his room. Dr. Shamala wanted to hold him longer, but he was antsy to get out. To Whiting's way of thinking, a hospital is no place to get well. He's certain he'll do better in his comped luxury suite at the Tangiers. It's quieter, better food, no one to tell him what he should and shouldn't do. *Fuck Shamala and his lectures on drug abuse.* All he needs is a Valium and a long nap.

Whiting enters the shiny brass express elevator and punches the button for the thirty-first floor. When the doors slide open, he exits and shuffles down the long hall. In front of his room's double doors, he fumbles for the card key. He inserts the card in the lock, grabs the levered handle and leans into one of the heavy doors. The suite's interior is dark with the blackout drapes closed—the only dim illumination comes from an ornate table lamp. Whiting shuffles through the marble tiled entryway, heading for the luxurious master bedroom with a relaxed smile on his face. He fails to notice two shadowy figures behind him on either side of the entry doors. One is tall and lanky, the shine on his alligator boots barely reflecting the dim light, his eyes aglow beneath the rim of his Stetson. The other's bull mastiff frame and beady black eyes reflect no light at all, much like his dead soul.

# IT'S A HIT

### [4:59 PM – Tuesday, April 12, 2011]

ON THE BUSTLING 101 Loop, traffic slows to a crawl at the I-17 Interchange. Frank Salmon drives on autopilot, his thoughts swirling around the events of the day. Still gutted over Connie's suicide attempt, he chews his bottom lip, hoping she makes it. Telafano's sad smile pops into his head, pushing his concern for Connie aside. He wonders if Denton got that list to Diane yet. Connie's condition still worries him. He needs to call Underphal.

Underphal answers on the sixth ring.

"Lance, it's Frank Salmon."

Salmon waits for a reply as a long silence ensues. "Underphal, ya still with me?"

"Yeah, uh yeah. Glad you called, actually. I was just getting ready to call you."

"I need to let you know about Rodriguez's wife."

"Oh … yeah. She okay?"

"She attempted suicide. They took her to Scottsdale General in critical condition. Don't know if she'll make it."

"Oh … sorry."

"Not your fault. You tried to warn me."

"I know, but …"

"Hey, you did your best," says Salmon. "More than I can say for the rest us."

"Bummer …"

"I know."

Neither man speaks for several moments.

"You were gonna call me?" Salmon asks.

"Yeah. More visions."

"Tell me."

"Not sure exactly. Does Rodriguez have a partner?"

"Several, in several different companies. Why?"

"One of them is in danger."

"Anything more you can tell me?"

"He might be killed, maybe an accident."

"Anything else?"

"I saw his face."

"You can identify him?"

"I'll try."

Salmon's police radio cackles with an incoming call.

"Lance, hold on a sec, I gotta take this."

Salmon pulls the mic off the console bracket. "One Forty-Seven, go ahead Two Twenty-Four."

Two Twenty-Four comes through loud and clear. "Thought you'd like to know, we've got a hit on that Lojack you've got us babysittin'."

"Give me a destination as soon as you've got one. And thanks. One Forty-Seven out."

"No problem. Two One Eleven is on his way. We'll keep you posted. Two Twenty-Four out."

Salmon re-clips the mic and picks up his cell. "Lance, ya still with me?"

"Yeah, I'm here."

"Look, something's come up."

"What?"

"We just gotta Lojack hit on Rodriguez's truck."

"Yeah, and?"

"Means it's hot."

"Someone stole it?"

"Yeah, and they're on the move. I'll have to get back to you on that partner thing—maybe have you come down, look at some photos. I'll get back to you."

Turning on his emergency flashers, Salmon accelerates. He swerves to the shoulder to bypass the gridlock then weaves in and out of traffic as he heads for the last known location of the Rodriguez vehicle—the MJR Development compound.

# TAKING CARE
# OF BUSINESS

**[5:01 PM – Tuesday, April 12, 2011]**

NORTH OF THE city, a giant lion's head stands atop a tall pole like a homing beacon to those seeking the lure of firm, fully exposed female flesh. Construction trucks and sport sedans fill the giant parking lot as rush hour turns into happy hour at the Lion's Den Gentlemen's Club.

A customized 4X4 pickup, its license plate smeared with mud, rumbles up to the private parking gate. Recognizing the silver F-150, the attendant waves it through. The killer nods, certain the attendant can't identify him behind the wraparound shades and wide-rimmed cowboy hat.

Backing into the space closest to the entrance, the killer jumps out and strides for the infamous rear entry. A wide grin breaks across his face in anticipation.

Once inside, the killer glides through the dining room and back kitchen into a dark narrow hall. He scans the rows of doors on either side, back access to the dancers' cubbies. Finding Sondra Du's cubby, his pulse quickens.

The killer twists the door knob, preparing to push through, but it's locked. Furious, his face reddens, veins bulging. He steps back, raises his long leg and smashes a cowboy boot through the flimsy door. A startled squeal erupts from inside as he reaches through the shattered door and turns the knob.

The killer explodes into the room, filling the small dark space with menace. A fat, flabby little man scrambles backwards over the divan, clutching his clothes, his pasty white belly jiggling like a nursing sow, his eyes wide with terror. Sondra Du huddles naked at the foot of the divan, wiping her mouth on her arm, eyes darting around, desperately looking for cover.

The killer pulls a 9mm semi-automatic from the back of his pants and points it at the pathetic excuse of a man. "Get out!"

Sondra's john runs naked to the other door, tightly gripping his pants in one hand. Fumbling with the lock, he panics, turns and attempts to run past the killer for the ruined back door.

The killer clubs the back of his head with his pistol butt as he passes, dropping the pathetic fuck to the floor in a quivering lump of flesh. He secretly wishes he had more time, he'd do them both. But Sondra is who he came for and he's bent on squeezing every last drop of exquisite agony out of her luscious flesh.

Sondra's soft smooth skin trembles. *That fucker's crazy!* The panic button is on the far end of the divan on the underside of the end table. She'll never get there without tipping him off. No way Jesse can get there in time. She clutches her knees to her perfect breasts, curling into a fetal position naked on the floor, playing dead, hoping he'll just go away.

The Lion's Den's thundering subwoofers pound out a deafening roar. No one hears the frenzied shrieks, the wails, the guttural grunts—or the double pop of a 9mm.

Sondra Du's broken body lies in a spreading pool of dark blood and fecal matter, arms askew, legs spread wide at an impossible angle exposing ruined genitalia. The twisted left foot twitches, the purplish-black big toe drumming erratically on soiled carpet. Film clouds lifeless eyes, one lid half closed, the other wide open in an unseeing stare. A purplish swollen tongue lolls out the side of her gaping mouth, stubs of broken teeth protrude from battered gums, blood oozing from torn, puffy lips. The head lays twisted back and around, dislocated from the crushed neck vertebrae, the blonde hair matted with black blood. Two black bullet penetrations in the left temple leak dark blood. The once-creamy flesh, plagued with blue-white

312 Michael Allan Scott

splotches discoloring to purplish grey. The vibrant curves now flaccid lumps of misshapen flesh.

The killer's head buzzes. His pits, back and chest are soaked with sweat from a heady mix of exertion and the thrill of the kill. He sucks at slobbery lips, strings of drool leaking from the corners of his mouth, the wet spot in his crotch spreading with his ejaculate. Panting heavily, he turns to make good his escape. Then like a bolt out of the blue, it hits him. He wipes down the 9mm with his shirttail and curls the unconscious little fat man's fingers around the still smoking gun.

Grinning like he's just won the Powerball jackpot, the killer tromps out to the truck. He laughs hysterically as he accelerates out of the back lot, waving at the lot attendant on his way through the gate. Steering the monster truck toward the road and back to the I-17 freeway, he revels in his good fortune. *The perfect crime.*

# THE CHASE

### [5:23 PM – Tuesday, April 12, 2011]

THE JET-BLACK MARAUDER rockets north on I-17, the throaty roar of its supercharged V-8 pushing effortlessly past ninety. Its grill's blue and red flashing lights warn civilians out of its path. Up ahead, but not yet in visual range, Two Twenty-Four is on an intercept course, tracking the Rodriguez truck by its Lojack signal. Two One Eleven piloted by Officer Denton is hot on their tail. Salmon's radio chatters away keeping him on track as he hustles to join the hunt. Salmon's pulse pounds in his ears, palms sweating in anticipation. With any luck, this is it. Whoever's in that silver F-150 is more than likely their killer.

Salmon's racing thoughts are sidelined by the crackle of his radio.

"One Forty-Seven, this is Two Twenty-Four."

He snatches the mic off the console. "Go ahead, Two Twenty-Four."

"Looks like your 11-54 is up ahead. We're closing fast."

"What's your 10-20?"

"Passing Thunderbird now."

"On my way. One Forty-Seven out."

Roughly two miles behind his team, Salmon accelerates, pushing the Marauder past a hundred and ten. He hits the siren and concentrates, preparing for erratic maneuvers from startled civilians as he streaks up I-17. As he passes the Thunderbird Road exit, he catches a glimpse of flashing lights up ahead. He pushes his speed up to one twenty-five in the wake cleared by his team. A couple seconds later he spots the other set of lights as well. As he settles in behind Denton, his speed drops below ninety.

Salmon grabs his mic. "Two Twenty-Four, it's One Forty-Seven."

"Go ahead One Forty-Seven."

"I'm right behind Two One Eleven. What's the status?"

"Looks like your 11-54 is roughly five miles up the road. But based on the close rate, he's either stopped or headed back this way. We'll know in a couple minutes."

"Got it, One Forty-Seven out."

Salmon reacts suddenly to Denton's bright brake lights, slamming on his brakes to avoid rear-ending the patrol car as its rear end lifts and its nose dives in a hard braking maneuver. Salmon regains his composure and drops back in behind Denton and Two Twenty-Four as they swerve right, cutting across three lanes to exit on Deer Valley Road.

"One Forty-Seven this is Two Twenty-Four, your 11-54 just passed us southbound. We're turning to pursue. Do you want us to apprehend?"

"Two Twenty-Four, 10-4 on course change and that's affirmative to apprehend. One Forty-Seven out."

"10-4. Calling for chopper backup. Two Twenty-Four out."

Traffic pulls over and stops dead on the interchange as civilians react. Two Phoenix police cruisers and a Mercury sedan scream by with sirens wailing—their emergency lights flashing in burst patterns. Lit like low flying UFOs, the police cars slide through the interchange. Lurching sideways, their tires squeal as they round the off-ramp's transition and blast back down the on-ramp. Their exhausts spew dark carbon as they accelerate hard off the ramp. Single-file, they rocket across three lanes of freeway traffic, heading south.


Up ahead, the tall F-150 goes with the flow, doing seventy in the center lane. The killer, unconcerned with his surroundings, relives the satiation of unspeakable appetites. His eyes squint as he revels in perverse pleasures derived from his victim's sacrifice. Licking his lips, he recalls each little detail in a crude attempt to re-experience the bloodlust. Laying her bare to her soul, then ripping the life out of her, and making good money to boot—a real coup. His hot face reddens as he bursts into a wicked laugh.

Out of the corner of his eye the killer catches a flash in his rearview mirror. *Cops!!!* His stomach clenches and pulse pounds. Verging on panic, he works to get a grip. *Not me.*

Muscles in knots, shoulders and neck rigid, he struggles to steady his death grip on the wheel as he slows to the exact speed limit, sixty-five, waiting for the cops to pass. Suddenly, they are right on his ass, lights flashing, sirens squealing like an electronic pig. *NO!* Terror rips through his feeble rationale like a detonating cruise missile. With a mind of its own, his right foot mashes the gas.

Salmon spots the Rodriguez truck as Two Twenty-Four pulls up behind it. Two One Eleven is just in front of Salmon and in line behind Two Twenty-Four. Background transmissions on his radio and the drone of rotors tell him the police chopper is in position overhead. He hears the warning blips from Two Twenty-Four's siren as it signals the big 4X4 to pull over. Suddenly the silver pickup leaps ahead and Salmon instantly steels himself for high-speed pursuit.

The truck scoots away, accelerating hard, lurching to the left, leaning dangerously as it cuts in front of traffic to dive into the HOV lane. Salmon's team speeds up in unison, sirens screaming, lights flashing, hot on the truck's tail. This late in the day the heavy traffic is northbound toward home in the suburbs. The southbound traffic is fairly light as the high-speed chase blasts its way down the carpool lane, racing back into the city. Salmon's speedometer rises past one twenty and keeps climbing as they fly down the HOV lane, working to keep pace with the truck.

At these speeds, the truck's high center of gravity causes it to pitch and lurch wildly, careening on the ragged edge as it barrels down the HOV lane. With the chopper tracking above, Two Twenty-Four backs off slightly, allowing a safer distance between the cruiser and the squirrely truck.

The demon truck's brake lights shine as its nose dives. Swerving right to dodge a Honda, the truck violently weaves its way through slower traffic in the center lanes. Two Twenty-Four follows the truck directly from behind while Two One Eleven sticks to the carpool and fast lanes. Salmon works his way to the far right in a coordinated effort to outflank the fleeing truck. The idea is to give the perp enough rope to hang himself and then carefully tighten the noose. A tricky business while dodging traffic at these speeds. Salmon breaks into a gritty grin as the standard disclaimer crosses his mind. *Professional driver on a closed course. Do not attempt.*

Then it happens. A confused motorist in a green SUV panics and slams on her brakes causing a chain reaction of flaring brake lights, squealing tires and skidding vehicles as they swerve out of control and slam into each other. In a split second, twisting steel, breaking glass, heavy thuds and the earsplitting screech of tearing metal explodes into chaos.

The silver truck violently veers to the right in a hopeless attempt to avoid the carnage. Tilting up on two wheels, the truck wavers in slow motion before finally slamming down on the driver's side. Sparks fly and metal screams as the truck slides on its side in a long arc. The renegade truck eventually slows, sliding to a stop against the back wheels of a jackknifed tanker.

Salmon and his team converge on the truck, sliding their cars to a stop, surrounding the dead truck on three sides. The chopper dutifully hovers overhead, its shiny fuselage glinting in the setting sun. First to arrive, Salmon opens his door and pulls his Beretta 9mm. He cautiously uses his door as a shield as he observes the truck. Smoke curls from the undercarriage as fluids spread on the asphalt. No sign of movement in the cab.

Signaling Denton and the rest of his crew, Salmon edges out from behind the door, pistol cocked and extended, ready to fire. He slowly approaches the downed vehicle, working his way up to the truck's bed. Salmon edges up to the truck's roof glancing through the rear window on his way by. Leaning against the roof, he peers through the top of the windshield looking for signs of life.

Behind the steering wheel a motionless torso slumps in the driver's seat, a slack face beneath a crumpled cowboy hat, wraparound shades pushed up at an angle across a bloody forehead, eyes closed, the head lolling to the side resting on bare asphalt where the driver's window once was, hair matted in a seeping smear of dark blood. There's a small rise in the chest signaling faint respiration. In the back of his mind, Salmon hears the sirens of the EMTs and ambulances as they arrive. He backs off, takes a deep breath, holsters his Beretta, and waves in the emergency crews.

Denton walks up as Salmon watches the emergency crews scramble over the truck. They've got the passenger door open on the truck's high side as the officers from Two Twenty-Four stand guard. Three EMTs are lowering a backboard and a first responder bag down to a couple of the EMTs already inside. Salmon glances at Denton.

"Is he gonna make it?" asks Denton.

"Can't tell. Why don't you check. And while you're at it, see who it is."

Salmon watches as Denton walks up to the truck's windshield, peers in then says something to one of the EMTs. After a short exchange, Denton walks back to Salmon.

"He's alive, but beat up pretty good. Ground off the side of his face on the pavement, but should make it."

"Hmm."

"EMT says no weapons, wallet or ID. I'll send a couple uniforms to the hospital with him."

"This guy's our killer. Tell those EMTs to be careful. It's a crime scene. Make sure you tell Forensics to get everything. And I want this guy shackled with two uniforms on him at all times." Salmon turns and heads for his car.

Early evening's grey light sets in over the carnage of the ten car pileup. The fading dimness cloaks the ragged edges of crashed vehicles and lives ruined in split-second collisions. Battered casualties litter the scene, hastily attended by EMTs. A constant stream of flashing red lights announces ambulance arrivals and departures.

Salmon ignores the chaos, concentrating on his mirrors as he carefully backs out of the disaster area.

The V-8 rumbles as he wheels around the worst of it. He picks his way through the debris and eases out into the empty lanes headed south. As he logs in, his radio crackles with static from Dispatch's call. Listening to his assignment, Salmon's face reddens as his heart sinks. *Shit!* He whips off the I-17 at the next exit. Hitting his siren and emergency lights, he hustles the big sedan through the interchange and heads north for the Lion's Den. Apparently, they didn't catch that fucker in time.

As Salmon exits I-17, his cell lights up with Lacey's number.

Hardened features betray Salmon's grim mood. "Lace, I'm in the middle of a call. I'll get back to ya later."

"You on your way to the Lions' Den?"

"Yup."

"I'm picking up Lance and am on my way."

"Why are you pickin' up Underphal?"

"I need photos and he's too out of it to drive. Says he hasn't slept in a week."

"Huh. And you're gonna have him do the shoot?"

"Yeah, I know. But he's still the best there is. See ya there."

"Yup." Salmon clicks off as he blasts down the empty road toward the Lion's Den. *Helluva day, so far.*

# LION TAMER

**[6:37 PM – Tuesday, April 12, 2011]**

I COULDN'T BELIEVE it when Lacey called, and I believe it even less now. Don't know why I'm so surprised. Another stripper dead. This time at the Lions' Den. And Lacey wants me to do the shoot. She apparently can't find anyone else to work this cheap. Don't know how many times I told her no—stubborn little wench. Salmon's got his hands full with her, I'm sure.

I stumble into my musty bedroom and rummage through drawers looking for anything clean enough to wear. She'll be here any minute and the drawers are mostly empty. It's just that I haven't slept and am half delirious. Don't know how much good I can do with a camera if I can't focus. Good thing it has autofocus. I pull on a pair of wrinkled cargo pants I found on the floor. At least she offered to come get me. No way I can drive. *Drive, shit, I can hardly see.* I sniff the pits of a stained T-shirt I found on the top of the chest—tolerable. I pull it on, grab my Nikes and head for the kitchen counter. Still can't tell if my eyes are open or closed as bizarre images swirl through my vision. Hearing must be fine. Lacey's pounding on the door. I grab my camera gear and head out.

Lacey chatters manically all the way out to her Prius. At the curb, my cynicism kicks in as I eye the Prius, waiting for her to hit the locks. The ultra-hip car for the environmentally pseudo-responsible and do-gooder celebs—way too much hype for little ol' me. Guess I probably wouldn't object, if it wasn't such a big fad. I contemplate sharing this with Lacey and my head spins so I keep my mouth shut and my cynicism to myself. *What the fuck do I know?* I drive a fifteen-year-old Sentra that smokes like a chimney.

I climb in and she hands me a latte and a sweet roll, bless her heart. Frank Salmon is one lucky son of a bitch.

We pull smoothly away from the curb and speed off for the scene of the latest homicide. *Nice car.* While Lacey continues her monologue I munch on the sweet roll and suck on the latte, determined not to think about another murder scene. *Fuck me. I can't believe I'm doing this.*

It's well after dark as we pull up to the Lion's Den. The black night, a velvety backdrop to the garish Lion's Den sign. A cluster of red and blue emergency lights flash, offsetting the sign's gold and red neon. Emergency and police vehicles are gathered around the front entrance, giving the scene a morbid carnival atmosphere. The news vans with their telescoping antennae add to the grim fray.

To distract myself, I run B movie titles through my mind—*Dancers of Death, Strip Tease Terror, Horror at the Whore House.* Better stick to still photography. In spite of efforts not to take it seriously, the throbbing at the back of my skull ratchets up a notch as we park.

I find myself immersed in dark swirling force fields. Crackling and writhing, they embroil the entire scene in an aura of raw energy. It's a wickedness that permeates everything. Its constricting pressure and static electric sting make my skin crawl.

I shoulder my gear bag and follow Lacey through the throng of TV news mongers and official personnel. We duck under the yellow crime scene tape and work our way inside, unobstructed. The uniforms guarding the perimeter seem to recognize Lacey's favored status and wave us through, much to the chagrin of the other news hounds.

We jostle our way through the entrance tunnel, crowded with police, firemen and EMTs. Caught in the crossfire, confused patrons are herded into long lines against the walls, some dazed, some indignant, all waiting for permission to leave. The rough tunnel empties out into a large showroom/bar area.

Detective Salmon sits at a table in front of the empty stage with a couple of uniforms and some guy who looks like he's in big trouble. Salmon seems to be grilling the disheveled little fat man. The guy is obviously overwrought. Can't tell if it's his circumstances or Salmon's intimidation. The poor guy is half naked, wearing nothing but a pair of torn slacks and a ratty blanket clutched tightly around his shoulders. Salmon's patience looks to be wearing thin as the pudgy little guy blubbers and hiccups his way through the interview.

Lacey beams as she closes on Salmon's table. I have to hustle to keep up. As we approach, Salmon gives us the stiff-arm. Holding out his hand for us to stop, he turns back to the sobbing fat man. Lacey pulls up short. We detour to a nearby table to wait our turn.

I watch as Salmon pushes away from his table. The two uniforms haul the fat guy out of the chair, cuff him, grab his elbows and escort him out. Salmon shakes his head as he moves to join us.

As Salmon drops into a chair, Lacey starts in. "What was all that about?"

Visibly discouraged, Salmon's face twists into a tight frown. "He's not a very solid suspect, but we'll have to clear him first."

"*He's* your murder suspect?"

"Like I said, probably not. Even though they found the murder weapon on him, the evidence doesn't add up. For instance, no residue. The guy didn't fire that gun."

Lacey leans forward, softening, her concern for Salmon showing. "Okay, so who do you like for it?"

"I've got a lot attendant that places the Rodriguez truck at the scene around the time of the shooting. We'll scour the crime scene until we find enough to nail that fucker, whoever he is."

"You mean you don't know who was in the truck?"

"They're workin' the perp at the hospital now. Should have a positive ID soon."

Salmon turns to me. "I want to see you downtown tomorrow. Need you for backup, need some IDs."

"Sure thing."

Salmon turns back to Lacey. "The stiff is gone, but you and Lance can get your pictures." He turns back to me with a severe look. "As long as you don't pass out and puke all over the place."

I give him a sheepish grin.

He waves over a uniform. "If he even looks like he could faint, you pick him up and drag his ass outta there, pronto. You got it?"

"Yessir."

Lacey and I follow the uniform off through a stage exit into a small dark hallway. As I trudge along behind, I pick up a faint odor that crinkles my nose, hints of rancid sweat, blood, urine, feces, all steeped in the reek of death. We round a corner into another tight hall. My chest constricts as the stench thickens. I tense, realizing this ain't gonna be pretty. *Don't blow it.*

We turn into a small room. The sickening miasma hits me like a sledgehammer. I gag as my stomach convulses, driving sour bile up my throat. Tightly clenching my jaw closed, I swallow hard, forcing my stomach contents back down my raw throat, determined not to hurl. Three of Forensics' high-intensity halogen floor lamps blaze away. Sitting on top of sturdy yellow tripods, they light up the murder scene bright as day. Yet there is an oily film suspended near the ceiling, drifting in dark licks and whorls of sinister hues, corrupting the bright light with blood-tainted shadows. I wonder if I'm the only one witnessing this phenomenon. No one else seems to notice. And there's something else, someone else, a presence. She ... yes, she's here.

I struggle to maintain and yet acknowledge the presence for what it is—her spirit, her ghost, her soul, her whatever the hell you want to call it—her essence. And she's pissed. Dark energies boil off her like black clouds of swarming insects. As I get her "communication" I feel I already know her. This is the same woman in my vision, the mysterious stripper, that first vision of an erotic dancer consumed and then dissipated by Rodriguez's rogue truck.

Salmon is right. This is the work of our guy in the truck, the compulsive maniac who killed Rodriguez and wounded his girlfriend, the drive-thru killer, the killer with the cowboy hat and wraparound sunglasses. It's all the same monster.

Soft and clear, I hear Sonja. "How does it seem to you now?"

I feel a lifting, a lightening, as though the eight hundred pound gorilla is off my back. Relief surges through me as I sigh. The room brightens, coming into sharp focus, a clear distinction between the harsh reality of the material universe and a netherworld of cryptic symbols and vapor. *Is it possible … could I be done with all this bullshit, now that we've got him?*

Sonja comes through, rich and full. "We're getting there. Please continue."

Testing my newfound freedom, I glance up at the dead stripper. She's still there, hovering near the ceiling, radiating a vehemence unmatched by Satan himself. Yet somehow I'm unaffected, nonchalant, almost indifferent to her presence as though it's *my* choice, *I'm* in control, take her or leave her, no problem. And it feels good. *Whew.*

I pull my Canon out of my gear bag and get down to it, suddenly the consummate professional. Carefully working my way around the small room, I fire away, capturing the grim scene in dozens of digital images. I absently notice that while I'm repulsed by the violent disarray of stained and broken furniture, noxious odors and puddles of thickening body fluids, I'm not incapacitated by nausea, dizziness, or a skull-cracking migraine. Maybe I'm getting jaded to it all, who knows? Maybe Sonja is right. Getting through it is the only way out. Guess I don't much care as long as it's getting better.

I signal to Lacey and the big uniform that I'm done.

# THE ROAD BACK
### [6:43 PM – Tuesday, April 12, 2011]

QUIET HUMMING IN soft illumination surround Connie Rodriguez. She wonders if she's been given a reprieve, if this could be Purgatory. Yet, how could it be? She's committed suicide, damning her soul to eternal Hell. There can be no reprieve for her. Tears well up. And as she attempts to blink them back, her eyes open. It's all a blur of soft white.

As her vision clears, white ceiling tiles in a white grid come into focus. Her head feels thick, as though stuffed with cotton—her mouth, dry as crypt dust. A vague weakness possesses her to the bone, interrupted only by fleeting dizziness and nausea's intermittent constrictions. Turning her head, she spots the IV stand, tubes running into her arm, her bandaged wrist, the bedside rail, lights and numbers on hospital monitoring equipment. A frisson of shame flushes through her at the thought of her survival. How can she face them now, after she's already tried to kill herself? What can she say? She closes her eyes, wishing she were dead.

When she opens her eyes again it's at the bidding of a mousey nurses' aide. A putty-colored tray with meager portions of bland hospital fare is placed in front of her. She resists the welling tears, resigning herself to a fate worse than death—living. *This must be Hell.*

After what seems like an eternity, the nurses' aide returns to quietly admonish her for the untouched meal. Handing her a small paper cup of meds, she stands watch as Connie dutifully pops them in her mouth and washes them down. Ms. Mouse brusquely smoothes sheets, lifts Connie's head to fluff her pillow, adjusts the remote, turns on the TV then lifts the tray and scurries away.

The murmur of the TV over the ventilation's quiet hum soothes her as the meds lull her into hypnotic bliss. She could stay like this forever, never having to think about what's to come, never having to worry.

Connie slowly rises to consciousness as she feels a soft hand gently shaking her shoulder. Blinking, she looks around, trying to remember where she is.

"Connie, it's me."

Connie struggles to think. "Who?"

"It's me, Brandy. Your sister."

Her speech slurs as she manages a drugged smile. "Oh ... Brandy ... What are *you* doing here?"

Brandy forces a smile. "I came to see *you*. How are you doing?"

"Oh, Brandy ... I'm so sorry, I've screwed it all up ... so sorry ..."

Brandy's tears force their way out. "Oh, Connie, it's all right ... everything's going to be all right."

Coming awake, Connie's sorrow grips her. "No, I ... screwed up. I just couldn't take it anymore ..."

"No. It's going to be all right, you'll see."

Despair fills Connie's voice. "How? How is it gonna be all right? I tried everything. Did everything the doctors told me to. Nothing helped—and the meds only made it worse. They drove me crazy! I couldn't ... OhMyGod." She breaks down and sobs.

Brandy sits quietly until Connie cries herself out. "Connie, listen, I know. Believe me, I know. I've been through this."

Connie looks up at Brandy, astonished. "You tried to kill yourself?"

"No, but I felt like it."

Incredulous, Connie's voice rises an octave. "Felt like it? Whaddaya mean, you felt like it? What's that? I nearly killed myself and now I wish I had!"

Brandy moves in close, looking into Connie's eyes. "Listen to me. I'm your sister and I'm here for you. You gotta listen to me. There *is* a way out of this. Now, come on!"

Connie looks dolefully at her sister. "Okay. I'm listening."

"First, you've gotta get off the antidepressants."

"I tried, but the doctor said ..."

"No, listen, you've *got* to get off them. There's a way. Trust me."

"Okay. How?"

"We need to get you home, then we'll get started. Don't worry, I'll help you. I've done it myself. It really helps."

Connie lets it all filter through, cooling her conflicted thoughts like powdery snow. "Home ... yes ... okay, let's go home."

Encouraged, Brandy stands to leave. "I'll check with your doctors and arrange it."

"Thanks, Sis. I love you."

"I love you, too. I'll be back."

Brandy's heartfelt reply rings in the air long after her departure. Connie feels blessed to have such a sister. And she doesn't know why, but she feels like there might be some small measure of hope for her after all. Brandy must know.

Smiling wistfully, Connie thumbs on the TV. The little screen lights with colorful pictures as she absently scrolls through the channels. She stops cold when she sees his face. It's Gary Whiting, her dead husband's partner. He's on the news. She turns up the volume to listen to the newscaster's polished melodrama.

"... found his body in his room, here, at the Tangiers Hotel & Casino ..."

A huge, brightly lit sign emblazoned with Tangiers Hotel & Casino slides onto the TV screen next to the color photo of Whiting.

"... heart failure appears to be drug related ... medical examiner's report showed toxic levels of cocaine in the bloodstream ..."

Saddened, Connie shakes her head. "Oh, no … Gary, what did you do?" Reflecting on her own troubles, she wonders if it was accidental. Or was he another lost soul who just couldn't take it anymore?

# INTERVIEW WITH
# A KILLER

**[9:09 AM – Wednesday, April 13, 2011]**


FRANK SALMON WEAVES through the squad room's maze of desks, running through a list of the morning's priorities in his head. The perp was treated at the hospital and cleared for incarceration last night, his injuries limited to a few contusions and a severe facial abrasion. Charged with grand theft auto, excessive speed and reckless endangerment, he's been cooling his jets in the City jail's infirmary, under constant observation while shackled to the sturdy steel frame of his bed. Salmon is having him brought down for questioning in thirty minutes, fully expecting to add three murder one raps to the charges.

As Salmon drops into his chair, he grabs a note pad. While they've managed to answer a number of key questions with the perp's ID, his capture has opened a Pandora's box of loose ends. At this point, to make the murder raps stick, they'll need a confession. So far, they have a ton of circumstantial evidence but not enough to guarantee conviction. They've yet to link him to the murder weapon. No question that Forensics will turn up more hard evidence, whether it turns out to be enough, only time will tell. Most of the eyewitness statements are suspect—too vague. Any good defense team could poke them full of holes. In the meantime, Salmon is determined not to let this perp walk. And he intends to use everything at his disposal to assure that outcome, including his reluctant psychic, Lance.

Salmon has taken quite a ribbing around the squad room for listening to Underphal at all. And he's extremely cautious in how he uses Underphal's information, mostly keeping it to himself. More to give him direction than as hard evidence, Salmon wants Underphal's insight into the perp's motivation, methods and connections between all three homicides— more details. To keep a lower profile, he's asked Lacey to drive Underphal rather than have a patrol car pick him up. Apparently, he's still not sleeping well and is in no condition to drive.

Haltingly, I approach the Violent Crimes reception counter, squinting at the fluorescent's glare. Feeling weak and shaky, I look around for a place to park my aching ass until Salmon shows. I've lost track of the days. All I know is that I haven't slept worth shit, plagued by the return of "communications" I don't yet fully understand. Lately, all my senses seem to be stuck wide open on volume 10 and it's wearing me out. This psychic bullshit is for the birds. Maybe getting a look at this guy will help. Given what I've had to go through to get here, I sincerely hope so. Sonja remains ominously silent. Still, Salmon seems to think it will help. I hope he's right.

*What the fuck?* I snap to with a start. Must've dozed off in the waiting room chair. Salmon's shaking my shoulder. I rub my eyes as he helps me up. He's trying to tell me something as I deadhead along behind, following him through an incomprehensible maze of corridors. It's all an irritating blur of grating noises and too-bright lights.

Salmon stops abruptly. Apparently we've arrived, but something's wrong here. My skin crawls with prickling electricity as though infested with fire ants. As I work to get my bearings, I notice all the racks of electronic gear in the dark little room, red and green LEDs lit up like mission control. A couple of uniforms stand by, ready for business. A hiss sizzles in my head, growing louder—can't tell where it's coming from. *I'm in trouble here.*

A large window exposes a stark room. Must be a two way mirror, not that it matters now. A well-used metal table dominates the room's center. Seated at the far side of the table is a big man in an orange jailhouse jumper a couple sizes too small. I see the top of his head as he stares at the tabletop. A large bandage bulges from the side of his face, the rest hidden by long shaggy hair, matted and greasy. He's manacled and in leg irons, thick connecting chains running through a waist belt and padlocked to a heavy-duty iron eyelet welded into the floor. The hissing in my head spits and crackles. My vision pulses, expanding and contracting with every heart-beat. I fight to control the agitation that has me cranked up this side of raw panic. *This is NOT going well.*

I stare spellbound at the prisoner. Slowly, his head raises, sending a shock of fright through me like a hammerhead shark through a darting school of mackerel. I can't look away as his eyes rise to capture mine. His glowing orbs shine with a malevolence I can't escape and I mutter under my breath. "It's him."

Salmon leans in. "What?"

Eyes locked with the prisoner's, I can't blink, can't avert my gaze, can't break this hypnotic stare. "It's HIM!"

Salmon carefully monitors Underphal's alarming transformation. Staring wide-eyed at the perp through the two-way mirror, Underphal's skin has gone bluish-white. He's trembling head to toe, sweating profusely, gasping in shallow rapid breaths—classic symptoms of shock. Salmon signals one of the uniforms to get help.

He turns back to Underphal. "You mean the shooter?"

"Yes! It's HIM, he killed them!"

Salmon steadies the wavering Underphal. His eyes cut to the other uni-form. "Great. Now all we gotta do is prove it."

He turns back to Underphal. "Is this the partner you were telling me about? The one that Rodriguez ran down?"

Underphal sputters, a long pause then more sputtering. "Uh … no, not that guy, different guy. Not the killer."

"But this is the guy that killed Rodriguez?"

"Yes!"

"And the guy that killed Rupert and Parkson, the drive-thru homicides?"

"Yes! Yes!"

"Also the Lion's Den homicide?"

"It's him. It's HIM!"

Salmon eases Underphal down to the floor next to a folding chair. "Okay, well ... help's on the way."

Stooping, Salmon cradles Underphal's head as he leans him back on the floor. "All right, put your feet up on the chair." He checks his pulse. "Okay, close your eyes, take slow deep breaths and relax."

He stands, and putting his hands on his hips, watches Underphal. "Hang in there."


After the EMTs wheel Underphal out, Salmon turns to stare at the prisoner. He's nicked up pretty good. A large patch of gauze taped to the left side of his face. They've kept him off all pain medication purposely, antibiotics only. He's been in there alone, chained to the floor, waiting a good hour or so— enough time to make him uncomfortable, should soften him up.

Salmon's iced plenty of suspects over the years. Innocent or guilty, they follow a predictable pattern: at first, all anxious bundles of nerves, then worry on the verge of tears. If they don't break down outright, it's followed by despair. Eventually they sink into a deep apathy, their defenses broken down to reveal the truth, whatever that truth might be. The whole process can take anywhere from a couple minutes to several hours, but it's inevitable, happens to nearly all of them. The only exceptions are the psychopaths. True psychopaths seem indifferent, disconnected, as though the whole thing has nothing to do with them.

As he watches his prisoner, Salmon sees hints of that same psychopathic disconnect, signs that the perp is certainly capable of the crimes as charged. Whether they can prove it or not is another matter. The good news is that most psychopaths don't care about anything, not even themselves, and easily confess their crimes without remorse or a second thought for the consequences. But that knife cuts both ways. They can just as easily refuse to talk, convinced that nothing could possibly happen to *them*. Salmon's hoping this dickhead goes for the glory and tells all. He looks like the bragging type, cocky, full of himself and according to his guards, a rough customer, a raging asshole. He figures he might get a lucky break on this one, a confession before lunch.

Salmon loosens his tie as he leaves the dimly-lit observation booth and heads into the harsh brightness of IR-1. Ready to tackle the perp head-on, he briskly strides to the steel table, pulls out a metal chair and sits.

Johnny Chavez shows no reaction to Salmon's entry, remaining hunched over, staring blankly at the tabletop.

Using the remote switches, Salmon starts both the audio and visual recording equipment. He focuses a penetrating stare on the perp and adds an introductory note to the record, getting the formalities out of the way. "Mr. Chavez, you understand the charges made against you?"

Without looking up, Chavez mumbles, "Bullshit."

Salmon leans forward. "Excuse me?"

Sneering at Salmon, Chavez seethes. "Charges are bullshit. You got nothin'."

He meets Chavez's hot stare head-on. "Mr. Chavez, you're in a world of hurt, here. You're about to go away for a long time. And there's more coming. Come clean and it'll go easier on ya."

Chavez's eyes dart back and forth. "Whaddaya mean more comin'?"

Salmon's eyes narrow as he grins. "Looks like you're about to go down for a few unsolved homicides we got kickin' around here."

Chavez jerks up, snapping the slack out of his chains, slamming back in his chair as his head turns beet red, veins popping, eyes flashing. Spittle erupts from his lips as he explodes. "FUCK YOU, you little needle-dick bug fucker!!! You're lucky you got these chains or I'd break your SCRAWNY LITTLE ASS IN HALF!!!"

Salmon jumps. Composing himself, he chuckles at Chavez's outburst. He's sure he's got him now, should start bragging about his exploits any second. "Easy there, tough guy. We'll see how tough you are when they slide that needle in your vein."

Chavez slumps, suddenly sullen. "Fuck you, I want a lawyer."

*SHIT!* That's it and Salmon knows it. Interview over.

# BACK ON THE TRAIL

**[6:49 PM – Thursday, April 14, 2011]**

IT'S BEEN A long shitty day. Lacey gave me a ride home from my overnighter at the hospital. That was this morning and it seems like ages. And here I thought I was done with all this shit, thought it was getting better. *Guess again.* My eyes burn, my head as thick as day-old oatmeal. I still haven't slept. Okay, maybe a couple of cat naps from the sedatives, but nothing really restful. As I drag my sorry ass to the fridge, my arms feel like I'm wallowing in sludge, my feet, made of concrete. I hang on the refrigerator door as I peer inside, bleary-eyed, hoping to find another beer. The fridge light illuminates vacant wire shelves, empty plastic drawers, a couple pieces of wadded up foil, an ancient tub of phony butter, an empty bottle of ketchup, but no beers. *I was afraid of that.*

Closing the fridge, I turn back to the dim kitchen, twilight seeping through threadbare curtains. What a fiasco at the police station. *At least I didn't throw up and pass out.* Still ... another day gone, evaporated with nothing much to show. I absently wonder how many days I have left. *And I was doing so good there, thought I was on my way, home free. How did it go wrong?*

Sonja's clear voice fills my head. "It's not wrong. Quit your whining. You've made real progress. You've helped find the killer. They couldn't have done it without you. You need to cowboy up. It's almost over."

"Yeah, a lotta good it'll do them. It don't mean shit if they haven't got enough evidence—just speculation, hearsay, nothing concrete they can use."

"It will all work out. This is no time to quit. Just see it through. Don't give up now."

"Great. Another fucking platitude from beyond the grave." But my cynicism is wasted. She's already gone and I'm talking to myself. Of course it's entirely possible that I've always been talking to myself, but I don't dare go there now. I'm on shaky ground as it is.

I waddle back to my broken recliner and flop, exhausted from the long excursion to the fridge. I gingerly lean back, readying myself for the horrors that await. *This ESP business is a real pain in the ass.* Glancing at my flatscreen, I hear it murmur as indistinct images splash across its face, background noise to help cope with the grinding monotony, the throbbing aches, the stabbing pains.

I ignore it all and glance up, directing my unfocused gaze past the ceiling, staring off into space. I'm listless with unfinished business, thinking about that dead stripper, thinking that the Rodriguez joyride isn't over, that he still has more to reveal. The question is, do I really want to know?

Sometimes I think Sonja just likes to jerk my chain. I mean, since they've already found the killer, why go through all this? Not that any of this makes any difference, I'm still stuck here, left to tough it out on my own. I resign myself to make it through. Like I have a choice. *Let's just get it over with.*

I hear Sonja's soothing tone. "You are not alone. I'm here. Just take a look."

My vision blurs, obscured by swirling mists condensing into thick fog. I feel the contour of the F-150's captain's chair and I'm Rodriguez's passenger once more. We bounce and swerve on that cattle-track of a road at breakneck speed. The dirt trail ahead is barely visible in the glare from the monster truck's running lights. Rodriguez cackles away, sawing at the wheel as he alternately mashes the gas and brake pedals to the floor. As usual, I'm just along for the ride, white-knuckling the dash and armrest. I keep repeating in my head, *it's only communication.*

I chance a question, yelling over the engine's roar. "Where we headed?"

Rodriguez's cackle explodes into barrel-chested hysterics. After a few moments, he winds down, tears streaming down his cheeks, his face, a mottled grey tinged with black. Wiping his eyes with the back of his free hand, he shakes his head and yells back, "Ain't death a bitch."

I content myself with his cryptic response and stare straight ahead. We round a sharp corner, nearly tipping over, dropping down into a wide arroyo. Standing near the arroyo's steep bank is a petite curly-headed beauty, stark naked with large full breasts and curvaceous hips. Her hips are tilted suggestively as she waves her thumb at us for a ride. *Do I know this woman?*

Rodriguez swerves and speeds up. We slam into the startled woman at an angle, her petite frame crumpling like a broken doll as she disappears under the truck with a thump. His head roars with deep laughter as he steers the truck back to the arroyo's sandy center. Laughing wildly, he bounces up and down in the seat with childish glee. We slow to a crawl as the truck's fat tires wallow in the deep sand.

He grins broadly as he turns to me. "Two down, one to go!"

*Dare I ask? What the hell.* I smile benignly as I turn to him. "Who was that?"

He spits fury. "A conniving little cunt, that bitch deserved it."

*Great.* Still no clue who she could be. "That bitch have a name?"

He glances over and grins. "That, my man, was crazy Marcia, the kinkiest fuck I ever knew."

Still no help. Maybe Salmon can make something of it.

As terror subsides, cynicism rears its ugly head and I absently wonder if any more of his ex-girlfriends are slated for roadkill. Hmm, he did say one to go. A cheerful thought. Hopefully, it's a short ride. Feeling like some tunes, I begin to hum Cindy Lauper's "Girls Just Want To Have Fun." Fitting background music for this bizarre little road trip. *We're all a bunch a fuckin' whackos on this bus. Remember, it's only communication.*

Rodriguez straightens up and punches it, spraying sand in large rooster-tails with all four wheels as we wildly weave through the arroyo.

Forget the humming, I'm hanging on. Back to white-knuckle flight status.

Rodriguez saws the wheel, then jerks it to head straight up the steep arroyo bank, mashing the throttle. The engine's roar elevates to a nerve-shattering scream as the pickup leaps out of the arroyo to sail into the darkness, all four wheels spinning in midair.

I brace myself, one hand against the ceiling and the other on the dash.

The truck plummets to Earth with a crunching thud, bouncing high off the desert floor, running lights carving bright white tunnels into empty space. Slamming back down, we skid from side to side as Rodriguez fights the wheel while laughing at the top of his lungs.

I'm thrown around like a rag doll, the seat belt the only thing keeping me from breaking my neck. I scramble to regain my seat, to get a grip. Glancing up, I see another figure running up ahead. *Shit!*

Rodriguez chortles to himself. "Go ahead, run you little fucker, I gotcha now!"

Stunned, I watch the chase unfold.

Rodriguez guns the engine. The pickup leaps ahead. He backs off and hits the brakes just short of his prey, toying with him like a big cat with a wounded mouse.

The little man sprints, trying to zigzag and dodge the pickup, but it's no use. Glancing back over his shoulder, I get a glimpse of Rodriguez's next victim. Beady little eyes set in a narrow face, sheer terror plastered all over his features as he realizes there's no escape.

Rodriguez runs up to within inches and backs off, cackling as he toys with his prey. Next run up, he pushes closer, tapping his victim with the chrome bull bar. The frantic little man stumbles and goes down. Rodriguez slams on the brakes, sliding on top of the hapless victim, fat off-road tires grinding his mangled carcass into the dirt as we jerk to a stop.

I'm horrified and amazed by this Rodriguez character. In spite of the gruesome outcome, I can't help but be impressed. The smell is getting really rank, but his precision driving skills are incredible. "Nice work."

Rodriguez turns to me, his zombie face beaming like a proud father at the birth of his firstborn. "Yeah, not bad, huh?"

"Who was *that* guy?"

Rodriguez chuckles. "That slimy little fuck was my lender."

I turn back to stare out the windshield, somehow knowing the joyride has reached its end. *His lender, wow … wonder what Salmon will make of that. Just more communication, huh?*

## [9:37 AM – Friday, April 15, 2011]

I come to, sprawled in my recliner, stinking of stale beer and BO—a rude awakening to be sure. Washed out like a limp dishrag, I struggle to sit up, flailing around like a turtle on its back, trying to push up and out of the chair. *Fuck!*

No point in checking the fridge again. I stumble to the kitchen, swirl yesterday's coffee dregs in the bottom of the pot, slosh them into my mug and brace myself. Cold and bitter, nothing like old burnt coffee to start your day.

Grimacing at the vile brew, I ponder my situation. At least I slept, or passed out. Regardless, I feel somewhat better, more human than zombie for a change—a good start. I need a shower. Then I'll make the call.

"Detective, it's Lance."

"Hey, haven't heard from you in a couple days. How ya feelin', Lance?"

"Better, thanks. Got some more stuff for ya."

"Whatcha got?"

"You remember that partner of Rodriguez's I was askin' about? Did you ever find anything?"

"Not yet, we've had other priorities."

"Right. Well, there's more to all that."

"Okay ..."

"Apparently Rodriguez had a girlfriend. Hot little number named Marcia."

"You're shittin' me. Marcia? Are you sure?"

"Pretty sure."

"No shit. His girlfriend ... Sure, why not?"

"Plus, there's another guy, his lender ... Any idea who that could be?"

"Like partners, he had several lenders, but I think I know where you're going with this."

"Whaddaya mean?"

"Chavez's attorney cut a deal. Chavez just gave up the people that hired him to whack Rodriguez, Rupert, and that stripper, Sondra Du.

Conspiracy charges all the way 'round. We're working on warrants now. One of them was Rodriguez's lender, a guy by the name of Martin Fellman and the other is Rupert's widow, Marcia Rupert."

I'm stunned. "Damn, *that's* what he was trying to tell me."

"Whaddaya mean?"

"The visions. Rodriguez was showing me more than just Chavez's victims, he was showing me Chavez's accomplices."

"Okay. Gotta go. Call me back in a few hours. You can give me more details and I'll fill ya in on the arrests."

# MARCIA'S DILEMMA

### [11:37 AM – Friday, April 15, 2011]

SALMON LEADS TWO police cruisers down the narrow street. The tall palms' late morning shadows dot the asphalt. He pulls into Marcia Lago-Rupert's driveway behind the Lexus SUV as the cruisers pull up to the curb. Four uniforms emerge from the two cruisers, dressed in crisp blues, all business.

As Salmon approaches the front door, two of the uniforms head around back to cover the rear of the house. The other two uniforms fall in behind Salmon, hanging back a bit, just in case. Salmon rings the doorbell as he surveys the slump block facade, checking the windows for signs of life.

Salmon rings the bell again. And as he's raising his fist to pound on the door, it opens a crack to reveal half of Marcia Lago-Rupert's pretty little face.

Marcia smiles provocatively. "Hello, Lieutenant."

Salmon firmly edges the door open. "It's Detective, actually. May we come in?"

Marcia backs away from the door as Salmon pushes through. In skimpy cutoffs and a tiny tank top, she poses for full advantage. She gazes seductively at the two uniforms following Salmon in. "Are you going to introduce me to your friends?"

Salmon's gaze hardens. "Marcia Lago-Rupert, you are under arrest for the murder of Daniel Rupert and Janice Parkson."

Lago-Rupert's eyes fly open wide as the blood drains from her face.

"You have the right to remain silent. Anything you say …"

Lago-Rupert's head and shoulders slump as a mournful keening emanates from deep within.

"… or do, can and will be held against you in the court of law. You have the right to speak …"

Her wail mutates into a screeching howl as her legs give way and she collapses into a heap.

A uniform clicks the mic on his shoulder, calling in for medical assistance.

Salmon rushes through the rest of the Miranda. *Shit!*

Lago-Rupert's eyes roll up in her head as she screams, arms and legs flailing away, pounding the floor with her fists and heels, in the throes of a frenzied fit.

The uniforms kneel down on each side of her, pinning her arms in an effort to subdue her.

Salmon calls in the other pair of uniforms and they set about pinning her legs, working to immobilize her.

Pinned, her frenzy ratchets up to fever pitch, exploding in a teeth-gnashing rage, her twisted face a dark red. Eyelids flutter spasmodically over the whites of her eyes as strings of spit fly from her quivering lips in convulsive gasps. She bangs the back of her head on the entry's ceramic tile. One of the uniforms attempts to hold her head off the floor in vain as she violently bangs her head, again and again.

Salmon hears a loud crack as Lago-Rupert goes limp. Unconscious.

Everyone breathes a sigh of relief as the uniforms release her limbs, stand up and back away.

She's as psychotic as he's ever seen and on her way to the mental ward for the criminally insane. Nothing Salmon can do about it now. He only hopes it's temporary and won't result in an insanity plea. In his view, anyone who commits murder is unquestionably insane, and no one should get away with murder.

# AT THE BANK

**[2:13 PM – Friday, April 15, 2011]**

INTENSE AFTERNOON GLARE reflects off hot pavement, concrete sidewalks, roadside signs and the shining windshields of fast moving traffic. Martin Fellman wheels his golden Mercedes through the intersection, turning right on Frank Lloyd Wright Boulevard. He's heading back to his office after a long tedious lunch with another pain-in-the-ass borrower.

Everybody's whining about how shitty things are, like it's the bank's fault and somehow they shouldn't have to pay. Fellman is tired of hearing about it. After all, the bank is in business to make money. Not the bank's fault that business is down. First Community is on the brink as it is. If one more of his loans goes into default, he's likely to lose his job. Everything he's worked for the past twenty-three years, his position, his stock, he'll lose everything. Then there's the big mortgage, the home equity line, the private schools, the leases on the Mercedes, and the wife's Lexus, not to mention all the credit cards. And where would he get another finance executive position in this economy? It just keeps getting worse.

Fellman's smartphone vibrates as it plays a few bars of Beethoven's Ninth. Checking the screen for the caller's ID, he sees it's his executive assistant. "Cherri, what's up?"

"Hey boss, the police are here waiting for you." Kiddingly, she adds, "What did you do, rob a bank?"

Fellman goes numb, hearing nothing after "… police are waiting for you." His thoughts scatter like panicky quail as he tries to guess why they're there. "Did they say what they wanted?"

Hearing the quaver in his voice, Cherri gets serious. "No, sir, they didn't say. There's a detective and a couple officers. They showed up a few minutes ago. And when I told them you were at a lunch appointment, they said they'd wait. What do you want me to tell them?"

Fellman's head buzzes, his heart palpitates—his face, blanching with fear. He tries to come up with a reason, any reason other than the obvious. *Nobody knows but Chavez* … He splutters, trying to talk. "Uh, uh … uh, just, uh, tell them I'm on my way." He hangs up without another word. Shame burns his face as his heart sinks with the realization. *Chavez must've told them.*

Fellman's head reels as panic gnaws at his core, ripping him to shreds from the inside out. He's got to think this through, got to figure things out. Making a hard left on Pima Road, Fellman automatically heads for home, his eyes darting in all directions as he tries to think, at a loss for what to do.

Salmon waits impatiently in First Community Bank's cathedral-like lobby. All hardwood and marble, the bank's lobby projects an image of discreet wealth. Out of the corner of his eye, Salmon catches Fellman's assistant coming his direction—her prim gait, an air of efficiency, high heels briskly clicking away. As he turns to face her, she stops, careful not to violate his personal space.

She forces a smile. "Mr. Fellman just called. He asked me to tell you he's on his way." She turns to leave. "I'll let you know when he's ready for you. Please have a seat."

"Did you tell him that a Homicide detective from the Phoenix Police is here to see him?"

Salmon's question stops her dead in her tracks. "I told him the police. I didn't know you were a Homicide detective."

Salmon turns to Officer Denton. "Keep one unit here in case he shows. You and I are going to his house." Salmon grabs one of the uniforms and turns back to the assistant. "This is Officer Galloway. Please let him know when Mr. Fellman arrives."

Denton follows Salmon as he hustles out of the lobby into the bank's parking lot, headed for the Mercury. As they sprint across the parking lot, Denton calls after Salmon, "How do ya know he's headed for his house?"

Without breaking stride, Salmon calls back over his shoulder. "I don't."

# NOBODY HOME

**[2:27 PM – Friday, April 15, 2011]**

AS THE GARAGE door rolls up, Fellman sees his wife's Lexus is gone. *Probably picking up the kids from school or soccer or whatever—good.* He parks, hits the garage door button and jumps out. He speed-dials his wife. It goes to voicemail on the third ring and thinking fast, he leaves a curt message. He tells her he's at the house and not to come home, but to take the kids to her sister's. There's an emergency electrical outage, no A/C. He'll call when the power's back on.

Fellman slams the anteroom door behind him and locks the deadbolt. Disarming the "Away" setting on the alarm's keypad, he activates the "Intruder" setting, barricading himself in his five thousand square foot, hacienda-style semi-custom. Rushing through the house, Fellman sheds his suit coat and tie as he heads upstairs to the master bedroom.

He strips down to his wife-beater and boxers as he rushes to his walk-in closet. Working the combination lock on a fireproof filing cabinet, he opens the top drawer and removes a heavy metal box with a keypad in its lid.

With the gun safe clutched under his arm he scurries out of the bed-room, across the mezzanine and down to the end of the hall. Punching his code into the door lock, he jerks open the door to his study and scoots in, locking the door behind him. His eyes dart around the room. The armchair, the flatscreen, the armoire, the bookcases, everything is as it should be, undisturbed. He breaths a heavy sigh of relief. *Safe.*

Setting the gun safe on the end table, he moves to the armoire, pulls out a crystal tumbler and a bottle of his favorite single-malt Scotch. He sets the half-filled tumbler on the end table and grabs his smoking jacket off the coat rack. Slipping into his velvety red smoking jacket, he slides into his house slippers and drops into his Chippendale. His hands shake as he reaches for his Scotch and the TV's remote. He absently scrolls through the channels as he nervously slurps his drink, landing on a local 24/7 news station.

He grabs the gun safe and presses a code into the keypad. The heavy metal lid pops open to reveal a loaded .357 Magnum. The news channel shows aerial footage of the recent ten-car pileup on I-17 with a mug shot of John M. Chavez superimposed in the upper right, chattering away about Chavez's recent arrest for multiple homicides. Slowly shaking his head, Fellman pulls the revolver out of the red velvet lining, eyeing it with a mix of fear and curiosity as he turns it over, feeling its unyielding weight, its deadly finality.

He bought the .357 eight years ago for home protection, figuring he'd never have to use it, better safe than sorry. He test-fired it at the gun shop's indoor range the day he bought it, hasn't fired it since. Staring blankly at the weapon, he realizes he doesn't have a clue. His scattered thoughts have yet to coalesce into a plan, he's just been running, looking for a place to hide. But now that he knows it's Chavez, he's screwed. Numb with terror, he sinks into deep despair. *What am I going to do?*

Checking his navigation for Fellman's home address, Salmon drives north on Pima Road, heading into the luxury neighborhoods of North Scottsdale. According to Officer Galloway, Fellman still hasn't shown up at the bank. Based on years of experience, Salmon figures it's a good bet Fellman will turn up at home. Denton is busy on the radio, calling in their location, destination and requesting backup.

Newshounds monitoring police scanners pick up Denton's transmissions. Based on police radio codes and request for backup, they mobilize their news units. News choppers and remote broadcast vans take off for the reported address, eager to be the first on the scene. The media's various in-house computer geeks busily mine the internet for all possible hits with the suspect's name or address. They instantly access data on Martin Fellman, his family, his personal history, his personal finances, everything about him.

Knowing full well the media is coming, Salmon switches on his emergency lights and throttles up the supercharged V-8. He needs a few minutes on the scene before the media arrive and all hell breaks loose.

Arriving at the entrance gate to the Desert Ranch planned community development, Salmon pulls up to the keypad and enters the default emergency/fire code. Denton watches mutely as the gates roll back and Salmon accelerates through. Winding left, then right, and left again, they pull up at the curb in front of the expansive Fellman residence. Late afternoon sun glares through the windshield, making it seem hotter than it really is. Salmon lets the engine idle, keeping the A/C cranked as heat shimmers off the hood. As soon as backup arrives, they'll cordon off the area.

Gritting his teeth, Denton hopes Salmon is right and Fellman is home. Otherwise, they'll look pretty fucking stupid. Salmon seems largely unconcerned, perfectly willing to risk a PR nightmare and the wrath of the department heads on a hunch. Maybe that's what it takes to make detective— *cojones grande.*


Burnt out, I lean against the cluttered counter, wondering where the day went. Is it ever going to stop? I've been wallowing in noxious images all day. Glimpses of the future or static from the dead, who knows? Keep trying to figure it out, but the horror movies never end. My cell breaks in with an obnoxious chirp. It's Lacey.

"Lance, get your gear together! I'm comin' to get ya!"

"What's up?"

"Scanner picked up a call. A murder suspect barricaded in his house."

"Figures. That'll be the lender, Fellman."

"How do *you* know!?!"

"Been gettin' those pictures all afternoon. Besides, your detective told me he was workin' on warrants earlier."

"What?! Why didn't you call me?"

"Figured you already knew. He's *your* boyfriend."

"Sonofabitch! No one ever tells me anything! Get your shit together, I'm almost there."

Salmon eyes the big house as he climbs the flagstone walk. Denton hitches up his pants as he follows along. At the front door, Salmon rings the bell and waits, hands on his hips, glancing at the windows for movement. Denton stands off, looking at the ground, chewing his bottom lip.

After several attempts at the door, Salmon and Denton turn back for the car.

"He's in there and knows we're after him," says Salmon. "How long 'til they get here with that warrant?"

"Should be any time. Let me check."

Denton climbs in and calls Dispatch as Salmon wanders around the front of the house. Salmon peers in the windows then moves to the garage.

As Salmon jerks on the door handle, he hears an alarm go off in the house. *Good. That'll get his attention.* He backs up to check the windows to see if anyone's watching, catching movement at a second story window. He hears the backup patrol cars roll up and the faint hum of an approaching chopper. Must be a news chopper, since they haven't called the police chopper yet. The three-ring media circus is about to begin.

As the alarm klaxon blares, Fellman jumps out of his chair, dropping the revolver on the floor, knocking the empty tumbler off the table. Wide eyed and trembling badly, he picks up the gun. Fellman creeps out of his study onto the mezzanine. He sneaks a quick peek at the street from its second floor window to see an unmarked black sedan at the curb. He jerks back suddenly when he spots the plainclothes cop in the driveway below. Dashing back to his study, he relocks the door, the alarm horn's incessant blasts jangling his frayed nerves.

Shakily, he picks up the tumbler. Setting the pistol on the armoire, he pours the tumbler full. He downs the Scotch in three gulps and fills the glass again. Looking at the full tumbler, he pauses. Chugging the fiery spirits, he drops the tumbler, grabbing the Scotch bottle with one hand and the .357 with the other. He stumbles back to his Chippendale and plops. Head spinning, panic and despair swirl through him like the burning Scotch. He can't hear for the alarm's frightful din. He can't think. It's as though his hair is on fire and all he can do is sit helplessly and watch his head blister, char, and burn to ash. The burning question remains. *What to do?*

All he knows is he has to stop that noise. He sets down the Scotch bottle and struggles to his feet. Staggering into the hall, he weaves his way to the master bedroom, the alarm's honking ringing in his ears. Leaning heavily against the wall, he resets the alarm. As the racket ceases he breathes a sigh of relief.

Fellman staggers back to his study, the ominous silence weighing on him. Without the blaring alarm, the more sinister elements of his situation grab hold of him like a terrier shaking a rat. Then he hears it—the background hum of a chopper.

In his chair with the revolver in his lap, he grabs the Scotch bottle and takes another swig. He's thinking hard, struggling to overcome the alcohol and work on a plan, nothing but disjointed ramblings. Resolute, he rants to himself. *Not goin' to jail. If they've got Chavez, it's a death penalty.* He takes another long pull on the Scotch. The only thing to do is find a way out, escape, make a run for it.

Glancing up at the flatscreen, he sees overhead images of a neighborhood, cop cars in the street in front of a big house. He leans forward and squints, peering at the pictures. *THAT'S MY HOUSE! OH SHIT! THEY'RE OUTSIDE MY HOUSE!!*

Until now he's been kidding himself, thinking there had to be some way out, thinking all he had to do was work it out, come up with a good plan. Now, harsh reality crashes in. *NO WAY OUT! TRAPPED!!!* Devastated, he takes another swig of Scotch and sets the bottle down. He drops his head into his hands. *They're comin' for me. What am I going to do?*

Breaking down, Fellman sobs, rocking back and forth as tears stream down his face. Awash in oceans of regret, his dark imaginings run aground, playing over and over in his head like a bad movie made for TV. *They'll kill me, shoot me down like a rabid dog. They'll call me a murderer. It'll be all over the news.*

*No one will ever know the real story. I didn't want to … they forced me … I had no choice. What else could I do?*

All he's worked for, all he's built, gone. What will happen to his children, his wife—what will they think of him? Him, a murderer. His wife and children ostracized, forced to abandon their lives, to move, to try and start their lives over. He's ruined all their lives, ruined everything. *They'll never forgive me.*

Fellman realizes too late he should never have gone along with all this. *It's that crazy fuck, Chavez. He's the killer!* Fellman never would have thought of killing Rodriguez if it wasn't for Chavez. Maybe, if he tells the police, maybe they'll understand, go after Chavez, the real murderer. After all, he wasn't even there, he *couldn't* have killed Rodriguez *or* that stripper, what's-her-name. *I've got to tell them, they've got to know it wasn't me!*

Lacey drives the little Prius with singular purpose, foot to the floor, dodging slower traffic like a fledgling Formula One driver.

I'm hanging on, but just barely. Ever since she picked me up, I've been nauseated. And it's getting worse the closer we get.

Crackling, buzzing energies swirl around me like a swarm of huge black wasps. Bitter bile rises in the back of my throat. I fight to hold it down. I want to tell Lacey to pull over so I don't vomit in her car, but we're almost there. I just want to get there and get it over with.

Lacey steals a quick glance. Seeing my distress, she tries to reassure me. "Hang in there."

I give her a weak smile, afraid to open my mouth in case I can't hold it down.

Wavering images of unfolding events swim in my head—the murderer in his red velvet smoking jacket, perched in his burgundy Chippendale. But instead of a cigar he's got a gun and he's going to use it. I want to warn Detective Salmon but sense it's already too late.

The normally quiet side street is cluttered with police cruisers, a SWAT van, an ambulance, a fire truck, and other assorted emergency response vehicles.

Overhead, half a dozen news choppers clog the sky, holding station a few hundred feet off the deck. In spite of the choppers' rotor racket, Salmon perks up at the sudden absence of the muffled alarm horn. Either it cycles off automatically or someone's in the house. Not that it matters much, Salmon has what he needs to proceed.

With the area cordoned off and warrant in hand, Salmon gathers the SWAT team and uniforms to brief them. High-risk busts like this are always filled with tension, unpredictable and risky. The seriousness of their situation isn't lost on anyone. They have trained endlessly to handle just such an occurrence. However, only three out of the entire crew have ever faced a live takedown under hostile circumstances. And given the odds, they're not likely to see action like this again in their careers. This is the true test. Any mistake could be fatal. Yet to a person, they fear endangering their fellow officers far more than their own mortality. The group breaks up and hustles to their assigned positions, adrenalin pumping, ready for anything.

Suited up in body armor, Salmon slowly approaches the front door, glancing at his crew, noting their positions, confirming their readiness. The first priority, safety. Safety of his crew, of civilians and safety of the perp. His goal is to make a clean arrest and make sure no one gets hurt in the process. Coordination and discipline are key and Salmon intends to carry it out by the book.

Following Salmon are three of the SWAT crew in full body armor carrying standard-issue weaponry and a battering ram for forced entry.

Salmon rings the doorbell, pounds on the door and announces, "Police! Open up!" He repeats this process three more times, orderly and by the book. He waits nearly a full minute after the last round—nothing. Shaking his head, he backs away, signaling the battering ram forward.

Officer Swenton positions his massive frame next to the door, rears back and slams the heavy ram through the solid wood door with a loud crack—splintered wood flying everywhere. With the door breached, the alarm horn blares. Swenton deftly reaches through the shattered door, turns the lock and pushes the remains of the door out of the way. As he steps back, Salmon bolts through with his crew following.

Just as Fellman resolves to get up and go tell the police his story, the news images stop him dead. Hunched forward in his chair, he watches the SWAT team deploy. Four of them headed for his front door. *Oh no!* Glued to the flatscreen, he stares dumbfounded as one of the cops rings his doorbell and pounds on his door. He's transfixed, hypnotized by the action unfolding on his screen. It's really happening and happening now.

Somewhere in the deep recesses of his mind he flails around helplessly, panicking as he struggles with the realization that there's nothing he can do. *They aren't going to listen to me.* No one will ever know he's not really a murderer, not his wife, not his children—no one.

He flinches as the battering ram crashes through the front door, the alarm klaxon blasting away. It's too late.

Glancing at the empty Scotch bottle, he clutches the .357 in both hands. His mind flits from ugly scenario to ugly scenario, all gruesome, all of his brutal death. Tears stream off his face as he sobs and splutters, staining the satin lapels of his smoking jacket. If he makes a last stand, they'll shoot him down, kill him like a common criminal—better than the long slow degrading agony of a death penalty. And at least his family will get the death benefits from his life insurance policy, enough for them to start over. He grimaces, if he's going to die a murderer, he might as well kill somebody. *It's the only way.*

Cried into a stupor, he doesn't care anymore. He knows what he has to do. Save his family. Lifting his puffy face, he glances over his shoulder at the door. Resigning himself to the inevitable, he scoots the armchair around to face the door. How long before they find him? Seems like it's taking forever. He can't hear anything with the alarm's infernal racket. His face twitches as his hands tremble. He's hearing things that make him think that they're on the other side of the door. Gritting his teeth, he grips the heavy revolver with both hands, his shaky finger on the trigger, pointing the .375 Magnum at the study door. Hesitating, he grapples with firing. Should he shoot now or wait until they come through the door? He wonders absently, *What if they only wound me? And what if I kill someone? What if they have a wife, a family?*

Salmon and his team have cleared and secured the ground floor. They storm the stairs and work their way through the master bedroom, clearing the bedroom, the closets and master bath. The honking klaxon keeps him on knife's edge. Robbed of his hearing, Salmon strains all senses past their limit, wary of what's next—can't afford surprises.

They cross the mezzanine and check the doors in the hall, a bedroom, a bathroom, another small bedroom used as a sewing room. Salmon tries the door handle at the next room. It's locked with a high-tech keypad system. Thumbing his mic, he calls for Swenton. Salmon pounds on the door, yelling, "Police," as Swenton arrives—his yells drowned out by the klaxon's incessant din.

The gunshot's booming crack makes them jump and duck. Looking around, they try to determine the report's origin. *Sonofabitch is shooting at us!* Salmon glances at the door looking for a bullet hole, then scans the crew behind him for signs of injury. *All safe.* He knows the report came from a larger caliber weapon, at least a .357 Magnum or possibly a .44 Magnum, it was no 9mm. He also knows full well that it came from the other side of the locked door. It's a brand new ball game.

Salmon has the men form up on either side of the door, crouching low, ready for anything. He signals Swenton forward as he inches up to the door frame, gun raised—the other three have his back. He glances over his shoulder making sure everyone is in position. Turning back to Swenton, he gives him the go-ahead.

Swenton rears back and slams the battering ram through the flimsy door, splintering the door and frame. He ducks and pulls back, next to the wall.

Salmon lunges through the gaping hole, crouching, ready to fire.

Slowly rising, Salmon lets his 9mm drop to his side as he takes it all in.

The body slumps in a high-backed burgundy armchair, its head tilted back, mouth agape. The top front teeth are broken off at the gum line, blood dribbling from the ruined hole of a mouth, oozing onto the chest and a blood-drenched smoking jacket—pieces of broken teeth stuck to its satin lapels. Eyeballs hang by fleshy cords on either side of a swollen bloody nose. Dark raw eye sockets stare emptily at the gore on the ceiling. Most of the top of the skull is gone, blown to a bloody pulp, leaving a jagged crater where the crown once was. Blood, ragged lumps of tissue and shards of skull are sprayed across the ceiling, back wall and furniture. The hands still grip the .357 Magnum backwards at odd angles, its barrel askew from where it blew back out of the mouth.

The alarm klaxon blasts as Salmon slowly scans. He notices the TV, blood and gore splattered down its face, the overhead images from the choppers flickering, red and distorted by the blood smears. Shaking his head, he thumbs his mic to let everyone know the perp ate his revolver, requesting Forensics and a tech to kill the alarm.

# END GAME

### [5:19 PM – Friday, April 15, 2011]

WHEN LACEY FINALLY pulls up, I fumble with the seatbelt and throw open the door, gagging, on the verge.

Lacey's face twists up. "Lance, you gonna be okay?"

My jaws knot, my stomach clenching and unclenching. Bile rises up the back of my throat. Then miraculously, it passes. Eyes watering, I sit up and get a first look at my surroundings.

Lacey's still staring at me.

"Yeah, I'm all right. Gimme a minute."

"Okay, hurry up. I'll be inside."

Lacey gets out of the car, weaves her way through emergency vehicles, heading for the yellow tape.

I tilt my head back as the nausea subsides. *Something's changed.* On the one hand I sense it's no longer a standoff, the emergency's over. On the other, I'm picking up a dark turbulent knot of energy. Boiling, writhing, it coalesces and dissipates to reform randomly in the vicinity of the house.

Sonja whispers in my head. "Pay attention. This is it."

The killer is hanging around. He's dead and he knows it. Frustrated, he's unsure if he can do anything about it—anguish, regret and bitterness spewing from his poisoned spirit like raw sewage.

"Identifying the source is the key," says Sonja.

It's clear the malevolence belongs to the dead killer. I need to keep him at bay if I'm going to survive this. Steeling myself, I grab my gear bag off the back seat. On high alert, I climb out of the Prius and work my way toward the yellow tape. *I can do this.*

As I walk up next to Lacey, the killer's energy crackles and fizzes, a roiling black mass. A large undulating orb, it eddies and spins. Currents reverse as whirlpools of violent energy disappear and then reappear, spitting glowing sparks. It hovers about fifteen feet off the ground next to a second story window. A loud pop, and it's gone. An unearthly howl, and it's back, floating over the garage, buzzing and hissing.

As I study the writhing mass, there's a sudden change. Every hair on my body rises on gooseflesh, electrified. Violent shivers shoot up my spine. *Shit! He's spotted me!*

The mass mutates into a large whirling vortex focusing on me, sucking me up into its black maw.

"Stay focused on the source. Remember, it's only communication." Sonja's calming tone attempts to reassure me.

*Fucking perfect. The killer is communicating.*

I reach out, feeling around in the inky blackness, trying to get my bearings. I haven't really gone anywhere, yet the swirling darkness obscures my physical senses. Swirling particles integrate as vague shapes form out of the murk, a small man seated at a scarred metal table, a much larger man seated across from him.

The smaller man's narrow pointy features remind me of a rodent, tiny black eyes sparkling with an evil gleam. He's wearing a red velvet smoking jacket that I'd recognize anywhere. It's Rodriguez's lender, Fellman. Don't know why I didn't make the connection before. Guess it's because when Rodriguez ran him down, he wasn't wearing the smoking jacket. He stares at me with a ravenous grin, like I'm fresh roadkill and he's the shrewd buzzard that spotted my carcass first.

"Looks like you've spotted the source," says Sonja. "Now take him down."

Everything slides toward me, expanding as it envelops me. Fellman, suddenly closer, staring me down. I hold Fellman's stare with an unblinking stare of my own. I don't dare look away. The next move is his.

Strain ripples through me, erratic high frequency vibrations moving at the speed of light. Feels like I'm about to explode. He's taking forever to make his move.

Finally, he breaks eye contact, turning away to face the large man seated across from him. Wraparound shades under the brim of a cowboy hat obscure the large man's identity. Yet it is unmistakably him—Chavez, the shooter. He grins at Fellman like a cornered wolf, teeth bared, ready to lunge at Fellman as a last resort.

A big revolver lies on its side in the middle of the table. Fellman casually picks up the gun. He looks it over, turning it in his hand as if admiring the look and feel of the hefty pistol. He releases the cylinder in a deft move, obviously familiar with the weapon. Looking at the chambers, he gives the cylinder a spin. He presses a pin to empty the chambers, releasing the cartridges, dropping them on the table to bounce and clatter. Reaching down, he picks up one of the cartridges and reinserts it. He gives the cylinder another spin and snaps it back in place. Aiming at Chavez's face, he grins and pulls the trigger. The cylinder rotates as the hammer draws back and snaps forward in one smooth mechanical action—click. Still grinning at Chavez, Fellman puts the barrel in his own mouth and pulls the trigger—click. His wicked grin widens as he slowly pulls the pistol's barrel out of his mouth. He turns his nasty grin on me. "Wanna play?"

"Don't take the bait," whispers Sonja.

I shake my head no.

"You gotta play. No one else left," he says.

Staring in his beady little eyes, I keep shaking my head no.

He leans back and points the pistol up into the darkness. "You don't get it, do you? If you don't play, they'll never know."

"Who will never know what?"

He replies smugly, like I'm an idiot for asking. "*They*—my kids, my wife, the cops, everyone—they'll never know it wasn't me."

"Whaddaya mean it wasn't you?"

"I didn't kill anyone." He points at Chavez with the pistol. "It was *this* crazy fuck. *He* killed them, not me!"

"And you want me to tell them …"

"Yes! They can still *hear* you, *see* you. They'll listen to you!"

I try to think this through, looking at all the angles, exploring all options. In the past, I would've given in, would've run, said yes just to get away. And I've been running ever since. Running my whole life only to end up here, a failure.

"Don't do it," whispers Sonja.

I don't dare cave now. The last speck of my integrity vanishes if I don't take him head on. I don't care anymore, no flinching. Whatever happens, this is it. Time to salvage what I can and start living my life, what's left of it. Time to stand my ground.

Slowly, I shake my head no. "Not a fucking chance. You're as much a murderer as he is."

Fellman's wicked little grin vanishes, his face contorting with rage. Electric-blue bolts of lightning snake off his crown, crackling and spitting. He points the gun at me and pulls the trigger—POW!

*I'm adrift in the clouds, cut loose from reality, nothing below but darkness, nothing above but light. And I'm drawn to the light like a moth to a flame.*

*Sonja's voice surrounds me, enveloping me in her soothing warmth. "That's not the way. When it's time, you'll take a different path. You'll be yourself for the first time in a long time and you'll finally be HOME."*

*She has me worried. "And what about you?"*

*Her voice radiates her smile. "I'll be here. And we'll be together, if that's what you choose. But it's up to you. You've done very well and I'm proud of you."*

My vision clears, darkness fading as light returns, my surroundings wavering dimly as I find myself firmly grounded in the material world—sky and house and people brightening around me. Lacey stands before me, giving me a brave smile, doing her best to conceal the concern in her eyes. I look around, exhaling a deep sigh of relief, feeling good, better than I've felt in a long time. Lacey watches me anxiously to see if I'm all there. Clusters of police and emergency workers mill around on the other side of the crime scene tape. Behind me, police and emergency vehicles huddle together to form a barrier from the media. News reporters and their entourages are jammed together, jostling for position. It all seems obnoxiously familiar, yet my relief grows.

I take it all in. There's a clarity to my perception. It's cleaner, sharper, brighter. I wonder why. A fundamental shift. I'm experiencing an inner peace, a quiet confidence. These traits are alien to me. I work to put my finger on the source of this newfound state. Everything's the same, except … something's missing. A profound absence, which by its very nature makes it invisible. The dark energy is gone, vanished. And with it, the nagging doubt that kept me tied to the "other side," held captive against my will, forced to communicate.

With that last pull of the trigger, the killer disappeared from this universe, evaporating with a small pop like a soap bubble swirling down the drain. So much for hollow intimidations from the "other side."

I've done nothing but struggle with this psychic bullshit from the beginning, lost in the void, with Sonja as my only link to sanity. And that, a tenuous one at best. The entities, spirits, or whatever, that pulled me in always seemed to be running the show. As it turns out, they never really had any power anyway. The only power they had, I gave them through my fear. Sonja's been right from the start. All I ever had to do was look them in the eye and they wilted like a used condom.

It's finally over. A brand new day, clean and clear—like clouds parting on a fresh spring morning after a gentle rain. And I think I'm going to like it.

Lacey looks at me with mild astonishment. "You're obviously feeling better."

I can't help it, I'm beaming, grinning ear to ear. "Yes … much … thank you."

"Good. Get your gear and let's get to work. Need some pictures."

"I'm ready."

"I'll go find Frank and come back for you."

I smile. "I'll be here."

# HOT CHILI

**[11:57 AM – Friday, May 20, 2011]**

I HUSTLE TO reach the crosswalk before the sign flashes DON'T WALK. The sun's bright glare glints off the tall mirrored buildings, radiating heat off the pavement. Nearly noon and it's hotter than hell in downtown Phoenix.

I duck under Chili Bean's burnt-orange canvas canopy, entering through the etched-glass door into the restaurant's cool waiting area. Scanning the dining room, I spot Frank Salmon and Lacey Friends in a booth near the back. Lacey sees me and raises a hand to wave me over. I've been looking forward to this. It's been more than a month since I've seen either of them and we've got a lot to talk about.

Smiles all around as I slide into the booth. "Hi guys."

Frank nods. "Lance."

Lacey beams. "Hi, Lance."

I grab a menu. "You guys order?"

"Not yet," Frank replies.

"Waitress will be right back," says Lacey.

Our waitress introduces herself, takes our orders, collects the menus and leaves. She hustles back to drop off three ice-cold Tecates with limes then disappears.

I tilt my glass and pour the Tecate as I look at Frank. "So tomorrow's the big day, huh?"

"Yup, Chavez is goin' down."

"Any idea what to expect?"

"His sentencing hearing is more or less a formality. The deal was done with the DA when he rolled over on his accomplices. Life instead of the needle."

"That mean he's eligible for parole in a few years?" Lacey asks.

"Not in this case," Frank replies. "That puke will likely get three life sentences to run consecutively, no parole."

"What about the Rupert woman?" I ask.

"No tellin'. She'll be undergoing psychiatric evaluation for months," says Frank.

I shake my head. "What a cluster. Glad it's over."

Frank smiles at me, gratitude in his eyes. "We couldn't have done it without you. Thanks."

The warmth of his appreciation makes me blush. I'm not used to people genuinely thanking me. I raise my glass in a toast. "Let's hope we never have to go through anything like that again."

Frank and Lacey raise their glasses.

"I'll drink to that," says Frank.

I take a drink and set my beer down. "Glad to hear Mrs. Rodriguez is doin' okay. Shame about the partner, Whiting."

Frank sets his glass down and gives me a stern look. "Yeah, well, there's more to that Whiting case than meets the eye."

"What do you mean?" asks Lacey.

"After I heard about his so-called heart attack, I was curious. Especially after Lance's warning. So I did some checking with the Vegas PD. He did in fact, have toxic amounts of cocaine in his system. And he was treated for a mild myocardial infarction associated with cocaine over-dose and released from a local hospital earlier that same day."

"Did he accidentally overdose or commit suicide?" I ask.

Frank gives a deadpan look. "Probably neither."

Curiosity lights Lacey's eyes. "Neither?"

Frank leans back, draping an arm on the top of the booth's uphol-stered back. "Problem is, when I dug deeper, it didn't add up. First off, there was no evidence of any cocaine in his room. None left over. No vials or containers with cocaine residue. They found all his prescription medication, but no trace of cocaine. Seems unlikely to me. Secondly, due to the needle mark in his arm, it was suspected that he injected the fatal overdose. Only, he had no other needle marks. And evidence suggests he always snorted his coke, never shot up. His nasal cavities were a mess. To top it off, they couldn't find his works. The needle and syringe he used to off himself, nowhere to be found."

"How would that work?" I ask.

"The investigating officer blew it off, figuring the OD was too obvious, attributing the missing evidence to the hotel cleaning staff or some such."

Lacey's eyes widen. "He was murdered?"

Frank pensively rotates his beer glass between thumb and middle finger. "We'll probably never know what really happened. But based on Lance's early warning, I doubt it was an accident."

Everyone goes quiet.

I think back through the images of Rodriguez running down his partner. Guess I saw it coming. I tell them, "It was no accident. They got to him, set him up—professionals. It was a hit."

"Who?" asks Lacey.

"Easy enough, just take a look at who benefited most," says Frank.

"And who would that be, Mrs. Rodriguez?" Lacey asks.

"No, not really," Frank replies. "She had insurance proceeds no matter what. Once you rule out Fellman and Chavez, it almost had to be Cohen & Company, the hard-money lenders. Probably couldn't cash in on the lender's life insurance unless both managing members were dead, both Rodriguez and Whiting. And they sure as hell didn't want to take the property back in this market. Makes sense, when you look at it. Bunch of lowlifes."

I think to myself, *No one deserves to die over money. Maybe I could have prevented it.* Nothing I can do about it now. *Time to move on.*

I look up to see that Frank and Lacey have moved on, too.

Lacey brightens as she looks at me, changing the subject. "Frank and I have some news."

I smile. "Yeah?"

Beaming, she turns to Frank. "Frank asked me to marry him and I said yes."

My smile widens. "That's great. Congratulations!"

Frank beams too. They're in love. It warms my heart and at the same time stirs up melancholy memories of Sonja. Guess I'll always miss her.

Seeing my mood, Lacey chimes in. "Lance has some news of his own. Don't you, Lance?"

Embarrassed, I drop my gaze. "Yeah."

Lacey turns back to Frank. "Lance has a book deal. He's going to be published!"

Frank looks at me. "Yeah?"

"Yeah," says Lacey. "My editor hooked him up with a publisher, and they're going to do an art book of his crime scene photos."

Looking down, I smile.

"They love his work. He's going to be a big-time artist, aren't you, Lance?"

I smile. "Yeah, well, maybe …"

Frank leans forward, smiling. "That's great! You're gonna be rich and famous."

"Thanks. I'll take the rich part, not sure about the famous part." I'm secretly elated by their enthusiasm.


It's been a long haul—brutal, ugly. Wasting away is not a pretty thing, but that part of my life is over. For the first time in a long time, I'm cautiously optimistic, getting a glimmer of how things might get better. I can't help thinking that Sonja's probably right, everything's going to work out … finally.

# AUTHOR'S NOTES

I hope you were entertained by this little tale of lust and greed. However, please note: This is entirely a work of fiction. You can find all the usual disclaimers elsewhere in this book. That said, much of this book is based on reality.

Unfortunately, the economic conditions depicted in the book were, and are, all too real. For in-depth insight into one of the most insidious causes of our recent economic woes, I highly recommend *Crises By Design*, written by author and former banker John Truman Wolfe. *Crises By Design* is available from Amazon and all major book stores.

Another unfortunate situation existing in the world today is the over-prescribing of psychoactive medications such as antidepressants. They are often prescribed for a wide variety of symptoms—in many cases without full disclosure of the health risks. A significant number of patients find themselves in trouble with these medications with nowhere to turn. If you or anyone you know is having difficulty with these medications and is looking for real solutions, I recommend the Road Back Program. Their website is http://www.theroadback.org.

Much more could be said on these points, but I'll leave that to the authors of nonfiction. I'm a storyteller, not an investigative reporter or scientific researcher. Please feel free to visit my website http://michaelallanscott.com for more.

I'd like to take this opportunity to personally acknowledge all the people who helped me with this project:

First, my wife, Cynthia for all her help and support. Our daughter, Julie for her back up, handling our bookkeeping and assisting with social media. Rachel Thompson of Bad Redhead Media for her brilliant work across all the social media venues. Linda Seed for her keen editing eye. Michael Duff of DuffWeb for amazing digital art and an ultracool website. Denice Duff Images for the creative genius embodied in the book trailer. Michael Manoogian of Michael Manoogian Logo Design for the ultimate in logos. All the folks at Telemachus Press for their professionalism and attention to detail. Then of course, all the thoughtful reviewers and wonderful readers that make this dream job possible.

Please note: any errors are mine, alone.

The following is an excerpt from the next Lance Underphal Mystery—

# FLIGHT

# OF THE

# TARANTULA HAWK

by

# MICHAEL ALLAN SCOTT

**Due for release in the Fall of 2013.**

# THE SHOWING

MIDDAY, AND A crisp scent of fall fills the balmy air of late October. Sun baked terrain has cooled, well below oven operating temperatures for several days in a row—the first time in nearly six months. Phoenix's last Indian summer is finally laid to rest. Snowbirds and other migratory fowl flock to town, clogging the freeways and surface streets, swelling the resort hotels, RV parks, and the wallets of local merchants. A veritable desert paradise ... almost, except for that fleshy, white underbelly that never sees the sun.

Crouched in the upscale suburb of Paradise Valley, a four-bedroom, two-and-a-half-bath contemporary ranch style sits vacant—its foyer, littered with MLS flyers and Realtors' business cards while dust bunnies breed in its corners. At the street, the For Sale sign declares it's Bank Owned—a sign of hard times, blighting nearly fifty thousand homes in the Phoenix area alone.

Carla Simon fumbles with the lockbox's key to open the empty house. Her hollow cheeks match the hunted look in her soft brown eyes. Nervously waiting in the foyer for her two o'clock showing, she smoothes the front of her skirt with sweaty palms. It's been a long time since she's shown property—too long.

Carla waves vigorously, her greeting overly effusive as her prospect trudges up the walk. She asks, "Any trouble finding it?"

Her prospect seems distracted, answering, "No ... no problem."

Carla starts in, leading the way. "You'll notice the hardwood flooring throughout the main living areas."

They cross through the foyer.

As they enter the living room, her prospect suddenly grabs Carla from behind and pushes her face-first into the wall, pinning Carla before she realizes what's happening.

"OhMyGod! What are you doing!?!" Stunned, Carla struggles to make sense of it. *This can't be happening!*

Her prospect spins Carla around, pinning Carla to the wall with a forearm.

Carla stares at her attacker's placid features in disbelief, frozen with terror. Her attacker's wide eyes bore through Carla like red hot lasers. Confusion scrambles her thoughts as she watches a hand rise over her head. Too late Carla sees the big syringe—the gleam of a large hypodermic needle as it thrusts deep into her neck, penetrating the carotid artery. Carla's eyes roll with panic as the stab of the big-bore needle pierces her throat. Burning fluid swells her neck as the contents are injected.

Racing to the brain like a predator possessed, the poison's fiery tendrils sizzle neurons as it fries then extinguishes cranial, optic and facial nerves. Burning numbness spreads, robbing Carla of all muscular control: eyelids drooping as facial muscles go slack, vision doubling, then blurring, then dark. Her attacker's retreat, the last image burned into the back of her fading retinas. Carla's shrieks echo in empty rooms, soon to be stillborn in her useless larynx as paralysis sets in.

*How is it possible?* The ultimate betrayal. Her life had just started to turn around after all the hard work and struggle to regain her family, her career, her sanity. She needs to ask why, but deadened lips refuse to move.

Her dry mouth hangs open uselessly as her last breaths flutter from paralyzed lungs. Maybe she wasn't meant to be happy. *But why now? And why like this?* Bladder and bowels let loose as arms and legs go limp. She slides down the wall to slump into a spreading puddle of her own urine. Slowly tilting over, her torso topples to the floor. Her head, bouncing off the hardwood like a ripe melon.

*No, No, NO!!!*

Fully conscious while trapped in a cooling carcass, Carla screams hysterically to no avail, only silence and darkness ensues.

Pale moonlight floods vacant rooms, streaming through bare windows. The consciousness that was Carla Simon watches cold blue-white light creep across hardwood floors to climb bare walls, exposing a swollen flyblown corpse. She's lost all track of time. How many nights has it been? She tries to remember … where she is, how she got there. Hollow spots, holes, nothing there when she's sure there must be. If only she could remember. Dr. Manson said there would be some confusion and short term memory loss, common side effects of electroconvulsive therapy (ECT).

Melancholy haunts her as thoughts flit from question to question, too many loose ends. *Did I lock the car? Did Howard make the house payment? Did Jimmy get his dinner?*

A fine layer of dust coats the smooth hardwood planking, absorbing its lustrous sheen. Dust motes gleam like tiny stars in the glowing blanket of moonlight that hugs the floor. Fragments whirl in Carla's thoughts, fluttering like wounded birds. A to-do list half done, the white sheen of a prom dress, a plastic wristband from the hospital—shards of a shattered past, nothing left but scraps.

It's so still she can almost hear the thrum of the cosmos, its pulse trembling at the edge of perception. The quiet house seems on the verge of telling her something, some deep revelation, a most intimate secret.

Something's not quite right, but she dare not think about it. She's certain that somehow it will miraculously all come to her and she'll be okay.

Moonlight sifts through dust streaked glass, exposing a void, an emptiness, as Carla absently reflects on her condition. But she's been done with all that for months now. Dr. Manson promised—told her it would be okay.

Cold light cuts through dead air with scalpel-like precision, illuminating tiny imperfections floating aimlessly in space. Yes, it will all be okay. Like gasping awake from a nightmare or coming to from a deep coma or a near-death experience—a grand mal seizure, like after an ECT treatment. Yet it has to be okay. How else could she still be seeing, hearing ... thinking? It's all just a bad dream, Carla's sure she'll wake up soon. Still, something's not right. If only Dr. Manson had explained it to her, maybe then she'd understand. And she really needs to understand.

# WAKE UP CALL

SIXTY MILES NORTHWEST of Phoenix, just outside Wickenburg, it's an unusually bright night for early November, the blood moon waxing full above a rugged mesa. A stiff breeze whips up into a gusty blow, kicking up dust and rolling tumbleweeds across the open desert to pile against long stretches of rusted barbwire fencing. As a lone coyote's howl dies off, the cold wind moans—a bone-chilling song, echoing through the dry creosote and down the rocky ravines.

Gritty gusts vibrate the metal sheeting of an aging doublewide. Anchored against the elements, the weather-beaten trailer clings to a five acre plot of raw desert. A ten-year-old Jeep Grand Cherokee is haphazardly parked nearby. The darkened trailer and old Jeep lie at the end of a narrow dirt track, the only evidence of civilization for miles. And that's fine with me. Just the way I like it.

I'm snoring away in my new La-Z-Boy recliner, a half-empty longneck Bud sweating on the side table. A new fifty-two-inch flatscreen flashes digital images—my new surround-sound system, whispering the satellite TV's endless monologue.

*Dreaming, I catch my breath as a new reality unfolds:*

*A bright summer day, clear and hot. A large jet-black wasp appears overhead before I hear the hum of its Halloween-orange wings. A tarantula hawk headed straight for me. Flashes of raw panic. She's enormous, big enough to carry me away. She lands in front of me, extending her hooked claws, wings flicking in anticipation. I rear back on hairy hind legs, baring my fangs and poking segmented forelegs at her in a valiant attempt to ward her off. She lunges, grappling with wicked claws, pulling me off balance and turning me over in one lightning-quick move. I flail wildly, arching my back, legs in the air, abdomen exposed and vulnerable. Holding fast, she thrusts her long black stinger deep into my belly, releasing her paralyzing venom. The shock-inducing sting slowly numbs me to the core as I silently scream from within its high voltage spell. Her vile excretion robs me of all muscular control, leaving me to crackle in a hellish limbo. I can't quite feel her dragging me away, but I fear the worst is yet to come.*

A ringing in my head distracts me, growing louder, more insistent as the nightmare fades.

My cell phone's obnoxious chirp drags me to semi-consciousness. I flail in my recliner, disoriented, trying to get my bearings. Grabbing my cell, I squint at the caller ID but can't focus—head spinning, drowning in dizziness.

The loud chirping stops and suddenly, it's quiet. All that's left is the ringing in my ears. As the ringing dies down, the dizziness fades. I decompress as the wind's inhuman wail seeps through cracks in old weatherstripping, competing with the TV's mindless drone.

Thinking it through, the nightmare was more than just another bad dream. I know, having had more than my share. And "the worst is yet to come" rings prophetic.


Visit http://michaelallanscott.com for the latest on the
Lance Underphal Mysteries.

# ABOUT THE AUTHOR

Photography by: Cynthia A. Scott

Born and raised at the edge of the high desert in Kingman, Arizona, Michael Allan Scott resides in Scottsdale with his wife, Cynthia, and their hundred-pound Doberman, Otto. In addition to writing mysteries and speculative fiction, his interests include music, photography, art, scuba diving and auto racing. For more, please visit http://michaelallanscott.com.

You can also find Michael Allan Scott on:

CPSIA information can be obtained at www.ICGtesting.com
Printed in the USA
LVOW11s2039211015

459180LV00007BA/811/P